Charles Harding Firth, Margaret Cavendish Newcastle

The Life of William Cavendish, Duke of Newcastle

The True Relation of my Birth, Breeding and Life

Charles Harding Firth, Margaret Cavendish Newcastle

The Life of William Cavendish, Duke of Newcastle
The True Relation of my Birth, Breeding and Life

ISBN/EAN: 9783744727716

Printed in Europe, USA, Canada, Australia, Japan

Cover: Foto ©Raphael Reischuk / pixelio.de

More available books at **www.hansebooks.com**

MEMOIRS OF

WILLIAM CAVENDISH

DUKE OF NEWCASTLE

AND MARGARET HIS WIFE

PUBLISHER'S NOTE.

Three hundred copies of this book printed for England, and two hundred for America.   No more will be printed.

THE LIFE OF

WILLIAM CAVENDISH

DUKE OF NEWCASTLE

TO WHICH IS ADDED

THE TRUE RELATION OF MY BIRTH, BREEDING, AND LIFE

BY

MARGARET, DUCHESS OF NEWCASTLE

EDITED BY C. H. FIRTH, M.A.

(Editor of "Memoirs of the Life of Colonel Hutchinson")

𝔚𝔦𝔱𝔥 𝔉𝔬𝔲𝔯 𝔈𝔱𝔠𝔥𝔢𝔡 𝔓𝔬𝔯𝔱𝔯𝔞𝔦𝔱𝔰

LONDON

JOHN C. NIMMO

14, KING WILLIAM STREET, STRAND, W.C.

1886

LIST OF ETCHED ILLUSTRATIONS.

[1] From the Duke's book on " Horsemanship," plates 32 and 34.

PREFACE.

THE first edition of this Life of the Duke of Newcastle was published in 1667. It is a thin folio
of about 200 pages. This was followed in 1668
by a Latin version, translated by Walter Charlton,
well known in his later days as President of the
College of Physicians. In 1675 was published the
third edition, a quarto ; for the translation, like the
original edition, is in folio. In 1872 a careful reprint of the first edition, edited by Mark Antony
Lower, was included in Russell Smith's "Library of
Old Authors." In the present, which is therefore
the fifth edition, the spelling has been modernised,
and the punctuation occasionally altered.

The three editions published during the lifetime
of the subject testify to the popularity of the book
at a time when the events recorded in it were still
fresh in the memories of those who read it, and
it still retains an enduring interest for later gene-
rations. Somewhat contradictory have been the
judgments passed upon it. The volume of " Letters

and Poems in Honour of the Incomparable Princess,
Margaret, Duchess of Newcastle," printed in 1676,
preserves the opinions of the learned persons and
learned bodies to whom the Duchess sent presentation copies. The response of the University
of Cambridge was worthy of the gift and the giver.
" Hereafter, if generous and highborn men shall
search our library for a model of a most accomplished general, they shall find it expressed to the
life, not in Xenophon's Cyrus, but in the Duchess
of Newcastle's William ! . . . In regard we could
not be admitted to the favour of kissing your hand,
we cease not to bestow ten thousand embraces
upon every page of that book which hath so noble
and immortal a subject as is his grace the Duke of
Newcastle." Whilst the heads of the University
were expressing themselves with the mixture
of gallantry and respect which becomes learned
bodies on such occasions, Pepys was confiding to
paper his contempt for the book and its writer :
"March 18, 1668—Thence home, and there in favour
to my eyes staid at home, reading the ridiculous
history of my Lord Newcastle, wrote by his wife ;
which shows her to be a mad, conceited, ridiculous
woman, and he an ass to suffer her to write what
she writes to him and of him. So to bed, my eyes
being very bad." Without stopping to inquire how
far the state of the worthy Secretary's eyes in-
fluenced his critical faculties, it may be taken for

granted that his recollections of the authoress in-
fluenced his judgment of her book. Describing
her visit to the Royal Society on May 30, 1667, he
had come to the conclusion that "her dress was so
antick and her deportment so ordinary" that he did
not like her at all, and expressed his terror lest
her conduct should make the Royal Society ridiculous. Perhaps it was these very eccentricities and
extravagances which had so shocked Pepys which
recommended the Duchess to Charles Lamb. Certainly his larger sympathy, and keener insight,
enabled him to perceive in the style and in the
writer those finer qualities which the more conventional judgment of Pepys had refused to recognise.
Lamb never mentions without praise "that princely
woman, thrice noble Margaret of Newcastle." For
a book such as the "Life of the Duke of Newcastle,"
a book "both good and rare," he held no binding
too good. "No casket is rich enough, no casing
sufficiently durable, to honour and keep safe such
a jewel."

To decide between these conflicting sentences,
and expound the precise amount of truth contained
in each, would be a tedious and ungrateful task.
This at least may be said, that the "generous and
highborn men" who follow the recommendation of
the Cambridge Senate and study this Life as a
contribution to military history will find little in it
which they could not learn more fully and accu-

b

rately from the pages of Rushworth or Whitelock.
An occasional incident or anecdote, the name of
a forgotten officer, or the locality of an obscure
skirmish, an account of the Duke's personal share
in one or two engagements, sum up the amount
of its contributions to the military history of the
civil wars. The special interest of the book lies
rather in the picture of the exiled royalist, cheerfully sacrificing everything for the King's cause,
struggling with his debts, talking over his creditors,
never losing confidence in the ultimate triumph of
the right, and on his return setting to work uncom-
plainingly to restore his ruined estate. It lies
rather in the portrait drawn of a great English
nobleman of the seventeenth century ; his manners
and his habits, his occupations and amusements,
his maxims and his opinions, his domestic policy
and his alliances with neighbouring potentates, all
are recorded and set down with the loving fidelity
of a Boswell. For the account of her husband's
exile and the description of his daily life the Duchess
depended on her own observations and recollections.
But for that part of the book which treats of his
warlike exploits she relied on the information she
received from his secretary, John Rolleston.

Rolleston had filled a position which must have
enabled him to know the truth on many doubtful
points, and to explain, had he thought fit, the
causes which determined the strategy of his General.

It is therefore much to be regretted that so meagre an account is given of many important incidents and resolutions during the Yorkshire campaigns. For these campaigns exercised a decisive influence on the course of the Civil War in the eastern and midland counties, and had Newcastle been a more capable general, the northern army might have forestalled the New-Model. The first and one of the most important services of Newcastle was the occupation of the town from which he took his title. The ports of the south and east of England, from Bristol to the towns of the Yorkshire coast, were all in the hands of the Parliament, and without communication with the Continent the King could hardly have conducted one campaign. The possession of Newcastle enabled him to receive the arms and ammunition which he urgently needed, and supplied a landing-place for the old soldiers who flocked from Holland and Germany to officer his armies. In the next place, the great territorial influence of Lord Newcastle enabled him to raise an army in the four northern counties with unusual speed ; and, at a period when 2000 or 3000 men was a large army, to advance with double that number into Yorkshire, and occupy York just when it was on the point of falling into the hands of Lord Fairfax. Considering the great superiority of his forces, Newcastle's operations against Lord Fairfax, which commenced in December 1642, can hardly be considered very creditable to his military talents. It required three separate attacks to expel the Fairfaxes from the West Riding. The first commenced with the attack on Tadcaster (December 7, 1642); was followed by the repulse of Sir William Savile from Bradford (December 18, 1642); and was brought to an end by the brilliant recapture of Leeds by Sir Thomas Fairfax (January 23, 1643). The second began in April with an unsuccessful attack on Leeds, and was marked by the capture of Rotherham (May 4) and Sheffield (May 9). Again Sir Thomas Fairfax, by the surprise of Wakefield on May 21, 1643, forced the royalists to retreat. The third and successful attack began with the capture of Howley Hall and the battle of Adwalton Moor (June 30), and ended with the capture of Bradford and Leeds, and the flight of the Fairfaxes to Hull.

In the interval between the first and second of these attacks occurred the controversy between New-castle and Lord Fairfax, recorded in the opposing proclamations printed by Rushworth. Newcastle sent Fairfax a characteristic challenge to come out and fight, to follow "the examples of our heroic ancestors, who used not to spend their time in scratching one another out of holes, but in pitched fields determined their doubts." Lord Fairfax replied by a refusal "to follow the rules of Amadis de Gaule, or the Knight of the Sun, which the language of the declaration seems to affect in offering pitched battles ; " but withal protested his willingness to offer battle wheresoever he found an opportunity. With these taunts were combined legal arguments on the rights of kings and subjects, discussions on the lawfulness of employing Catholics and sectaries, and accusations of plunder and indiscipline against each other's armies.

The conquest of the West Riding left Hull the only important place in Yorkshire in the hands of the Parliament. Charles summoned Newcastle to move southwards, and ordered him to march through the Eastern association on London.[1] He obeyed so far as to march into Lincolnshire, where he recaptured Gainsborough (July 30) and garrisoned Lincoln, but at the end of August he returned into Yorkshire to besiege Hull. The combined movement on London planned by the King might have changed the fortune of the war, for at the end of July the Parliament had no army capable of keeping the field. Waller's forces had been reduced to a few hundred horse, Essex's troops were diminished by disease and desertion, and disheartened by failure, and the army of the Eastern association was still in the process of

---

[1] " He had orders to march into the associated counties, when, upon the taking of Bristol, his Majesty had a purpose to have marched towards London on the other side."— Clarendon, Rebellion, viii. 86. See also vii. 177. Other statements are quoted in the note to p. 57.

formation. Even if the march on London had been unattempted, a vigorous invasion of the Eastern association might have made a breach in that stronghold of Puritanism, and would almost certainly have prevented the relief of Gloucester. The reasons which led Newcastle to disobey the King's command are differently stated. Warwick asserts that his desire to retain his independent command, and fear of being placed under the orders of Rupert, was the chief motive. That this was one reason is certain. The Queen made use of it to incite Newcastle to refuse obedience, and her influence was thrown into the scale against the King's orders. To this was added the opposition of the gentlemen of Yorkshire to the proposed scheme, their objections to leaving their own county, and their urgent appeals to Newcastle to capture Hull and put a stop to Fairfax's inroads into Yorkshire. It was on this last ground that Newcastle based his refusal, but there is little doubt that it coincided with his own inclinations.[1] From the time that Newcastle turned back into Yorkshire his good fortune ended. One day (October 11, 1643) saw the defeat of his field army at Winceby, and the rout of the besieging army under the walls of Hull. November and December were spent in recruiting his shattered forces, and in January 1644

---

[1] See Clarendon, vii. 177, and passages quoted on p. 57.

he was called northwards to oppose the entry of
the Scots into England. Slowly the Scots forced
their way south, Newcastle ever attempting to
bring on a general action, and ever failing through
Lesly's judicious choice of positions. Though he
was able by means of his great superiority in
cavalry to cut off their provisions, he could never
absolutely reduce them to extremity, and his best
horse were ruined by the severity of the season.
At the same time, he had to contend against the
criticisms of his own party, and even thought of
laying down his commission to escape their complaints. " I perceive," wrote the King to him,
" that the Scots are not the only, or the least
enemies you contest with at this time; wherefore
I must tell you in a word you must as much con-
temn the impertinent or malicious tongues and pens
of those that are or profess to be your friends, as
well as you despise the sword of an equal enemy.
The truth is, if either you or my Lord Ethyn leave
my service, I am sure all the north is lost. Remember all courage is not in fighting, constancy in
a good cause being the chief, and the despising of
slanderous tongues and pens being not the least
ingredient." [1] This letter was written on April 6,
1644, and on the 11th of the same month Newcastle's lieutenant, Bellasis, was defeated and taken

---

[1] Ellis, Original Letters, I. iii. 298.

prisoner, and the Marquis himself forced to make a hurried retreat to York, where the united armies of Fairfax, Lesly, and Manchester closed in upon him, and made his surrender only a question of time. Prince Rupert raised the siege; but, not content with that, and misunderstanding the King's orders, pursued the retreating enemy, and, against the advice of the Marquis, forced on the battle of Marston Moor. In that battle the Marquis held no command, but fought as a private gentleman at the head of a company of volunteers. The day after, he, with his immediate friends, made his way to Scarborough and embarked for the Continent. If he had been content to remain in England, and laboriously recommence the task of raising armies for the King, he might have considerably retarded the loss of the north. There were a hundred examples of men, less eminent in position and command, who struggled cheerfully, even though with little hope of success, until all further resistance was impossible. But Newcastle, loyal though he was, held no such troublesome and exacting a view of his duty. His wife represents him as leaving England because he saw there was nothing else to be done, and was "loath to have aspersions cast upon him" for failing to do what was impossible. Another account makes him reply to Rupert's persuasions to recruit his forces for another effort, by saying, "I will not endure the laughter of the court."

Clarendon, whilst discussing the causes of this retirement, seizes the opportunity to draw one of those
portraits which no biographer can leave unquoted:—

" All that can be said for the Marquis is, that he
was utterly tired with a condition and employment
so contrary to his humour, nature, and education,
that he did not at all consider the means or the
way that would let him out of it, and free him for
ever from having more to do with it. And it was
a greater wonder, that he sustained the vexation
and fatigue of it so long, than that he broke from
it with so little circumspection. He was a very
fine gentleman, active and full of courage, and most
accomplished in those qualities of horsemanship,
dancing, and fencing which accompany a good
breeding ; in which his delight was. Besides that,
he was amorous in poetry and music, to which he
indulged the greatest part of his time ; and nothing
could have tempted him out of those paths of
pleasure, which he enjoyed in a full and ample
fortune, but honour and ambition to serve the
King, when he saw him in distress, and abandoned by most of those who were in the highest
degree obliged to him, and by him. He loved
monarchy, as it was the foundation and support
of his own greatness ; and the Church, as it was
well constituted for the splendour and security of
the Crown ; and religion, as it cherished and maintained that order and obedience that was necessary

to both; without any other passion for the particular opinions which were grown up in it, and
distinguished it into parties, than as he detested
whatsoever was like to disturb the public peace.
. . . He liked the pomp and absolute authority
of a general well, and preserved the dignity of it
to the full; and for the discharge of the outward
state and circumstances of it, in acts of courtesy,
affability, bounty, and generosity he abounded;
which in the infancy of a war became him, and
made him for some time very acceptable to men
of all conditions. But the substantial part, and
fatigue of a general, he did not in any degree
understand, (being utterly unacquainted with war,)
nor could submit to;[1] but referred all matters of
that nature to his lieutenant-general, King. . . .
In all actions of the field he was still present, and
never absent in any battle; in all which he gave
instances of an invincible courage and fearless-
ness in danger; in which the exposing of himself
notoriously did sometimes change the fortune of
the day when his troops began to give ground.
Such articles of action were no sooner over, than
he retired to his delightful company, music, or his
softer pleasures, to all which he was so indulgent,
and to his ease, that he would not be interrupted

---

[1] Clarendon's private opinion is quoted in a note to p.
102, *post.*

upon what occasions soever ; insomuch as he some-times denied admission to the chiefest officers of the army, even to General King himself, for two days together ; from whence many inconveniences fell out. . . . The strange manner of the Prince's coming, and undeliberated throwing himself, and all the King's hopes, into that sudden and unneces-sary engagement, by which all the force the Marquis had raised, and with so many difficulties preserved, was in a moment cast away and destroyed, so transported him with passion and despair, that he could not compose himself to think of beginning the work again, and involving himself in the same undelightful condition of life, from which he might now be free. He hoped his past meritorious actions might outweigh his present abandoning the thought of future action ; and so without further consideration, as hath been said, he trans-ported himself out of the kingdom."[1]

Very similar is the judgment passed on New-castle by another contemporary, Sir Philip Warwick. " He was a gentleman of grandeur, generosity, loyalty, and steady and forward courage ; but his edge had too much of the razor in it : for he had a tincture of a romantic spirit, and had the mis-fortune to have somewhat of the poet in him ; so as he chose Sir William Davenant, an eminent

---

[1] Rebellion, viii. 82, 85, 87.

good poet, and loyal gentleman, to be lieutenant-general of his ordnance. This inclination of his own and such kind of witty society (to be modest in the expression of it) diverted many counsels, and lost many opportunities, which the nature of that affair this great man had now entered into required." [1]

The very defects which, according to these two authorities, prevented Newcastle from being a successful general, have given him an additional claim to the remembrance of posterity. His own writings, and his patronage of other writers, combine to secure him a niche in the literature of his age. He was not only a dramatic author himself, but the friend and protector of most of the dramatic authors of his time.

"Since the time of Augustus," says Langbaine, "no person better understood dramatic poetry, nor more generously encouraged poets ; so that we may truly call him our English Mæcenas." [2] Jonson dedicated to him elegies on his riding and fencing, wrote the epitaphs of his father, mother, and other members of his family, composed an interlude for the christening of his son Charles, and the two Masques entitled "Love's Welcome at Welbeck," and "Love's Welcome at Bolsover," for his entertainments to the King and Queen. Three of the poet's letters have been printed. In one he offers

---

[1] Memoirs, p 235.   [2] Dramatic Poets, p. 386.

his patron "the faith of a fast friend with the duties of an humble servant, and the hearty prayers of a religious bedesman." In another, which probably accompanied "Love's Welcome at Welbeck," he thanks the Earl for "a timely gratuity, which fell like the dew of heaven on my necessities." "God sends you," he continues, "these chargeable and magnificent honours of making feasts, to mix with your charitable succours, dropt upon me your servant; who have nothing to claim of merit but a cheerful undertaking whatsoever your lordship's judgment thinks me able to perform."[1]

James Shirley also addressed a poem to Newcastle, and dedicated to him in 1638 his play of "The Traitor." When the Civil War broke out, and Shirley was forced to leave London, "he was invited," says Wood, "by his most noble patron, William, Earl of Newcastle, to take his fortune with him in the wars; for that Count had engaged him so much by his generous liberality towards him, that he thought he could not do a worthier act than to serve him, and consequently his Prince." According to the same author, "Shirley did much assist the Duke in the composure of certain plays, which the Duke afterwards published." On which Dyce remarks—"The style of his Grace's dramas

---

[1] Cunningham's "Jonson," vol. iii. p. 459, Preface, pp. lvii.–lix., and Underwoods Epigrams, 72 and 89. See also pp. 3, 7, 195, and 209 of these Memoirs.

would certainly have induced me to suspect the truth of this statement, if I had not discovered that a drinking song which is inserted in the Duke's comedy called 'The Country Captain' is printed amongst our author's poems." [1]

Newcastle's relations with Davenant have already been mentioned. It is very likely that the poet owed his post in Newcastle's army to the recommendation of the Queen rather than to the merits of his verse.[2] It is somewhat remarkable that Davenant makes no mention of the Duke in his poems, and that, with the exception of a brief poem on the marriage of one of the Duke's daughters, there is no trace of this connection in his works. Dryden, who also shared the favours of Newcastle, takes the opportunity, in his florid dedication of " The Mock Astrologer " to the Duke, to refer to his kindnesses to former poets. " The manes of Jonson and Davenant seem to require from me, that those favours which you placed on them, and which they wanted opportunity to own in public, yet might not be lost to the knowledge of posterity, with a forgetfulness unbecoming of the Muses who are the daughters of memory. . . .

---

[1] Wood, " Athenæ Oxonienses," ed. Bliss, iii. 737. Dyce's Shirley, Preface, p. xliii. The song referred to is in act iv. of " The Country Captain," and commences " Come let us throw the dice."

[2] " Letters of Queen Henrietta Maria," ed. Green, p. 134.

I am proud to be their remembrancer : for by relating how gracious you have been to them, and
are to me, I, in some measure, join my name to
theirs; and the continued descent of your favours
to me is the best title which I can plead for my
succession." Dryden's enemy, Shadwell, shared the
Duke's bounty, and dedicated to him "The Vir-
tuoso" and "The Libertine." Flecknoe, another
of the victims of Dryden's satire, rhymes assidu-
ously in praise of the Duke and Duchess.[1] But
Dryden's connection with Newcastle was that of
collaborateur as well as client. The Duke translated or adapted Molière's "L'Étourdi," which
Dryden converted into "Sir Martin Mar-all." It
was performed under the name of the Duke, and is
entered on the books of the Stationer's Company
as his work.[2] Not till 1697 did it appear under
Dryden's name, but according to Pepys the secret
of its authorship was well known at the time.

Newcastle's own plays are four in number, viz. :
"The County Captain" and "The Variety," pub-
lished in 1649, and the "Humorous Lovers" and
"Triumphant Widow," published in 1677. Of the

---

[1] See Walpole's "Royal and Noble Authors," edited by
Park, where specimens of Flecknoe's verses are given.
Richard Brome also prefixes to his play of "The Covent
Garden Weeded," verses on the Duke's play entitled "The
Variety."

[2] Scott's "Dryden," vol. iii.

first of these, Pepys observes, "so silly a play as
in all my life I never saw ; " of the third, " the most
silly thing that ever came upon a stage."[1]   Shadwell, however, who knew what was likely to succeed
as well as most men, thought sufficiently well of
" The Triumphant Widow " to transcribe a large
part of it into his " Bury Fair."   And whether
fitted for the stage or not, the plays are certainly
readable and amusing.   There is less to be said
in favour of the Duke's poems.   They consist
chiefly of songs in his own plays and those of the
Duchess, of adulatory verses prefixed to his wife's
publications, and some tales in verse in her "Nature's
Pictures."   They are as far inferior to her poems as
his plays are superior to those of the Duchess.

Walpole, who never loses an opportunity of
sneering at Newcastle, says, referring to his plays
and poems, " He would soon have been forgotten in
the walk of fame which he chose for himself.   Yet
as an author he is familiar to those who scarce know
any other author from his book of horsemanship."[2]
Horsemanship was a study to which Newcastle had
devoted himself from his youth.   His father, Sir
Charles Cavendish, " kept him several masters in
the art of horsemanship, and sent him to the Mews

---

[1] See the passages quoted from Pepys on p. 203. Geneste,
who describes the Duke's plays (x. 73–75), sums up by saying
that they " ought not to have been forgotten."

[2] Royal and Noble Authors, iii. 175.

to Mons. Antoine, who was then accounted the
best master in that art." As governor of Prince
Charles he also taught him to ride, and continually
celebrates the progress of his pupil (see the passages quoted in the note to p. 121), to whom he
afterwards dedicated his " Méthode Nouvelle de
Dresser les Chevaux." The same pursuit filled the
enforced leisure of his exile, and relieved its tedium.

Early in 1648, towards the end of his stay in
France, Newcastle contrived to obtain credit, and
promptly bought a couple of Barbary horses, " resolving for his own recreation and divertisement to
exercise the art of manage." After his removal to
Antwerp he increased his stable to eight horses,
" in which he took so much delight and pleasure
that, though he was then in distress for money,
yet he would sooner have tried all other ways than
parted with any of them." No stranger of note
thought of passing through Antwerp without coming
to see Newcastle's riding-house. " It would fill a
volume," he writes, " to repeat all the commendations that were given to horses and horsemanship,
by several worthy gentlemen of all nations, High
and Low Dutch, Italians, English, French, Spaniards,
Polacks, and Swedes, in my own private riding-
house at Antwerp, which, though very large, was
often so full that my esquier, Captain Mazin, had
hardly room to ride." He relates in detail the
compliments of some of his more important visitors,

c

tells us how he himself mounted and performed before them, whilst Spaniards "crossed themselves and cried Miraculo." And that "though the French think that all the horsemanship in the world is in France," one said, " Par Dieu, Monsieur, il est bien hardi qui monte devant vous," and another, "Il n'y a plus seigneur comme vous en Angleterre." [1] The fruit of these experiences and studies was published in 1658 at Antwerp under the title of " La Methode et Invention Nouvelle de Dresser les Chevaux." It is a magnificent folio, with two title-pages and 42 fine plates. The Marquis wrote in English, but had his work translated into French for publication.[2]

A letter which is printed in the Appendix shows that it was owing to the help of his two friends, Sir Hugh Cartwright and Mr. Loving, that Newcastle was able to produce so sumptuous an edition of his book. In the numerous diagrams which adorn it, we see the Duke and Captain Mazin alternately exhibiting the various figures of their art in the riding-house. Other plates represent Newcastle himself performing " capriolles " and

---

[1] Preface to the " New Method and Extraordinary Invention," 1667. Some extracts are quoted in the notes to pp. 116, 119.

[2] According to Lowndes (ed. Bohn) the book was published in 1657, and the printed title is sometimes altered by hand to 1658. But the copies I have myself seen are dated 1658.

" balottades " before the windows of Welbeck, or under the towers of Bolsover. The frontispiece pictures him mounted and upon a pedestal, crowned by flying Cupids, with verses beneath stating that if he were to mount "un diable tres robuste" it would become immediately as docile as one of his own trained steeds. One emblematic design displays the author driving a chariot drawn by centaurs through a circle of kneeling horses ; in another he is seen flying on a winged horse betwixt heaven and earth, below are submissively adoring horses, whilst from above the gods look down and admire. The verses attached to this last picture are so much superior to most of those supplied by Mons. D. V., the poet employed by the Duke, that they deserve quotation :—

> " Il monte avec la main, les éperons et gaule,
> Le cheval de Pégase, qui volle en capriole ;
> Il monte si haut qu'il touche de sa tête les cieux,
> Et par ses merveilles ravit en extases les Dieux.
> Les chevaux corruptibles qui là bas sur terre sont,
> En courbettes demi-airs, terre à terre vont,
> Avec humilité soumission et bassesse,
> L'adorer comme Dieu auteur de leur addresse."

When the Duke returned from exile he continued to occupy himself with his favourite pursuit. "In his old age," writes his wife, "though he doth not ride himself, as he hath done, yet he takes delight in seeing his horses of manage rid by his escuyers,

whom he instructs in that art for his own pleasure."
In 1667 he published a second book, under the
following title : " A New Method and Extraordinary
Invention to Dress Horses, and Work them, according to Nature ; as also to perfect Nature by the
subtlety of Art; which was never found out but
by the thrice noble, high, and puissant Prince,
William Cavendish," &c.   In the preface the Duke
explains the relation of the later to the earlier
work. " I did (during my long exile) publish in
French a book of Horsemanship ; and having
again, since my return to my native country, had
much leisure, in my solitary country life, to recollect
my thoughts, and try new experiments about that
art ; I now, for the more particular satisfaction of
my countrymen, print this second book in English,
which, being neither a translation of the first, nor
an absolutely necessary addition to it, may be of
use by itself without the other, as the other hath
been hitherto, and is still, without this ; but both
together will questionless do best."

But though the Duke's contribution to literature
is by no means insignificant, his works are far
surpassed in number by those of the Duchess.
Poems and Plays, Letters, Orations, and Stories,
combined with a whole series of works on Natural
Philosophy, flowed from her facile pen. It was
during her exile, more especially during her visit
to England with Sir Charles Cavendish, that she

published her earliest works. The volume of
" Poems and Fancies" was first printed in 1653 ;
a second edition followed in 1664, and a third in
1668 ; all three were published at London and in
folio form. This volume contains some of her best
work—" The Pastime and Recreation of the Queen
of the Fairies in Fairyland," and " The Dialogue
between Melancholy and Mirth," both of which
will be found in the little volume of selections
published by Mr. Jenkins. Other poems are
scattered through the volume entitled " Nature's
Pictures by Fancy's Pencil." The first edition of
the last-named book was published in 1656, and the
second in 1671. It contains the autobiography of
the Duchess, and several poems by the Duke, in
addition to the tales in verse and prose which form
the bulk of her volume. There should be a frontispiece representing the Duchess seated with her
husband and his children telling them stories, but
this is generally missing. In one of the very numerous prefaces she prides herself on the tendency of
her fictions, and condemns the romances of the day.
" As for those tales I name Romancicall, I would not
have my readers think I writ them, either to please
or to make foolish whining lovers, for it is a humour
of all humours I have an aversion to ; but my
endeavour is to express the sweetness of Virtue,
and the Graces, and to dress and adorn them in
the best expressions I can. . . . Neither do I

know the rule or method of Romancy writing; for
I never read a Romancy Book throughout in all
my life, I mean such as I take to be Romances,
wherein little is writ which ought to be practised,
but rather shunned as foolish amorosities, and
desperate follies, not noble love's discreet virtues,
and true valour.   The most I ever read of Romances
was but part of three books, as the three parts of one,
and the half of the two others.   And if I thought
those tales I call my Romancicall Tales, should or
could neither benefit the life, nor delight the mind
of my readers, no more than those pieces of
Romances I read did me, I would never suffer
them to be printed. . . . Likewise if I could
think that any of my writings should create amorous
thoughts in idle brains, I would make blots instead
of letters; but I hope this work of mine will rather
quench amorous passions than inflame them, and
beget chaste thoughts, nourish love of Virtue,
kindle humane Pity, warm Charity, increase Civility,
strengthen fainting Patience, encourage noble
Industry, crown Merit, instruct Life, and recreate
Time."

The book entitled " The World's Olio " is a collection of essays, observations, and aphorisms, published in 1655, with a second edition dated 1671
(London, folio). "The CCXI. Sociable Letters," published in 1664 (London, folio), consist of descriptions
of imaginary scenes, persons, and conversations, with

one or two letters to real persons intermixed, and
one or two on critical subjects, such as the works
of Shakespeare and Davenant. A still more curious
proof of the versatility of the Duchess is the volume
called "Orations of Divers Sorts accommodated to
Divers Places" (first edition 1662, London, folio;
second 1668, do. do.) It contains orations for all times
and places—for funerals, for weddings, for law courts
and battlefields, speeches seditious and loyal, some
to stir up mutiny, some to prevent civil war, some
for and some against taxes, speeches to the King
in council and to the citizens in market-place,
and dying speeches for all conditions, from kings
to courtesans. There is a collection of speeches
for a convivial meeting of country gentlemen in a
market town, ending with "a speech of a quarter-
drunk gentleman," and "a speech of a half-drunken
gentleman." Another little collection, headed
"Female Orations," reports the speeches delivered
at a meeting of women on the great question of
combining together to make themselves as "free,
happy, and famous as men," and concludes with
an oration persuading them to remain as they are
and be content with their present position. It is
hardly necessary to say that the orations are all
singularly alike in style and expression, for the
Duchess, with a considerable power of description,
was entirely devoid of any dramatic instinct. In
all her plays there is hardly a single character with

any semblance of life; her characters are mere
abstractions, qualities, and humours, uttering the
fantastic speeches and quaint conceits which she
loved to write.[1] The plots are original enough,
but there is no skill in the construction to redeem
the weakness of the character-drawing. All that can
be said for the dialogue is that it contains occasional passages of poetic beauty, and some amusing
descriptions, but it is too strained and affected to
be spoken on the stage. Nevertheless the Duchess
was an indefatigable playwright: in 1662 she
published a volume containing twenty-one plays
(" Plays," London, 1662, folio); this was followed in
1668 by a second containing five more (" Plays
Never Before Printed," London, 1668, folio). They
were not particularly well received by the world;
the Duchess complains that the critics condemned
in them the very things she had admitted in her
preface. " My plays, they say, are not made up so
exactly as they should be, having no plots, designs,
catastrophes, and such like, I know not what, which

[1] Some of the figures represent the authoress herself. " In
a scene in the second part of 'Youth's Glory and Death's
Banquet,' she appears under the character of Lady Sans-
pareile, and gives what may be supposed to be a picture of
her own reception at Court. As the Lady Contemplation
in the play of that name, as the Lady Chastity of the ' Matri-
monial Trouble,' and in a score of other characters, the
Duchess is recognisable."—Dictionary of National Biography.

I expressed in the Epistles prefixed before them ; acknowledging that I had neither skill nor art to form them as they should be" (Preface to Orations). For this reason she boldly states, in the address to the readers in her second volume—"When I call this new one 'Plays' I do not believe to have given it a very proper title ; for it would be too great a fondness to my works to think such plays as these suitable to ancient rules, in which I pretend no skill ; or agreeable to the modern humour, to which I dare acknowledge my aversion : but having pleased my fancy in writing many dialogues upon several subjects, and having afterwards ordered them into acts and scenes, I will venture in spite of the critics to call them 'Plays ;' and if you like them so, well and good ; if not, there is no harm done.",

But the philosophical, or rather scientific works of the Duchess, were those of which she herself was most proud, and those which were most famous in her time. The first of these was the "Philosophical Fancies" (London, 1653), afterwards developed into "Philosophical Opinions" (London, 1655), and still further enlarged and amended in the second edition of "Philosophical Opinions" in 1663. In some verses on this book, quoted in the note to page 303, she terms it "of all that I have writ,

---

[1] There is a very fine portrait of the Duchess by Diepenbeck as frontispiece to this volume.

my best beloved and greatest favourite." Already, in her Poems in 1653, and in "The World's Olio," published in 1655, she had set forth some of her views on natural philosophy. One of the dozen prefaces to her Poems is specially addressed "to natural philosophers." She pleads her complete ignorance of the works of former writers on the subject, and the fact that she understands no language but her own, and only colloquial English, as reasons for a kindly judgment of her speculations. In the remarks attached to "Philosophical Opinions" she prides herself that her views are all her own, and all new. "I desire all those that are friends to my book to believe that whatsoever is new is my own, which I hope all is; for I never had any guide to direct me, nor intelligence from any authors to advertise me, but writ according to my own natural cogitations." As might be expected from these confessions, the ponderous tomes on science and philosophy which the Duchess published are entirely valueless. This was not only due to the ignorance of the writings of others, which the Duchess admits, but to the method which she adopted in reasoning on physical science. One of her correspondents, Glanville, points this out to her. "There are two sorts of reasoning," he says, "those that the mind advanceth from its inbred store, such are all metaphysical contemplations; and those natural researches which are raised from experiment and the objects of sense. Now, what I have said about these matters is to tie down the mind in physical things to consider nature as it is, to lay a foundation in sensible collections, and from thence to proceed to general propositions and discourses. So that my aim is that we may arise according to the order of nature, from the exercise of our senses to that of our reason; which indeed is most noble and most perfect when it concludes aright, but not so when it is mistaken; and that it may so conclude and arrive to that perfection it must begin in sense; and the more experiments our reasons have to work on, by so much they are the more likely to be certain in their conclusions, and consequently more perfect in their actings." Whilst the Royal Society and all those to whom the progress of physical science in England during the latter half of the seventeenth century was due were eagerly pursuing the experimental method, the Duchess continued to spin her "metaphysical cogitations" like a spider, as she says, from her own brain.[1]

[1] In addition to these works the Duchess published the following:—

(1.) "Philosophical Letters, or Modest Reflections upon some Opinions in Natural Philosophy maintained by several learned authors of the age." London, 1664, folio.

(2.) "Observations upon Experimental Philosophy, to which is added the Description of a New World." London, 1666, folio; second edition, 1668.

(3.) "Grounds of Natural Philosophy." London, 1668,

It is not surprising that her husband praised them, for he held that nobody knew or could know the cause of anything, all were but guessers, and so his wife's opinions were as likely to be correct as any one else's. But it is rather a shock to find learned bodies and learned men lavishing unmeasured praise upon them. Dr. Walter Charlton gravely writes to her, bidding her not be discouraged, if her philosophy have not the fate to be publicly read in all the Universities of Europe, and discusses the question whether the jealousy of philosophical teachers, the dislike of dogmatism which had recently sprang up in England, or the influence of the opposing philosophy of Aquinas, was the cause of this delay.[1] Some such reward of her labours the Duchess seems to have expected, for she liberally supplied the public libraries of Oxford and Cambridge, and those of many of their Colleges, with copies of her works, and dedicated her " Philosophical Opinions " to the Universities of England, and her " Grounds of Natural Philosophy " to the Universities of Europe.

Passing from the consideration of her works to the consideration of the Duchess herself, the task of

---

folio. This is a second edition, much altered, of " Philosophical and Physical Opinions."

[1] " Letters and Poems in Honour of the incomparable Princess, Margaret, Duchess of Newcastle, written by severa persons of honour and learning," 1676, p. 111.

the critic is more delicate and more difficult. She has been unduly praised and unjustly depreciated. Clever people have sneered at her as a pedant, and dull people still term her "the mad Duchess." Her reputation has suffered something from the pens of others, but more from her own. She wrote a number of excellent things, but carefully buried them in a vast heap of rubbish. No woman ever more frankly described herself in her autobiography, or more carelessly displayed herself in her writings. Even those who admire and love her most must admit that some of her defects are too highly developed for the character of a perfect heroine. Her love of singularity amounted to a passion; in her philosophy as in her clothes she was determined above all things to be original. Her vanity was enormous and insatiable. "Vanity," she says somewhere, "is so natural to our sex that it were unnatural not to be so;" but her vanity was something superfeminine.

Yet her weaknesses were very largely the results of the circumstances in which she grew up, and the position in which Fortune placed her. Her education was neglected, her youth solitary and secluded. She associated only with the members of her own family, and shunned the company of even near connections. Her stay in the court of Henrietta Maria was too brief to give her a taste for society, or to fit her for it. After her marriage with the Marquis of Newcastle she continued her secluded and contemplative way of living, immuring herself in a little world of speculations and fancies, out of sight and out of sound of the real world outside. She had no children, and the management of an exile's household afforded her little occupation; writing became to her a resource, a pleasure, and a necessity. "Be not too severe in your censures," she says in one of the prefaces to her first book, "for first, I have no children to employ my care and attendance on. Next, my Lord's estate being taken away in those times when I writ this book, I had nothing for huswifery or thrifty industry to employ myself in, having no stock to work on. ᛫ Thirdly, you are desired to spare your severe censures, because I had not so many years of experience when I wrote this book, as could make me a garland to crown my head; only I had so much time, as to gather a little posy to stick upon my breast. Lastly, the time I have been writing them hath not been very long, but since I came into England, being eight years out and nine months in; and of these nine months, only some hours in the day, or rather in the night; for my rest being broken with discontented thoughts, because I was from my Lord and husband, knowing him to be in great wants, and myself in the same condition; to divert them I strove to turn the stream, and, shunning the muddy and

foul ways of vice, I went to the well of Helicon, and
by the well's side I did sit, and wrote this work."
And again: "Since all times must be spent
either ill, or well, or indifferently, I thought this
was the most harmless pastime : for sure this
work is better than to sit still, and censure my
neighbour's actions, which nothing concern me ;
or to condemn their humours, because they do not
sympathise with mine ; or their lawful recreations,
because they are not agreeable to my delight ; or
ridiculously to laugh at my neighbour's clothes, if
they are not of the mode, colour, or cut, or the
ribbons tied with a mode-knot ; or to busy myself
out of the sphere of our sex, in politics of state,
or to preach false doctrine in a tub ; or to entertain myself in hearkening to vain flatteries, or to
the incitements of evil persuasions ; whereas all
these follies, and many more, may be cut off by
such innocent work as this."

Another motive urged the Duchess to write, and
she owns it with charming simplicity. " I confess
my ambition is restless, and not ordinary, because
it would have an extraordinary fame : and since
all heroic actions, public employments, powerful
governments, and eloquent pleadings, are denied
our sex in this age, or at least would be condemned
for want of custom, is the cause I write so much ;
for my ambition being restless, though rather busy
than industrious, yet it hath made that little wit

I have to run upon every subject I can think of, or is fit for me to write on" (Epistle to the Reader, "Nature's Pictures," 1656).

"It will satisfy me," says she elsewhere, "if my writing please the readers, though not the learned; for I had rather be praised, in this, by the most, although not the best; for all I desire is fame, and fame is nothing but a great noise, and noise lives most in a multitude." By a curious reversal of her wishes, exactly the contrary of what she hoped for has happened. What fame she has is with the few, and not with the many, with the best and not with the most. To some she is still the "incomparable Princess," as contemporary panegyrists termed her, and Lamb delighted to style her. But to most she is and will be merely the fantastic figure which flits for a moment across the pages of Pepys.

The last work written by the Duchess was the "Grounds of Natural Philosophy," published in 1668. She died on December 15, 1673, leaving, it is said, three volumes of poems in manuscript. She was buried in Westminster Abbey, on January 7, 1674, near the chapel of St Michael. Her husband survived her three years, dying on December 25, 1676.[1] On their monument, erected

[1] The date of the death of the Duchess is given by Anthony Wood in his account of Walter Charlton, who

by the Duke during his lifetime, is the following inscription :—

"Here lyes the Loyall Duke of Newcastle, and his Dutches, his second wife, by whom he had noe issue: Her name was Margarett Lucas, yongest sister to the Lord Lucas of Colchester, a noble familie; for all the Brothers were Valiant, and all the Sisters virtuous. This Dutches was a wise, wittie, and Learned Lady, which her many Bookes do well testifie; she was a most Virtuous and a Loveing and carefull wife, and was with her Lord all the time of his banishment and miseries, and when he came home, never parted from him in his solitary retirements."

---

translated her life of the Duke into Latin (Athenæ Oxonienses). The date of the Duke's death, and the epitaph, are from Collins, who gives an engraving of the monument (Collins, "Historical Collections," p. 44).

THE LIFE

OF THE

Thrice noble, high and puissant PRINCE,

WILLIAM CAVENDISH,

Duke, Marquis, and Earl of Newcastle; Earl of
Ogle; Viscount Mansfield; and Baron of Bolsover,
of Ogle, Bothal and Hepple: Gentleman of His
Majesty's Bed-chamber; one of His Majesty's
most Honourable Privy Council; Knight of the
most noble Order of the Garter; His Majesty's
Lieutenant of the county and town of Nottingham; and Justice in Eyre Trent-North: who had
the honour to be Governor to our most glorious
King and gracious Sovereign, in his youth, when
he was Prince of Wales; and soon after was made
Captain-General of all the provinces beyond the
river of Trent, and other parts of the kingdom of
England, with power, by a special commission,
to make Knights.

Written by the thrice noble, illustrious, and excellent Princess,
Margaret, Duchess of Newcastle, his Wife.

LONDON,
Printed by *A. Maxwell,* in the Year 1667.

CHARLES THE SECOND,

By the Grace of God, of England, Scotland, France, and Ireland King, Defender of the Faith, &c.

MAY IT PLEASE YOUR MAJESTY,—I have, in confidence of your gracious acceptance, taken the boldness, or rather the presumption, to dedicate to your Majesty this short history (which is as full of truths, as words) of the actions and sufferings of your most loyal subject, my lord and husband (by your Majesty's late favour) Duke of Newcastle; who when your Majesty was Prince of Wales, was your most careful governor, and honest servant. Give me therefore leave to relate here, that I have heard him often say, he loves your royal person so dearly, that he would most willingly, upon all occasions, sacrifice his life and posterity for your Majesty : whom that Heaven will ever bless, is the prayer of your most obedient, loyal, humble subject and servant,

MARGARET NEWCASTLE.

THE DUKE OF NEWCASTLE.

My Noble Lord,—It hath always been my hearty prayer to God, since I have been your wife, that first I might prove an honest and good wife, whereof your Grace must be the only judge: next, that God would be pleased to enable me to set forth and declare to after ages, the truth of your loyal actions and endeavours, for the service of your King and country; for the accomplishing of which design, I have followed the best and truest observations of your secretary John Rolleston, and your Lordship's own relations, and have accordingly writ the history of your Lordship's life, which, although I have endeavoured to render as perspicuous as ever I could, yet one thing I find hath much darkened it; which is, that your Grace commanded me not to mention any thing or passage to the prejudice or disgrace of any family or particular person (although they might be of great truth, and would illustrate much the actions of your life) which I have dutifully performed to satisfy your Lordship,[1] whose nature is so generous, that you are as well pleased to obscure the faults of your enemies, as you are to divulge the virtues of your friends. And certainly, my Lord, you have had as many enemies, and as many friends, as ever any one particular person had; and I pray God to forgive the one, and prosper the other. Nor do I so much wonder at it, since I, a woman, cannot be exempt from the malice and aspersions of spiteful tongues, which they cast upon my poor writings, some denying me to be the true authoress of them; for your Grace remembers well, that those books I put out first to the judgment of this censorious age, were accounted not to be written by a woman, but that somebody else had writ and published them in my name; by which your Lordship was moved to prefix an Epistle before one of them in my vindication, wherein you assure the world upon your honour, that what was written and printed in my name, was my own;[2] and I have also made known, that your Lordship was my only tutor, in declaring to me what you had found and observed by your

---

[1] This is probably the reason for the obliteration of so many proper names in the first edition, which was done by hand after the book had been printed.

[2] "An Epistle to justify the Lady Newcastle, and truth against falsehood, laying those false and malicious aspersions of her, that she was not author of her books," prefixed to "Philosophical and Physical Opinions," 1655.

own experience; for I being young when your Lordship married me, could not have much knowledge of the world; but it pleased God to command his servant Nature to indue me with a poetical and philosophical genius, even from my birth; for I did write some books in that kind, before I was twelve years of age, which for want of good method and order, I would never divulge. But though the world would not believe that those conceptions and fancies which I writ were my own, but transcended my capacity, yet they found fault that they were defective for want of learning; and on the other side, they said I had plucked feathers out of the universities; which was a very preposterous judgment. Truly, my Lord, I confess that for want of scholarship, I could not express myself so well as otherwise I might have done, in those philosophical writings I published first; but after I was returned with your Lordship into my native country, and led a retired country life, I applied myself to the reading of philosophical authors, of purpose to learn those names and words of art that are used in schools; which at first were so hard to me, that I could not understand them, but was fain to guess at the sense of them by the whole context, and so write them down as I found them in those authors, at which my readers did wonder, and thought it impossible that a woman could have so much learning and understanding in terms of art, and scholastical ex-

pressions; so that I and my books are like the old
apologue, mentioned in Æsop, of a father, and his
son, who rid on an ass through a town when his
father went on foot, at which sight the people
shouted and cried shame, that a young boy should
ride, and let his father, an old man, go on foot:
whereupon the old man got upon the ass, and let
his son go by.   But when they came to the next
town, the people exclaimed against the father, that
he, a lusty man, should ride, and have no more pity
of his young and tender child, but let him go on
foot.   Then both the father and his son got upon the
ass, and coming to the third town, the people blamed
them both for being so unconscionable as to over-
burden the poor ass with their heavy weight.   After
this both father and son went on foot, and led the
ass; and when they came to the fourth town, the
people railed as much at them as ever the former
had done, and called them both fools, for going on
foot, when they had a beast able to carry them.
The old man, seeing he could not please mankind
in any manner, and having received so many blemishes and aspersions, for the sake of his ass, was at
last resolved to drown him when he came to the
next bridge.   But I am not so passionate to burn
my writings for the various humours of mankind,
and for their finding fault, since there is nothing in
this world, be it the noblest and most commendable
action whatsoever, that shall escape blameless.   As

for my being the true and only authoress of them,
your Lordship knows best, and my attending servants are witness that I have had none but my own
thoughts, fancies, and speculations to assist me; and
as soon as I have set them down, I send them to
those that are to transcribe them, and fit them for
the press; whereof since there have been several, and
amongst them such as only could write a good hand,
but neither understood orthography, nor had any
learning (I being then in banishment with your
Lordship, and not able to maintain learned secretaries), which hath been a great disadvantage to my
poor works, and the cause that they have been
printed so false and so full of errors; for besides
that I want also the skill of scholarship and true
writing, I did many times not peruse the copies
that were transcribed, lest they should disturb my
following conceptions; by which neglect, as I said,
many errors are slipt into my works, which yet I
hope learned and impartial readers will soon rectify,
and look more upon the sense, than carp at words.
I have been a student even from my childhood;
and since I have been your Lordship's wife, I have
lived for the most part a strict and retired life, as
is best known to your Lordship, and therefore my
censurers cannot know much of me, since they have
little or no acquaintance with me. 'Tis true, I have
been a traveller both before and after I was married
to your Lordship, and sometimes show myself at

your Lordship's command in public places or assemblies; but yet I converse with few. Indeed, my Lord, I matter not the censures of this age, but am rather proud of them; for it shows that my actions are more than ordinary, and according to the old proverb, it is better to be envied, than pitied: for I know well, that it is merely out of spite and malice, whereof this present age is so full, that none can escape them, and they'll make no doubt to stain even your Lordship's loyal, noble, and heroic actions, as well as they do mine, though yours have been of war and fighting, mine of contemplating and writing: yours were performed publicly in the field, mine privately in my closet: yours had many thousand eye-witnesses, mine none but my waiting-maids. But the great God, that hath hitherto blessed both your Grace and me, will, I question not, preserve both our fames to after ages, for which we shall be bound most humbly to acknowledge His great mercy; and I myself, as long as I live, be your Grace's honest wife, and humble servant,

M. Newcastle.

THE PREFACE.

—+—

WHEN I first intended to write this history, knowing myself to be no scholar, and as ignorant of the
rules of writing histories, as I have in my other
works acknowledged myself to be of the names and
terms of art; I desired my Lord, that he would be
pleased to let me have some elegant and learned
historian to assist me; which request his Grace
would not grant me; saying, that having never
had any assistance in the writing of my former
books, I should have no other in the writing of his
life, but the informations from himself, and his
secretary, of the chief transactions and fortunes
occurring in it, to the time he married me. I
humbly answered, that without a learned assistant,
the history would be defective: but he replied,
that truth could not be defective. I said again,
that rhetoric did adorn truth: and he answered,
that rhetoric was fitter for falsehoods than truths.
Thus I was forced by his Grace's commands, to
write this history in my own plain style, without

elegant flourishings, or exquisite method, relying
entirely upon truth, in the expressing whereof, I
have been very circumspect; as knowing well,
that his Grace's actions have so much glory of their
own, that they need borrow none from anybody's
industry.

Many learned men, I know, have published rules
and directions concerning the method and style of
histories, and do with great noise, to little purpose,
make loud exclamations against those historians,
that keeping close to the truth of their narrations,
cannot think it necessary to follow slavishly such
instructions; and there is some men of good understandings, as I have heard, that applaud very much
several histories, merely for their elegant style, and
well-observed method; setting a high value upon
feigned orations, mystical designs, and fancied
policies, which are, at the best, but pleasant
romances.   Others approve, in the relations of
wars, and of military actions, such tedious descriptions, that the reader, tired with them, will imagine
that there was more time spent in assaulting, defending, and taking of a fort, or a petty garrison,
than Alexander did employ in conquering the
greatest part of the world: which proves, that such
historians regard more their own eloquence, wit, and
industry, and the knowledge they believe to have of
the actions of war, and of all manner of governments, than of the truth of the history, which is the

main thing, and wherein consists the hardest task,
very few historians knowing the transactions they
write of, and much less the counsels and secret
designs of many different parties, which they confidently mention.

Although there be many sorts of histories, yet
these three are the chiefest: (1.) a general history;
(2.) a national history; (3.) a particular history.
Which three sorts may, not unfitly, be compared
to the three sorts of governments, democracy,
aristocracy, and monarchy. The first is the history
of the known parts and people of the world; the
second is the history of a particular nation, kingdom,
or commonwealth. The third is the history of the
life and actions of some particular person. The
first is profitable for travellers, navigators, and
merchants; the second is pernicious, by reason it
teaches subtle policies, begets factions, not only
between particular families and persons, but also
between whole nations, and great princes, rubbing
old sores, and renewing old quarrels, that would
otherwise have been forgotten. The last is the
most secure; because it goes not out of its own
circle, but turns on its own axis, and for the most
part keeps within the circumference of truth. The
first is mechanical, the second political, and the
third heroical. The first should only be written by
travellers and navigators; the second by statesmen; the third by the prime actors, or the

spectators of those affairs and actions of which they
write, as Cæsar's Commentaries are, which no pen
but of such an author, who was also actor in the
particular occurrences, private intrigues, secret
counsels, close designs, and rare exploits of war he
relates, could ever have brought to so high
perfection.

This history is of the third sort, as that is; and
being of the life and actions of my noble lord and
husband, who hath informed me of all the particular
passages I have recorded, I cannot, though neither
actor nor spectator, be thought ignorant of the
truth of what I write. Nor is it inconsistent with
my being a woman, to write of wars, that was
neither between Medes and Persians, Greeks and
Trojans, Christians and Turks, but among my own
countrymen, whose customs and inclinations, and
most of the persons that held any considerable place
in the armies, was well known to me; and besides
all that (which is above all) my noble and loyal Lord
did act a chief part in that fatal tragedy, to have
defended (if human power could have done it) his
most gracious sovereign, from the fury of his
rebellious subjects.

This history being (as I have said) of a particular
person, his actions and fortunes, it cannot be
expected that I should here preach of the beginning
of the world; nor seem to express understanding
in the politics, by tedious moral discourses, with

long observations upon the several sorts of government that have been in Greece and Rome, and upon others more modern. I will neither endeavour to make show of eloquence, making speeches that never were spoken, nor pretend to great skill in war, by making mountains of molehills, and telling romancical falsehoods for historical truths; and much less will I write to amuse my readers, in a mystical and allegorical style, of the disloyal actions of the opposite party, of the treacherous cowardice, envy, and malice of some persons, my Lord's enemies, and of the ingratitude of some of his seeming friends; wherein I cannot better obey his Lordship's commands to conceal those things, than in leaving them quite out, as I do, with submission to his Lordship's desire, from whom I have learned patience to overcome my passions, and discretion to yield to his prudence.

Thus am I resolved to write, in a natural plain style, without Latin sentences, moral instructions, politic designs, feigned orations, or envious and malicious exclamations, this short history of the loyal, heroic, and prudent actions of my noble Lord, as also of his sufferings, losses, and ill-fortunes, which in honour and conscience I could not suffer to be buried in silence; nor could I have undertaken so hard a task, had not my love to his person, and to truth, been my encourager and supporter.

I might have made this book larger, in transcribing (as is ordinary in histories) the several letters,[1] full of affection, and kind promises he received from his Gracious Sovereign, Charles the First, and from his royal consort, in the time he was in the actions of war, as also since the war, from his dear sovereign and master, Charles the Second: but many of the former letters having been lost, when all was lost, I thought it best, seeing I had not them all, to print none. As for orations, which is another way of swelling the bulk of histories, it is certain, that my Lord made not many; choosing rather to fight than to talk; and his Declarations having been printed already, it had been superfluous to insert them in these narrations.

This book would, however, have been a great volume, if his Grace would have given me leave to publish his enemy's actions. But being to write of

---

[1] Seven of these letters of the King's have been published by Sir Henry Ellis, " Original Letters," series I. vol. iii. pp. 291-303. Those of the Queen will be found in Mrs. M. E. Green's " Letters of Queen Henrietta Maria."

The Declarations referred to below are reprinted in Rushworth's Collection—"A Declaration made by the Earl of Newcastle for his resolution of marching into Yorkshire, as also a just vindication of himself from that unjust aspersion laid upon him for entertaining some Popish recusants in his service."—Rushworth, III. i. 78-81. " A Declaration of his Excellency the Earl of Newcastle, in answer to the aspersions cast upon him by the Lord Fairfax in his warrant bearing date February 2d."—Rushworth, III. i. 133.

his own only, I do it briefly and truly; and not as
many have done, who have written of the late Civil
War, with but few sprinklings of truth, like as heat-
drops upon a dry barren ground; knowing no more
of the transactions of those times, than what they
learned in the gazettes, which, for the most part
(out of policy to amuse and deceive the people),
contain nothing but falsehoods and chimeras; and
were such parasites, that after the King's party was
overpowered, the government among the rebels
changing from one faction to another, they never
missed to exalt highly the merits of the chief commanders of the then prevailing side, comparing some
of them to Moses, and some others to all the great
and most famous heroes, both Greeks and Romans.[1]
Wherein, unawares, they exceedingly commended
my noble Lord; for if those ringleaders of factions
were so great men as they are reported to be, by
those time-servers, how much greater must his
Lordship be, who beat most of them, except the
Earl of Essex, whose employment was never in the
northern parts, where all the rest of the greatest
strength of the Parliament was sent, to oppose my
Lord's forces, which was the greatest the King's
party had anywhere.

Good fortune is such an idol of the world, and is
so like the golden calf worshipped by the Israelites,

---

[1] This is evidently a hit at May.

that those arch-rebels never wanted astrologers to foretell them good success in all their enterprises, nor poets to sing their praises, nor orators for panegyrics; nay, which is worse, nor historians neither, to record their valour in fighting, and wisdom in governing. But being, so much as I am, above base profit, or any preferment whatsoever, I cannot fear to be suspected of flattery, in declaring to the world the merits, wealth, power, loyalty, and fortunes of my noble Lord, who hath done great actions, suffered great losses, endured a long banishment, for his loyalty to his King and country; and leads now, like another Scipio, a quiet country life. If, notwithstanding all this, any should say, that those who write histories of themselves, and their own actions, or of their own party, or instruct and inform those that write them, are partial to themselves; I answer, that it is very improbable worthy persons, who having done great, noble, and heroic exploits, deserving to be recorded, should be so vain as to write false histories; but if they do, it proves but their folly; for truth can never be concealed, and so it will be more for their disgrace than for their honour and fame. I fear not any such blemishes in this present history, for I am not conscious of any such crime as partiality or falsehood, but write it whilst my noble Lord is yet alive, and at such a time where truth may be declared, and falsehood contradicted; and I chal-

lenge any one (although I be a woman) to contra-
dict anything that I have set down, or prove it to
be otherwise than truth ; for be there never so many
contradictions, truth will conquer all at last.

Concerning my Lord's actions in war, which are
comprehended in the first Book, the relation of
them I have chiefly from my Lord's secretary, Mr.
Rolleston, a person that has been an eye-witness
thereof, and accompanied my Lord as secretary in
his army, and gave out all his commissions ; his
honesty and worth is unquestionable by all that
know him. And as for the second Book, which
contains my Lord's actions and sufferings, during
the time of his exile, I have set down so much as I
could possibly call to mind, without any particular
expression of time, only from the time of his banishment, or rather (what I can remember) from the
time of my marriage, till our return into England.
To the end of which I have joined a computation
of my Lord's losses, which he hath suffered by those
unfortunate wars. In the third Book I have set
down some particular chapters concerning the
description of his person, his natural faculties, and
personal virtues, &c. And in the last, some essays
and discourses of my Lord's, together with some
notes and remarks of mine own ; which I thought
most convenient to place by themselves at the end
of this work, rather than to intermingle them with
the body of the history.

It might be some prejudice to my Lord's glory, and the credit of this history, not to take notice of a very considerable thing I have heard, which is, that when his Lordship's army had got so much strength and reputation, that the rebellious Parliament finding themselves overpowered with it, rather than to be utterly ruined (as was unavoidable), did call the Scots to their assistance, with a promise to reward so great a service with the four northern counties of Northumberland, Cumberland, Westmoreland, and the bishopric of Durham, which I have not mentioned in the book.

And it is most certain, that the Parliament's forces were never powerful, nor their commanders or officers famous, until such time as my Lord was overpowered; neither could loyalty have been overpowered by rebellion, had not treachery had better fortune than prudence.

When I speak of my Lord's pedigree, where Thomas, Earl of Arundel, grandfather to the now Duke of Norfolk, is mentioned, they have left out William, Viscount Stafford, one of his sons, who did marry the heir of the last Baron Stafford, descended from the Dukes of Buckingham; which was set down in my original manuscript.

Some of those omissions, and very probably others, are happened, partly for want of timely information, and chiefly by the death of my secretary, who did copy my writings for the press, and died in

London, attending that service, afore the printing of the book was quite finished. And as I hope of your favour to be excused for omitting those things in the book; so I expect of your justice to be approved in putting them here, though somewhat unseasonably.

Before I end this Preface, I do beseech my readers not to mistake me when I speak of my Lord's banishment, as if I would conceal that he went voluntarily out of his native country; for it is most true, that his Lordship prudently perceiving all the King's party lost, not only in England, but also in Scotland and Ireland; and that it was impossible to withstand the rebels, after the fatal overthrow of his army; his Lordship, in a poor and mean condition, quitted his own country, and went beyond sea; soon after which, the rebels having got an absolute power, and granted a general pardon to all those that would come in to them, upon composition, at the rates they had set down, his Lordship, with but few others, was excepted from it, both for life and estate, and did remain thus banished till his Majesty's happy restoration.

I must also acknowledge, that I have committed great errors in taking no notice of times as I should have done in many places of this history: I mention in one place the Queen Mother's being in France, when my Lord went thither, but do not say in what year that was; nor do I express when his Majesty (our now gracious Sovereign) came in, and went out again several times from that kingdom, which has happened for want of memory, and I desire my readers to excuse me for it.

Nobody can certainly be more ready to find faults in this work, than I am to confess them; being very conscious that I have, as I told my Lord I should, committed many for want of learning, and chiefly of skill in writing histories. But having, according to his Lordship's commands, written his actions and fortunes truly and plainly, I have reason to expect, that whatsoever else shall be found amiss, will be favourably pardoned by the candid readers, to whom I wish all manner of happiness.

THE DUCHESS OF NEWCASTLE.

MAY IT PLEASE YOUR GRACE,—I have been taught, and do believe, that obedience is better than sacrifice; and know, that both are due from me to your Grace; and since I have been so long in obeying your commands, I shall not presume to use any arguments for my excuse, but rather choose ingenuously to confess my fault, and beg your Grace's pardon. And because forgiveness is a glory to the supremest powers, I will hope that your Grace by that great example will make it yours. And now I humbly take leave to represent to your Grace, as faithfully and truly as my memory will serve me, all my observations of the most memorable actions, and honourable deportments of his Grace, my most noble lord and master, William, Duke of Newcastle, in the execution and performance of the trusts and high employments committed and commended to his care and charge by three Kings of England; that is to say, King James, King Charles

the First, of ever blessed memory; and our gracious
King, Charles the Second; under whom he hath
had the happiness to live, and the honour to serve
them in several capacities. And because I humbly
conceive, that it is not within the intention of your
Grace's commands, that I should give you a particular relation of his Grace's high birth, his noble
and princely education and breeding, both at home
and abroad; his natural faculties, and personal
virtues; his justice, bounty, charity, friendship;
his right approved courage, and true valour, not
grounded upon, or governed by passion, but reason;
his magnificent manner of living and supporting
his dignity, testified by his great entertainments of
their Majesties, and his private friends, upon all fit
occasions, besides his ordinary and constant housekeeping and attendants, some for honour, and some
for business, wherein he exceeded most of his quality;
and that he was, and is, an incomparable master to
his servants, is sufficiently testified by all or most of
the chiefest of them, living and dying in his Grace's
service, which is an argument that they thought
themselves as happy therein, as the world could
make them; nor of his well-chosen pleasures, which
were principally horses of all sorts, but more particularly horses of manage;[1] his study and art of

---

[1] Horses trained in the riding-school. Manage is from
the French *manège*, the training of a horse in a riding-

the true use of the sword; his magnificent buildings. These are his chiefest delights, wherein his Grace spared for no cost nor charge, which are sufficiently manifested to the world ; for other delights, as those of running horses, hawking, hunting, &c, his Grace used them merely for society's sake, and out of a generous and obliging nature to please others, though his knowledge in them excelled, as well as in the other. And yet, notwithstanding these this large and vast expenses, before his Grace was called to the court, he increased his revenue by way of purchase to a great value; and when he was called to the court, he was then free from debts, and, as I have heard, some thousands of pounds in his purse. These particulars, and as many more of this kind as would swell a volume, I could enumerate to your Grace; but that they are so well known to your Grace, it would be a presumption in me, rather

---

school ; Italian *maneggiare*, to handle, train, from Latin *manus*. In Book II. of these Memoirs the Duchess speaks of her husband buying horses "to exercise the art of manage, which he is a great lover and master of." "They vault from hunters to the managed steed," says Young, and Scott even speaks of a "managed hawk." Orlando, when complaining of his brother's neglect, says, "His horses are bred better ; for, besides that they are fair with their feeding, they are taught their manage, and to that end riders dearly hired."—As You Like It, i. 1. Lady Hotspur also tells her husband that she has heard him in his sleep "speak terms of manage to thy bounding steed."—1 Henry IV. ii. 3.

than a service, to give your Grace that trouble ; and therefore I humbly forbear, and proceed, according to my intention, to give your Grace a faithful account of your Grace's commands, as becomes, may it please your Grace, your Grace's most humble and most obedient servant,

JOHN ROLLESTON.

THE LIFE

OF

THE MOST ILLUSTRIOUS PRINCE,

WILLIAM, DUKE OF NEWCASTLE.

—✳—

THE FIRST BOOK.

SINCE my chief intent in this present work is to describe the life and actions of my noble Lord and husband, William, Duke of Newcastle, I shall do it with as much brevity, perspicuity, and truth, as is required of an impartial historian. The history of his pedigree I shall refer to the Heralds, and partly give you an account thereof at the latter end of this work ; only thus much I shall now mention, as will be requisite for the better understanding of the following discourse.

His grandfather by his father's side was Sir William Cavendish, Privy Counsellor and Treasurer of the Chamber to King Henry the Eighth, Edward the Sixth, and Queen Mary. His grandfather by his mother was Cuthbert, Lord Ogle, an ancient

A

Baron.   His father, Sir Charles Cavendish, was the youngest son to Sir William, and had no other children but three sons, whereof my Lord was the second ; but his elder brother dying in his infancy, left both his title and birthright to my Lord, so that my Lord had then but one only brother left, whose name was Charles after his father, whereas my Lord had the name of his grandfather.[1]

These two brothers were partly bred with Gilbert, Earl of Shrewsbury, their uncle-in-law, and their aunt Mary, Countess of Shrewsbury, Gilbert's wife, and sister to their father ; for there interceded an entire and constant friendship between the said Gilbert, Earl of Shrewsbury, and my Lord's father, Sir Charles Cavendish, caused not only by the marriage of my Lord's aunt, his father's sister, to the aforesaid Gilbert, Earl of Shrewsbury, and by the marriage of George, Earl of Shrewsbury, Gilbert's father, with my Lord's grandmother, by his father's

---

[1] Sir William Cavendish died in 1557.   His widow, Elizabeth Hardwick, married George Talbot, Earl of Shrews-bury, and thus began the connection between the Talbot and Cavendish families, which was strengthened and com-pleted by the marriage of Mary Cavendish, youngest daughter of Sir William, to Gilbert Talbot, the eldest son of Earl George, whilst Henry Cavendish, eldest son of Sir William, married Grace Talbot, youngest daughter of the same Earl.   William Cavendish, the hero of this Memoir, was born in 1592.   Gilbert, Earl of Shrews-bury died May 8, 1616, and Sir Charles Cavendish died

side ; but Sir Charles Cavendish, my Lord's father, and Gilbert, Earl of Shrewsbury, being brought up and bred together in one family, and grown up as parts of one body, after they came to be beyond children, and travelled together into foreign countries, to observe the fashions, laws, and customs of other nations, contracted such an entire friendship which lasted to their death. Neither did they outlive each other long, for my Lord's father, Sir Charles Cavendish, lived but one year after Gilbert, Earl of Shrewsbury.

But both my Lord's parents, and his aunt and uncle-in-law, showed always a great and fond love

---

April 4, 1617. Ben Jonson wrote the following epitaph upon him :—

Charles Cavendish to his Posterity.

" Sons, seek me not amongst these polished stones,
These only hide part of my flesh and bones,
Which, did they ne'er so neat or proudly dwell,
Will all turn dust, and may not make me swell.

Let such as justly have outlived all praise,
Trust in the tombs their careful friends do raise ;
I made my life my monument and yours,
To which there's no material that endures.

Nor yet inscription like it. Write but that,
And teach your nephews it to emulate :
It will be matter loud enough to tell
Not when I died, but how I lived—farewell."

Collins' Historical Collections, p. 22, and
Cunningham's Jonson, iii. 459.

to my Lord, endeavouring, when he was but a child, to please him with what he most delighted in. When he was grown to the age of fifteen or sixteen, he was made Knight of the Bath, an ancient and honourable order, at the time when Henry, King James, of blessed memory, his eldest son, was created Prince of Wales :[1] and soon after he went to travel with Sir Henry Wotton,[2] who was sent as ambassador extraordinary to the then Duke of Savoy; which Duke made very much of my Lord, and when he would be free in feasting, placed him next to himself. Before my Lord did return with the ambassador into England, the said Duke proffered my Lord, that if he would stay with him, he would not only confer upon him the best titles of honour he could, but also give him an honourable command in war, although my Lord was but young, for the Duke had then some designs of war. But the ambassador, who had taken the care of my Lord, would not leave him behind without his parents' consent.

At last, when my Lord took his leave of the Duke, the Duke being a very generous person,

---

[1] Prince Henry was created Prince of Wales, June 4, 1610. William Cavendish was made Knight of the Bath, June 3.—Birch, "Life of Henry Prince of Wales," p. 192.

[2] Sir Henry Wotton. See the account of him in Walton's Lives and Reliquiæ Wottonianæ.

presented him with a Spanish horse, a saddle very richly embroidered, and with a rich jewel of diamonds.[1]

Some time after my Lord's return into England, Gilbert, Earl of Shrewsbury, died, and left my Lord, though he was then but young, and about twenty-two years of age, his executor; a year after, his father, Sir Charles Cavendish, died also. His mother, being then a widow, was desirous that my Lord should marry: in obedience to whose commands, he chose a wife both to his own good liking, and his mother's approving; who was daughter and heir to William Basset of Blore, Esq.; a very honourable and ancient family in Staffordshire, by whom was added a great part to his estate, as hereafter shall be mentioned.[2] After my Lord was married, he lived, for the most part, in the country, and pleased himself and his neighbours with hospitality, and such delights as the country afforded; only now and then he would go up to London for some short time to wait on the King.

---

[1] I can find no mention of Sir William Cavendish in Wotton's published letters, nor any of this offer of the Duke of Savoy's.

[2] The rents of the Duke of Newcastle's Staffordshire estates amounted to £2349, 17s. 4d. per annum. See the account of the Duke's estates given later. This lady was the widow of Henry Howard, third son of the Earl of Suffolk. The marriage probably took place in 1618.

About this time King James, of blessed memory, having a purpose to confer some honour upon my Lord, made him Viscount Mansfield, and Baron of Bolsover;[1] and after the decease of King James, King Charles the First, of blessed memory, constituted him Lord Warden of the Forest of Sherwood and Lieutenant of Nottinghamshire, and restored his mother, Catharine, the second daughter of Cuthbert, Lord Ogle, to her father's dignity, after the death of her only sister Jane, Countess of Shrewsbury, publicly declaring, that it was her right;[2] which title, after the death of his mother, descended also upon my Lord, and his heirs general, together with a large inheritance of £3000 a year, in Northumberland.

About the same time, after the decease of William, late Earl of Devonshire, his noble cousin-german, my Lord was by his said Majesty made Lord Lieutenant of Derbyshire; which trust and honour, after he had enjoyed for several years, and managed it, like as all other offices put to his

---

[1] This took place after the King's visit to Welbeck in 1619. The patent creating Sir William Cavendish Lord Ogle of Bothal and Viscount Mansfield is dated November 3, 1620.—Collins, "Historical Collections of the Noble Families of Cavendish, Holles," &c., p. 29.

[2] Lady Jane Ogle died in 1625. Her epitaph was written by Jonson, *vide* Jonson's works, ed. Cunningham, p. 460. Lady Catharine was created Baroness Ogle, Decem-

trust, with all possible care, faithfulness, and dexterity, during the time of the said Earl's son, William, the now Earl of Devonshire, his minority, as soon as this same Earl was come to age, and by law made capable of that trust, he willingly and

---

ber 4, 1628 (Collins, p. 24). Jonson's epitaph on this lady is as follows :—

> " She was the light (without reflex
> Upon herself) of all her sex,
> The best of women !—Her whole life
> Was the example of a wife,
> Or of a parent, or a friend !
> All circles had their spring and end
> In her, and what could perfect be
> And without angles, *It was she.*
>
> All that was solid in the name
> Of virtue ; precious in the frame,
> Or else magnetic in the force,
> Or sweet, or various in the course ;
> What was proportion, or could be
> By warrant called just symmetry,
> In number, measure, or degree
> Of weight or fashion, *It was she.*
>
> Her soul possessed her flesh's state
> In freehold, not as an inmate,
> And when the flesh here shut up day,
> Fame's heat upon the grave did stay,
> And hourly brooding o'er the same,
> Keeps warm the spice of her good name,
> Until the ashes turned be
> Into a Phœnix—*Which is she.*"

This is followed by two other pieces of verse on the same subject.—Jonson, ed. Cunningham, iii. 460.

freely resigned it into his hands, he having hitherto
kept it only for him, that he and nobody else
might succeed his father in that dignity.

In these, and all other both public and private
employments, my Lord hath ever been careful to
keep up the King's rights to the uttermost of his
power, to strengthen those mentioned counties with
ammunition, and to administer justice to every one ;
for he refused no man's petition, but sent all that
came to him, either for relief or justice, away from
him fully satisfied.[1]

Not long after his being made Lieutenant of
Nottinghamshire, there was found so great a defect
of arms and ammunition in that county, that the
Lords of the Council being advertised thereof, as
the manner then was, his Majesty commanded a levy
to be made upon the whole county for the supply
thereof. Whereupon the sum of £500, or thereabout, was accordingly levied for that purpose, and
three persons of quality, then Deputy Lieutenants,
were desired by my Lord to receive the money,
and see it disposed ; which being done accordingly,
and a certain account rendered to my Lord, he voluntarily ordered the then Clerk of the Peace of that
county, that the same account should be recorded

---

[1] A letter from the Duke (as Viscount Mansfield) to
Strafford is printed in the Strafford correspondence, vol. i.
p. 43, *vide* Appendix.

amongst the sessions rolls, and be published in open sessions, to the end that the country might take notice how their monies were disposed of; for which act of justice my Lord was highly commended.

Within some few years after, King Charles the First, of blessed memory, his gracious Sovereign, in regard of his true and faithful service to his King and country, was pleased to honour him with the title of Earl of Newcastle, and Baron of Bothal and Heple;[1] which title he graced so much by his noble actions and deportments, that some seven years after, which was in the year 1638, his Majesty called him up to Court, and thought him the fittest person whom he might intrust with the government of his son Charles, then Prince of Wales, now our most gracious King, and made him withal a member of the Lords of his Majesty's most honourable Privy Council; which, as it was a great honour and trust, so he spared no care and industry to discharge his duty accordingly; and to that end, left all the care of governing his own family and estate, with all fidelity attending his master, not without consider- able charges, and vast expenses of his own.[2]

---

[1] "On the 7th day of March in the third year of King Charles I. he was further advanced to the dignity of Baron Cavendish of Bolsover and Earl of Newcastle-upon-Tyne." —Collins, "Historical Collections," p. 26.

[2] The patent appointing the Earl of Newcastle governor of the Prince is dated June 4, 1638, and has been printed by Collins ("Historical Collections," p. 27). Windebanke's

In this present employment he continued for the space of three years, during which time there happened an insurrection and rebellion of his Majesty's discontented subjects in Scotland, which forced his Majesty to raise an army, to reduce them to their obedience, and his treasury being at that time exhausted he was necessitated to desire some supply and assistance of the noblest and richest of his loyal subjects. Amongst the rest, my Lord lent his Majesty £10,000 and raised himself a volunteer troop of horse, which consisted of 120 knights and gentlemen of quality,[1] who marched to Berwick by

---

letter offering this post to the Earl, and the Earl's reply, are both contained in the Clarendon State Papers, and dated 19th and 21st March 1638. For these see the Appendix. "It is certainly a mighty mark of his Majesty's estimation of you," writes Strafford, "that he intrusts you with the keeping of so precious a jewel." The Lord Deputy sends at the same time a number of counsels for the Earl's guidance at court (Strafford Papers, ii. 174). The advice given by the Earl to his pupil, originally printed by Sir Henry Ellis, is also given in the Appendix. A letter in the Record Office, written by one Thomas Wiseman on Newcastle's retirement from this post, states that the Earl ran himself into debt to the amount of £40,000 during his employment.

[1] Mrs. Hutchinson's testimony to the Earl's great popularity is worth quoting ; it will be observed that her account of the volunteer troop differs slightly from that given by the Duchess. "The Earl of Newcastle . . . a lord once so much beloved in his country, that when the first expedition was against the Scots, the gentlemen of the country set him forth two troops, one all of gentlemen, the

his Majesty's command, where it pleased his Majesty to set this mark of honour upon that troop, that it should be independent, and not commanded by any general officer, but only by his Majesty himself. The reason thereof was upon this following occasion.

His Majesty's whole body of horse, being commanded to march into Scotland against the rebels, a place was appointed for their rendezvous ; immediately upon their meeting, my Lord sent a gentleman of quality of his troop [1] to his Majesty's then General of the Horse, to know where his troop should march ; who returned this answer, That it was to march next after the troops of the General Officers of the Field. My Lord conceiving that his troop ought to march in the van, and not in the rear, sent the same messenger back again to the General, to inform him, that he had the honour to march with the Prince's colours, and therefore he thought it not fit to march under any of the Officers

other of their men, who waited on him into the north at their own charges. He had, indeed, through his great estate, his liberal hospitality, and constant residence in his country, so endeared them to him, that no man was a greater prince than he was in all that northern quarter ; till a foolish ambition of glorious slavery carried him to court, where he ran himself much into debt, to purchase neglects of the King and Queen, and scorns of the proud courtiers."—Memoirs, vol. i. p. 163.

[1] Sir William Carnaby, Kt.

of the Field; yet nevertheless the General ordered
that troop as he had formerly directed.   Whereupon, my Lord thinking it unfit at that time to
dispute the business, immediately commanded his
Cornet[1] to take off the Prince's colours from his
staff, and so marched in the place appointed, choosing rather to march without his colours flying, than
to lessen his master's dignity by the command of
any subject.

Immediately after the return from that expedition to his Majesty's leaguer, the General made a
complaint thereof to his Majesty; who being truly
informed of the business, commended my Lord's
discretion for it, and from that time ordered that
troop to be commanded by none but himself.   Thus
they remained upon duty, *without receiving any
payment or allowance from his Majesty,*[2] until his
Majesty had reduced his rebellious subjects, and
then my Lord returned with honour to his charge,
viz., the government of the Prince.

At last when the whole army was disbanded,
then, and not before, my Lord thought it a fit time
to exact an account from the said General for the
affront he passed upon him, and sent him a challenge;
the place and hour being appointed by both their

---

[1] Mr. Gray, brother to the Lord Gray of the North.
[2] The words in italic have been carefully obliterated
with ink.

consent: where and when to meet, my Lord appeared
there with his second,[1] but found not his opposite.
After some while his opposite's second came all
alone, by whom my Lord perceived that their design
had been discovered to the King by some of his
opposite's friends, who presently caused them both
to be confined until he had made their peace.[2]

My Lord having hitherto attended the Prince,
his master, with all faithfulness and duty befitting
so great an employment, for the space of three
years, in the beginning of that rebellious and
unhappy Parliament, which was the cause of all the
ruins and misfortunes that afterwards befell this
kingdom, was privately advertised, that the Parliament's design was to take the government of the
Prince from him, which he apprehending as a disgrace to himself, wisely prevented, and obtained the

---

[1] Francis Palmes.

[2] This General of the Horse was the Earl of Holland. Clarendon's account of this incident is very similar to that given
in the text, and was very probably derived from the Duke himself. As soon as the army was disbanded, says Clarendon,
Newcastle "sent a challenge to the Earl of Holland, by a
gentleman very punctual and well acquainted with those
errands ; who took a proper season to mention it to him,
without a possibility of suspicion. The Earl of Holland
was never suspected to want courage, yet in this occasion he
showed not that alacrity, but that the delay exposed it to
notice ; and so by the King's authority the matter was composed."—History of the Rebellion, ii. 23.

consent of his late Majesty, with his favour, to deliver up the charge of being governor to the Prince, and retire into the country.[1]   Which he

---

[1] Newcastle resigned his post in May 1641, and was succeeded by the Marquis of Hertford, whose appointment is dated by Whitelock May 17 (vol. i. p. 44).   Clarendon's account of the Earl's retirement is, that he, knowing the hostility of the Earls of Essex and Holland to himself, knowing also " that they liked not his having the government of the Prince as one who would infuse such principles into him as would not be agreeable to their designs, and would not rest till they saw another man in that province," therefore, " upon these considerations *and some other imaginations upon the prospect of affairs* he very wisely resolved to retire from the court," and suggested the Marquis of Hertford to the King as his successor.   (Rebellion, iv. 293.)   The real cause of this retirement, however, seems to have been the *other imaginations* alluded to by Clarendon.   The Earl was implicated in the Army plot, and his share in it became publicly known early in May. Suckling and Jermyn selected the Earl of Newcastle to be titular General of the Army in place of the Earl of Northumberland, and Goring was to be his Lieutenant-General. Though the King disapproved of the proposal and did not make the suggested appointment, the Queen encouraged the plot, and the plan for bringing the army up to London was persisted in.   It was proposed to the officers, testifies Lieutenant-Colonel Ballard, " that, if there were occasion, the army should remove their quarters into Nottinghamshire, where the Prince and the Earl of Newcastle should meet them with a thousand horse, and all the French that were in London should be mounted, and likewise meet them."   " Sergeant-Major Willis said, moreover," according to Captain Chudleigh, " that the army would be very

did in the beginning of the year 1641, and settled himself, with his lady, children, and family, to his great satisfaction, with an intent to have continued there, and rested under his own vine, and managed his own estate. But he had not enjoyed himself long, but an express came to him from his Majesty, who was then unjustly and unmannerly treated by the said Parliament, to repair with all possible speed and privacy to Kingston-upon-Hull, where the greatest part of his Majesty's ammunition and arms then remained in that magazine, it being the most considerable place for strength in the northern parts of the kingdom.

Immediately upon the receipt of these his Majesty's orders and commands, my Lord prepared for their execution, and about twelve of the clock at night, hastened from his own house when his family were all at their rest, save two or three servants which he appointed to attend him. The

---

well kept together, for that the Prince was to be brought thither, which would confirm their affections ; . . . and Willis told them also, that if my Lord of Newcastle was their General, he would feast them in Nottinghamshire, and would not use them roughly, but that they should be governed by a council of war."—Husband's " Exact Collection," quarto 1643, p. 222 ; Gardiner, " Fall of the Monarchy of Charles I.," ii. 117–126. With these facts before them it would have been impossible for the Parliament to trust the Prince longer in Newcastle's hands, and he therefore avoided an attack by retiring.

next day early in the morning he arrived at Hull, in the quality of a private gentleman, which place was distant from his house forty miles ; and none of his family that were at home knew what was become of him, till he sent an express to his lady to inform her where he was.

Thus being admitted into the town, he fell upon his intended design, and brought it to so hopeful an issue for his Majesty's service, that he wanted nothing but his Majesty's further commission and pleasure to have secured both the town and magazine for his Majesty's use : and to that end by a speedy express [1] gave his Majesty, who was then at Windsor, an account of all his transactions therein, together with his opinion of them, hoping his Majesty would have been pleased either to come thither in person, which he might have done with much security, or at least have sent him a commission and orders how he should do his Majesty further service.

But instead thereof he received orders from his Majesty to observe such directions as he should receive from the Parliament then sitting : whereupon he was summoned personally to appear at the House of Lords, and a committee chosen to examine the grounds and reasons of his undertaking that design ; but my Lord showed them his commission,

---

[1] Captain Mazine.

and that it was done in obedience to his Majesty's
commands, and so was cleared of that action.[1]

---

[1] The warrant to Newcastle is dated Hampton Court,
January 11, 1642 (Lords' Journals, iv. 585). Captain Legg
was despatched to Hull to prepare the citizens to receive
Lord Newcastle as their governor. The Parliament obtained information of the King's purpose, and sent off
Captain Hotham with orders to his father, Sir John Hotham,
to secure Hull by means of the Yorkshire Trained Bands,
and not to deliver it up till he was ordered to do so by
"the King's authority, signified unto him by the Lords
and Commons now assembled in Parliament." Newcastle
was despatched by the King in person as soon as Captain
Hotham's journey was known. The King's object was not
only to secure the munitions stored up at Hull, but to obtain
possession of a port where the Danish soldiers he was then
purposing to hire might be safely landed. (Gardiner, "Fall
of the Monarchy of Charles I.," vol. ii. p. 409.) A letter
from Legg to Sir E. Nicholas states that Newcastle arrived
at Hull on January 14; Newcastle himself announced his
arrival to the King in a letter dated January 15, which is
given in the Appendix. (Domestic State Papers, Charles I.,
vol. 488, Nos. 55 and 62.) According to Rushworth (III. i.
564), the Earl "desired to pass unknown, calling himself Sir
John Savage, and at his first coming was brought before the
Mayor under that name, till being known by some bystanders
he was forced to own both his name and his errand." The
Mayor refused to admit either Hotham's or Newcastle's
troops, and humbly desired the King and Parliament to join
in appointing a garrison. "A strong party bestirred themselves for the Earl with great expectations of the King's
royal favour to the town thereby," continues Rushworth,
and he might possibly have secured the town if the King's
ill success elsewhere had not obliged him to yield and

B

Not long after, my Lord obtained the freedom
from his Majesty to retire again to his country life,
which he did with much alacrity.   He had not
remained many months there, but his Majesty was
forced, by the fury of the said Parliament, to repair
in person to York, and to send the Queen beyond
the seas for her safety.

No sooner was his Majesty arrived at York but
he sent his commands to my Lord to come thither
to him ; which, according to his wonted custom
and loyalty, he readily obeyed, and after a few
days spent there in consultation, his Majesty was

---

recall Newcastle.   On January 20, the House of Lords
passed a resolution ordering him to attend the House.
He made no haste to return upon the summons of the
House, but sent to the King to know his pleasure ; who,
not thinking matters yet ripe enough to make any such
declaration, appointed him to come away. (Clarendon,
Rebellion, iv. 215.)   " But the same day that the Earl
departed, Mr. Hotham was freely received into the town,
with three companies of Trained Bands, and the keys of
the ports, and the magazine, were surrendered into his
hands " (Rushworth).   This took place before the end of
January.   The Earl did not appear in the House of Lords
till after the 9th February, and was finally, on the 14th
February, after delivering up his commission, granted
leave to go into the country for his health's sake.   (Lords'
Journals, February 14, 1642.)   See also Sanford, " Studies
and Illustrations of the Great Rebellion," p. 474 ; and Buff,
" Die Politik Karls des Ersten in den ersten Wochen nach
seiner Flucht von London," pp. 5–18.

pleased to command him to Newcastle - upon-
Tyne, to take upon him the government of that
town, and the four counties next adjoining;[1] that
is to say, Northumberland, Cumberland, Westmoreland, and the Bishopric of Durham. Which
my Lord did accordingly, although he wanted men,
money, and ammunition, for the performance of
that design; for when he came thither he neither
found any military provision considerable for the
undertaking that work, nor generally any great
encouragement from the people in those parts,
more than what his own interest created in them.
Nevertheless, he thought it his duty rather to
hazard all, than to neglect the commands of his
Sovereign; and resolved to show his fidelity, by
nobly setting all at stake, as he did, though he well
knew how to have secured himself, as too many
others did, either by neutrality or adhering to the
rebellious party; but his honour and loyalty was too
great to be stained with such foul adherences.

---

[1] The King's commission to the Earl is dated June 20,
1642 (Collins, "Historical Collections," p. 30). Brand, referring to Rymer's Fœdeia, tom. xx. p. 531, says June 29.
The earlier date is most probable, for the Commons' Journals
(June 30) mention the Earl having sent out his warrants from
Newcastle into the county of Durham commanding 600 foot
and 100 horse of the trained band of Durham to come into
Newcastle. Moreover, a news letter in the Record Office
dated June 17, says that the Earl left York for Newcastle on
the preceding Wednesday, *i.e.*, June 15.

As soon as my Lord came to Newcastle, in the first place he sent for all his tenants and friends in those parts, and presently raised a troop of horse consisting of 120, and á regiment of foot, and put them under command, and upon duty and exercise in the town of Newcastle ; and with this small beginning took the government of that place upon him ; where with the assistance of the townsmen, particularly the Mayor [1] (whom, by the power of his forces, he continued Mayor for the year following, he being a person of much trust and fidelity, as he approved himself), and the rest of his brethren, within few days he fortified the town, and raised men daily, and put a garrison of soldiers into Tynmouth Castle, standing upon the river Tyne, betwixt Newcastle and the sea, to secure that port, and armed the soldiers as well as he could. And thus he stood upon his guard, and continued them upon duty ; playing his weak game with much prudence, and giving the town and country very great satisfaction by his noble and honourable deportment.[2]

---

[1] Sir John Marlay, Kt.

[2] Our information concerning the Earl's conduct at Newcastle is very scanty. Something, however, may be gathered from a paper amongst the Clarendon State Papers, attributed to Sir John Marlay, No 2064—"An Account of the military proceedings in the North from 1641 to 1645 inclusive, chiefly those in which the Marquis of Newcastle was concerned, and which relate to the town of Newcastle."

In the meantime, there happened a great mutiny of the train-band soldiers of the Bishopric at Durham, so that my Lord was forced to remove thither in person, attended with some forces to appease them ; where at his arrival (I mention it by the way, and as a merry passage) a jovial fellow used this expression, that he liked my Lord very well, but not his company (meaning his soldiers).

After my Lord had reduced them to their obedience and duty, he took great care of the Church government in the said bishopric (as he did no less in all other places committed to his care and protection, well knowing that schism and faction in religion is the mother of all or most rebellions, wars, and disturbances in a state or government) and constituted that learned and eminent divine the then Dean of Peterborough, now Lord Bishop of Durham,[1] to view all sermons that were to be preached, and suffer nothing in them that in the least reflected against his Majesty's person and government, but to put forth and add whatsoever he thought convenient, and punish those that should trespass against it. In which that worthy person used so much care and industry, that never the Church could be more happily governed then it was at that present.

---

[1] Dr. Cosin ; unfortunately there occurs at this point a gap of five years in the letters of Cosin collected by Mr. Ornsby.

Some short time after, my Lord received from her Majesty the Queen,[1] out of Holland, a small supply of money, viz., a little barrel of ducatoons, which amounted to about £500 sterling ; which my Lord distributed amongst the officers of his new-raised army, to encourage them the better in their service ; as also some arms, the most part whereof were consigned to his late Majesty ; and those that were ordered to be conveyed to his Majesty, were sent accordingly, conducted by that only troop of horse, which my Lord had newly raised, with orders to return again to him ; but it seems his Majesty liked the troop so well, that he was pleased to command their stay to recruit his own army.

About the same time the King of Denmark was likewise pleased to send his Majesty a ship, which

---

[1] The Queen's correspondence with Newcastle is contained in the " Letters of Queen Henrietta Maria," edited by Mrs. M. E. Green. "The Queen herself intended at first to land at Newcastle and join the Earl. She writes to the King on November 20, 1642 : 'As I was ready to set out, and had fixed the day, the wind changed, which has made me change my resolution. I have received letters from the Earl of Newcastle, by which he begs me not to come yet, for he is constrained to march into Yorkshire. Hotham is playing the devil. So that I shall await the issue of his march, of which in a week I hope to hear tidings.'"—Letters, p. 145. Brand states that on October 13 a small vessel arrived at Newcastle with arms for a thousand men, and £10,000 in money. History of Newcastle, i. 461.

arrived at Newcastle, laden with some ammunition, arms, regiment pieces, and Danish clubs;[1] which my Lord kept for the furnishing of some forces which he intended to raise for his Majesty's service. For he perceiving the flames increase more and more in both the Houses of Parliament then sitting at Westminster, against his Majesty's person and government; upon consultation with his friends and allies, and the interest he had in those northern parts, took a resolution to raise an army for his Majesty's service, and by an express acquainted his Majesty with his design; who was so well pleased with it, that he sent him commissions for that purpose, to constitute him General of all the forces raised and to be raised in all the parts of the

---

[1] Vicars mentions the capture in August 1643 of a Danish ship bringing arms to the King, including 1000 "piked clubs or Roundheads" (God's Ark, p. 22). One of the chief reasons which induced the King to attempt the seizure of Hull, in January 1642, was its convenience for landing Danish troops. The King was still seeking to obtain troops and munitions from Denmark, *vide* "Letters of Queen Henrietta Maria," pp. 148, 153, and an intercepted letter from the Hague, dated November 26, 1642, addressed to Secretary Nicholas, and printed by order of the Parliament. "From Denmark are likewise sent arms for 10,000 foot, and 1500 horse, with a train of artillery and everything proportionable, to the very drums and halberds. Two good men of war come their convoy, and in them an ambassador to his Majesty, a person of great quality in Denmark."—Rushworth, III. ii. 69.

kingdom, Trent-North, and moreover in the several
counties of Lincoln, Nottingham, Derby, Lancashire,
Cheshire, Leicester, Rutland, Cambridge, Huntingdon, Norfolk, Suffolk, and Essex, and Commander-
in-Chief for the same ; as also to empower and
authorise him to confer the honour of knighthood
upon such persons as he should conceive deserved
it, and to coin money and print whensoever he saw
occasion for it.   Which as it was not only a great
honour, but a great trust and power ; so he used it
with much discretion and wisdom, only in such
occurrences where he found it tending to the
advancement of his Majesty's service, and conferred
the honour of knighthood sparingly, and but on
such persons whose valiant and loyal actions did
justly deserve it, so that he knighted in all to the
number of twelve.[1]

Within a short time, my Lord formed an army
of 8000 foot, horse and dragoons, and put them
into a condition to march in the beginning of
November 1642.   No sooner was this effected,
but the insurrection grew high in Yorkshire, inso-

---

[1] The Earl of Essex in Queen Elizabeth's reign also
enjoyed, and, according to the Queen, too freely exercised,
this power of making knights.   Amongst his knights were
Sir John Harington (Nugæ Antiquæ, ed. Park, i. 318) and
Sir Robert Cary (Lord Orrery's preface to the "Memoirs of
Sir Robert Cary," p. xxiv. ed. 1808, where many similar cases
are cited).

much, that most of his Majesty's good subjects of that country, as well the nobility as gentry, were forced, for the preservation of their persons, to retire to the city of York, a walled town, but of no great strength ; and hearing that my Lord had not only kept those counties in the northern parts generally faithful to his Majesty, but raised an army for his Majesty's interest, and the protection of his good subjects ; thought it convenient to employ and authorise some persons of quality to attend upon my Lord, and treat with him on their behalf, that he would be pleased to give them the assistance of his army, which my Lord granted them upon such terms as did highly advance his Majesty's service, which was my Lord's chief and only aim.[1]

Thus my Lord being with his army invited into Yorkshire, he prepared for it with all the speed that the nature of that business could possibly permit ; and after he had fortified the town of Newcastle, Tynmouth Castle, Hartlepool (a haven town), and some other necessary garrisons in those

---

[1] The letters relating to Newcastle's march into York-shire, and the terms finally agreed upon, are printed in a pamphlet entitled, "A New Discovery of Hidden Secrets," 1645. The first letter is dated September 26, three days before the treaty of neutrality between the Yorkshire Cava-liers and Parliamentarians was signed at Rodwell. The correspondence is printed in the Appendix.

parts, and manned, victualled, and ordered their constant supply, he thought it fit in the first place, before he did march, to manifest to the world, by a Declaration in print, the reasons and grounds of his undertaking that design; [1] which were in general, for the preservation of his Majesty's person and government, and the defence of the orthodox Church of England ; where he also satisfied those that murmured for my Lord's receiving into his army such as were of the Catholic religion, and then he presently marched with his army into Yorkshire to their assistance, and within the time agreed upon, came to York, notwithstanding the enemy's forces gave him all the interruption they possibly could, at several passes. Whereof the chief was at Piercebridge, at the entering into

---

[1] "A Declaration made by the Earl of Newcastle for his resolution of marching into Yorkshire, as also a just vindication of himself from that unjust aspersion laid upon him for entertaining some Popish recusants in his service." Rushworth, III. ii. 78–81.

The Earl had been not merely permitted, but instructed by the King to employ Catholics who offered their services. See the King's letter to Newcastle (Ellis, Original Letters, series I. vol. iii. p. 291, quoted also in the "Memoirs of Col. Hutchinson," vol. i. p. 215): "Therefore, I do not only permit, but command you to make use of all my loving subjects' services, without examining their consciences (more than their loyalty to me) as you shall find most to conduce to the upholding of my just regal power."

Yorkshire, where 1500 of the enemy's forces, commanded in chief by Colonel Hotham, were ready to interrupt my Lord's forces, sent thither to secure that pass, consisting of a regiment of dragoons, commanded by Colonel Thomas Howard, and a regiment of foot, commanded by Sir William Lambton, which they performed with so much courage, that they routed the enemy, and put them to flight, although the said Colonel Howard in that charge lost his life by an unfortunate shot.[1]

The enemy thus missing of their design, fled until they met with a conjunction of their whole forces at Tadcaster, some eight miles distant from York, and my Lord went on without any other considerable interruption. Being come to York, he drew up his whole army before the time, both horse and foot, where the Commander-in-Chief, the then Earl of Cumberland, together with the gentry of the country, came to wait on my Lord, and the then Governor of York, Sir Thomas Glenham, presented him with the keys of the city.[2]

Thus my Lord marched into the town with

---

[1] A brief account of this action is contained in Rushworth, III. ii. 77. It is there said to have taken place on December 1, 1642.

[2] According to Drake's Eboracum, Newcastle arrived at York on November 30. "It cannot be denied," says Clarendon, "that the Earl of Newcastle, by his quick march with his troops, as soon as he had received his commission to be

great joy, and to the general satisfaction both of
the nobility and gentry, and most of the citizens;
and immediately without any delay, in the later
end of December 1642, fell upon consultations how
he might best proceed to serve his King and
country; and particularly, how his army should
be maintained and paid (as he did also afterwards
in every country wheresoever he marched), well
knowing, that no army can be governed without
being constantly and regularly supported by provision and pay. Whereupon it was agreed, that
the nobility and gentry of the several counties,
should select a certain number of themselves to
raise money by a regular tax, for the making provisions for the support and maintenance of the
army, rather than to leave them to free-quarter,
and to carve for themselves; and if any of the
soldiers were exorbitant and disorderly, and that
it did appear so to those that were authorised to
examine their deportment, that presently order
should be given to repair those injuries out of the
moneys levied for the soldiery; by which means the
country was preserved from many inconveniences,
which otherwise would doubtless have followed.

And though the season of the year might well

---

general, and in the depth of winter, redeemed or rescued the
city of York from the rebels, when they looked upon it as their
own, and had it even within their grasp."—Rebellion, viii. 84.

have invited my Lord to take up his winter quarters, it being about Christmas; yet after he had put a good garrison into the city of York, and fortified it, upon intelligence that the enemy was still at Tadcaster, and had fortified that place, he resolved to march thither. The greatest part of the town stands on the west side of a river not fordable in any place near thereabout, nor allowing any passage into the town from York, but over a stone-bridge, which the enemy had made impassable by breaking down part of the bridge and planting their ordnance upon it, and by raising a very large and strong fort upon the top of a hill, leading eastward from that bridge towards York, upon design of commanding the bridge and all other places fit to draw up an army in, or to plant cannon against them.[1]

But notwithstanding all these discouragements, my Lord, after he had refreshed his army at York, and recruited his provisions, ordered a march before the said town in this manner: that the

---

[1] Lord Fairfax mentions merely " some breastworks for our musketeers." Sir Thomas, in his " Short Memorial," says : " In a council of war the town was judged untenable, and that we should draw out to an advantageous piece of ground by the town ; but, before we could all march out, the enemy advanced so fast that we were necessitated to leave some foot in a slight work above the bridge to secure our retreat ; but, the enemy pressing on us, forced us to draw back, to maintain that ground."—Short Memorial, Maseres' Tracts, i. 417.

greatest part of his horse and dragoons should in the night march to a pass at Weatherby, five miles distant from Tadcaster, towards north-west, from thence under the command of his then Lieutenant-General of the army, to appear on the west side of Tadcaster early the next morning, by which time my Lord with the rest of his army resolved to appear at the east side of the said town. Which intention was well designed, but ill executed; for though my Lord with that part of the army which he commanded in person, that is to say, his foot and cannon, attended by some troops of horse, did march that night, and early in the morning appeared before the town on the east side thereof, and there drew up his army, planted his cannon, and closely and orderly besieged that side of the town, and from ten in the morning till four o'clock in the afternoon, battered the enemy's forts and works, as being in continual expectation of the appearance of the troops on the other side, according to his order; yet (whether it was out of neglect or treachery that my Lord's orders were not obeyed) that day's work was rendered ineffectual as to the whole design.[1]

However, the vigilancy of my Lord did put the

---

[1] The battle took place on Tuesday, December 6;—at least Lord Fairfax, in his letter of December 10, mentions the preceding Tuesday as the day of the battle. Vicars, how-

enemy into such a terror, that they forsook that fort, and secretly fled away with all their train that very night to another stronghold not far distant from Tadcaster, called Cawood Castle, to which, by reason of its low and boggy situation, and foul and narrow lanes and passages, it was not possible for my Lord to pursue them without too great an hazard to his army.[1] Whereas had the

ever (Jehovah Jireh, p. 230), fixes Wednesday, December 7, as the date. But December 7 was a Tuesday in 1642.

The Lieutenant-General of Newcastle's army was then the Earl of Newport. His delay is thus explained by Drake (Eboracum, 161): "Captain Hotham, at the beginning o the fight, wrote a letter to the Earl of Newport signed ' Will. Newcastle,' and sent it by a running footboy to tell him that, though his commission was to come and assist him, yet he might now spare his pains, and stay till he sent him order the next morning." Newport was deceived by this trick, delayed his march, and gave Lord Fairfax time to escape. Sir Henry Slingsby, however, says that Newport's march "was so troublesome, having with him two drakes, that it grew too late, and a counter-order (was) sent him on Clifford Moor to march back to Wetherby and there quarter."—Memoirs, p. 86.

[1] Fairfax thus explains his retreat: "In this fight our men behaved themselves with very great resolution far beyond expectation, insomuch as I conceive we might have maintained the place still, if we had been furnished with powder and shot, but having spent in a manner all our whole store of bullet, match, and powder, I advised with the commanders, and by general consent I was thought fit to rise with our forces and march to Cawood and Selby, to secure those places, and there receive supplies of ammunition and men ; which was accordingly done : and now I am

Lieutenant-General performed his duty, in all probability the greatest part of the principal rebels
in Yorkshire would that day have been taken in
their own trap, and their further mischief prevented.
My Lord, the next morning, instead of storming the
town (as he had intended), entered without interruption, and there stayed some few days to refresh
his army, and order that part of the country.

In December 1642, my Lord thought it fit to
march to Pomfret,[1] and to quarter his army in that
part of the country which was betwixt Cawood and
some garrisons of the enemy, in the west part of
Yorkshire, viz., Halifax, Bradford, Leeds, Wakefield, &c., where he remained some time to recruit
and enlarge his army, which was much lessened by
erecting of garrisons, and to keep those parts in
order and obedience to his Majesty.[2]   And after

---

at Selby with part of the army, and the rest with Captain
Hotham at Cawood."—Letter of Lord Fairfax to the Speaker,
December 10, 1642, Rushworth, III. ii. 92.

[1] Pontefract.

[2] The Duchess does not mention an important episode in
the Yorkshire civil war which took place during this halt at
Pomfret. Sir William Savile was detached by the Earl of
Newcastle to subdue the manufacturing towns of the West
Riding. Leeds and Wakefield submitted without fighting,
and Sir William attacked Bradford on December 18, 1642.
The men of Halifax came to the aid of the men of Bradford,
and the royalists were beaten off with considerable loss. Sir
Thomas Fairfax, with four or five hundred men, made his way

he had thus ordered his affairs, he was enabled to give protection to those parts of the country that were most willing to embrace it, and quartered his army for a time in such places which he had reduced. Tadcaster, which stood upon a pass, he made a garrison, or rather a strong quarter, and put also a garrison into Pomfret Castle, not above eight miles distant from Tadcaster, which commanded that town, and a great part of the country.

During the time that his army remained at Pomfret, my Lord settled a garrison at Newark in Nottinghamshire, standing upon the river Trent, a very considerable pass, which kept the greatest part of Nottinghamshire, and part of Lincolnshire, in obedience;[1] and after that he returned, in the beginning of January 1642, back to York, with an intention to supply himself with some ammunition, which he had ordered to be brought from Newcastle. A convoy of horse that were employed to conduct it from thence, under the command of the Lieutenant-General of the Army, the Lord Ethyn,

---

to Bradford a few days later, and took command of the local levies. With these forces he attacked Sir William Savile at Leeds on January 23, 1643, and captured the town and about 500 prisoners.

[1] The garrisoning of Newark took place about Christmas 1642, under Sir John Henderson.—Hutchinson's Memoirs, vol i. p. 360. Newcastle returned to York on January 27, 1643.—Markham's Fairfax, p. 91.

was by the enemy at a pass, called Yarum
Bridge, in Yorkshire, fiercely encountered; in
which encounter my Lord's forces totally routed
them, slew many, and took many prisoners, and
most of their horse colours, consisting of seventeen
cornets; and so marched on to York with their
ammunition, without any other interruption.[1]

My Lord, after he had received this ammunition,
put his army into a condition to march, and having
intelligence that the Queen was at sea, with intention to land in some part of the East Riding of
Yorkshire, he directed his march, in February 1642,
into those parts, to be ready to attend her Majesty's
landing, who was then daily expected from Holland.
Within a short time, after it had pleased God to
protect her Majesty both from the fury of wind and
waves, there being for several days such a tempest
at sea that her Majesty, with all her attendance,
was in danger to be cast away every minute, as
also from the fury of the rebels, which had the
whole naval power of the kingdom then in their
hands, she arrived safely at a small port in the
East Riding of Yorkshire called Burlington Key.
Where her Majesty was no sooner landed, but the
enemy at sea made continual shot against her ships
in the port, which reached not only her Majesty's

---

[1] This fight at Yarum Bridge took place on February 1,
1643. Lord Ethyn is better known as General King.j

landing, but even the house where she lay (though without the least hurt to any), so that she herself, and her attendants, were forced to leave the same, and to seek protection from a hill near that place, under which they retired ; and all that while it was observed that her Majesty showed as much courage as ever any person could do ; for her undaunted and generous spirit was like her royal birth, deriving itself from that unparalleled king, her father, whose heroic actions will be in perpetual memory whilst the world hath a being.[1]

---

[1] The Queen landed at Burlington on February 22nd. She gives the following account of her adventure (" Letters," p. 166). " God, who took care of me at sea, was pleased to continue his protection by land, for that night, four of the Parliament ships arrived at Burlington without our knowledge, and in the morning (February 24), about four o'clock, the alarm was given that we should send down to the harbour to secure our ammunition boats, which had not yet been able to be unloaded ; but, about an hour after, these four ships began to fire so briskly, that we were all obliged to rise in haste, and leave the village to them : at least the women, for the soldiers remained very resolutely to defend the ammunition. One of these ships had done me the honour to flank my house, which fronted the pier, and before I could get out of bed, the balls were whistling upon me in such style that you may easily believe I loved not such music. Everybody came to force me to go out, the balls beating so on all the houses, that, dressed just as it happened, I went on foot to some distance from the village, to the shelter of a ditch, like those at Newmarket ; but before we could reach it, the balls were singing round

My Lord, finding her Majesty in this condition, drew his army near the place where she was, ready to attend and protect her Majesty's person, who was pleased to take a view of the army as it was drawn up in order; and immediately after, which was in March 1643, took her journey towards York, whither the whole army conducted her Majesty, and brought her safe into the city. About this time, her Majesty having some present occasion for money, my Lord presented her with £3000 sterling, which she graciously accepted of, and having spent sometime there in consultation about the present affairs, she was pleased to send some arms and ammunition to the King, who was then in Oxford. To which end, my Lord ordered a party, consisting of 1500, well commanded, to conduct the same, with whom the Lord Percy, who then had waited upon her

---

us in fine style, and a sergeant was killed twenty paces from me. We placed ourselves then under this shelter, during two hours that they were firing upon us, and the balls passing always over our heads, and sometimes covering us with dust. At last, the Admiral of Holland sent to tell them, that if they did not cease, he would fire upon them as enemies. . . . On this they stopped, and the tide went down, so that there was not water enough for them to stay where they were. . . . I am told that one of the captains of the Parliament ships had been beforehand to reconnoitre where my lodging was, and I assure you that it was well marked, for they always shot upon it." The Queen arrived at York, March 7th, 1643.—Rushworth.

Majesty from the King, returned to Oxford ; which party his Majesty was pleased to keep with him for his own service.[1]

Not long after, my Lord, who always endeavoured to win any place or persons by fair means, rather than by using of force, reduced to his Majesty's obedience a strong fort and castle upon the sea, and a very good haven, called Scarborough Castle, persuading the governor thereof, who heretofore had opposed his forces at Yarum Bridge, with such rational and convincible arguments, that he willingly rendered himself, and all the garrison, unto his Majesty's devotion. By which prudent action my Lord highly advanced his Majesty's interest ; for by that means the enemy was much annoyed and prejudiced at sea, and a great part in the East Riding of Yorkshire kept in due obedience.[2]

After this, my Lord having received intelligence

---

[1] This convoy left Newark under the conduct of Col. Hastings on May 8 (Dugdale's Diary), and arrived at Oxford on May 15. A note in "Mercurius Aulicus," May 15, 1643, says, "The conductors were Col. Hastings, the Lord of Dover, and Mr. Percy ; they brought with them twenty troops of horse and 2000 foot, and about two and fifty cart loads of arms and ammunition."

[2] This governor was Sir Hugh Cholmley, who declared for the King on March 25.—Rushworth, III. ii. 264. See also Sir Hugh Cholmley's Autobiography.

that the enemy's General of the Horse [1] had designed
to march with a party from Cawood Castle, whither
they were fled from Tadcaster, as before is mentioned, to some garrisons which they had in the
west of Yorkshire, presently ordered a party of
horse, commanded by the General of the Horse, the
Lord George Goring, to attend the enemy in their
march, who overtook them on a moor, called Seacroft Moor, and fell upon their rear, which caused
the enemy to draw up their forces into a body; to
whom they gave a total rout (although their number
was much greater), and took about 800 prisoners,
and 10 or 12 colours of horse, besides many that
were slain in the charge; which prisoners were
brought to York, about 10 or 12 miles distant from
that same place. [2]

Immediately after, in pursuit of that victory, my
Lord sent a considerable party into the west of Yorkshire, where they met with about 2000 of the enemy's
forces, taken out of their several garrisons in those
parts, to execute some design upon a moor called
Tankerly Moor, and there fought them, and routed
them; many were slain, and some taken prisoners.

---

[1] Sir Thomas Fairfax.

[2] The best account of the battle at Seacroft Moor is given
in Sir Thomas Fairfax's "Short Memorial," Maseres'
Tracts, vol. i. p. 422; Markham's "Life of the Great Lord
Fairfax," p. 95. The battle took place on March 30, 1643
(see "Mercurius Aulicus," April 4).

Not long after, the remainder of the army that were left at York marched to Leeds,[1] in the west of Yorkshire, and from thence to Wakefield, being both the enemies' quarters, to reduce and settle that part of the country. My Lord having possessed himself of the town of Wakefield, it being large and of great compass, and able to make a strong quarter, ordered it accordingly ; and receiving intelligence that in two market-towns south-west from Wakefield, viz. Rotherham and Sheffield, the enemy

---

[1] The Queen's Letters give an account of this second advance into the West Riding. Newcastle's army numbered, according to her, 7000 foot and 3500 horse. The Parliamentarians quitted Pontefract at their approach, and retired to Leeds, where they were besieged by Newcastle. General King and the officers of experience were against an assault, and thought an effectual siege impossible. Newcastle, after two or three days' inffectual cannonading, thought best to follow their advice and raise the siege. This was done under colour of a cessation of arms for four days for the purpose of treating, and the army retired to Wakefield (see also " Mercurius Aulicus," April 25). There Newcastle left them for a few days. "I am still waiting the return of the Earl of Newcastle," writes the Queen on April 23 ; "he is gone to bury his wife, who has died, and is not yet returned. . . . He is staying," she adds, "to treat with Hotham's son ; if he succeeds, our affairs will go well " (" Letters," p. 188). According to Dugdale's Diary, the Earl of Newcastle came privately to Welbeck on April 13. Four letters from young Hotham to Newcastle, written between April 20 and May 1, are printed by Sanford (" Studies and Illustrations of the Great Rebellion," p. 553).

was very busy to raise forces against his Majesty, and had fortified them both about four miles distant from each other, hoping thereby to give protection and encouragement to all those parts of the country which were populous, rich, and rebellious, he thought it ncessary to use his best endeavours to blast those their wicked designs in the bud; and thereupon took a resolution, in April 1643, to march with part of his army from Wakefield into the mentioned parts, attended with a convenient train of artillery and ammunition, leaving the greatest part of it at Wakefield, with the remainder of his army, under the care and conduct of his General of the Horse, and Major General of the Army,[1] which was so considerable, both in respect of their number and provision, that they did, as they might well, conceive themselves master of the field in those .parts, and secure in that quarter, although in the end it proved not so, as shall hereafter be declared, which must necessarily be imputed to their invigilancy and carelessness.

My Lord first marched to Rotherham, and finding that the enemy had placed a garrison of soldiers in that town, and fortified it, he drew up his army in the morning against the town, and summoned it;

---

[1] "The Lord Goring and Sir Francis Mackworth, Knight." These names were printed in a side note, and carefully obliterated by hand before publication.

but they refusing to yield, my Lord fell to work with his cannon and musket, and within a short time took it by storm, and entered the town that very night; some enemies of note that were found therein were taken prisoners; and as for the common soldiers, which were by the enemy forced from their allegiance, he showed such clemency to them, that very many willingly took up arms for his Majesty's service, and proved very faithful and loyal subjects and good soldiers.[1]

After my Lord had stayed two or three days there, and ordered those parts, he marched with his army to Sheffield, another market-town of large extent, in which there was an ancient castle; which

---

[1] Lord Fairfax, in his letter of May 23rd to Lenthal, says, "The forces in Rotherham held out two days' siege, and yielded up the town upon treaty : wherein it was agreed, that the town should not be plundered ; and that all the gentlemen, commanders and soldiers (six only excepted that were especially named), leaving their arms, should have free liberty to go whither they pleased. But when the enemy entered, contrary to their articles, they have not only plundered the town, but have also made all the commanders and soldiers prisoners ; and do endeavour to constrain them to take up arms on their party."—Rushworth, III. ii. 268. This statement as to the breach of the capitulation, is confirmed by the Rev. John Shaw, at that time the Vicar of Rotherham. See the dedication to his sermon, entitled, "The Three Kingdoms Case," 1646. Shaw states that the town was taken on Thursday, May 4.

when the enemy's forces that kept the town came
to hear of, being terrified with the fame of my
Lord's hitherto victorious army, they fled away
from thence into Derbyshire, and left both town
and castle (without any blow) to my Lord's mercy.
And though the people in the town were most of
them rebelliously affected, yet my Lord so prudently
ordered the business, that within a short time he
reduced most of them to their allegiance by love,
and the rest by fear, and recruited his army daily ;
he put a garrison of soldiers into the castle, and
fortified it in all respects, and constituted a gentleman of quality [1] governor both of the castle, town,
and country ; and finding near that place some iron
works, he gave present order for the casting of iron
cannon for his garrisons, and for the making of
other instruments and engines of war.[2]

---

[1] Sir William Savile, knight and baronet.

[2] The commanders at Sheffield, says Lord Fairfax in the
letter before quoted, hearing of the loss of Rotherham, and
seeing some of the enemy's forces advanced in view of the
town, they all presently deserted the place, as not tenable
with so few against so "potent an army ; and fled away
with their arms, some to Chesterfield and some to Manchester." The Earl of Newcastle appointed Sir William
Savile governor of Sheffield on May 9, 1643.—Hunter's
Hallamshire, ed. Gatty, p. 136. "Mercurius Aulicus," for
May 9, thus notes the capture of these two places :—
"News that Rotherham and Sheffield, two towns of principal note in the West Riding of Yorkshire, were yielded

Within a short time after, my Lord receiving
intelligence that the enemy in the garrisons near
Wakefield had united themselves, and being drawn
into a body in the night time, and surprised and
entered the town of Wakefield, and taken all, or
most of the officers and soldiers left there, prisoners
(amongst whom was also the General of the Horse,
the Lord Goring, whom my Lord afterwards redeemed by exchange), and possessed themselves
of the whole magazine, which was a very great loss
and hindrance to my Lord's designs, it being the
moiety of his army, and most of his ammunition,[1]

up to his Majesty : by getting which his Majesty had
obtained two convenient passes, the one by Sheffield into
Derbyshire, the other by Rotherham into those parts of
Nottinghamshire which are most helpful unto Gell and his
associates : and that besides the use his Majesty might have
of the Sheffield cutlers (for which that town is very famous)
in the employment of his armoury, there were found 1400
arms in Rotherham fit for present use, together with £5000
in ready money."

[1] This victory took place on Sunday, May 21, 1643.—
Rushworth, III. ii. 269, where the despatches of Lord Fairfax
and Sir Thomas are given, and the "Short Memorial" in
Maseres' Tracts, p. 423. Sir Thomas says, "This appeared
the greater mercy when we saw our mistake ; for we found
3000 men in the town and expected but half the number.
We brought away 1400 prisoners, 80 officers, 28 colours,
and great store of ammunition." His own force numbered
only 1100 men, and he concludes by observing, "This was
more a miracle than a victory."

he fell upon new counsels, and resolved without any delay to march from thence back towards York, which was in May 1643, where after he had rested some time, her Majesty being resolved to take her journey towards the southern parts of the kingdom, where the king was, designed first to go from York to Pomfret, whither my Lord ordered the whole marching army to be in readiness to conduct her Majesty, which they did, he himself attending her Majesty in person. And after her Majesty had rested there some small time, she being desirous to proceed in her intended journey, no less than a formed army was able to secure her person : wherefore my Lord was resolved out of his fidelity and duty to supply her with an army of 7000 horse and foot, besides a convenient train of artillery, for her safer conduct ; choosing rather to leave himself in a weak condition (though he was even then very near the enemy's garrisons in that part of the country) than suffer her Majesty's person to be exposed to danger. Which army of 7000 men, when her Majesty was safely arrived to the King, he was pleased to keep with him for his own service.[1]

---

[1] The Queen left York on June 4 (Drake's Eboracum) ; she arrived at Newark on June 16 (Dugdale's Diary), and left that place on July 3, reaching Oxford on July 14 (*ibid*). The Queen at first thought of bringing with her merely her own two regiments of foot and horse, consisting of about two thousand men (" Letters," pp. 180–191). On the 14th of May,

After her Majesty's departure out of Yorkshire, my Lord was forced to recruit again his army, and within a short time, viz. in June 1643, took a resolution to march into the enemy's quarters, in the western parts ; in which march he met with a strong stone house well fortified, called Howley House, wherein was a garrison of soldiers, which my Lord summoned ; but the governor disobeying the summons, he battered it with his cannon, and so took it by force. The governor, having quarter given him contrary to my Lord's orders, was brought before my Lord by a person of quality, for which the officer that brought him received a check ; and though he resolved then to kill him, yet my Lord would not suffer him to do it, saying, it was inhuman to kill any man in cold blood. Hereupon the governor kissed the key of the house door, and presented it to my Lord ; to which my Lord returned this answer : "I need

---

the Queen speaks of bringing 4000 men ; the King desired at least 1000 foot and 1500 horse ("Letters," pp. 200–205). Most of these troops were armed with the weapons brought by the Queen, but raised by the Earl of Newcastle. "I carry with me," writes Henrietta to the King from Newark, "3000 foot, thirty companies of horse and dragoons, six pieces of cannon and two mortars."—"Letters of Queen Henrietta Maria," ed. Green, p. 222. The number given in the text is certainly exaggerated ; 4500 or 5000 men probably represents the total strength of the Queen's army.

it not," said he, " for I brought a key along with
me, which yet I was unwilling to use, until you
forced me to it." [1]

At this house my Lord remained five or six days,
till he had refreshed his soldiers; and then a
resolution was taken to march against a garrison
of the enemy's called Bradford, a little but a strong
town. In the way he met with a strong interruption by the enemy drawing forth a vast number
of musketeers, which they had very privately gotten
out of Lancashire, the next adjoining county to

---

[1] Howley House was garrisoned by the Parliamentarians
on January 16, 1642; its owner, Lord Savile, had made a
composition with young Hotham in the preceding October,
and also received a similar promise of protection from Lord
Fairfax, and had in consequence declined to receive a
detachment sent by Newcastle to occupy the house. The
suspicions raised by these transactions caused Newcastle to
arrest Savile, and to send to the King a lengthy information
against him. (Information against the Lord Viscount Savile,
in " Papers relating to the delinquency of Lord Savile,"
Camden Miscellany, vol. viii.) The King, however, decided
that though Newcastle had very good cause for suspicion,
and was justified in what he did, yet Savile's explanations
were satisfactory. Howley House was about half way
between Wakefield and Leeds. The capture mentioned
above took place on June 22, 1643. (Rushworth III. ii.
279.) The governor referred to was Sir John Savile of
Lupset, cousin of Lord Savile. The House was retaken by
the Parliament forces in February 1644 (Scottish Dove,
23rd February to 1st March).

those parts of Yorkshire which had so easy an access to them at Bradford, by reason the whole country was of their party, that my Lord could not possibly have any constant intelligence of their designs and motions. For in their army there were near 5000 musketeers, and 18 troops of horse, drawn up in a place full of hedges, called Atherton Moor, near to their garrison at Bradford, ready to encounter my Lord's forces, which then contained not above half so many musketeers as the enemy had; their chiefest strength consisting in horse, and these made useless for a long time together by the enemy's horse possessing all the plain ground upon that field; so that no place was left to draw up my Lord's horse, but amongst old coal-pits. Neither could they charge the enemy, by reason of a great ditch and high bank betwixt my Lord's and the enemy's troops, but by two on a breast, and that within musket shot; the enemy being drawn up in hedges, and continually playing upon them, which rendered the service exceeding difficult and hazardous.

In the meanwhile the foot of both sides on the right and left wings encountered each other, who fought from hedge to hedge and for a long time together overpowered and got ground of my Lord's foot, almost to the environing of his cannon; my Lord's horse (wherein consisted his greatest strength) all this while being made, by reason of the ground,

incapable of charging. At last the pikes of my
Lord's army having had no employment all the day,
were drawn against the enemy's left wing, and
particularly those of my Lord's own regiment, which
were all stout and valiant men, who fell so furiously
upon the enemy, that they forsook their hedges,
and fell to their heels. At which very instant my
Lord caused a shot or two to be made by his
cannon against the body of the enemy's horse,
drawn up within cannon shot, which took so
good effect, that it disordered the enemy's troops.
Hereupon my Lord's horse got over the hedge, not
in a body (for that they could not), but dispersedly
two on a breast; and as soon as some considerable
number was gotten over, and drawn up, they
charged the enemy, and routed them. So that in
an instant there was a strange change of fortune,
and the field totally won by my Lord, notwithstanding he had quitted 7000 men, to conduct her
Majesty, besides a good train of artillery, which in
such a conjuncture would have weakened Cæsar's
army. In this victory the enemy lost most of their
foot, about 3000 were taken prisoners, and 700
horse and foot slain, and those that escaped fled
into their garrison at Bradford, amongst whom was
also their General of the Horse.[1]

---

[1] Sir Thomas Fairfax. The battle of Atherton, or Adwalton Moor, took place on June 30th. He estimates the number

After this my Lord caused his army to be rallied, and marched in order that night before Bradford, with an intention to storm it the next morning; but the enemy that were in the town, it seems, were so discomfited, that the same night they escaped all various ways, and amongst them the said General of the Horse, whose Lady being behind a servant on horseback, was taken by some of my Lord's soldiers, and brought to his quarters, where she was treated and attended with all civility and respect, and within few days sent to York in my Lord's own coach, and from thence very shortly after to Kingston-upon-Hull, where she desired to be attended by my Lord's coach and servants.[1]

---

of the Parliamentary troops at 3000. All accounts agree that the battle began favourably to the Parliamentarians. The enemy, says Fairfax, were thinking of retreating, and some had actually marched off the field. "Whilst they were in this wavering condition, one Colonel Skirton desired his general to let him charge once with a stand of pikes, with which he broke in upon our men; and, they not being relieved by our reserves (which were commanded by some ill-affected officers, chiefly Major-General Gifford, who did not his part as he ought to do), our men lost ground, which the enemy seeing, pursued this advantage by bringing on fresh troops; ours being herewith discouraged began to fly, and were soon routed."—"Short Memorial," Maseres' Tracts, i. 426. Where is the letter of July 5th, in which Lord Fairfax gave an account of these events to the Speaker of the House of Commons?

[1] Sir Thomas Fairfax had married, in 1637, Anne, daughter of Horace, Lord Vere of Tilbury. "My wife," says Sir

D

Thus my Lord, after the enemy was gone, entered the town and garrison of Bradford, by which victory the enemy was so daunted, that they forsook the rest of their garrisons, that is to say, Halifax, Leeds, and Wakefield, and dispersed themselves severally, the chief officers retiring to Hull, a strong garrison of the enemy; and though my Lord, knowing they would make their escape thither, as having no other place of refuge to resort to, sent a letter to York to the Governor of that city, to stop them in their passage; yet by neglect of the post, it coming not timely enough to his hands, his design was frustrated.

The whole county of York, save only Hull, being now cleared and settled by my Lord's care and conduct, he marched to the city of York, and having a competent number of horse well armed and commanded, he quartered them in the East Riding, near Hull, there being no visible enemy then to oppose

---

Thomas, "ran the same hazard with us in this retreat, and with as little expression of fear; not from any zeal or delight in the war, but through a willing and patient suffering of this undesirable condition." Lady Fairfax was captured during the passage from Bradford to Leeds, being mounted behind an officer named Hill.—" Short Memorial," p. 428. "Not many days after the Earl of Newcastle sent my wife back again in his coach, with some horse to guard her; which generous act of his gained him more reputation than he could have got by detaining a lady prisoner upon such terms."—*Ibid.* p. 431.

them. In the meanwhile my Lord, receiving news that the enemy had made an invasion into the next adjoining county of Lincoln, where he had some forces, he presently despatched his Lieutenant-General of the Army[1] away with some horse and dragoons, and soon after marched thither himself with the body of the army, being earnestly desired by his Majesty's party there. The forces which my Lord had in the same county, commanded by the then Lieutenant-General of the Horse, Mr. Charles Cavendish, second brother to the now Earl of Devonshire, though they had timely notice, and orders from my Lord to make their retreat to the Lieutenant-General of the Army, and not to fight the enemy; yet the said Lieutenant-General of the Horse being transported by his courage (he being a person of great valour and conduct), and having charged the enemy, unfortunately lost the field, and himself was slain in the charge, his horse lighting in a bog;[2] which news being brought to my

---

[1] The Lord Ethyn.

[2] The Queen, in her letter to the King from Newark on 27th June, writes that she leaves behind her, for the protection of Nottinghamshire and Lincolnshire, 2000 foot and twenty companies of horse ; "all this to be under Charles Cavendish, whom the gentlemen of the county have desired me not to carry with me—against his will, for he desired extremely to go." Cavendish, on the petition of the King's Commissioners for those two counties, had been appointed Commander-in-

Lord when he was on his march, he made all the haste he could, and was no sooner joined with his Lieutenant-General, but fell upon the enemy, and put them to flight.

The first garrison my Lord took in Lincolnshire

Chief of their forces, with the rank of Colonel-General.   On April 11, he had defeated young Hotham and the Lincolnshire Parliamentarians at Ancaster, and on July 2, whilst convoying the Queen to Oxford, took Burton.   Now, whilst attempting to prevent the raising of the siege of Gainsborough, he was defeated by Cromwell, and slain on July 28, 1643.   The cavaliers were at one moment of the fight nearly gaining the victory.   The main body of the Parliamentarians charged and routed the main body of the Royalists.   Charles Cavendish, with their reserve, almost changed the fortune of the day ; but Cromwell, with three troops he had kept in hand, retrieved the battle.   " Whilst the enemy was following our flying troops, I charged him on the rear with my three troops ; drove him down the hill, brake him all to pieces : forced Lieutenant-General Cavendish into a bog, who fought in this reserve : one officer cut him on the head, and as he lay, my Captain-Lieutenant Berry thrust him into the short ribs, of which he died about two hours after in Gainsborough."— Carlyle's Cromwell, Appendix 5, and also Letter XII.   "Mercurius Aulicus," of August 1, contains the Royalist account of the battle.   It is stated there that Cavendish, "being cut most dangerously on the head, was struck off his horse, and so, unfortunately, shot with a trace of bullets after he was on the ground."   Lloyd, in his " Memoirs of Excellent Personages," says, " He died magnanimously, refusing quarter, and throwing the blood that ran from his wounds in their faces that shed it " (p. 673).

was Gainsborough, a town standing upon the river Trent, wherein (not long before) had been a garrison of soldiers for his Majesty, under the command of the then Earl of Kingston, but surprised, and the town taken by the enemy's forces, who having an intention to convey the said Earl of Kingston from thence to Hull in a little pinnace, met with some of my Lord's forces by the way, commanded by the Lieutenant of the Army, who being desirous to rescue the Earl of Kingston, and making some shots with their regiment pieces, to stop the pinnace, unfortunately slew him and one of his servants.[1]

My Lord drawing near the mentioned town of Gainsborough, there appeared on the top of a hill, above the town, some of the enemy's horse drawn up in a body; whereupon he immediately sent a party of his horse to view them; who no sooner

---

[1] Gainsborough was taken by Lord Willoughby on the 16th of July.—Ricraft's Champions, p. 35. See also "The Kingdom's Weekly Intelligencer," 18–25 July; Rushworth III. ii. 278.

"Lord Willoughby having sent away many of his carriages towards Lincoln, and put his prisoners aboard a pinnace which was sent from Hull, did intend to quit the place, as not being able to defend it. But before those intents were put in execution, he was surrounded by a part of the Earl of Newcastle's forces, who sat down before it."—"Mercurius Aulicus," July 30.

The death of the Earl of Kingston is also told in Mrs. Hutchinson's Memoirs, vol. i. pp. 216 and 223.

came within their sight, but they retreated fairly so
long as they could well endure; but the pursuit
of my Lord's horse caused them presently to break
their ranks, and fall to their heels, where most of
them escaped, and fled to Lincoln, another of their
garrisons.   Hereupon my Lord summoned the town
of Gainsborough; but the Governor thereof refusing
to yield, caused my Lord to plant his cannon, and
draw up his army on the mentioned hill; and
having played some little while upon the town, put
the enemy into such a terror, that the Governor
sent out and offered the surrender of the town
upon fair terms, which my Lord thought fit rather
to embrace than take it by force; and though,
according to the articles of agreement made between
them, both the enemy's arms and the keys of the
town should have been fairly delivered to my Lord,
yet it being not performed as it was expected, the
arms being in a confused manner thrown down, and
the gates set wide open, the prisoners that had been
kept in the town began first to plunder; which my
Lord's forces seeing, did the same, although it was
against my Lord's will and orders.[1]

---

[1] Gainsborough was surrendered on July 30.   The breach
of the capitulation is also mentioned by Mrs. Hutchinson
(Memoirs, vol. i. p. 233).   " Mercurius Aulicus," for August
3, gives the following account :—" It was advertised this day
that Gainsborough was yielded to the Earl of Newcastle ;
on whose first coming before the town, with the rest of his

After my Lord had thus reduced the town, and put a good garrison of soldiers into it, and better fortified it, he marched before Lincoln,[1] and there

forces, the Lord Willoughby and other of the rebels in it did desire a parley, which being granted upon Saturday night last, July 29, the Commissioners for both parts did agree, in the next morning early (that is to say, about two of the clock), that the town should be delivered, by five of the clock that morning, to such as his Excellency the Earl of Newcastle should appoint to receive it for his Majesty ; the Lord Willoughby and other officers of the rebels to go away, with such arms as they brought into the town ; no common soldier to go forth with any arms at all, nor with more baggage than he brought thither with him ; neither the officers nor soldiers to take with them any colours of horse or foot ; no ordnance, nor any kind of ammunition, to be carried out of the town, or destroyed in it, nor any part of the town or of the goods thereof to be burnt or hurt. All prisoners belonging to the army of the Earl of Newcastle, or which were there when the Lord Willoughby first entered, to be left behind ; and finally, no townsman to go out of the town under pretence of being soldiers."

1 Lord Willoughby on surrendering Gainsborough marched to Lincoln. " But seeing an impossibility that Cromwell should time enough recruit his beaten and distracted forces, or that he could receive any seasonable supplies from London, on the first news that the Earl of Newcastle was coming towards him, he forsook the place, and made what haste he could to Boston."—" Mercurius Aulicus," August 10. Willoughby writes to Cromwell from Boston on August 5, "Since the business of Gainsborough, the hearts of our men have been so deaded that we have lost most of them by running away, so that we were forced to leave Lincoln

he entered with his army without great difficulty, and placed also a garrison in it, and raised a considerable army, both horse, foot, and dragoons, for the preservation of that county, and put them under commanders, and constituted a person of honour [1] Commander-in-Chief, with intention to march towards the South, which, if it had taken effect, would doubtless have made an end of that war.[2]   But he being daily importuned by the

---

upon a sudden ; and if I had not done it, then I should have been left alone in it."—Carlyle's Cromwell, i. p. 140.

Lincoln was recaptured by Manchester on October 20, 1643, evacuated by the Parliamentary forces in March 1644, after the relief of Newark by Prince Rupert, and surrendered again to Manchester on May 6, 1644.

[1] The Lord Widdrington.

[2] The King repeatedly desired Newcastle to march southwards.   The Queen writes to Newcastle, on the 18th June, that the King "had sent me a letter to command you absolutely to march to him, but I do not send it you, since I have taken a resolution with you that you remain " (" Letters," p. 219) ; and again, on August 13 she writes—" He had written me to send you word to go into Suffolk, Norfolk, or Huntingdonshire.   I answered him that you were a better judge than he of that, and that I should not do it.   The truth is, that they envy your army ("Letters," p. 225).   Sir Philip Warwick was sent by the King to persuade Newcastle to march south, apparently about the end of July.   "But I found him very averse to this, and perceived, that he apprehended nothing more, than to be joined to the King's Army, or to serve under Prince Rupert ; for he designed himself to be the man that should turn the scale, and to be a

nobility and gentry of Yorkshire, to return into
that county, especially upon the persuasions of the
Commander-in-Chief of the forces left there, who
acquainted my Lord that the enemy grew so strong
every day, being got together in Kingston-upon-
Hull, and annoying that country, that his forces
were not able to bear up against them ; alleging

---

self-subsisting and distinct army, wherever he was. Yet he
told me that when he could quit Yorkshire, and leave it in a
condition to defend itself against the before-mentioned
enemies in it (which the Yorkshire men would not have been
unwilling to have adventured, if he had left them in some
measure their own forces, and marched with his own more
northerly army ; for they knew the Parliament would
command Fairfax after him), he would march through
Lincolnshire, and recruit himself there, and so over the
Washes into Norfolk, and Suffolk, and the associated
counties ; which had been a noble design." This march into
Lincolnshire was Newcastle's first step towards carrying
out this design. "He took in Gainsborough and Lincoln,"
says Sir T. Fairfax, "and intended to take in Boston, which
was the key of the associated counties ; for his orders (which
I have seen) were to go into Essex, and block up London
on that side. Having laid a great while still, and being now
strong enough for those forces which remained in the
country, we sent out a good party to make an attempt upon
Stamford Bridge, near York. But the enemy upon the alarm
fled thither, which put them also in such a fear, that they
sent earnestly to my Lord of Newcastle to desire him to
return, or the country would again be lost. Upon this he
returned again into Yorkshire, and not long after came to
besiege Hull."—"Short Memorial," Maseres' Tracts, i. 431.

withal, that my Lord would be suspected to betray
the trust reposed in him, if he came not to succour
and assist them; he went back with his army for
the protection of that same country; and when he
arrived there, which was in August 1643, he found
the enemy of so small consequence, that they did all
fly before him.   About this time his Majesty was
pleased to honour my Lord, for his true and faithful
service, with the title of Marquis of Newcastle.[1]

My Lord, being returned into Yorkshire, forced the
enemy first from a town called Beverley,[2] wherein
they had a garrison of soldiers; and from thence,
upon the entreaty of the nobility and gentry of
Yorkshire (as before is mentioned), who promised
him ten thousand men for that purpose, though
they came short of their performance, marched near
the town of Kingston-upon-Hull, and besieged that
part of the garrison that bordered on Yorkshire, for
a certain time,—in which time the enemy took the
courage to sally out of the town with a strong party
of horse and foot very early in the morning, with

---

[1] The patent is dated 27th October, 19 Charles I.   It is
quoted at length by Collins (Historical Collections, p. 13), and
also by the Duchess in the third book of these Memoirs.

[2] "The town (Hull) being little, I was sent to Beverley
with the horse and 600 foot," says Sir T. Fairfax, who gives
a detailed account of his retreat from Beverley to Hull
("Short Memorial," Maseres' Tracts, i. 431).   Newcastle
occupied Beverley on August 25 (Dugdale's Diary).   See
also "Mercurius Britannicus," 5–12 September.

purpose to have forced the quarters of a regiment of my. Lord's horse that were quartered next the town ; but by the vigilancy of their commander, Sir Marmaduke Langdale, afterwards Lord Langdale, his forces being prepared for the reception, they received such a welcome as cost many of them their lives, most of their foot (but such as were slain) being taken prisoners ; and those of their horse that escaped got into their hold at Hull.[1]

The enemy, thus feeling that they could do my Lord's army no further damage on that side of the river in Yorkshire, endeavoured by all means (from Hull, and other confederate places in the eastern

---

[1] The siege began on September 2, and ended on October 11 (Rushworth III. ii. 280). Warwick says the policy of besieging Hull was attributed to General King's advice. Warwick was sent on a second mission to Newcastle during September 1643, and found him before Hull. "I went down," says Sir Philip, "to see his trenches and works, and found (the season having been very wet) his men standing ankle deep in dirt a great distance from the town ; so as I conceived those without were likelier to rot than those within to starve ; and by assault there was not the least probability to carry it. Upon my return to him, relating but faintly and modestly my thoughts (for he knew I had not the least part of a soldier to warrant a discourse upon that subject) he merrily put it off, saying, 'You often hear us called the Popish Army : but you see we trust not in our good works.'"—Memoirs, p. 265. An account of the sally mentioned in the text is given in "Mercurius Aulicus" for September 16, *vide* Appendix.

parts of the kingdom) to form a considerable party
to annoy and disturb the forces raised by my Lord
in Lincolnshire, and left there for the protection of
that county ; where the enemy being drawn together
in a body, fought my Lord's forces in his absence,
and got the honour of the day near Hornby Castle
in that county ;[1] which loss, caused partly by their
own rashness, forced my Lord to leave his design
upon Hull, and to march back with his army to York,
which was in October 1643, where he remained
but a few days to refresh his army ; and receiving

---

[1] The battle of Winceby, or Horncastle, fought on October
11 (Rushworth III. ii. 281 ; Vicar's " God's Ark," pp. 43–8 ;
and Fairfax Correspondence, " Memorials of the Civil War,"
i. p. 62). When the siege of Hull commenced, the Earl of
Manchester, with the army of the Eastern Association, was
occupied in the siege of Lynn. Its surrender, on September
16, enabled him to despatch his horse under Cromwell into
Lincolnshire, to join Sir Thomas Fairfax with the horse of
the garrison of Hull, and Lord Willoughby with the local
levies of Lincolnshire. The union of Fairfax and Cromwell
took place on September 26. Manchester also sent 500
men, under Sir John Meldrum, into Hull, which they entered
on October 5 ; and he himself, with his foot, joined Fairfax
and Cromwell at Kirby in Lincolnshire on October 10. In
the battle the Royalists lost 1000 prisoners and 35 colours.
" We have in a manner totally lost our foot and dragoons
that were there, being near 800 horse, extremely disseverd
but no great number cut off," reports Sir William Widdington
to Newcastle. The consequences of the battle were the
evacuation of Gainsborough by the Royalists, the capture
of Lincoln, and the blockade of Newark.

intelligence that the enemy was got into Derbyshire, and did grow numerous there, and busy in seducing the people, that country being under my Lord's command, he resolved to direct his March thither in the beginning of November 1643, to suppress their further growth ; and to that end quartered his army at Chesterfield, and in all the parts thereabout, for a certain time.[1]

Immediately after his departure from York to Pomfret, in his said march into Derbyshire, the city of York sent to my Lord to inform him of their intention to choose another Mayor for the year following, desiring his pleasure about it. My Lord, who knew that the Mayor for the year before

---

[1] "Mercurius Aulicus," for Jan. 1, 1644, contains the following : " The first day of this year brought us in good news from the Lord Marquis of Newcastle, who, as we are advertised lately, put in execution the commission of array at Chesterfield in Derbyshire ; where he was met with the greatest concourse of people that hath been seen in those parts these many years. And (as it was for certain advertised) his Excellency had then gathered up above 2300 stout Derbyshire volunteers, resolved to venture their lives for their King and country against this rebellion ; whereof Sir John Gell, by his meekness and humanity, hath made them very sensible. And as a further testimony of the people's loyalty, that noble knight, Sir John Harpur, had received very fair contributions of that county for the maintenance of those forces." An account of the proceedings of Newcastle's forces in Derbyshire is given in a contemporary pamphlet, reprinted in the Appendix.

was a person of much loyalty and discretion, declared his mind to them, that he thought it fit to continue him Mayor also for the year following; which it seems they did not like, but resolved to choose one which they pleased, contrary to my Lord's desire. My Lord perceiving their intentions, about the time of the election, sent orders to the Governor of the city of York to permit such forces to enter into the city as he should send; which being done accordingly, they upon the day of the election repaired to the Town Hall, and with their arms stayed there until they had continued the said Mayor according to my Lord's desire.

During the time of my Lord's stay at Chesterfield in Derbyshire, he ordered some part of his army to march before a strong house and garrison of the enemy's, called Wingfield Manor, which in a short time they took by storm.[1]   And when my

---

[1] Certain informations, 6–13 March 1643, gives the following account of the first garrisoning of Wingfield at Chesterfield.   It says, " They are extremely pestered with the Earl of Newcastle's forces that lie in Bolsover, who, in the night, came out of that town and took thirty horses from the adjacent people ; whereupon the inhabitants of Chesterfield, to secure their town, have taken Wingfield Manor, and placed there thirty soldiers to guard it ; and they have also put forty musketeers into Chatsworth, under the command of Lieutenant Bagshaw, to defend it."   The capture mentioned in the text is thus related in "Mercurius Aulicus : "—Letters came from my Lord Marquis of Newcastle,

Lord had raised in that county as many forces, horse and foot, as were supposed to be sufficient to preserve it from the fury of the enemy, he armed them, and constituted an honourable person [1] Commander-in-Chief of all the forces of that county and of Leicestershire; and so leaving it in that condition, marched, in December 1643, from Chesterfield to Bolsover in the same county, and from thence to Welbeck in Nottinghamshire, to his own house and garrison, in which parts he stayed some time, both to refresh his army and to settle and

---

advertising us that yesterday was seven night, December 15, Sir Francis Mackworth, with five hundred horse and foot and some cannon, came before Wingfield Manor, a house of the late Earl of Shrewsbury, strengthened with a strong embattled wall of fifteen foot high and ten foot thick. The rebels refused to yield it up upon summons, whereupon Sir Francis played upon it with his cannon, but (through the great strength of the wall) did not much harm to the house. At length, upon exchange of the body of a gentleman slain by the King's forces for one killed near the walls who could not be brought off, some words passed, when Sir Francis told them, that if yet they would surrender they might find favour, which offer was soon embraced : and after a short treaty they were allowed to march away, leaving all their arms behind them, being about 160, with good store of ammunition and above three months' provision, all which was taken in the house, which through its strength and situation, standing in the middle way between Derby and Chesterfield, will be very advantageous to his Majesty's affairs." Dugdale dates the surrender December 18.

[1] The Lord of Loughborough.

reform some disorders he found there, leaving no
visible enemy behind him in Derbyshire, save only
an inconsiderable party in the town of Derby, which
they had fortified, not worth the labour to reduce it.

About this time the report came, that a great
army out of Scotland was upon their march towards
the northern parts of England, to assist the enemy
against his Majesty,[1] which forced the nobility and
gentry of Yorkshire to invite my Lord back again
into those parts, with promise to raise for his service
an army of 10,000 men. My Lord (not upon this
proffer, which had already heretofore deceived him,
but out of his loyalty and duty to preserve those
parts which were committed to his care and protection) returned in the middle of January 1643.
And when he came there, he found not one man
raised to assist him against so powerful an army,
nor an intention of raising any. Wherefore he
was necessitated to raise himself, out of the country,

---

[1] According to Warwick, the Marquis had some time
before received notice from the Marquis of Hamilton, that
the Scots were at last going to march into England, with
the recommendation to seize and garrison Carlisle and
Berwick. He replied that this would be against the treaty,
and waited for instructions from Oxford. Whilst he waited
Berwick was occupied for the Parliament ("Memoirs of
Sir Philip Warwick," p. 267). This statement is confirmed
by Burnet, "Lives of the Hamiltons," ed. 1852, p. 310.
These events apparently took place in August and September 1643.

what forces he could get; and when he had settled the affairs in Yorkshire, as well as time and his present condition would permit, and constituted an honourable person [1] Governor of York and Commander-in-Chief of a very considerable party of horse and foot for the defence of the county (for Sir Thomas Glemham was then made Colonel-General, and marched into the field with the army), he took his march to Newcastle in the beginning of February 1643, to give a stop to the Scots army. [2]

Presently after his coming thither with some of his troops, before his whole army was come up, he received intelligence of the Scots army's near approach, whereupon he sent forth a party of horse to view them, who found them very strong, to the number of 22,000 horse and foot, well armed and commanded. They marched up towards the town with such confidence, as if the gates had been opened for their reception; and the General of their army seemed to take no notice of my Lord's being in it, for which afterwards he excused himself. But as they drew near, they found not such entertainment as they expected; for though they

---

[1] The Lord Bellasis.

[2] A full account of the progress of the Scotch army is given in Rushworth III. ii. 612, *et seq*. The Scots arrived before the town of Newcastle on February 3; the Marquis entered the town the day before.

assaulted a work that was not finished, yet they were beaten off with much loss.

The enemy being thus stopped before the town, thought fit to quarter near it, in that part of the country; and so soon as my Lord's army was come up, he designed one night to have fallen into their quarter; but by reason of some neglect of his orders in not giving timely notice to the party designed for it, it took not an effect answerable to his expectation. In a word, there were three designs taken against the enemy, whereof if one had but hit, they would doubtless have been lost; but there was so much treachery, juggling, and falsehood in my Lord's own army, that it was impossible for him to be successful in his designs and undertakings. However, though it failed in the enemy's foot-quarters, which lay nearest the town, yet it took good effect in their horse-quarters, which were more remote; for my Lord's horse, commanded by a very gallant and worthy gentleman,[1] falling upon them, gave them such an alarm, that all they could do was to draw into the field, where my Lord's forces charged them, and in a little time routed them totally, and killed and took many prisoners, to the number of 1500.[2]

---

[1] The Lord Langdale.

[2] This skirmish took place on Monday, February 5 (Rushworth III. ii. 614). The loss of the Scots appears to

Upon this the enemy was forced to draw their whole army together, and to quarter them a little more remote from the town, and to seek out inaccessible places for their security, as afterwards appeared more plainly ; for so soon as my Lord had prepared his army for a march, he drew them forth against the Scots, which he found quartered upon high hills close by the river Tyne, where they could not be encountered but upon very disadvantageous terms ; besides, that day proved very stormy and tempestuous, so that my Lord was necessitated to withdraw his forces, and retire into his own quarters.[1]

The next day after, the Scots army, finding ill harbour in those quarters, marched from hill to hill into another part of the bishopric of Durham, near the sea coast, to a town called Sunderland ; and

---

be exaggerated by the Duchess. See also the letter of the Marquis and General King, quoted in the Appendix.

[1] The Scots marched from before Newcastle on February 22, leaving a detachment to blockade the town ; they passed the Tyne on February 28, and entered Sunderland on March 4. See the letter of the Marquis in the Appendix. During the latter part of the campaign the great aim of the Marquis was to cut off the supplies of the Scots by means of his great superiority in cavalry. This he partially effected, " so that sometimes their whole army had neither meat nor drink, and never had above twenty-four hours' provision beforehand " (Rushworth, p. 615.) Nevertheless, owing to the severity of the season, Newcastle's army, and especially his cavalry, was greatly diminished in numbers and efficiency.

thereupon my Lord thought fit to march to Durham, to stop their further progress, where he had contrived the business so, that they were either forced to fight or starve within a little time. The first was offered to them twice, that is to say, at Pensher hills one day, and at Bowden hills another day, in the bishopric of Durham. But my Lord found them at both times drawn up in such places, as he could not possibly charge them;[1] wherefore he retired again to Durham, with an intention to straiten their quarters, and to wait upon them, if ever they left their holds and inaccessible places. In the meantime it happened that the Earl of Montrose came to the same place, and having some design for his Majesty's service in Scotland, desired my Lord to give him the assistance of some of his forces; and although my Lord stood then in present need of them, and could not conveniently spare any, having so great an army to oppose, yet out of a desire to advance his Majesty's service as much as lay in his power, he was willing to part with 200 horse and dragoons to the said earl.[2]

---

[1] The Marquis offered battle on the 7th and 8th of March at Bowden hills, near Sunderland, and again on the 23rd, 24th, and 25th of the same month at Hilton. An account of the proceedings of these days from " Mercurius Aulicus" is given in the Appendix. The Marquis began his march back to York on April 13.

[2] Montrose writes to Sir R. Spottiswood from York on March 13, 1644—" At our arrival here, being uncertain of

The Scots perceiving my Lord's vigilancy and care, contented themselves with their own quarters, which could not have served them long, but that a great misfortune befell my Lord's forces in Yorkshire ; for the Governor whom he had left behind with sufficient forces for the defence of that country, although he had orders not to encounter the enemy, but to keep himself in a defensive posture ; yet he being a man of great valour and courage, it transported him so much, that he resolved to face the enemy, and offering to keep a town that was not tenable,[1] was utterly routed, and himself taken prisoner, although he fought most gallantly.[2]

So soon as my Lord received this sad intelligence,

---

all business, I directed Cornet Cochrane to my Lord Newcastle to learn the condition of affairs, and inform him particularly of what we had to expect ; which necessarily occasioned our stay here for some days. His return to us was, that for supplies he would dispense none for the present ; for monies he had none, neither was he owing to the Lord Jermyn any ; for arms and ammunition he had not to the two parts of his own, but had been so long expecting them beyond sea, as he was now out of hopes." Finally, Montrose followed Newcastle to Durham, and obtained from him, according to Wishart, " an hundred horse, and those very lean and ill appointed, and two small brass field-pieces."—Napier's " Memorials of Montrose," ii. 124.

[1] Selby in Yorkshire.

[2] This defeat took place at Selby on April 11, 1644. Lord Fairfax's despatch is given in Rushworth III. ii. 618. Sir Thomas gives an account of the battle in his " Short

he upon consultation, and upon very good grounds
of reason, took a resolution not to stay between the
two armies of the enemy's, viz. the Scots and the
English, that had prevailed in Yorkshire ; but immediately to march into Yorkshire with his army, to
perserve (if possible) the city of York out of the
enemy's hands : which retreat was ordered so well,
and with such excellent conduct, that though the army
of the Scots marched close upon their rear, and
fought them every day of their retreat, yet they gained
several passes for their security, and entered safe
and well into the city of York, in April 1643.[1]

My Lord being now at York, and finding three
armies against him, viz. the army of the Scots, the
army of the English that gave the defeat to the
Governor of York, and an army that was raised out
of associate counties, and but little ammunition and

Memorial," Maseres' Tracts, ii. Bellasis himself was taken
prisoner with 1600 men, and his artillery and baggage.

[1] Newcastle arrived at York on April 19. Next day
Fairfax and Leven joined at Tadcaster and beleaguered the
city, and on June 3, they were joined by Manchester (Rushworth III. ii. 620). There is a good letter from Lord Fairfax to the committee of both kingdoms on these occurrences,
printed from the Duke of Manchester's papers in the Eighth
Report of the Royal Commission on Historical Manuscripts,
part ii. p. 60. See also Newcastle's letter of 18th April ;
Warburton's Prince Rupert, ii. 434. In the Report on the
Eglinton MSS., p. 53, is a letter from a Scotch officer describing the pursuit.

provision in the town, was forced to send his horse away to quarter in several counties, viz. Derbyshire, Nottinghamshire, Leicestershire, for their subsistence, under the conduct of his Lieutenant-General of the Horse, my dear brother Sir Charles Lucas, himself remaining at York, with his foot and train for the defence of that city.[1]

In the meantime, the enemy, having closely besieged the city on all sides, came to the very gates thereof, and pulled out the earth at one end, as those in the city put it in at the other end ; they planted their great cannons against it, and threw in granadoes at pleasure : but those in the city made several sallies upon them with good success.   At

---

[1] Sir Charles Lucas had only recently received a command in Newcastle's army. He writes to Rupert from Doncaster on February 2, 1644, beginning, "Your Highness having been pleased to dispense with my service to be employed for a time in these parts, where I know not at first coming almost where I am," &c. He continues—"Here I live and move by the warmth of your liberal recommendations of me to my Lord Marquis of Newcastle ;" and ends by saying, that the Marquis has gone north, leaving him behind with 2000 horse to protect the country, whilst Doncaster is being fortified (Warburton's *Prince Rupert*, vol. ii. p. 370). Lucas joined Newcastle, with twelve troops of horse, near Sunderland, some time before March 6 (Rushworth III. ii. 615). After parting from the Marquis, as described in the text, the body of horse Lucas commanded passed under the command of Goring, and joined Rupert on his march to York.

last, the General of the Associate army of the enemy,
having closely beleaguered the north side of the
town, sprung a mine under the wall of the Manor
Yard, and blew part of it up; and having beaten
back the town forces (although they behaved themselves very gallantly), entered the Manor House with
a great number of their men, which as soon as my
Lord perceived, he went away in all haste—even to
the amazement of all that were by, not knowing
what he intended to do—and drew 80 of his own
regiment of foot, called the White Coats, all stout
and valiant men, to that post, who fought the
enemy with that courage, that within a little time
they killed and took 1500 of them; and my Lord
gave present order to make up the breach which
they had made in the wall.[1]   Whereupon the enemy
remained without any other attempt in that kind, so

---

[1] The breach was made by the blowing up of St. Mary's
Tower, whence the Manor House was easily reached (Markham's Fairfax, p. 148).   The assault was made prematurely,
and in insufficient force, by General Crawford, who was
eager to monopolise the honour of the expected success.
The Duchess greatly exaggerates the loss of the besiegers,
which Rushworth puts at a total of 300 (Rushworth III.
ii. 631).   Baillie blames "the foolish rashness of Major
Crawford, and his great vanity to assault alone the breach
made by his mine, without the acquainting Lesley or Fairfax with it" ("Letters," ii. 195).   Slingsby, who was there,
speaks only of 200 prisoners, and estimates the strength of
the storming party at 500 (Memoirs, p. 109, ed. 2).

long, till almost all provision for the support of the soldiery in the city was spent, which nevertheless was so well ordered by my Lord's prudence, ·that no famine or great extremity of want ensued.

My Lord having held out in that manner above two months, and withstood the strength of three armies; and seeing that his Lieutenant-General of the Horse whom he had sent for relief to his Majesty, could not so soon obtain it (although he used his best endeavour), for to gain yet some little time, began to treat with the enemy; ordering in the meanwhile, and upon the treaty, to double and treble his guards.[1]   At last after three months

---

[1] The Marquis made overtures for a treaty on June 8, and the negotiations were carried on till the 15th. The correspondence is printed in Rushworth III. ii. 624–631. Newcastle demanded that the garrison should be allowed to march out with arms, ammunition, and baggage, to join the King or Prince Rupert. These terms were of course refused by the besiegers, who sent counter-propositions, to which Newcastle replied :—

" MY LORDS,—I have perused the conditions and demands your Lordships sent ; but when I considered the many professions made to avoid the effusion of Christian blood, I did admire to see such propositions from your Lordships, conceiving this not the way to it ; for I cannot suppose that your Lordships do imagine, that persons of honour can possibly condescend to any of these propositions, and so remain, my Lords, your Lordships most humble servant,

" WILL. NEWCASTLE.

" YORK, 15*th June* 1644."

time from the beginning of the siege, his Majesty was pleased to send an army, which, joining with my Lord's horse that were sent to quarter in the aforesaid countries, came to relieve the city under the conduct of the most gallant and heroic Prince Rupert, his nephew; upon whose approach near York, the enemy drew from before the city into an entire body, and marched away on the west side of the river Ouse, that runs through the city, his Majesty's forces being then of the east side of that river.[1]

My Lord immediately sent some persons of quality to attend his Highness, and to invite him into the city to consult with him about that important affair, and to gain so much time as to open a port to march forth with his cannon and foot which were in the town, to join with his Highness' forces; and went himself the next day in person to wait on his Highness; where, after some conferences, he declared his mind to the Prince, desiring his Highness not to attempt anything as yet upon the

---

[1] The siege was raised on July 1. The allied army were retreating towards Tadcaster on July 2, when Rupert's pursuit forced them to halt and give battle. A letter from Newcastle to Rupert on the raising of the siege in the Pythouse Papers, p. 19. Rupert and Newcastle did not meet till the morning of the fight. A detailed account of the preliminaries of the battle is given in Sir Hugh Cholmley's Memorials touching the battle of York, which I hope to print in full in a subsequent volume of this series.

enemy ; for he had intelligence that there was some discontent between' them, and that they were resolved to divide themselves, and so to raise the siege without fighting : besides, my Lord expected within two days Colonel Cleavering, with above three thousand men out of the North, and two thousand drawn out of several garrisons (who also came at the same time, though it was then too late). But his Highness answered my Lord, that he had a letter from his Majesty (then at Oxford), with a positive and absolute command to fight the enemy ; which in obedience, and according to his duty, he was bound to perform.[1] Whereupon my Lord

---

[1] The King's letter is printed in the Nicholas correspondence at the end of Evelyn's Diary, iv. 152, and in Warburton's " Prince Rupert and the Cavaliers," ii. 437. The King's words are : " If York be lost I shall esteem my crown little less ; unless supported by your sudden march to me ; and a miraculous conquest in the south, before the effects of their northern power can be found here. But if York be relieved, and you beat the rebel's army of both kingdoms, which are before it ; then (but otherwise not) I may possibly make a shift (upon the defensive) to spin out time until you come to assist me. Wherefore, I command and conjure you, by the duty and affection which I know you bear me, that all new enterprises laid aside, you immediately march, according to your first intention, with all your force to the relief of York. But if that be either lost, or have freed themselves from the besiegers, or that for want of powder you cannot undertake that work, that you immediately march with your whole strength directly to Worcester, to

replied, That he was ready and willing, for his part, to obey his Highness in all things, no otherwise than if his Majesty was there in person himself; and though several of my Lord's friends advised him not to engage in battle, because the command (as they said) was taken from him: yet my Lord answered them, that happen what would, he would not shun to fight, for he had no other ambition but to live and die a loyal subject to his Majesty.

Then the Prince and my Lord conferred with several of their officers, amongst whom there were several disputes concerning the advantages which the enemy had of sun, wind, and ground. The horse of his Majesty's forces was drawn up in both wings upon that fatal moor called Hessom Moor; and my Lord asked his Highness what service he would be pleased to command him; who returned this answer, that he would begin no action upon the enemy, till early in the morning; desiring my Lord to repose himself till then. Which my Lord did, and went to rest in his own coach that was close by in the field, until the time appointed.[1]

---

assist me and my army; without which, or your having relieved York by beating the Scots, all the successes you can afterwards have must infallibly be useless unto me." The letter is dated "Ticknell, June 14, 1644."

[1] There is an interesting account of this discussion amongst the Clarendon State Papers (No. 1805), which Dr. Gardiner was kind enough to point out to me. It is a

Not long had my Lord been there, but he heard a great noise and thunder of shooting, which gave him notice of the armies being engaged. Whereupon he immediately put on his arms, and was no sooner got on horseback, but he beheld a dismal

---

paper of rough notes on the northern campaign, drawn up by Clarendon himself, and based, no doubt, on the information of some of the persons concerned in it.

"The next morning the Marquis went out of the city to attend the Prince, and found him upon his march and the enemy having placed themselves upon a hill ; and when the Marquis overtook the Prince they both alighted, and after salutations went again to horse, and the Prince said, "My Lord, I hope we shall have a glorious day. So the Earl asked whether he meant to put it to a day, and urged many reasons against it ; the Prince replied, "Nothing venture, nothing have," &c. Several persons had that morning reported that the Prince had an absolute commission to command those parts, and that the Marquis's power was at an end. When Major-General King came up Prince Rupert showed the Marquis and the Earl a paper, which he said was the draught of the battle as he meant to fight it, and asked them what they thought of it. King answered, "By God, sir, it is very fine in the paper, but there is no such thing in the fields." The Prince replied, "Not so," &c. The Marquis asked the Prince what he would do ? His Highness answered, "We will charge them to-morrow morning." My Lord asked him, whether he were sure the enemy would not fall on them sooner ; he answered No ; and the Marquis goes to his coach hard by, and calling for a pipe of tobacco, before he could take it the enemy charged, and instantly all the Prince's horse were routed. Goring beat the other wing, &c."

sight of the horse of his Majesty's right wing, which out of a panic fear had left the field, and run away with all the speed they could; and though my Lord made them stand once, yet they immediately betook themselves to their heels again, and killed even those of their own party that endeavoured to stop them. The left wing in the meantime, commanded by those two valiant persons, the Lord Goring and Sir Charles Lucas, having the better of the enemy's right wing, which they beat back most valiantly three times, and made their general retreat, insomuch that they sounded victory.

In this confusion my Lord (accompanied only with his brother Sir Charles Cavendish, Major Scot, Captain Mazine, and his page), hastening to see in what posture his own regiment was, met with a troop of gentlemen volunteers, who formerly had chosen him their captain, notwithstanding he was general of an army; to whom my Lord spake after this manner. "Gentlemen," said he, "you have done me the honour to choose me your captain, and now is the fittest time that I may do you service; wherefore if you will follow me, I shall lead you on the best I can, and show you the way to your own honour." They being as glad of my Lord's proffer as my Lord was of their readiness, went on with the greatest courage; and passing through two bodies of foot, engaged with each other not at forty yards' distance, received not the least hurt, although they fired quick upon each other; but marched towards a Scots regiment of foot, which they charged and routed; in which encounter my Lord himself killed three with his page's half-leaden sword, for he had no other left him; and though all the gentlemen in particular offered him their swords, yet my Lord refused to take a sword of any of them. At last, after they had passed through this regiment of foot, a pikeman made a stand to the whole troop; and though my Lord charged him twice or thrice, yet he could not enter[1] him; but the troop despatched him soon.

In all these encounters my Lord got not the least hurt, though several were slain about him; and his White Coats showed such an extraordinary valour and courage in that action, that they were killed in rank and file. And here I cannot but mention by the way, that it is remarkable, that in all actions and undertakings where my Lord was in person himself, he was always victorious, and prospered in the execution of his designs; but whatsoever was lost or succeeded ill, happened in his absence, and was caused either by the treachery or negligence and carelessness of his officers.

My Lord being last in the field, and seeing that all was lost, and that every one of his Majesty's

---

[1] Enter, *i.e.*, get within his guard.

party made their escapes in the best manner they could ; he being, moreover, inquired after by several of his friends, who had all a great love and respect for my Lord, especially by the then Earl of Craw- ford (who loved my Lord so well that he gave 20s. to one that assured him of his being alive and safe, telling him, that that was all he had), went towards York late at night, accompanied only with his brother and one or two of his servants ; and coming near the town, met his Highness Prince Rupert, with the Lieutenant-General of the Army, the Lord Ethyn. His Highness asked my Lord how the business went ? To whom he answered, that all was lost and gone on their side.[1]

That night my Lord remained in York ; and having nothing left in his power to do his Majesty any further service in that kind ; for he had neither ammunition, nor money to raise more forces, to keep either York, or any other towns that were yet

---

[1] Warburton quotes from Rupert's Diary the following notes of this conversation :—Says General King, " What will you do ? " Says the Prince, " I will rally my men." Says General King, " Now you what Lord Newcastle will do ?" ("Now what will you Lord Newcastle do ?") Says Lord Newcastle, "I will go to Holland," looking upon all as lost. The Prince would have him endeavour to recruit his forces. " No," says he, " I will not endure the laughter of the court," and King said he would go with him.—Warburton's Prince Rupert, vol. ii. p. 468.

in his Majesty's devotion, well knowing that those which were left could not hold out long, and being also loath to have aspersions cast upon him, that he did sell them to the enemy, in case he could not keep them, he took a resolution, and that justly and honourably, to forsake the kingdom; and to that end, went the next morning to the Prince, and acquainted him with his design, desiring his Highness would be pleased to give this true and just report of him to his Majesty, that he had behaved himself like an honest man, a gentleman, and a loyal subject. Which request the Prince having granted, my Lord took his leave; and being conducted by a troop of horse and a troop of dragoons to Scarborough, went to sea, and took shipping for Hamburgh; the gentry of the country, who also came to take their leaves of my Lord, being much troubled at his departure, and speaking very honourably of him, as surely they had no reason to the contrary.[1]

---

[1] Clarendon severely blames both Rupert and Newcastle. "This may be said of it, that the like was never done or heard or read of before ; that two great generals, whereof one had still a good army left, his horse, by their not having performed their duty, remaining upon the matter entire, and much the greater part of his foot having retired into the town, the great execution having fallen upon the northern foot ; and the other having the absolute commission over the northern counties, and very many considerable places in them still remaining under his obedience, should both agree in nothing else but in leaving that good ally and the

F

whole country as a prey to the enemy. . . . All that can be said for the Marquis is, that he was utterly tired with a condition and employment so contrary to his humour, nature, and education ; that he did not at all consider the means or the way that would let him out of it, and free him for ever from having more to do with it. . . . The strange manner of the Prince's coming, and undeliberated throwing himself and all the King's hopes into that sudden and unnecessary engagement, by which all the force the Marquis had raised, and with so many difficulties preserved, was in a moment cast away and destroyed, so transported him with passion and despair that he could not compose himself to think of beginning the work again, and involving himself in the same undelightful condition of life, from which he might now be free."—Clarendon, Rebellion, viii. 76-87.

Sir Hugh Cholmley, in his Memorials touching the battle of York, says—" General King, considering the King's affairs absolutely destroyed by loss of this battle, persuaded the Marquis, against all the power of his other friends, to quit the kingdom."

THE LIFE

OF

THE MOST ILLUSTRIOUS PRINCE,

WILLIAM, DUKE OF NEWCASTLE.

—✦—

THE SECOND BOOK.

HAVING hitherto faithfully related the life of my noble Lord and husband, and the chief actions which he performed during the time of his being employed in his Majesty's service for the good and interest of his King and country, until the time of his going out of England, I shall now give you a just account of all that passed during the time of his banishment till the return into his native country.

My Lord being a wise man, and foreseeing well what the loss of that fatal battle upon Hessam Moor, near York, would produce, by which not only those of his Majesty's party in the northern parts of the kingdom, but in all other parts of his Majesty's dominions, both in England, Scotland, and

Ireland, were lost and undone, and that there was
no other way but either to quit the kingdom or
submit to the enemy, or die, he resolved upon the
former, and preparing for his journey, asked his
steward how much money he had left; who
answered that he had but £90. My Lord, not
being at all startled at so small a sum, although his
present design required much more, was resolved
to seek his fortune, even with that little; and
thereupon, having taken leave of his Highness
Prince Rupert and the rest that were present,
went to Scarborough (as before is mentioned),
where two ships were prepared for Hamburgh to
set sail within twenty-four hours, in which he
embarked with his company, and arrived in four
days' time to the said city, which was on the 8th
of July 1644.

In one of these ships was my Lord, with his two
sons, Charles Viscount Mansfield and Lord Henry
Cavendish now Earl of Ogle; as also Sir Charles
Cavendish, my Lord's brother; the then Lord
Bishop of Londonderry, Dr. Bramhall; the Lord
Falconbridge; the Lord Widdrington; Sir William
Carnaby, who after died at Paris, and his brother
Mr. Francis Carnaby, who went presently in the
same ship back again for England, and soon after was
slain by the enemy near Sherborne, in Yorkshire;
besides many of my Lord's and their servants. In
the other ship was the Earl of Ethyn, Lieutenant

General of my Lord's Army, and the Lord Corn-
worth.[1]   But before my Lord landed at Hamburgh,
his eldest son Charles, Lord Mansfield, fell sick of
the smallpox ; and not long after his younger son,
Henry, now Earl of Ogle, fell likewise dangerously

---

[1] At Sherborne, on October 15, 1645, Colonel Copley
defeated Lord Digby and Sir Marmaduke Langdale on
their way from Newark to join Montrose in Scotland.
Colonel Sir Francis Carnaby is in the list of slain given
by Vicars ("Burning Bush," 299).   Lord Widdrington, before mentioned in this Memoir, p. 56, was slain in Lord
Derby's defeat at Bolton in 1651.   Clarendon speaks of
him thus—"The Lord Withrington was one of the most
goodly persons of that age, being near the head higher than
most tall men, and a gentleman of the best and most
ancient extraction of the county of Northumberland, and of
a very fair fortune, and one of the four which the last king
made choice of to be about the person of his son the prince,
as gentleman of his privy-chamber, when he first erected
his family. . . . As soon as the war broke out, he was of
the first who raised both horse and foot at his own charge,
and served eminently with them under the Marquis of
Newcastle, from whom he had a very particular and entire
friendship, as he was very nearly allied to him ; and by his
testimony that he had performed many signal services, he
was, about the middle of the war, made a peer of the realm."
—Rebellion, xiii. 68.   Clarendon concludes by saying, " He
was a man of great courage and choler."
    Lord Carnworth, or rather Carnwath, was the Scottish
peer who seized the King's bridle rein at Naseby, and prevented him heading a last charge.   The Earl of Ethyn, so
often mentioned in these pages, deserves a fuller biography,
which will be found in the Appendix.

ill of the measles; but it pleased God that they both happily recovered.

My Lord, finding his company and charge very great, although he sent several of his servants back again into England, and having no means left to maintain him, was forced to seek for credit; where at last he got so much as would in part relieve his necessities; and whereas heretofore he had been contented, for want of a coach, to make use of a waggon, when his occasions drew him abroad, he was now able (with the credit he had got) to buy a coach and nine horses of an Holsatian breed; for which horses he paid £160, and was afterwards offered for one of them an hundred pistoles at Paris, but he refused the money, and presented seven of them to her Majesty the Queen-Mother of England, and kept two for his own use.

After my Lord had stayed in Hamburgh from July 1644 till February 1645, he being resolved to go into France, went by sea from Hamburgh to Amsterdam, and from thence to Rotterdam, where he sent one of his servants with a compliment and tender of his humble service to her Highness the then Princess Royal, the Queen of Bohemia, the Princess Dowager of Orange, and the Prince of Orange, which was received with much kindness and civility.

From Rotterdam he directed his journey to Antwerp, and from thence, with one coach, one chariot, and two waggons, he went to Mechlin and Brussels, where he received a visit from the Governor, the Marquis of Castle Rodrigo, the Duke of Lorraine, and Count Piccolomini.

From thence he set forth for Valenciennes and Cambray, where the Governor of the town used my Lord with great respect and civility, and desired him to give the word that night. Thence he went to Peronne, a frontier town in France (where the Vice-Governor, in absence of the Governor of that place, did likewise entertain my Lord with all respect, and desired him to give the word that night), and so to Paris without any further stay.

My Lord being arrived at Paris, which was in April 1645, immediately went to tender his humble duty to her Majesty, the Queen-Mother of England, where it was my fortune to see him the first time, I being then one of the Maids of Honour to her Majesty ; and after he had stayed there some time, he was pleased to take some particular notice of me, and express more than an ordinary affection for me ; insomuch that he resolved to choose me for his second wife.[1] For he, having but two sons, purposed to marry me, a young woman that might prove fruitful to him and increase his posterity by a masculine offspring. Nay, he was so desirous of

---

[1] They were married in Sir Richard Browne's chapel at Paris (Evelyn's Diary, vol. ii. p. 217, ed. Wheatley).

male issue that I have heard him say he cared not (so God would be pleased to give him many sons) although they came to be persons of the meanest fortunes ; but God (it seems) had ordered it otherwise, and frustrated his designs by making me barren, which yet did never lessen his love and affection for me.

After my Lord was married, having no estate or means left him to maintain himself and his family, he was necessitated to seek for credit, and live upon the courtesy of those that were pleased to trust him ; which, although they did for some while, and showed themselves very civil to my Lord, yet they grew weary at length, insomuch that his steward was forced one time to tell him that he was not able to provide a dinner for him, for his creditors were resolved to trust him no longer. My Lord, being always a great master of his passions, was— at least showed himself—not in any manner troubled at it, but in a pleasant humour told me that I must of necessity pawn my clothes to make so much money as would procure a dinner. I answered that my clothes would be but of small value, and therefore desired my waiting-maid[1] to pawn some small toys which I had formerly given her, which she willingly did. The same day, in the afternoon, my Lord spake himself to his creditors, and both

---

[1] Mrs. Chaplain, now Mrs. Top.

by his civil deportment and persuasive arguments, obtained so much that they did not only trust him for more necessaries, but lent him money besides to redeem those toys that were pawned. Hereupon I sent my waiting-maid into England to my brother, the Lord Lucas, for that small portion which was left me, and my Lord also immediately after despatched one of his servants,[1] who was then governor to his sons, to some of his friends, to try what means he could procure for his subsistence. But though he used all the industry and endeavour he could, yet he effected but little, by reason everybody was so afraid of the Parliament that they durst not relieve him who was counted a traitor for his honest and loyal service to his King and country.

Not long after, my Lord had proffers made him of some rich matches in England for his two sons, whom, therefore, he sent thither with one Mr. Loving, hoping by that means to provide both for them and himself; but they, being arrived there, out of some reasons best known to them, declared their unwillingness to marry as yet, continuing, nevertheless, in England, and living as well as they could.[2]

---

[1] Mr. Benoist.

[2] Charles Viscount Mansfield married the eldest daughter and heir of Mr. Richard Rogers; Henry, afterwards Earl

Some two years after my Lord's marriage, when he had prevailed so far with his creditors that they began to trust him anew, the first thing he did was, that he removed out of those lodgings in Paris where he had been necessitated to live hitherto, to a house which he hired for himself and his family, and furnished it as well as his new-gotten credit would permit ; and withal, resolving for his own recreation and divertisement, in his banished condition, to exercise the art of manage, which he is a great lover and master of, bought a Barbary horse for that purpose, which cost him 200 pistoles, and, soon after, another Barbary horse from the Lord Crofts, for which he was to pay him £100 when he returned into England.

About this time there was a council called at St. Germain, in which were present, besides my Lord, her Majesty the now Queen-Mother of England ; his Highness the Prince, our now gracious King ; his cousin Prince Rupert ; the Marquis of Worcester ; the then Marquis, now Duke of Ormond ; the Lord Jermyn, now Earl of St. Albans, and several others ; where, after several debates concerning the then present condition of his Majesty

---

of Ogle, married a daughter of Mr. William Pierrepont, who is so frequently mentioned by Mrs. Hutchinson. But see Section 16, in Book III. of this Memoir, which treats of the Duke's pedigree.

King Charles the First, my Lord delivered his sentiment, that he could perceive no other probability of procuring forces for his Majesty but an assistance of the Scots. But her Majesty was pleased to answer my Lord that he was too quick.

Not long after, when my Lord had begun to settle himself in his mentioned new house, his gracious master the Prince having taken a resolution to go into Holland upon some designs, her Majesty the Queen-Mother desired my Lord to follow him, promising to engage for his debts which hitherto he had contracted at Paris, and commanding her Controller[1] and Treasurer[2] to be bound for them in her behalf; which they did, although the creditors would not content themselves until my Lord had joined his word to theirs. So great and generous was the bounty and favour of her Majesty to my Lord!—considering she had already given him heretofore near upon £2000 sterling, even at the time when her Majesty stood most in need of it.

My Lord, after his Highness the Prince was gone, being ready to execute her Majesty's commands in following him and preparing for his journey, wanted the chief thing, which was money; and having much endeavoured for it, at last had the good fortune to obtain upon credit three or

---

[1] Sir Henry Wood.   [2] Sir Richard Foster.

four hundred pounds sterling; with which sum he set out of Paris in the same equipage he entered, viz., one coach, which he had newly caused to be made (wherein were the Lord Widdrington, my Lord's brother, Sir Charles Cavendish, Mr. Loving, my waiting-maid, and some others, whereof the two latter were then returned out of England), one little chariot that would only hold my Lord and myself; and three waggons, besides an indifferent number of servants on horseback.

That day, when we left Paris, the creditors, coming to take their farewell of my Lord, expressed so great a love and kindness for him, accompanied with so many hearty prayers and wishes, that he could not but prosper on his journey.

Being come into the King of Spain's dominions, my Lord found a very noble reception. At Cambray the Governor was so civil that my Lord coming to that place somewhat late, and when it was dark, he commanded some lights and torches to meet my Lord and conduct him to his lodgings. He offered my Lord the keys of the city, and desired him to give the word that night, and, moreover, invited him to an entertainment which he had made for him of purpose; but it being late, my Lord (tired with his journey) excused himself as civilly as he could; the Governor notwithstanding being pleased to send all manner of provisions to my Lord's lodgings, and charging our landlord to take no pay for anything we had : which extraordinary civilities showed that he was a right noble Spaniard.

The next morning early my Lord went on his journey, and was very civilly used in every place of his Majesty of Spain's dominions where he arrived. At last coming to Antwerp, he took water to Rotterdam (which town he chose for his residing-place during the time of his stay in Holland), and sent thither to a friend of his,[1] a gentleman of quality, to provide him some lodgings ; which he did, and procured them at the house of one Mrs. Beynham, widow to an English merchant who had always been very loyal to his Majesty the King of England, and serviceable to his Majesty's faithful subjects in whatsoever lay in his power.[2]

My Lord, being come to Rotterdam, was informed that his Highness the Prince (now our gracious King) was gone to sea. Wherefore he resolved to follow him, and for that purpose hired a boat, and victualled it ; but since nobody knew whither his Highness was gone, and I being unwilling that my Lord should venture upon so uncertain a voyage, and (as the proverb is) seek a needle in a bottle of hay, he desisted from that design. The Lord Widdrington, nevertheless, and Sir William Throckmorton, being resolved to find

---

[1] Sir William Throckmorton, Knight.

[2] Probably the widow of Theophilus Baynham, concerning whom see the Journals of the House of Lords, July 6, 1644.

out the Prince, but having by a storm been driven towards the coast of Scotland, and endangered their lives, they returned without obtaining their aim.[1]

After some little time, my Lord having notice that the Prince was arrived at the Hague, he went to wait on his Highness (which he also did afterwards at several times, so long as his Highness continued there), expecting some opportunity where he might be able to show his readiness to serve his King and country, as certainly there was no little hopes for it; for, first, it was believed that the English fleet would come and render itself into the obedience of the Prince; next, it was reported that the Duke of Hamilton was going out of Scotland with a great army, into England, to the assistance of his Majesty, and that his Majesty had then some party at Colchester. But it pleased God that none of these proved effectual; for the fleet

---

[1] Sir William Throckmorton afterwards succeeded in reaching Scotland, when the King went thither in 1650, took part in the expedition to England, and was dangerously wounded in Lord Derby's defeat at Wigan. " He received so many wounds that he was looked upon as dead, and not fit to.be carried away with the prisoners; and so fell into such charitable and generous hands in the town, that, being believed to be dead, he was afterwards so well recovered, though with great maims and loss of limbs, that he at last got himself transported into Holland, where he was at first appearance taken for a ghost, all men having believed him to be buried long before."—Clarendon, Rebellion, xiii. 67.

did not come in, the Duke of Hamilton's army was destroyed, and Colchester was taken by the enemy, where my dear brother, Sir Charles Lucas, and his dear friend, Sir George Lisle, were most inhumanly murdered and shot to death, they being both valiant and heroic persons, good soldiers, and most loyal subjects to his Majesty ; the one an excellent commander of horse, the other of foot.[1]

---

[1] Sir Charles Lucas and Sir George Lisle were shot on August 28, 1648, by sentence of a court-martial after the surrender of Colchester. This can hardly be termed a murder. By the fourth article of the capitulation the Lords, Captains, superior officers, and gentlemen of quality were "to render themselves to the mercy of My Lord General," which, in answer to a question from the Commissioners of the besieged, was defined to mean, "without certain assurance of quarter ; so as the Lord General may be free to put some immediately to the sword, if he see cause" (Rushworth IV. ii. 1247). The executions therefore involved no breach of the terms of the treaty.

On the question of the justice of their sentence, however, there is more room for doubt. Lisle, when surrendering Farringdon, had promised not to bear arms against the Parliament in the future. Fairfax claimed that Lucas had been under a similar engagement to himself as his prisoner, and had forfeited his parole by taking up arms. Lucas admitted that he had been under such an engagement to Fairfax, but asserted the payment of the fine imposed on him by the Parliament squared the account and released him from this promise. He pleaded also that the law of nature justified him in taking the sword in hand again, in that the Derby House Committee set a price upon his head when he

My Lord having now lived in Rotterdam almost six months, at a great charge, keeping an open and noble table for all comers, and being pleased especially to entertain such as were excellent soldiers and noted commanders of war, whose kindness he took as a great obligation, still hoping that some occasion would happen to invite those worthy persons into England to serve his Majesty; but seeing no probability of either returning into England or doing his Majesty any service in that kind, he resolved to retire to some place where he might live privately; and having chosen the city of Antwerp for that purpose, went to the Hague to take his leave of his Highness the Prince, our now gracious Sovereign. My Lord had then but a small stock of money left; for though the then Marquis of Hertford (after Duke of Somerset) and

---

was peaceably living in London (Letter in Fairfax's Correspondence, "Memorials of the Civil Wars," ii. 56). The second of these excuses is obviously the better of the two, but the statement requires proof. The first is hardly tenable, for the composition implied an obligation to keep the peace in the future, as well as an indemnity for having broken it in the past. But, besides "the satisfaction of military justice," Fairfax gives as a reason—"Avenge for the innocent blood they have caused to be spilt, and the trouble, damage, and mischief they have brought upon the town, this country, and the kingdom." If it is just in any case to impose the penalty of death on the instigators and leaders of a civil war, it was just to inflict it in this instance.

his cousin-german, once removed, the now Earl of Devonshire had lent him £2000 between them; yet all that was spent, and above £1000 more, which my Lord borrowed during the time he lived in Rotterdam, his expense being the more, by reason (as I mentioned) he lived freely and nobly.

However my Lord, notwithstanding that little provision of money he had, set forth from Rotterdam to Antwerp, where for some time he lay in a public inn, until one of his friends that had a great love and respect for my Lord, Mr. Endymion Porter, who was Groom of the Bed-chamber to his Majesty King Charles the First (a place not only honourable, but very profitable) being not willing that a person of such quality as my Lord should lie in a public-house, proffered him lodgings at the house where he was, and would not let my Lord be at quiet, until he had accepted of them.

My Lord, after he had stayed some while there, endeavouring to find out a house for himself which might fit him and his small family (for at that time he had put off most of his train), and also be for his own content, lighted on one that belonged to the widow of a famous picture-drawer, Van Ruben,[1] which he took.

About this time my Lord was much necessitated

---

[1] This "picture-drawer" was Rubens. Mr. Lower says that he "had a magnificent museum, which the Duke afterwards purchased for £1000."

for money, which forced him to try several ways
for to obtain so much as would relieve his present
wants. At last Mr. Aylesbury, the only son to Sir
Thomas Aylesbury, Knight and Baronet, and brother
to the now Countess of Clarendon, a very worthy
gentleman,[1] and great friend to my Lord, having
some moneys that belonged to the now Duke of
Buckingham, and seeing my Lord in so great distress, did him the favour to lend him £200 (which
money my Lord since his return hath honestly
and justly repaid). This relief came so seasonably,
that it got my Lord credit in the city of Antwerp,
whereas otherwise he would have lost himself to
his great disadvantage ; for my Lord having hired
the house afore-mentioned, and wanting furniture
for it, was credited by the citizens for as many
goods as he was pleased to have, as also for meat
and drink, and all kind of necessaries and provisions, which certainly was a special blessing of
God, he being not only a stranger in that nation,
but, to all appearance, a ruined man.

After my Lord had been in Antwerp some time,
where he lived as retiredly as it was possible for
him to do, he gained much love and respect of all
that knew or had any business with him. At the

---

[1] William Aylesbury, the translator of Davila's " History
of the Civil Wars of France," born 1615, died 1656. Hyde
married his sister Frances. See his life in the " Dictionary
of National Biography," vol. ii.

beginning of our coming thither, we found but few English (except those that were merchants) but afterwards their number increased much, especially of persons of quality ; and whereas at first there were no more but four coaches that went the Tour,[1] viz., the Governor's of the Castle, my Lord's, and two more, they amounted to the number of above a hundred, before we went from thence ; for all those that had sufficient means, and could go to the price, kept coaches, and went the Tour for their own pleasure. And certainly I cannot in duty and conscience but give this public testimony to that place. That whereas I have observed, that most commonly such towns or cities where the prince of that country does not reside himself, or where there is no great resort of the chief nobility and gentry, are but little civilised ; certainly, the inhabitants of the said city of Antwerp are the civilest and best-behaved people that ever I saw. So that my Lord lived there with as much content as a man of his condition could do, and his chief pastime and divertisement consisted in the manage of the two afore-mentioned horses ; which he had not enjoyed long, but the Barbary horse, for which

---

[1] The Duchess, in her Life, explains this to signify driving about the town and the principal streets in a coach, "which we call here a Tour, where all the chief of the town go to see and be seen, likewise all strangers, of what quality soever."

he paid 200 pistoles in Paris, died, and soon after the horse which he had from the Lord Crofts ; and though he wanted present means to repair these his losses, yet he endeavoured and obtained so much credit at last that he was able to buy two others, and by degrees so many as amounted in all to the number of eight. In which he took so much delight and pleasure, that though he was then in distress for money, yet he would sooner have tried all other ways, than parted with any of them ; for I have heard him say, that good horses are so rare, as not to be valued for money, and that he who would buy him out of his pleasure (meaning his horses), must pay dear for it. For instance I shall mention some passages which happened when my Lord was in Antwerp.

First, a stranger coming thither, and seeing my Lord's horses, had a great mind to buy one of them, which my Lord loved above the rest, and called him his favourite, a fine Spanish horse ; entreating my Lord's escuyer to acquaint him with his desire, and ask the price of the said horse. My Lord, when he heard of it, commanded his servant, that if the chapman returned, he should be brought before him ; which being done accordingly, my Lord asked him, whether he was resolved to buy his Spanish horse ? Yes, answered he, my Lord, and I'll give your Lordship a good price for him. I make no doubt of it, replied my

Lord, or else you shall not have him : but you must know, said he, that the price of that horse is £1000 to-day, to-morrow it will be £2000, next day £3000, and so forth. By which the chapman perceiving that my Lord was unwilling to part with the said horse for any money, took his leave, and so went his ways.

The next was, that the Duke de Guise, who was also a great lover of good horses, hearing much commendation of a grey leaping horse, which my Lord then had, told the gentleman that praised and commended him, that if my Lord was willing to sell the said horse, he would give 600 pistoles for him. The gentleman knowing my Lord's humour, answered again, that he was confident my Lord would never part with him for any money, and to that purpose sent a letter to my Lord from Paris ; but my Lord was so far from selling that horse, that he was displeased to hear that any price should be offered for him : so great a love hath my Lord for good horses ! And certainly I have observed, and do verily believe, that some of them had also a particular love to my Lord; for they seemed to rejoice whensoever he came into the stables, by their trampling action, and the noise they made ; nay, they would go much better in the manage [1] when my Lord was by, than when he

---

[1] Manage = *manège*, riding-school.

was absent ; and when he rid them himself, they seemed to take much pleasure and pride in it.   But of all sorts of horses, my Lord loved Spanish horses and barbs best ; saying, that Spanish horses were like princes, and barbs like gentlemen, in their kind.   And this was the chief recreation and pastime my Lord had in Antwerp.

I will now return to my former discourse, and the relation of some important affairs and actions which happened about this time.   His Majesty (our now gracious King, Charles the Second) some time after he was gone out of Holland, and returned into France, took his journey from thence to Breda (if I remember well) to treat there with his subjects of Scotland, who had then made some offers of agreement.[1]   My Lord, according to his duty, went

---

[1] These negotiations took place at Breda in the spring of 1650.   Charles sailed for Scotland on June 2.   In his letter from Jersey to the Estates of Scotland Charles had fixed March 15 for the opening of the negotiations (Carte, Original Letters, i. 356).   Nicholas writes to Ormonde on April 3, 1650 : "The King hath lately sworn of his Privy Council here, the Dukes of Buckingham and Hamilton and the Marquis of Newcastle" (p. 376).   According to Doyle's Official Peerage, Newcastle entered the Council on April 6, 1650.   Hopton and Nicholas were excluded from the Council for opposing the concessions made by the King to the Scots.   Hyde, referring to this, writes to Nicholas : "You have a very precious junto to determine concerning three kingdoms ; you will find the Marquis of Newcastle a very lamentable man, and as fit to be a general as a bishop,

thither to wait on his Majesty, and was there in council with his Majesty, his Highness the then Prince of Orange, his Majesty's brother-in-law, and some other privy-counsellors ; in which, after several debates concerning that important affair, his Highness the Prince of Orange, and my Lord, agreed in one opinion, viz., that they could perceive no other and better way at that present for his Majesty, but to make an agreement with his subjects of Scotland, upon any condition, and to go into Scotland in person himself, that he might but be sure of an army, there being no probability or appearance then of getting an army anywhere else. Which counsel, either out of the then alleged reasons, or some others best known to his Majesty,

---

but I doubt though you choose officers you are not in the way of raising armies."—Clarendon State Papers, iii. 20.

Hyde was at Madrid during this treaty, but his letters show that he was thoroughly opposed to the policy which dictated it. "What secret spirit possesses the hearts of all the King's party, that from all parts they cry out, 'Agree with the Scots upon any terms.' It were as possible for me to rebel as to govern myself by those senseless sayings ; and yet people of all kinds sing that tune." If any agreement was to be made with the Scots, it ought to be straightforward and sincere. The Scots required the acceptance of the Covenant. Hopton and Nicholas urged the King to refuse ; others urged that the King should take it and break it afterwards, which Clarendon characterised as "such folly and atheism that we should be ashamed to avow it or think it."—Clarendon State Papers, iii. 15.

was embraced; his Majesty agreeing with the
Scots so far (notwithstanding they were so unreasonable in their treaty, that his Majesty had
hardly patience to hear them), that he resolved to
go into Scotland in person; and though my Lord
had an earnest desire to wait on his Majesty
thither, yet the Scots would not suffer him to come,
or be in any part of that kingdom. Wherefore,
out of his loyalty and duty, he gave his Majesty
the best advice he could, viz., that he conceived it
most safe for his Majesty to adhere to the Earl
of Argyle's party, which he supposed to be the
strongest; but especially, to reconcile Hamilton's
and Argyle's party, and compose the differences
between them; for then his Majesty would be
sure of two parties, whereas otherwise he would
leave an enemy behind him, which might cause his
overthrow, and endanger his Majesty's person;
and if his Majesty could but get the power into his
own hands, he might do hereafter what he pleased.

His Majesty being arrived in Scotland, ordered
his affairs so wisely, that soon after he got an army
to march with him into England; but whether they
were all loyal, is not for me to dispute. However,
Argyle was discontented, as it appeared by two
complaining letters he sent to my Lord, which my
Lord gave his Majesty notice of; so that only the
Duke of Hamilton went with his Majesty, who
fought and died like a valiant man, and a loyal

subject. In this fight between the English and Scots, his Majesty expressed an extraordinary courage ; and though his army was in a manner destroyed, yet the glory of an heroic prince remained with our gracious sovereign.

In the meantime, whilst his Majesty was yet in Scotland, and before he marched with his army into England, it happened that the Elector of Brandenburg, and Duke of Neuburg, upon some differences, having raised forces against each other, but afterwards concluded a peace between them, were pleased to proffer those forces to my Lord for his Majesty's use and service, which (as the Lord Chancellor, who was then in France, sent word to my Lord) was the only foreign proffer that had been made to his Majesty. My Lord immediately gave his Majesty notice of it ; but whether it was for want of convenient transportation, or money, or that the Scots did not like the assistance, that proffer was not accepted.[1]

---

[1] Nicholas writes to Ormond on June 20, 1651, that he hears from the Hague "that the Marquess of Brandenburgh and his lady arrived there Friday last, and on Sunday following he and his lady (when the Princess Royal was at sermon) went to see the young Prince of Orange, and on Tuesday following intended to leave the Hague, without making one visit to her Highness Royal. The Marquess resolves to make war against the Duke of Neuburg, who will be assisted by the King of Spain and the Duke of Lorraine, as the Marquess hopes to be by the Swede."—

Concerning the affairs and intrigues that passed in Scotland and England, during the time of his Majesty's stay there, I am ignorant of them; neither doth it belong to me now to write, or give an account of anything else but what concerns the history of my noble Lord and husband's life, and his own actions; who, so soon as he had intelligence that the Scottish army, which went with his Majesty into England, was defeated, and that no-

---

Carte, Original Letters, ii. 38. On August 8, however, the Elector of Brandenburgh wrote to the Marquess of Newcastle that his being obliged to take up arms against the Duke of Neuburg hindered his helping Charles at present, but that as soon as matters were settled he would not fail to let his soldiers put themselves at the service of the King. On September 11, he wrote further congratulating him on the success of the King of Great Britain, and saying that as he hoped soon to have no further need of his troops he would willingly enter into a treaty for their employment in the King's service. A letter from one of the Elector's Ministers stated that his sovereign would provide 6000 infantry and 4000 cavalry, adding that he had been employed to proceed to Denmark to solicit ships, and asking in what British harbour the troops were to land. The Marquess replied saying that he was about to send a messenger to make arrangements with the King of Denmark. "Calendar of the Clarendon State Papers," vol. ii. pp. 105–107. But the battle of Worcester put an end to all these hopes. Nevertheless the Elector of Brandenburgh continued to exercise his good offices on behalf of Charles in the Diet of the Empire, and in January 1654 the King sent him the Order of the Garter (p. 303).

body knew what was become of his Majesty, fell into so violent a passion, that I verily believed it would have endangered his life; but when afterwards the happy news came of his Majesty's safe arrival in France, never any subject could rejoice more than my Lord did.

About this time it chanced, that my Lord's brother, Sir Charles Cavendish, and myself, took a journey into England, occasioned both by my Lord's extreme want and necessity, and his brother's estate; which having been under sequestration from the time (or soon after) he went out of England, was then, in case he did not return and compound for it, to be sold outright. Sir Charles was unwilling to receive his estate upon such conditions, and would rather have lost it, than compounded for it. But my Lord, considering it was better to recover something, than lose all, entreated the Lord Chancellor, who was then in Antwerp, to persuade his brother to a composition, which his Lordship did very effectually, and proved himself a noble and true friend in it.[1] We had so

---

[1] See Clarendon's letter to Nicholas, November 1, 1657. Newcastle had placed most of his lands in the hands of trustees; nevertheless the Commonwealth laid hands on them. "Where any clauses of revocation are," writes Hyde, "the Commonwealth takes the advantage to do that which the persons dead in law might do; and so they disappoint all those engagements, as they have done or declare they will do in the case of my Lord Newcastle, who before these times

small a provision of money when we set forth our
journey for England, that it was hardly able to
carry us to London, but were forced to stay at
Southwark ; where Sir Charles sent into London
for one that had formerly been his steward, and
having declared to him his wants and necessities,
desired him to try his credit.   He seemed ready
to do his master what service he could in that
kind ; but pretending withal, that his credit was
but small, Sir Charles gave him his watch to
pawn, and with that money paid those small scores
we had made in our lodging there.   From thence
we went to some other lodgings that were prepared

---

conveyed his lands for the payment of debts and raising
younger children's portions, with a power of revocation,
which the sovereign power will now execute, and so defraud
the creditors and all other intentions.   In very good earnest
the whole business of proceeding with them is so intricate
and perplexed and ridiculous, that I do not intend to trouble
myself at all about it ; and I fear whosoever does, except he
resolves to do that which he is to be damned for doing, will
get nothing by it ; and yet my Lady Marquis of Newcastle
ventures thither this week ; and no question it is wisely done,
and with her Sir Charles Cavendish, as well to urge some
deeds of trust, which he hath long been in for his brother,
as to endeavour to enjoy the benefit of a composition which
was made long since for his own estate."—Clarendon State
Papers, iii. 34.   Sir Charles Cavendish compounded for
£2048, 6s. 8d.   Dring's Catalogue, ed. 1733, p. 27.   The
arguments by which Clarendon converted Sir Charles
Cavendish are given in his Life, Book vi. § 30–34.

for us in Covent Garden ; and having rested ourselves some time, I desired my brother, the Lord
Lucas, to claim in my behalf some subsistence
for myself out of my Lord's estate (for it was
declared by the Parliament, that the lands of
those that were banished, should be sold to any
that would buy them, only their wives and children
were allowed to put in their claims) : but he received this answer, that I could not expect the
least allowance, by reason my Lord and husband
had been the greatest traitor of England (that is to
say, the honestest man, because he had been most
against them).

Then Sir Charles entrusted some persons to
compound for his estate ; but it being a good while
before they agreed in their composition, and then
before the rents could be received, we having in
the meantime nothing to live on, must of necessity
have been starved, had not Sir Charles got some
credit of several persons, and that not without
great difficulty ; for all those that had estates, were
afraid to come near him, much less to assist him,
until he was sure of his own estate.   So much is
misery and poverty shunned !

But though our condition was hard, yet my dear
Lord and husband, whom we left in Antwerp, was
then in a far greater distress than ourselves ; for
at our departure he had nothing but what his
credit was able to procure him ; and having run

upon the score so long without paying any the least part thereof, his creditors began to grow impatient, and resolved to trust him no longer. Wherefore he sent me word, that if his brother did not presently relieve him, he was forced to starve. Which doleful news caused great sadness and melancholy in us both, and withal made his brother try his utmost endeavour to procure what moneys he could for his subsistence, who at last got £200 sterling upon credit, which he immediately made over to my Lord.

But in the meantime, before the said money could come to his hands, my Lord had been forced to send for all his creditors, and declare to them his great wants and necessities; where his speech was so effectual, and made such an impression in them, that they had all a deep sense of my Lord's misfortunes: and instead of urging the payment of his debts, promised him, that he should not want anything in whatsoever they were able to assist him ; which they also very nobly and civilly performed, furnishing him with all manner of provisions and necessaries for his further subsistence ; so that my Lord was then in a much better condition amongst strangers, than we in our native country.

At last when Sir Charles Cavendish had compounded for his estate, and agreed to pay £4500 for it, the Parliament caused it again to be surveyed, and made him pay £500 more, which was more

than many others had paid for much greater estates ;
so that Sir Charles, to pay this composition, and
discharge some debts, was necessitated to sell
some land of his at an under-rate. My Lord's
two sons (who were also in England at that time)
were no less in want and necessity than we, having
nothing but bare credit to live on ; and my Lord's
estate being then to be sold outright, Sir Charles,
his brother, endeavoured, if possible, to save the
two chief houses, viz., Welbeck and Bolsover, being
resolved rather to part with some more of his land,
which he had lately compounded for, than to let
them fall into the enemy's hands.   But before such
time as he could compass the money, somebody
had bought Bolsover, with an intention to pull it
down, and make money of the materials ; of whom
Sir Charles was forced to buy it again at a far
greater rate then he might have had it at first, notwithstanding a great part of it was pulled down
already ; and though my Lord's eldest son Charles,
Lord Mansfield, had those mentioned houses some
time in possession, after the death of his uncle, yet
for want of means he was not able to repair them.

I having now been in England a year and a
half, some intelligence which I received of my
Lord's being not very well, and the small hopes I
had of getting some relief out of his estate, put me
upon design of returning to Antwerp to my Lord,
and Sir Charles, his brother, took the same resolu-

tion, but was prevented by an ague that seized upon
him.   Not long had I been with my Lord, but we received the sad news of his brother's death, which was
an extreme affliction both to my Lord and myself,
for they loved each other entirely.   In truth, he was a
person of so great worth, such extraordinary civility,
so obliging a nature, so full of generosity, justice
and charity, besides all manner of learning, especially
in the mathematics, that not only his friends, but
even his enemies, did much lament his loss.[1]

---

[1] The death of Sir Charles Cavendish took place on
the 4th of February, 1654.   Clarendon announces it to
Nicholas in a letter dated March 6, 1654 (Clarendon State
Papers, iii. 223).   In his Life (vi. 29) he draws the following
portrait :—

"The conversation the Chancellor took most delight in
was that of Sir Charles Cavendish, brother to the Marquis,
who was one of the most extraordinary persons of that age,
in all the noble endowments of the mind.   He had all the
disadvantages imaginable in his person, which was not only
of so small a size that it drew the eyes of men upon him,
but with such deformity in his little person, and an aspect
in his countenance, that was apter to raise contempt than
application ; but in this unhandsome or homely habitation,
there was a mind and a soul lodged, that was very lovely
and beautiful ; cultivated and polished by all the knowledge and wisdom that arts and sciences could supply it
with.   He was a great philosopher, in the extent of it, and
an excellent mathematician ; whose correspondence was
very dear to Gassendus and Descartes, the last of which
dedicated some of his works to him.   He had very notable
courage, and the vigour of his mind so adorned his body,

After my return out of England, to my Lord, the creditors supposing I had brought great store of money along with me, came all to my Lord to solicit the payment of their debts; but when my Lord had informed them of the truth of the business, and desired their patience somewhat longer, with assurance that so soon as he received any money, he would honestly and justly satisfy them, they were not only willing to forbear the payment of those debts he had contracted hitherto, but to credit him for the future, and supply him with such necessaries as he should desire of them. And this was the only happiness which my Lord had in his

---

that being with his brother the Marquis in all the war, he usually went out in all parties, and was present and charged the enemy in all battles, with as keen a courage as could dwell in the heart of man. But then the gentleness of his disposition, the humility and meekness of his nature, and the vivacity of his wit, was admirable. He was so modest that he could hardly be prevailed with to enlarge himself on subjects he understood better than other men, except he were pressed by his very familiar friends, as if he thought it presumption to know more than handsomer men use to do. Above all, his virtue and piety was such that no temptation could work upon him to consent to anything that swerved in the least degree from the precise rules of honour, or the most severe rules of conscience."

Several letters from Sir Charles Cavendish to Pell are printed in the second volume of Robert Vaughan's "Protectorate of Cromwell," others have been printed by Halliwell, "Letters on Scientific Subjects" (1841).

H

distressed condition, and the chief blessing of the eternal and merciful God, in whose power are all things, who ruled the hearts and minds of men, and filled them with charity and compassion. For certainly it was a work of Divine Providence, that they showed so much love, respect, and honour to my Lord, a stranger to their nation ; and notwithstanding his ruined condition, and the small appearance of recovering his own, credited him wheresoever he lived, both in France, Holland, Brabant, and Germany ; that although my Lord was banished his native country, and dispossessed from his own estate, could nevertheless live in so much splendour and grandeur as he did.

In this condition (and how little soever the appearance was) my Lord was never without hopes of seeing yet (before his death) a happy issue of all his misfortunes and sufferings, especially of the restoration of his most gracious King and master, to his throne and kingly rights, whereof he always had assured hopes, well knowing, that it was impossible for the kingdom to subsist long under so many changes of government ; and whensoever I expressed how little faith I had in it, he would gently reprove me, saying, I believed least, what I desired most ; and could never be happy if I endeavoured to exclude all hopes, and entertained nothing but doubts and fears.

The city of Antwerp, in which we lived, being a

place of great resort for strangers and travellers, his Majesty (our now gracious King, Charles the Second) passed through it, when he went his journey towards Germany ; and after my Lord had done his humble duty, and waited on his Majesty, he was pleased to honour him with his presence at his house. The same did almost all strangers that were persons of quality ; if they made any stay in the town, they would come and visit my Lord, and see the manage of his horses : and, amongst the rest, the Duke of Oldenburg, and the Prince of East Friesland, did my Lord the honour, and presented him with horses of their own breed.

One time it happened, that his Highness Dom John d'Austria (who was then governor of those provinces) came to Antwerp, and stayed there some few days ; and then almost all his court waited on my Lord, so that one day I reckoned about seventeen coaches, in which were all persons of quality, who came in the morning of purpose to see my Lord's manage. My Lord receiving so great an honour thought it fit to show his respect and civility to them, and to ride some of his horses himself, which otherwise he never did but for his own exercise and delight.[1] Amongst the rest of

---

[1] In the introduction to the Duke's second book on horse-manship ("A New Method and Extraordinary Invention to Dress Horses"), the Duke tells the following story :—

those great and noble persons, there were two of our nation, viz., the then Marquis, now Duke of Ormond, and the Earl of Bristol; but Dom John was not there in person, excusing himself afterwards to my Lord (when my Lord waited on him) that the multiplicity of his weighty affairs had hindered his coming thither, which my Lord accounted as a very high honour and favour from so great a Prince; and conceiving it his duty to

---

"When I had the honour to wait on Don John of Austria, at Antwerp, brought to him by my Lord of Bristol, his Highness was pleased to use me extreme civilly; and to ask both then, and at several other times, for my book of horsemanship, before it was printed; and to receive it with great satisfaction, when I presented his Highness with one. But he did not see my horses, which, in above twenty coaches, all the Spaniards of his court went to my mannage to see; with many noblemen of Flanders, as the Duke of Ascot, and others, before whom I rid myself three horses, and my esquire, five. Being returned to Don John, he asked them, whether my horses were as rare, as their reputation was great; to which they answered, that my horses were such that they wanted nothing of reasonable creatures but speaking. And the Marquess of Seralvo, Master of the Horse to his Highness, and Governor of the Castle of Antwerp, told his Highness, that he had asked me, what horses I liked best? and that I had answered, there were good and bad of all nations; but that the Barbs were the gentlemen of horse-kind, and Spanish horses the princes. Which answer did infinitely please the Spaniards; and it is very true, that horses are so as I said."

wait on his Highness, but being unknown to him, the Earl of Bristol, who had acquaintance with him, did my Lord the favour, and upon his request, presented him to his Highness; which favour of the said Earl my Lord highly resented.[2]

Dom John received my Lord with all kindness and respect; for although there were many great and noble persons that waited on him in an out-room, yet so soon as his Highness heard of my Lord's and the Earl of Bristol's being there, he was pleased to admit them before all the rest. My Lord, after he had passed his compliments, told his Highness, that he found himself bound in all duty to make his humble acknowledgments for the favour he received from his Catholic Majesty for permitting and suffering him (a banished man) to live in his dominions, and under the government of his Highness. Whereupon Dom John asked my Lord whether he wanted anything, and whether he lived peaceably without any molestation or disturbance? My Lord answered, that he lived as much to his own content as a banished man could do; and received more respect and civility from that city than he could have expected, for which he returned his most humble thanks to his Catholic Majesty, and his Highness. After some short discourse, my Lord took his leave of Dom John,

---

[1] Resented, felt.

several of the Spaniards advising him to go into Spain, and assuring him of his Catholic Majesty's kindness and favour; but my Lord being engaged in the city of Antwerp, and besides in years, and wanting means for so long and chargeable a voyage, was not able to embrace their motions. And surely he was so well pleased with the great civilities he received from that city, that then he was resolved to choose no other residing place all the time of his banishment but that; he being not only credited there for all manner of provisions and necessaries for his subsistence, but also free both from ordinary and extraordinary taxes, and from paying excise, which was a great favour and obligation to my Lord.[1]

After his Highness Dom John had left the government of those provinces the Marquis of Caracena succeeded in his place, who having a great desire to see my Lord ride in the manage, entreated a gentleman of the city, that was acquainted with my Lord, to beg that favour of him. My Lord having not been at that exercise

---

[1] This indulgence was granted to most of the exiles. On August 7, 1656, Hyde writes to Talbot :—"In consequence of being incognito, the King is the only gentleman who has lived in this country without being exempt from paying excise and other similar impositions," an exemption enjoyed by Lord Newcastle at Antwerp, Hyde himself while at Antwerp, and Lord Hopton and many others at Bruges. Calendar of Clarendon State Papers, iii. 154.

six weeks, or two months, by reason of some sickness that made him unfit for it, civilly begged his excuse; but he was so much importuned by the said gentleman that at last he granted his request, and rid one or two horses in presence of the said Marquis of Caracena, and the then Marquis, now Duke of Ormond, who often used to honour my Lord with his company. The said Marquis of Caracena seemed to take much pleasure and satisfaction in it, and highly complimented my Lord; and certainly I have observed, that noble and meritorious persons take great delight in honouring each other.[1]

---

[1] In the preface to the book before mentioned the Duke thus relates this incident:—

"The Marquess of Caracena was so civilly earnest to see me ride, that he was pleased to say, it would be a great satisfaction to him to see me on horseback, though the horse should but walk. And seeing that no excuses would serve (though I did use many) I was contented to satisfy his so obliging a curiosity; and told him, I would obey his commands, though I thought I should hardly be able to sit in the saddle. Two days after he came to my manage, and I rid first a Spanish horse, called ' Le Superbe,' of a light bay, a beautiful horse, and though hard to be rid, yet when he was hit right, he was the readiest horse in the world. He went in corvets forward, backward, sideways, on both hands; made the cross perfectly upon his voltoes; and did change upon his voltoes so just, without breaking time, that a musician could not keep time better; and went terra a terra perfectly. The second horse I rid, was

But not only strangers, but his Majesty himself
(our now gracious Sovereign) was pleased to see
my Lord ride, and one time did ride himself, he
being an excellent master of that art, and instructed
by my Lord, who had the honour to set him first
on a horse of manage, when he was his governor;
where his Majesty's capacity was such, that being
but ten years of age, he would ride leaping horses,
and such as would overthrow others, and manage
them with the greatest skill and dexterity, to the
admiration of all that beheld him.[1]

---

another Spanish, called Le Genty; and was rightly named
so, for he was the finest-shaped horse that ever I saw, and
the neatest; a brown bay with a white star in his forehead;
no horse ever went terra a terra like him, so just, and so
easy; and for the piroyte in his length, so just and so swift
that the standers-by could hardly see the rider's face when
he went, and truly when he had done, I was so dizzy, that
I could hardly sit in the saddle. The third and last horse
I rid then was a Barb, that went a metz-ayre, very high,
both forward and upon his voltoes, and terra a terra. And
when I had done riding the Marquess of Caracena seemed
to be very well satisfied; and some Spaniards that were
with him, crossed themselves, and cried, Miraculo!"

For an explanation of the terms of horsemanship used I
must refer readers to the Duke's two books on the subject.

[1] The Duke himself says, in the preface before quoted—
"Having had the honour, when I was his governor, to be the
first that set him on horseback, and did instruct him in the
art of horsemanship, it is a great satisfaction to me, to
make mention here of the joy I had then, to see that his
Majesty made my horses go better than any Italian or French

Nor was this the only honour my Lord received from his Majesty,—but his Majesty and all the royal race, that is to say, her Highness the then Princess-Royal, his Highness the Duke of York, with his brother the Duke of Gloucester (except the Princess Henrietta, now Duchess of Orleans), being met one time in Antwerp, were pleased to honour my Lord with their presence, and accept of a small entertainment at his house, such as his present condition was able to afford them.[1]   And

riders (who had often rid them) could do." And again at p. 7 of the Dublin edition of the same book—" Our gracious and most excellent King is not only the handsomest, and most comely horseman in the world, but as knowing and understanding in the art as any man ; and no man makes a horse go better than I have seen some go under his Majesty the first time that ever he came upon their backs, which is the height and quintessence of the art."

[1] This entertainment is probably the one mentioned as taking place in February 1658. Sir Charles Cotterell writes to Nicholas :—"At the ball at Lord Newcastle's was the Duchess of Lorraine and her son and daughter, with the King and his brothers and sister, several French people, and some of the town. The King was brought in with music, and all being placed, Major Mohun, the player, in a black satin robe and garland of bays, made a speech in verse of his lordship's own poetry, complimenting the King in his highest hyperbole. Then there was dancing for two hours, and then my Lady's Moor, dressed in feathers, came in and sang a song of the same author's, set and taught him by Nich. Lanier. Then was the banquet brought in in eight great chargers, each borne by two gentlemen of the court,

some other time his Majesty passing through the city was pleased to accept of a private dinner at my Lord's house; after which. I receiving that gracious favour from his Majesty, that he was pleased to see me, he did merrily, and in jest, tell me that he perceived my Lord's credit could procure better meat than his own.   Again, some other time, upon a merry challenge playing a game at butts with my Lord (when my Lord had the better of him), What (said he) my Lord, have you invited me to play the rook with me?[1] although their stakes were not at all considerable, but only for pastime.

These passages I mention only to declare my Lord's happiness in his miseries, which he received by the honour and kindness not only of foreign princes, but of his own master and gracious sovereign.   I will not speak now of the good esteem and repute he had by his late Majesty King Charles the First, and her Majesty the now Queen-mother,

---

and others bringing wines, drinks, &c.   Then they danced again two hours more, and Major Mohun ended all with another speech, prophesying his Majesty's re-establishment."—Calendar of State Papers, 1657–58, pp. 296, 311.

[1] Rook, a sharper.   Cotton, describing an ordinary at night, says:—"This is the time (when ravenous beasts naturally seek their prey) wherein comes shoals of Huffs, Hectors, Setters, Gills, Pads, Biters, Divers, Listers, Filers, Budgies, Droppers, Crossbiters, &c., and these may all pass under the general and common appellation of Rooks."—The Complete Gamester.

who always held and found him a very loyal and faithful subject, although fortune was pleased to oppose him in the height of his endeavours ; for his only and chief intention was to hinder his Majesty's enemies from executing that cruel design which they had upon their gracious and merciful King. In which he tried his uttermost power, insomuch that I have heard him say out of a passionate zeal and loyalty, that he would willingly sacrifice himself and all his posterity, for the sake of his Majesty and the royal race. Nor did he ever repine either at his losses or sufferings, but rejoiced rather that he was able to suffer for his King and country. His army was the only army that was able to uphold his Majesty's power ; which, so long as it was victorious, it preserved both his Majesty's person and crown. But so soon as it fell, that fell too ; and my Lord was then in a manner forced to seek his own preservation in foreign countries, where God was pleased to make strangers his friends, who received and protected him when he was banished his native country, and relieved him when his own countrymen sought to starve him, by withholding from him what was justly his own, only for his honesty and loyalty ; which relief he received more from the commons of those parts where he lived, than from princes, he being unwilling to trouble any foreign prince with his wants and miseries, well knowing, that gifts of great princes came slowly, and not without much difficulty; neither loves he to petition any one but his own Sovereign.

But though my Lord by the civility of strangers, and the assistance of some few friends of his native country, lived in an indifferent condition, yet (as it hath been declared heretofore) he was put to great plunges and difficulties, insomuch that his dear brother Sir Charles Cavendish would often say, that though he could not truly complain of want, yet his meat never did him good by reason my Lord, his brother, was always so near wanting, that he was never sure after one meal to have another : and though I was not afraid of starving or begging, yet my chief fear was, that my Lord for his debts would suffer imprisonment, where sadness of mind, and want of exercise and air, would have wrought his destruction, which yet by the mercy of God he happily avoided.

Some time before the restoration of his Majesty to his royal throne, my Lord, partly with the remainder of his brother's estate (which was but little, it being wasted by selling of land for compounding with the Parliament, paying of several debts, and buying out the two houses aforementioned, viz., Welbeck and Bolsover), and the credit which his sons had got, which amounted in all to £2400 a year, sprinkled something amongst his creditors, and borrowed so much of Mr. Top and Mr. Smith (though without assurance) that he could pay such scores as were most pressing, contracted from the poorer sort of tradesmen, and send ready money to market, to avoid cozenage (for small scores run up most unreasonably, especially if no strict accounts be kept, and the rate be left to the creditor's pleasure) by which means there was in a short time so much saved, as it could not have been imagined.

About this time, a report came of a great number of sectaries, and of several disturbances in England, which heightened my Lord's former hopes into a firm belief of a sudden change in that kingdom, and a happy restoration of his Majesty, which it also pleased God to send according to his expectation;[1] for his Majesty was invited by his subjects, who were not able longer to endure those great confusions and encumbrances they had sustained hitherto, to take possession of his hereditary rights, and the power of all his dominions: and being then at the Hague in Holland, to take shipping in those parts for England, my Lord went thither to wait on his Majesty, who used my Lord very graciously; and his Highness the Duke of York was pleased to offer him one of those ships that were ordered to transport his Majesty; for which he returned his most humble thanks to his High-

---

[1] See the Duke's letters to Nicholas in the Appendix.

ness, and begged leave of his Highness that he might hire a vessel for himself and his company.

In the meantime, whilst my Lord was at the Hague, his Majesty was pleased to tell him, that General Monk, now Duke of Albemarle, had desired the place of being Master of the Horse : to which my Lord answered, that that gallant person was worthy of any favour that his Majesty could confer upon him : and having taken his leave of his Majesty, and his Highness the Duke of York, went towards the ship that was to transport him for England (I might better call it a boat, than a ship ; for those that were intrusted by my Lord to hire a ship for that purpose, had hired an old rotten frigate that was lost the next voyage after ; insomuch, that when some of the company that had promised to go over with my Lord, saw it, they turned back, and would not endanger their lives in it, except the now Lord Widdrington, who was resolved not to forsake my Lord).

My Lord (who was so transported with the joy of returning into his native country, that he regarded not the vessel) having set sail from Rotterdam, was so becalmed, that he was six days and six nights upon the water, during which time he pleased himself with mirth, and passed his time away as well as he could ; provisions he wanted not, having them in great store and plenty. At last, being come so far that he was able to discern the smoke of London, which he had not seen in a long time, he merrily was pleased to desire one that was near him, to jog and awake him out of his dream, for surely, said he, I have been sixteen years asleep, and am not thoroughly awake yet. My Lord lay that night at Greenwich, where his supper seemed more savoury to him, than any meat he had hitherto tasted; and the noise of some scraping fiddlers he thought the pleasantest harmony that ever he had heard.

In the meantime my Lord's son, Henry, Lord Mansfield, now Earl of Ogle, was gone to Dover with intention to wait on his Majesty, and receive my Lord his father, with all joy and duty, thinking he had been with his Majesty; but when he missed of his design, he was very much troubled, and more, when his Majesty was pleased to tell him that my Lord had set to sea, before his Majesty himself was gone out of Holland, fearing my Lord had met with some misfortune in his journey, because he had not heard of his landing. Wherefore he immediately parted from Dover, to seek my Lord, whom at last he found at Greenwich. With what joy they embraced and saluted each other, my pen is too weak to express.

But all this while, and after my Lord was gone from Antwerp, I was left alone there with some of my servants; for my Lord being in Holland with his Majesty, declared in a letter to me his intention of going for England, withal commanding me to stay in that city, as a pawn for his debts, until he could compass money to discharge them ; and to excuse him to the magistrates of the said city for not taking his leave of them, and paying his due thanks for their great civilities, which he desired me to do in his behalf. And certainly my Lord's affection to me was such, that it made him very industrious in providing those means ; for it being uncertain what or whether he should have anything of his estate, made it a difficult business for him to borrow money. At last he received some of one Mr. Ash, now Sir Joseph Ash, a merchant of Antwerp, which he returned to me ; but what with the expense I had made in the meanwhile, and what was required for my transporting into England, besides the debts formerly contracted, the said money fell too short by £400, and although I could have upon my own word taken up much more, yet I was unwilling to leave an engagement amongst strangers. Wherefore I sent for one Mr. Shaw, now Sir John Shaw, a near kinsman to the said Mr. Ash, entreating him to lend me £400, which he did most readily, and so discharged my debts.

My departure being now divulged in Antwerp, the magistrates of the city came to take their leaves of me, where I desired one Mr. Duart,[1] a very

---

[1] Letters ccii. and ccvi. in the Duchess of Newcastle's " Sociable Letters " are addressed to Eleanora Duarte, and

worthy gentleman, and one of the chief of the city, though he derives his race from the Portuguese (to whom and his sisters, all very skilful in the art of music, though for their own pastime and recreation, both my Lord and myself were much bound for their great civilities) to be my interpreter. They were pleased to express that they were sorry for our departure out of their city, but withal rejoiced at our happy returning into our native country, and wished me soon and well to the place where I most desired to be. Whereupon I having excused my Lord's hasty going away without taking his leave of them, returned them mine and my Lord's hearty thanks for their great civilities, declaring how sorry I was that it lay not in my power to make an acknowledgment answerable to them. But after their departure from me, they were pleased to send their under-officers (as the custom there is) with a present of wine, which I received with all respect and thankfulness.

I being thus prepared for my voyage, went with my servants to Flushing, and finding no English man-of-war there, being loath to trust myself with a less vessel, was at last informed that a Dutch man-of-war lay there ready to convoy some merchants. I forthwith sent for the captain thereof,

---

in the Letters and Poems in honour of the Duchess, p. 131, is a letter from J. Duarte in 1671, thanking her for some of her books.

whose name was Bankert, and asked him whether it was possible to obtain the favour of having the use of his ship to transport me into England? To which he answered, that he questioned not but I might; for the merchants which he was to convey, were not ready yet, desiring me to send one of my servants to the State, to request that favour of them; with whom he would go himself, and assist him the best he could; which he also did. My suit being granted, myself and my chief servants embarked in the said ship; the rest, together with the goods, being conveyed in another good strong vessel, hired for that purpose.

After I was safely arrived at London, I found my Lord in lodgings; I cannot call them unhandsome; but yet they were not fit for a person of his rank and quality, nor of the capacity to contain all his family. Neither did I find my Lord's condition such as I expected: wherefore out of some passion I desired him to leave the town, and retire into the country; but my Lord gently reproved me for my rashness and impatience, and soon after removed into Dorset House; which, though it was better than the former, yet not altogether to my satisfaction, we having but a part of the said house in possession. By this removal I judged my Lord would not hastily depart from London; but not long after, he was pleased to tell me, that he had despatched his business, and was now resolved to remove into the country, having already given order for waggons to transport our goods, which was no unpleasant news to me, who had a great desire for a country life.[1]

My Lord, before he began his journey, went to his gracious Sovereign, and begged leave that he might retire into the country, to reduce and settle, if possible, his confused, entangled, and almost ruined estate. " Sir," said he to his Majesty, " I am not ignorant, that many believe I am discontented ; and 'tis probable they'll say, I retire through discontent : but I take God to witness, that I am in no kind or ways displeased ; for I am so joyed at your Majesty's happy restoration, that I cannot be sad or troubled for any concern to my own particular ; but whatsoever your Majesty is pleased to command me, were it to sacrifice my life, I shall most obediently perform it ; for I have no other will, but your Majesty's pleasure."

---

[1] Clement Ellis, Newcastle's chaplain, thus comments on his retirement in the prefatory epistle to a sermon preached on May 29, 1661 : " With much pleasure I have hearkened to you discoursing of that satisfaction you reaped from that sweet privacy and retirement his Majesty is pleased to grant your Lordship here in the country. Indeed, the greatest reward his Majesty can possibly recompense your services withal, is thus to bestow yourself upon yourself, and I know you think it greater happiness to enjoy my Lord Marquis of Newcastle at Welbeck, than all the offices and honours which your exemplary loyalty has merited."—Kennet's " Ecclesiastical and Civil Register," 455.

Thus he kissed his Majesty's hand, and went the next day into Nottinghamshire, to his manor-house called Welbeck; but when he came there, and began to examine his estate, and how it had been ordered in the time of his banishment, he knew not whether he had left anything of it for himself or not, till by his prudence and wisdom he informed himself the best he could, examining those that had most knowledge therein. Some lands, he found, could be recovered no further than for his life, and some not at all: some had been in the rebels' hands, which he could not recover, but by his Highness the Duke of York's favour, to whom his Majesty had given all the estates of those that were condemned and executed for murdering his Royal Father of blessed memory, which by the law were forfeited to his Majesty; whereof his Highness graciously restored my Lord so much of the land that formerly had been his, as amounted to £730 a year.[1] And though my Lord's children had their claims granted, and bought out the life of my Lord,

---

[1] The grant restoring these lands is amongst the Egerton MSS. in the British Museum (No. 2551). The King grants to Newcastle three manors sold under the Commonwealth and bought by regicides, viz.—Sibthorpe in Nottinghamshire, purchased by Edward Whalley; certain lands in the said county in Carcolston, purchased by Colonel Hacker; and the Granges of Kirby Woodhouse and Annesley Woodhouse, purchased by Gilbert Millington. The grant is dated September 5, 1660.

their father, which came near upon the third part, yet my Lord received nothing for himself out of his own estate, for the space of eighteen years, viz., during the time from the first entering into war, which was June 11, 1642, till his return out of banishment, May 28, 1660. For though his son Henry, now Earl of Ogle, and his eldest daughter, the now Lady Cheiny, did all what lay in their power to relieve· my Lord their father, and sent him some supplies of moneys at several times when he was in banishment, yet that was of their own, rather than out of my Lord's estate ; for the Lady Cheiny sold some few jewels which my Lord, her father, had left her, and some chamber-plate which she had from her grandmother, and sent over the money to my Lord, besides £1000 of her portion ; and the now Earl of Ogle did at several times supply my Lord, his father, with such moneys as he had partly obtained upon credit, and partly made by his marriage.

After my Lord had begun to view those ruins that were nearest, and tried the law to keep or recover what formerly was his (which certainly showed no favour to him, besides that the Act of Oblivion proved a great hindrance and obstruction to those his designs, as it did no less to all the royal party), and had settled so much of his estate as possibly he could, he cast up the sum of his debts, and set out several parts of land for the payment of them, or of some of them (for some of his lands could not be easily sold, being entailed) and some he sold in Derbyshire to buy the Castle of Nottingham, which, although it is quite ruined and demolished, yet, it being a seat which had pleased his father very much, he would not leave it since it was offered to be sold.[1]

His two houses Welbeck and Bolsover he found much out of repair, and this later half pulled down;[2] no furniture or any necessary goods were left in them, but some few hangings and pictures, which had been saved by the care and industry of his

---

[1] After the restoration, George Villiers, second Duke of Buckingham, having claimed the Castle of Nottingham in right of his mother, the sole daughter and heiress of Francis Earl of Rutland, to whom it had been granted by James I., sold it to the Duke of Newcastle in 1674. Bailey, "Annals of Nottinghamshire," vol. ii. p. 971.

[2] On June 23 the Council of State ordered Bolsover to be made untenable. On July 2, 1649, the Council of State wrote to the Committee of Derbyshire :—"To avoid the charge of a garrison in Bolsover Castle, and yet to prevent danger if it should be surprised and kept by an enemy, we refer it to your care to do it so as the house itself, as it relates to private habitation, may be as little prejudiced as may be ; but let the outworks abroad, and garden walls, with the turrets and walls of the frontier court that are of strength be demolished, and all the doors of the house be taken away, and slight ones set in their place ; as also the iron bars of the windows, and the materials of the walls that are taken down be improved to the best, and the charge of demolishing defrayed out of the revenue thereof."—Calendar of Domestic State Papers, 1649, p. 217.

eldest daughter the Lady Cheiny, and were bought over again after the death of his eldest son Charles, Lord Mansfield. For they being given to him, and he leaving some debts to be paid after his death, my Lord sent to his other son Henry, now Earl of Ogle, to endeavour for so much credit, that the said hangings and pictures (which my Lord esteemed very much, the pictures being drawn by Van Dyke) might be saved; which he also did, and my Lord hath paid the debt since his return.

Of eight parks, which my Lord had before the wars, there was but one left that was not quite destroyed, viz., Welbeck Park, of about four miles' compass; for my Lord's brother, Sir Charles Cavendish, who bought out the life of my Lord in that lordship, saved most part of it from being cut down; and in Blore Park there were some few deer left. The rest of the parks were totally defaced and destroyed, both wood, pales, and deer; [1] amongst which was also Clipston Park, of seven

---

[1] On the destruction of these woods see the "Calendar of Domestic State Papers" for 1655, p. 137. The verderers of Sherwood Forest complained to Lord Clare, who had been made Warden in Newcastle's place—" The forest is ruined, especially Clipston Woods, where the inhabitants have right of estovers, by Mr. Clark, on pretence of a grant from the Committee for Sale of Traitors' Estates. He has felled 1000 trees, and daily fells more. He fells in the heart of the forest, where the deer have their greatest relief. There is much good ship-timber in the forest."

miles' compass, wherein my Lord had taken much
delight formerly, it being rich of wood, and containing the greatest and tallest timber-trees of all
the woods he had; insomuch, that only the pale-
row was valued at £2000. It was watered by a
pleasant river that runs through it, full of fish and
otters; was well-stocked with deer, full of hares,
and had great store of partridges, poots,[1] pheasants,
&c., besides all sorts of water-fowl; so that this
park afforded all manner of sports, for hunting,
hawking, coursing, fishing, &c., for which my Lord
esteemed it very much. And although his patience
and wisdom is such, that I never perceived him
sad or discontented for his own losses and misfortunes, yet when he beheld the ruins of that park,
I observed him troubled, though he did little
express it, only saying, he had been in hopes it
would not have been so much defaced as he found
it, there being not one timber-tree in it left for
shelter. However, he patiently bore what could
not be helped, and gave present order for the
cutting down of some wood that was left him in a
place near adjoining, to repale it, and got from
several friends deer to stock it.

Thus, though his lawsuits and other unavoidable

---

[1] According to Mr. Lower's note on this passage in the
edition of 1872, poot means either blackcock or red grouse,
probably the former. Poot or pout means a young bird of
any kind.—*Halliwell.*

expenses were very chargeable to him, yet he ordered his affairs so prudently, that by degrees he stocked and manured those lands he keeps for his own use, and in part repaired his manor-houses, Welbeck and Bolsover, to which latter he made some additional building; and though he has not yet built the seat at Nottingham, yet he hath stocked and paled a little park belonging to it.[1]

Nor is it possible for him to repair all the ruins of the estate that is left him, in so short a time, they being so great, and his losses so considerable, that I cannot without grief and trouble remember them; for before the wars my Lord had as great an estate as any subject in the kingdom, descended upon him most by women, viz., by his grandmother of his father's side, his own mother, and his first wife.

What estate his grandfather left to his father Sir Charles Cavendish, I know not; nor can I exactly tell what he had from his grandmother, but

---

[1] Not yet, *i.e.*, in 1667. Bailey, in the passage previously quoted from his " History of Nottinghamshire," is evidently wrong in saying that the castle was not acquired by the Duke till 1674. It was in that year that the Duke commenced rebuilding, as stated in the "inscription on an oblong square white marble tablet in the wall over the back door : " " This house was begun by William, Duke of Newcastle, in the year 1674 (who died in the year 1676), and according to his appointment by his last will, and by the model he left, was finished in the year 1679."—Bailey, " Annals of Nottinghamshire," p. 971.

she was very rich; for her third husband, Sir
William Saint Loo, gave her a good estate in the
west, which afterwards descended upon my Lord,
my Lord's mother being the younger daughter of
the Lord Ogle, and sole heir, after the death of her
eldest sister Jane, Countess of Shrewsbury, whom
King Charles the First restored to her father's
dignity, viz., Baroness of Ogle. This title descended upon my Lord and his heirs general,
together with £3000 a year in Northumberland;
and besides the estate left to my Lord, she gave
him £20,000 in money, and kept him and his
family at her own charge for several years.

My Lord's first wife, who was daughter and
heir to William Basset, of Blore, Esq.; widow to
Henry Howard, younger son to Thomas, Earl of
Suffolk, brought my Lord £2400 a year inheritance,
between six and seven thousand pounds in money,
and a jointure for her life of £800 a year. Besides,
my Lord increased his own estate, before the wars,
to the value of £100,000, and had increased it more,
had not the unhappy wars prevented him; for
though he had some disadvantages in his estate,
even before the wars, yet they are not considerable
to those he suffered afterwards for the service of
his King and country. For example, his father
Sir Charles Cavendish had lent his brother-in-law
Gilbert, Earl of Shrewsbury, £16,000, for which,
although afterward before his death he settled

£2000 a year upon him, yet he having enjoyed the said money for many years without paying any use for it, it might have been improved to my Lord's better advantage, had it been in his father's own hands, he being a person of great prudence in managing his estate ; and though the said Earl of Shrewsbury made my Lord his executor, yet my Lord was so far from making any advantage by that trust, even in what the law allowed him, that he lost £17,000 by it ; and afterwards delivered up his trust to William, Earl of Pembroke, and Thomas, Earl of Arundel, who both married two daughters of the said Earl of Shrewsbury; and since his return into England, upon the desire of Henry Howard, second son to the late Earl of Arundel, and heir-apparent (by reason of his eldest brother's distemper), he resigned his trust and interest to him, which certainly is a very difficult business, and yet questionable whether it may lawfully be done or not ? But such was my Lord's love to the family of the Shrewsburys, that he would rather wrong himself than it.

To mention some lawful advantages which my Lord might have made by the said trust, it may be noted in the first place, that the Earl of Shrewsbury's estate was let in long leases, which, by the law, fell to the executor. Next, that after some debts and legacies were paid out of those lands, which were set out for that purpose, they were settled so, that they fell to my Lord. Thirdly, seven hundred pounds a year was left as a gift to my Lord's brother, Sir Charles Cavendish, in case the Countess of Kent, second daughter to the said Earl of Shrewsbury, had no children. But my Lord never made any advantage for himself, of all these ; neither was he inquisitive whether the said Countess of Kent cut off the entail of that land, although she never had a child ; for my Lord's nature is so generous, that he hates to be mercenary, and never minds his own profit or interest in any trust or employment, more than the good and benefit of him that entrusts or employs him.

But, as I said heretofore, these are but petty losses in comparison of those he sustained by the late Civil Wars, whereof I shall partly give you an account. I say partly ; for though it may be computed what the loss of the annual rents of his lands amounts to, of which he never received the least worth for himself and his own profit, during the time both of his being employed in the service of war, and his sufferings in banishment ; as also the loss of those lands that are alienated from him, both in present possession, and in reversion ; and of his parks and woods that were cut down ; yet it is impossible to render an exact account of his personal estate.

As for his rents during the time he acted in the wars ; though he suffered others to gather theirs for their own use, yet his own either went for the use of the army, or fell into the hands of the enemy, or were suppressed and withheld from him by the cozenage of his tenants and officers, my Lord being then not able to look after them himself.

About the time when his late Majesty undertook the expedition into Scotland for the suppressing of some insurrection that happened there ; my lord, as afore is mentioned, amongst the rest, lent his Majesty £10,000 sterling ; but having newly married a daughter to the then Lord Brackly, now Earl of Bridgwater, whose portion was £12,000, the moiety whereof was paid in gold on the day of her marriage, and the rest soon after (although she was too young to be bedded);—this, together with some other expenses, caused him to take up the said £10,000 at interest, the use whereof he paid many years after.[1]

Also, when, after his sixteen years' banishment, he returned into England, before he knew what estate was left him, and was able to receive any rents of his own, he was necessitated to take £5000 upon use for the maintenance of himself and his family ; whereof the now Earl of Devonshire, his cousin-german, once removed, lent him £1000, for which and the former £1000 mentioned heretofore, he never desired nor received any use from my Lord, which I mention, to declare the favour and bounty of that noble Lord.

---

[1] Use—*i.e.*, interest.

But though it is impossible to render an exact account of all the losses which my Lord has sustained by the said wars, yet as far as they are accountable, I shall endeavour to represent them in these following particulars :

In the first place, I shall give you a just particular of my Lord's estate in lands, as it was before the wars, partly according to the value of his own surveyors, and partly according to the rate it is let at this present.

Next, I shall accompt the woods cut down by the rebellious party, in several places of my Lord's estate.

Thirdly, I shall compute the value of those lands which my Lord hath lost, both in present possession, and in reversion ; that is to say, those which he has lost altogether, both for himself and his posterity ; and those he has recovered only during the time of his life, and which his only son and heir, the now Earl of Ogle, must lose after his father's decease.

Fourthly, I shall make mention, how much of land my Lord hath been forced to sell for the payment of some of his debts, contracted during the time of the late Civil Wars, and when his estate was sequestered ; I say some, for there are a great many to pay yet.

To which I shall, fifthly, add the composition of his brother's estate ; and the loss of it for eight years.

A particular of my Lord's estate in plain rents, as it was partly surveyed in the year 1641, and partly is let at this present.[1]

NOTTINGHAMSHIRE.

The Manor of Welbeck . . .	£600	0	0
The Manor of Norton, Carburton, and the Granges . . .	454	19	1
Warsop.	51	6	8
The Manor-house of Sookholm .	308	10	3
The Manor of Clipston and Edwinstowe	334	9	8
Drayton	8	16	6
Dunham	99	17	8
Sutton	185	0	5
The Manor of Kirby, &c. . .	1075	7	2
The Manor of Cotham . . .	833	18	8
The Manor of Sibthorpe . .	704	1	0
Carcolston	450	3	0
Hawksworth, &c.	139	4	2
Flawborough.	512	11	8
Mearing and Holm Meadow . .	471	2	0
	£6229	7	11

LINCOLNSHIRE.

Wellingore and Ingham Meales [2] . £100 0 0

[1] When the places mentioned could be identified the modern spelling of their names has been adopted.

[2] Camden, in his map of Lincolnshire, places Ingold-meles just above Skegness, and elsewhere explains "meales" or "meles" to mean sand-hills.

DERBYSHIRE.[1]

The Barony of Bolsover and Wood- thorp.	£846	8	11
The Manor of Chesterfield . .	378	0	0
The Manor of Barlow . . .	796	17	6
Tissington	159	11	0
Dronfield	486	15	10
The Manor of Brampton . .	142	4	8
Little Longston	87	2	0
The Manor of Stoke . . .	212	3	0
Beard Hall, and Peak Forest . .	131	8	0
The Manor of Grindlow . .	156	8	0
The Manor of Hucklow . .	162	10	8
The Manor of Blackwall . .	306	0	4
Buxton and Tideswell . . .	153	2	0
Mansfield Park	100	0	0
Mapleton and Thorpe . . .	207	5	0
The Manor of Win Hill . .	238	18	0
. The Manor of Litchurch and Mackworth	713	15	1
Church and Meynel Langly Manor	850	1	0
	£6128	11	10

STAFFORDSHIRE.

The Manor of Blore with Caulton .	£573	13	4
The Manor of Grindon, Cauldon, with Waterfall	822	3	0
The Manor of Cheadle with Kingsley	259	18	0
The Manor of Barlaston, &c. . .	694	3	0
	£2349	17	4

[1] Birth Hall, Tids Hall, and Windly Hill are the names given by the Duchess to three of these manors.

GLOUCESTERSHIRE.

The Manor of Tormorton with Litleton	£1193	16	0
The Manor of Acton Turvil	388	3	2
	£1581	19	2

SOMERSETSHIRE.

The Manor of Chewstoke	£816	15	6
Knighton Sutton	300	14	4
Stroud and Kingsham (Keynsham ?) Park	186	4	0
	£1303	13	10

YORKSHIRE.

The Manors of Slingsby, Hoverngham (Hovingham) and Friton, Northinges and Pomfret	£1700	0	0

NORTHUMBERLAND.

The Barony of Bothal, Ogle and Hepple, &c.	£3000	0	0
Total	£22,393	10	1

That this particular of my Lord's estate was no less than is mentioned, may partly appear by the rate, as it was surveyed, and sold by the rebellious Parliament; for they raised, towards the later end of their power, which was in the year 1652, out of my Lord's estate, the sum of £111,593, 10s. 11d.,

K

at five years' and a half purchase, which was at above the rate of £18,000 a year, besides woods ; and his brother Sir Charles Cavendish's estate, which estate was £2000 a year, which falls not much short of the mentioned account ; and certainly, had they not sold such lands at easy rates, few would have bought them, by reason the purchasers were uncertain how long they should enjoy their purchase : besides, under-officers do not usually refuse bribes ; and it is well known that the surveyors did underrate estates according as they were fee'd by the purchasers.

Again, many of the estates of banished persons were given to soldiers for the payment of their arrears, who again sold them to others which would buy them at easier rates. But chiefly, it appears by the rate as my Lord's estate is let at present, there being several of the mentioned lands that are let at a higher rate now than they were surveyed ; nor are they all valued in the mentioned particular according to the survey, but many of them which were not surveyed, are accounted according to the rate they are let at this present.

The loss of my Lord's estate, in plain rents, as also upon ordinary use, and use upon use, is as followeth :[1]

The annual rent of my Lord's lands, viz.,

---

[1] "Use," interest ; "use upon use," compound interest.

£22,393, 10s. 1d., being lost for the space of eighteen years, which was the time of his acting in the wars, and of his banishment, without any benefit to him, reckoned without any interest, amounts to £403,083. But being accounted with the ordinary use at six in the hundred, and use upon use for the mentioned space of eighteen years, it amounts to £733,579.

But some perhaps will say, that if my Lord had enjoyed his estate, he would have spent it, at least so much as to maintain himself according to his degree and quality.

I answer, that it is very improbable my Lord should have spent all his estate, if he had enjoyed it, he being a man of great wisdom and prudence, knowing well how to spend, and how to manage; for though he lived nobly before the time of the wars, yet not beyond the compass of his estate. Nay, so far he would have been from spending his estate, that no doubt but he would have increased it to a vast value, as he did before the wars; where, notwithstanding his hospitality and noble housekeeping, his charges of building came to about £31,000; the portion of his second daughter, which was £12,000; the noble entertainments he gave King Charles the First, one whereof came to almost £15,000, another to above £4000, and a third to £1700, as hereafter shall be mentioned; and his great expenses during the time of his being

governor to his Majesty that now is, he yet
increased his estate to the value of £100,000,
which is £5000 per annum, when it was by so
much less.

But if any one will reckon the charges of his
housekeeping during the time of his exile, and
when he had not the enjoyment of his estate, he
may substract [1] the sum accounted for the payment
of his debts, contracted in the time of his banishment, which went to the maintenance of himself
and his family; or in lieu thereof, considering that
I do not account all my Lord's losses, but only
those that are certainly known, he may compare it
with the loss of his personal estate, whereof I
shall make some mention anon, and he'll find that
I do not heighten my Lord's losses, but rather
diminish them.   For surely the losses of his
personal estate, and those I account not, will
counterbalance the charges of his housekeeping, if
not exceed them.

Again, others will say, that there was much
land sold in the time of my Lord's banishment by
his sons, and feoffees in trust.

I answer, first, that whatsoever was sold, was
first bought of the rebellious power: next, although
they sold some lands, yet my Lord knew nothing
of it, neither did he receive a pennyworth for him-

---

[1] Substract, subtract.

self, neither of what they purchased, nor sold, all the time of his banishment till his return.[1]

And thus much of the loss of my Lord's estate in rents. Concerning the loss of his parks and woods, as much as is generally known (for I do not reckon particular trees cut down in several of his woods yet standing), 'tis as follows :

1. Clipston Park and woods, cut down to the value of £20,000.

2. Kirkby Woods, for which my Lord was formerly proffered £10,000.

3. Woods cut down in Derbyshire, £8000.

4. Red Lodge Wood, Rome Wood, and others near Welbeck, £4000.

5. Woods cut down in Staffordshire, £1000.

6. Woods cut down in Yorkshire, £1000.

7. Woods cut down in Northumberland, £1500.

The total, £45,000.

The lands which my Lord hath lost in present possession are £2015 per annum, which at twenty years' purchase come to £40,300 ; and those which he hath lost in reversion are £3214 per annum, which at sixteen years' purchase amount to the value of £51,424.

The lands which my Lord since his return has

---

[1] See the Duke's letter to Secretary Nicholas on this subject, written during his exile, in the Appendix.

sold for the payment of some of his debts, occasioned by the wars (for I do not reckon those he sold to buy others), come to the value of £56,000, to which out of his yearly revenue he has added £10,000 more, which is in all £66,000.

Lastly, the composition of his brother's estate was £5000, and the loss of it for eight years comes to £16,000.

All which, if summed up together, amounts to £941,303.[1]

These are the accountable losses, which my dear Lord and husband has suffered by the late Civil Wars, and his loyalty to his King and country. Concerning the loss of his personal estate, since (as I often mentioned) it cannot be exactly known; I shall not endeavour to set down the particulars thereof, only in general give you a note of what partly they are:

1. The pulling down of several of his dwelling or manor-houses.

2. The disfurnishing of them, of which the furniture at Bolsover and Welbeck was very noble

---

[1] The amount of the losses incurred by the Duke on behalf of the royal cause finds a parallel only in the somewhat similar statement drawn up by the Marquis of Worcester, and presented by him to Charles II. His total "spent, lent, &c., for my King and country, £918,000." Warburton's " Prince Rupert," iii. 515.

and rich. Out of his London house at Clerkenwell, there were taken, amongst other goods, suits of linen, viz., table-cloths, sideboard-cloths, napkins, &c., whereof one suit cost £160 ; they being bought for an entertainment which my Lord made for their Majesties, King Charles the First, and the Queen, at Bolsover Castle ; and of 150 suits of hangings of all sorts in all his houses, there were not above ten or twelve saved.

Of silver plate, my Lord had so much as came to the value of £3800, besides several curiosities of cabinets, cups, and other things, which after my Lord was gone out of England, were taken out of his manor-house, Welbeck, by a garrison of the King's party that lay therein,[1] whereof he recovered

---

[1] Welbeck was captured by the Earl of Manchester about August 2, 1644 (Rushworth, III. ii. 64 : Manchester's letter of August 6, in a volume published by the Camden Society under the title "Manchester's Quarrel with Cromwell," p. 5). An account of some of the spoils found there is given in Mrs. Hutchinson's Memoirs, vol. ii. p. 24. Welbeck was retaken by the Royalists on July 16, 1645 (Mercurius Belgicus). Symonds gives the following account of its capture :—"Welbeck was surprised by Newark horse under the command of Sir Richard Willis, about three weeks since. In a wood near the port stood his horse in ambush, and when the trevall was beat, and they let down their bridge for their scouts, our horse, under the command of Major Jarnot, a Frenchman, rid hard, and though they pulled up the bridge a foot high yet they got in and took it. They disputed every yard, and our men alighted and with

only £1100, which money was sent him beyond the seas ; the rest was lost.

As for pewter, brass, bedding, linen, and other household stuff, there was nothing else left but some few old feather-beds, and those all spoiled, and fit for no use.

3. My Lord's stock of corn, cattle, &c., was very great before the wars, by reason of the largeness and capacity of those grounds, and the great number of granges he kept for his own use ; as, for example, Barlow, Carcolston, Gleadthorp, Welbeck, and several more, which were all well manured and stocked.   But all this stock was lost, besides his race of horses in his grounds, grange horses, hackney-horses, manage-horses, coach-horses, and others he kept for his use.

·To these losses I may well and justly join the charges which my Lord hath been put to since his return into England, by reason they were caused by the ruins of the said wars ; whereof I reckon :

1. His law-suits, which have been very charge-able to him, more than advantageous.

---

their pistols scaled and got in."—Symonds, p. 224.   Major Jarnot, more properly (as in the " Memoirs of Colonel Hut-chinson ") Jammot, was a Walloon.   Welbeck was finally disgarrisoned, by arrangement between the two parties, in November 1645.   (Note in " Memoirs of Colonel Hutchin-son," ii. 24.)

2. The stocking, manuring, paling, stubbing,[1] hedging, &c., of his grounds and parks ; where it is to be noted, that no advantage or benefit can be made of grounds, under the space of three years, and of cattle not under five or six.

3. The repairing and furnishing of some of his dwelling-houses.

4. The setting up a race or breed of horses, as he had before the wars ; for which purpose he hath bought the best mares he could get for money.

In short, I can reckon £12,000 laid out barely for the repair of some ruins, which my Lord could not be without, there being many of them to repair yet ; neither is this all that is laid out, but much more which I cannot well remember ; nor is there more but one grange stocked, amongst several that were kept for furnishing his house with provisions. As for other charges and losses, which my Lord hath sustained since his return, I will not reckon them, because my design is only to account such losses as were caused by the wars.

By which, as they have been mentioned, it may easily be concluded, that although my Lord's estate was very great before the wars, yet now it is shrunk into a very narrow compass, that it puts

---

[1] "Stub," to grub up stumps or roots.—Halliwell, "Dictionary of Archaic and Provincial Words."

his prudence and wisdom to the proof, to make it serve his necessities, he having no other assistance to bear him up; and yet notwithstanding all this, he hath since his return paid both for himself and his son, all manner of taxes, loans, levies, assessments, &c., equally with the rest of his Majesty's subjects, according to that estate that is left him, which he has been forced to take upon interest.

THE LIFE

OF

THE MOST ILLUSTRIOUS PRINCE,

WILLIAM, DUKE OF NEWCASTLE.

—•—

THE THIRD BOOK.

THUS having given you a faithful account of all my Lord's actions, both before, in, and after the Civil Wars, and of his losses, I shall now conclude with some particular heads concerning the description of his own person, his natural humour, disposition, qualities, virtues ; his pedigree, habit, diet, exercises, &c., together with some other remarks and particulars which I thought requisite to be inserted, both to illustrate the former books, and to render the history of his life more perfect and complete.

1. *Of his Power.*

After his Majesty King Charles the First had entrusted my Lord with the power of raising forces for his Majesty's service, he effected that which never any subject did, nor was (in all probability) able to do; for though many great and noble persons did also raise forces for his Majesty, yet they were brigades, rather than well-formed armies, in comparison to my Lord's. The reason was, that my Lord, by his mother, the daughter of Cuthbert, Lord Ogle, being allied to most of the most ancient families in Northumberland, and other the northern parts, could pretend a greater interest in them, than a stranger; for they, through a natural affection to my Lord as their own kinsman, would sooner follow him, and under his conduct sacrifice their lives for his Majesty's service, than anybody else, well knowing, that by deserting my Lord, they deserted themselves. And by this means my Lord raised first a troop of horse, consisting of a hundred and twenty, and a regiment of foot; and then an army of eight thousand horse, foot and dragoons, in those parts; and afterwards upon this ground, at several times, and in several places, so many several troops, regiments and armies, that in all, from the first to the last, they amounted to above 100,000 men, and those most upon his own interest, and without any other considerable help or assistance; which was much for a particular subject, and in such a conjuncture of time; for since armies are soonest raised by covetousness, fear, and faction; that is to say, upon a constant and settled pay, upon the ground of terror, and upon the ground of rebellion; but very seldom or never upon uncertainty of pay; and when it is as hazardous to be of such a party, as to be in the heat of a battle; also when there is no other design but honest duty. It may easily be conceived that my Lord could have no little love and affection when he raised his army upon such grounds as could promise them but little advantage at that time.

Amongst the rest of his army, my Lord had chosen for his own regiment of foot, 3000 of such valiant, stout, and faithful men (whereof many were bred in the moorish grounds of the northern parts) that they were ready to die at my Lord's feet, and never gave over, whensoever they were engaged in action, until they had either conquered the enemy, or lost their lives. They were called White-coats, for this following reason : my Lord being resolved to give them new liveries, and there being not red cloth enough to be had, took up so much of white as would serve to clothe them, desiring withal, their patience until he had got it dyed; but they, impatient of stay, requested my Lord, that he would be pleased to let them have it un-dyed as it was, promising they themselves would dye it in the enemy's blood. Which request my Lord granted them, and from that time they were called White-coats.

To give you some instances of their valour and courage, I must beg leave to repeat some passages mentioned in the first book. The enemy having closely besieged the city of York, and made a passage into the manor-yard, by springing a mine under the wall thereof, was got into the manor-house with a great number of their forces ; which my Lord perceiving, he immediately went and drew eighty of the said White-coats thither, who with the greatest courage went close up to the enemy, and having charged them, fell pell-mell with the butt-ends of their muskets upon them, and with the assistance of the rest that renewed their courage by their example, killed and took 1500, and by that means saved the town.[1]

How valiantly they behaved themselves in the last fatal battle upon Hessom Moor near York, has been also declared heretofore ; insomuch, that although most of the army were fled, yet they would not stir, until by the enemy's power they were overcome, and most of them slain in rank and file.[2]

---

[1] See p. 72.

[2] "A most memorable action happened on that day. There was one entire regiment of foot belonging to Newcastle, called the Lambs, because they were all new clothed in white woollen cloth, two or three days before the fight. This sole regiment, after the day was lost, having got into a small parcel of ground ditched in, and not of easy access of horse, would take no quarter ; and by mere valour, for one whole hour, kept the troops of horse from entering amongst them at near push of pike : when the horse did enter, they would have no quarter, but fought it out till

Their love and affection to my Lord was such, that it lasted even when he was deprived of all his power, and could do them little good; to which purpose I shall mention this following passage:

My Lord being in Antwerp, received a visit from a gentleman, who came out of England, and rendered my Lord thanks for his safe escape at sea; my Lord being in amaze, not knowing what the gentleman meant, he was pleased to acquaint him, that in his coming over sea out of England, he was set upon by pickaroons,[1] who having examined him, and the rest of his company, at last some asked him, whether he knew the Marquess of Newcastle? To whom he answered, that he knew him very well, and was going over into the same city where my Lord lived. Whereupon they did not only take nothing from him, but used him with all civility,

---

there was not thirty of them living; those whose hap it was to be beaten down upon the ground as the troopers came near them, though they could not rise for their wounds, yet were so desperate as to get either a pike or sword, or piece of them, and to gore the troopers' horses, as they came over them, or passed by them. Captain Camby, then a trooper under Cromwell, and an actor, who was the third or fourth man that entered amongst them, protested he never, in all the fights he was in, met with such resolute brave fellows, or whom he pitied so much, and said, 'He saved two or three against their wills.'"—Diary of William Lilly, p. 178, ed. 1822.

[1] Rogues, from the Spanish *Picaro.*

and desired him to remember their humble duty
to their Lord-General, for they were some of his
White-coats that had escaped death; and if my
Lord had any service for them, they were ready
to assist him upon what designs soever, and to
obey him in whatsoever he should be pleased to
command them.

This I mention for the eternal fame and memory
of those valiant and faithful men.   But to return
to the power my Lord had in the late wars : as he
was the head of his own army, and had raised it
most upon his own interest for the service of his
Majesty; so he was never ordered by his Majesty's
privy council (except that some forces of his were
kept by his late Majesty (which he sent to him),
together with some arms and ammunition heretofore
mentioned) until his Highness Prince Rupert came
from his Majesty, to join with him at the siege of
York.   He had, moreover, the power of coining,
printing, knighting, &c., which never any subject
had before, when his sovereign himself was in the
kingdom ;   as   also   the   command   of   so   many
counties, as is mentioned in the first book, and the
power of placing and displacing what governors
and commanders he pleased, and of constituting
what garrisons he thought fit; of the chief whereof
I shall give you this following list :

*A Particular of the Principal Garrisons, and the
Governors of them, constituted by my Lord.*[1]

IN NORTHUMBERLAND.[2]

Newcastle-upon-Tyne, Sir John Marley, Knight.
Tynmouth Castle and Shields, Sir Thomas Riddal,
Knight.

IN THE BISHOPRIC OF DURHAM.[3]

Hartlepool, Lieutenant-Colonel Henry Lambton.
Raby Castle, Sir William Savile, Knight and Baronet.

IN YORKSHIRE.[4]

The city of York, Sir Thomas Glenham, Knight and
Baronet ; and afterwards, when he took the field,
the Lord John Bellasis.

---

[1] I have endeavoured to give as far as possible the dates
of the capture of these garrisons, as they show the fate of
the royalist cause in the North after Newcastle's departure.

[2] Newcastle-upon-Tyne. The town captured by the Scots,
October 20, 1644 ; the Castle, October 27. Vicars' "Burning
Bush," pp. 46–61.
Tynmouth Castle, October 27, 1644. Burning Bush, p. 63.

[3] Hartlepool, July 24, 1644. Thurloe, State Papers, i. 41.
Raby Castle. The date of its first capture I have not
been able to find. Whitelock notes on July 7, 1645, " the
King's forces from Bolton surprised Raby Castle, belonging
to Sir Henry Vane, but were again close blocked up by
forces raised by Sir George Vane," and notes its surrender
to the Parliament on July 28. Whitelock, vol. i. pp. 465, 487,
ed. 1853.

[4] York. Articles signed July 16, 1644. Rushworth, III.ii.640.

L

Pomfret Castle, Colonel Mynn, and after him Sir John
   Redman.
Sheffield Castle, Major Beaumont.
Wortley Hall, Sir Francis Wortley.
Tickhill Castle, Major Mounteney.
Doncaster, Sir Francis Fane, Knight of the Bath, after-
   wards Governor of Lincoln.
Sandal Castle, Captain Bonivant.
Skipton Castle, Sir John Mallary, Baronet.
Bolton Castle, Mr. Scroope.
Hemsley Castle, Sir Jordan Crosland.
Scarborough Castle and town, Sir Hugh Cholmley.

Pomfret Castle, July 21, 1645. Burning Bush, p. 202. See
also the Surtees Society's Volume of Miscellanies containing
the history of the siege of Pontefract.

Sheffield Castle, 11th August 1644. Hunter's Hallamshire, ed. Gatty, p. 142.

Wortley Hall. Possibly Walton Hall is meant, captured
with Sir Francis Wortley in it on 3d June 1644. Rushworth, III. ii. 622.

Tickhill Castle, July 26, 1644. Vicars' "God's Ark," p. 293.

Doncaster, fortified in January 1644. Rushworth, III. ii.
305. In the "Kingdom's Weekly Intelligencer" for April 2–10,
1644, it is stated that the royalists had abandoned Doncaster.

Sandal Castle, October 2, 1645.

Skipton Castle, December 21, 1645. Burning Bush, 337.

Bolton Castle, beginning of November 1645. Vicar's
"Burning Bush," p. 318.

Helmsley Castle, November 22, 1644. The Articles are
printed in the Fairfax Correspondence, vol. iii. p. 121.

Scarborough, the town taken 17th February 1645 ; the
castle, July 22, 1645.

Stamford Bridge, Colonel Galbraith.
Halifax, Sir Francis Mackworth.
Tadcaster, Sir Gamaliel Dudley.
Eyrmouth, Major Kaughton.

In Cumberland.[1]

The city of Carlisle, Sir Philip Musgrave, Knight and
   Baronet.
Cockermouth, Colonel Kirby.

In Nottinghamshire.[2]

Newark-upon-Trent, Sir John Henderson, Knight; and
   afterwards Sir Richard Byron, Knight, now Lord
   Byron.
Wyrton House, Colonel Rowland Hacker.

Stamford Bridge. On the history of this garrison see
Slingsby's Memoirs, p. 93. It was captured about the same
time as Tadcaster.

Tadcaster, March 3, 1644. Ricraft's Champions.

Eyrmouth, 24th May 1644, taken by Sir John Meldrum.
Mercurius Civicus, May 23-30, 1644. He had also captured
Cawood Castle on May 19.

[1] Carlisle, July 1645. Vicars' "Burning Bush," p. 186.
Whitelock notes its surrender under July 2.

[2] Newark. The articles for the surrender of Newark
are signed 6th May, the garrison marched out May 8, 1646.
Rushworth, IV. i. 269.

Wyrton, or Wiverton, before November 6, 1645. Vicars'
"Burning Bush," p. 316.

Welbeck, Colonel Van Peire ; and after Colonel Beeton.
Shelford House, Colonel Philip Stanhop.

In Lincolnshire.[1]

The city of Lincoln, first Sir Francis Fane, Knight of
    the Bath ; secondly Sir Peregrine Bartu.
Gainsborough, Colonel St. George.
Bullingbrook Castle, Lieutenant-Colonel Chester.
Belvoir Castle, Sir Gervas Lucas.

In Derbyshire.[2]

Bolsover Castle, Colonel Muschamp.
Wingfield Manor, Colonel Roger Molyneux.
Staveley House, the now Lord Fretchvile.

Welbeck, August 2, 1644. Rushworth, III. ii. 644. Manchester's Quarrel with Cromwell, p. 6.

Shelford, November 3, 1645. Memoirs of Col. Hutchinson, vol. ii. pp. 82, 376, ed. 1885.

[1] Lincoln, taken by Manchester's forces after the battle of Winceby, about October 24, 1643. Vicars' "God's Ark," p. 51. Abandoned in March 1644, after Prince Rupert's relief of Newark ; reoccupied by the Cavaliers, and taken again by Manchester, May 6, 1644. Rushworth, III. ii. 621. Gainsborough was taken the same October 1643.

Bullingbrook Castle is mentioned as captured in the Scottish Dove, October 27 to November 3, 1643.

Belvoir, surrendered January 31, 1646. Peck's " Desiderata Curiosa," p. 345.

[2] Bolsover Castle, August 12, 1644.

Wingfield Manor, August 14, 1644.

Staveley House, August 21, 1644. These three houses were all taken by Major-General Crawford with a detachment of Manchester's army, after the battle of Marston Moor. Rushworth, III. ii. 644.

A List of the General Officers of the Army.

1. The Lord-General, the now Duke of Newcastle, the noble subject of this book.

2. The Lieutenant-General of the Army; first the Earl of Newport, afterwards the Lord Eythin.

3. The General of the Ordnance, Charles, Viscount Mansfield.

4. The General of the Horse, George, Lord Goring.

5. The Colonel-General of the Army, Sir Thomas Glenham.

6. The Major-General of the Army, Sir Francis Mackworth.

7. The Lieutenant-General of the Horse, first Mr. Charles Cavendish, after him Sir Charles Lucas.

8. Commissary-General of Horse, first Colonel Windham, after him Sir William Throckmorton, and after him Mr. George Porter.

9. Lieutenant-General of the Ordnance, Sir William Davenant.

10. Treasurer of the Army, Sir William Carnaby.

11. Advocate-General of the Army, Dr. Liddal.

12. Quartermaster-General of the Army, Mr. Ralph Errington.

13. Providore-General [1] of the Army, Mr. Gervas Nevil, and after Mr. Smith.

14. Scout-Master-General of the Army, Mr. Hudson. [2]

15. Waggon-Master-General of the Army, Baptist Johnson.

---

[1] The precise duties of these officers can best be gathered from Markham's " Five Decades of Epistles of War." Providore-General is what he calls Victual-Master, Provant-Master, or Purveyor.

[2] Michael Hudson, D.D., of Queen's College, Oxford, the

William, Lord Widdrington, was President of the Council of War, and Commander-in-Chief of the three counties of Lincoln, Rutland, and Nottingham, and the forces there.

When my Lord marched with his army to Newcastle against the Scots, then the Lord John Bellasis was constituted Governor of York, and Commander-in-Chief, or Lieutenant-General of Yorkshire.

As for the rest of the officers and commanders of every particular regiment and company, they being too numerous, cannot well be remembered, and therefore I shall give you no particular account of them.

2. *Of his Misfortunes and Obstructions.*

Although Nature had favoured my Lord, and endued him with the best qualities and perfections she could inspire into his soul; yet Fortune hath ever been such an inveterate enemy to him, that she invented all the spite and malice against him that lay in her power; and notwithstanding his prudent counsels and designs, cast such obstructions in his way, that he seldom proved successful, but where he acted in person. And since I am not ignorant that this unjust and partial age is apt to suppress the worth of meritorious persons, and that many will endeavour to obscure my Lord's noble

King's guide and companion in his flight from Oxford. He was killed at the capture of Woodcroft House in Northamptonshire, June 6, 1648. See the numerous documents relating to him in Peck's " Desiderata Curiosa," pp. 347, 379.

actions and fame, by casting unjust aspersions upon him, and laying (either out of ignorance or malice) Fortune's envy to his charge, I have purposed to represent these obstructions which conspired to render his good intentions and endeavours ineffectual, and at last did work his ruin and destruction, in these following particulars.

1. At the time when the kingdom became so infatuated, as to oppose and pull down their gracious King and Sovereign, the treasury was exhausted, and no sufficient means to raise and maintain armies to reduce his Majesty's rebellious subjects; so that my Lord had little to begin withal but what his own estate would allow, and his interest procure him.

2. When his late Majesty, in the beginning of the unhappy wars, sent my Lord to Hull, the strongest place in the kingdom, where the magazine of arms and ammunition was kept, and he by his prudence had gained it to his Majesty's service; my Lord was left to the mercy of the Parliament, where he had surely suffered for it (though he acted not without his Majesty's commission), if some of the contrary party had not quitted him, in hopes to gain him on their side.

3. After his Majesty had sent my Lord to New-castle-upon-Tyne, to take upon him the government of that place, and he had raised there, of friends and tenants, a troop of horse and regiment of foot, which he ordered to convey some arms and

ammunition to his Majesty, sent by the Queen out of Holland; his Majesty was pleased to keep the same convoy with him to increase his own forces, which, although it was but of a small number, yet at that present time it would have been very serviceable to my Lord, he having then but begun to raise forces.

4. When her Majesty, the now Queen Mother, after her arrival out of Holland to York, had a purpose to convey some arms to his Majesty, my Lord ordered a party of 1500 to conduct the same, which his Majesty was pleased to keep with him for his own service.

5. After her Majesty had taken a resolution to go from York to Oxford, where the King then was, my Lord for her safer conduct quitted 7000 men of his army, with a convenient train of artillery, which likewise never returned to my Lord.

6. When the Earl of Montrose was going into Scotland, he went to my Lord at Durham, and desired of him a supply of some forces for his Majesty's service ; when my Lord gave him 200 horse and dragoons, even at such a time when he stood most in need of a supply himself, and thought every day to encounter the Scottish army.[1]

7. When my Lord out of the northern parts went into Lincoln- and Derby- shires with his army, to order and reduce them to their allegiance and duty

---

[1] See p. 68.

to his Majesty, and from thence resolved to march into the Associate Counties (where in all probability he would have made an happy end of the war), he was so importuned by those he left behind him, and particularly the Commander-in-Chief, to return into Yorkshire (alleging the enemy grew strong and would ruin them all, if he came not speedily to succour and assist them), that in honour and duty he could do no otherwise but grant their requests; when as yet being returned into those parts, he found them secure and safe enough from the enemy's attempts.[1]

---

[1] See p. 57. Slingsby says Lord Newcastle marched in Lincolnshire, took Gainsborough, "and had done greater matters in that county had he not been too hastily called away by the gentlemen of Yorkshire, who began again to fear my Lord Fairfax's power; for after he was once got to Hull, his shattered troops began to drop in one after another, and what he wanted in foot he made the country supply him with out of the East Riding. He begins to enlarge his quarters, and held Beverley too, and doubted not within a while to be able to visit his dearly beloved the West Riding again. This I say was the cause that moved the gentlemen to send to his Excellency to desire him to come back; and being come gave their opinions that his only way would be to besiege him in Hull; and of that opinion was Lieutenant-General King, and that it might be won if the gentlemen would undertake to raise an addition of force to those out of the country. They go about it and in several parts of the country sits in commission, makes great levies if they could be kept together."—Slingsby, Memoirs, p. 99.

8. My Lord (as heretofore mentioned) had as great private enemies about his Majesty, as he had public enemies in the field, who used all the endeavour they could to pull him down.

9. There was such juggling, treachery, and falsehood in his own army, and amongst some of his own officers, that it was impossible for my Lord to be prosperous and successful in his designs and undertakings.

10. My Lord's army being the chief and greatest army which his Majesty had, and in which consisted his prime strength and power, the Parliament resolved, at last, to join all their forces with the army of the Scots (which when it came out of Scotland, was above 20,000 men), to oppose, and if possible, to ruin it; well knowing, that if they did pull down my Lord, they should be masters of all the three kingdoms; so that there were three armies against one. But although my Lord suffered much by the negligence (and sometimes treachery) of his officers, and was unfortunately called back into Yorkshire, from his march he designed for the Associate Counties, and was forced to part with a great number of his forces and ammunition, as afore-mentioned; yet he would hardly have been overcome, and his army ruined by the enemy, had he but had some timely supply and assistance at the siege of York, or that his counsel had been taken in not fighting the enemy

then, or that the battle had been deferred some two or three days longer, until those forces were arrived which he expected, namely, 3000 men out of Northumberland, and 2000 drawn out of several garrisons. But the chief misfortune was that the enemy fell upon the King's forces, before they were all put into a battallia, and took them at their great disadvantage; which caused such a panic fear amongst them, that most of the horse of the right wing of his Majesty's forces betook themselves to their heels; insomuch, that although the left wing (commanded by the Lord Goring and my brother Sir Charles Lucas) did their best endeavour, and beat back the enemy three times, and my Lord's own regiment of foot charged them so courageously, that they never broke, but died most of them in their ranks and files; yet the power of the enemy being too strong, put them at last to a total rout and confusion. Which unlucky disaster put an end to all future hopes of his Majesty's party; so that my Lord, seeing he had nothing left in his power to do his Majesty any further service in that kind (for had he stayed, he would have been forced to surrender all those towns and garrisons in those parts, that were yet in his Majesty's devotion, as afterwards it also happened), resolved to quit the kingdom, as formerly is mentioned.

And these are chiefly the obstructions to the

good success of my Lord's designs in the late Civil Wars; which being rightly considered, will save him blameless from what otherwise would be laid to his charge. For, as according to the old saying, "'Tis easy for men to swim, when they are held up by the chin :" so, on the other side, it is very dangerous and difficult for them to endeavour it, when they are pulled down by the heels, and beaten upon their heads.

3. *Of his Loyalty and Sufferings.*

I dare boldly and justly say, that there never was, nor is a more loyal and faithful subject than my Lord, not to mention the trust he discharged in all those employments, which either King James, or King Charles the First, or his now gracious master King Charles the Second, were pleased to bestow upon him, which he performed with such care and fidelity, that he never disobeyed their commands in the least; I will only note—

1. That he was the first that appeared in arms for his Majesty, and engaged himself and all his friends he could for his Majesty's service; and though he had but two sons which were young, and one only brother, yet they all were with him in the wars. His two sons had commands, but his brother, though he had no command, by reason of the weakness of his body, yet he was never from my Lord when he was in action, even to the last;

for he was the last with my Lord in the field in that fatal battle upon Hessom Moor, near York; and though my brother, Sir Charles Lucas, desired my Lord to send his sons away, when the said battle was fought, yet he would not, saying, his sons should show their loyalty and duty to his Majesty, in venturing their lives, as well as himself.

2. My Lord was the chief and only person, that kept up the power of his late Majesty; for when his army was lost, all the King's party was ruined in all three of his Majesty's kingdoms; because in his army lay the chief strength of all the royal forces; it being the greatest and best formed army which his Majesty had, and the only support both of his Majesty's person and power, and of the hopes of all his loyal subjects in all his dominions.

3. My Lord was sixteen years in banishment, and hath lost and suffered most of any subject, that suffered either by war, or other ways, except those that lost their lives, and even that he valued not, but exposed it to so imminent dangers that nothing but Heaven's decree had ordained to save it.

4. He never minded his own interest more than his loyalty and duty, and upon that account never desired nor received anything from the Crown to enrich himself, but spent great sums in his Majesty's service; so that after his long banishment and return into England, I observed his ruined estate was like an earthquake, and his debts like thunder-

bolts, by which he was in danger of being utterly undone, had not patience and prudence, together with Heaven's blessings, saved him from that threatening ruin.

5. He never repined at his losses and sufferings, because he lost and suffered for his King and country; nay, so far was he from that, that I have heard him say, if the same wars should happen again, and he was sure to lose both his life and all he had left him, yet he would most willingly sacrifice it for his Majesty's service.

6. He never connived or conspired with the enemy, neither directly nor indirectly; for though some person of quality being sent in the late wars to him into the north,[1] from his late Majesty, who was then at Oxford, with some message, did withal in private acquaint him, that some of the nobility that were with the King, desired him to side with them against his Majesty, alleging that if his Majesty should become an absolute conqueror, both himself and the rest of the nobility would lose all their rights and privileges; yet he was so far from

---

[1] Sir Philip Warwick was twice employed on errands from Oxford to the northern army, and may possibly be the person referred to, but there is no hint of any such intrigue in his Memoirs. Wilmot may have been concerned in it, for, as Sir Philip remarks, "he that marks Wilmot's whole progress through the war shall find him much affected to be an arbiter of peace."

consenting to it, that he returned him this answer, namely, that he entered into actions of war, for no other end, but for the service of his king and master, and to keep up his Majesty's rights and prerogatives, for which he was resolved to venture both his life, posterity, and estate ; for certainly, said he, the nobility cannot fall if the King be victorious, nor can they keep up their dignities if the King be overcome.

This message was delivered by word of mouth, but none of their names mentioned ; so that it is not certainly known whether it was a real truth or not ; more probable it was, that they intended to sound my Lord, or to make, if possible, more division. For certainly not all that pretended to be for the King, were his friends ; and I myself remember very well, when I was with her Majesty, the now Queen Mother, in Oxford (although I was too young to perceive their intrigues, yet I was old enough to observe), that there were great factions both amongst the courtiers and soldiers. But my Lord's loyalty was such, that he kept always faithful and true to his Majesty, and could by no means be brought to side with the rebellious party, or to juggle and mind his own interest more than his Majesty's service ; and this was the cause that he had as great private enemies at court, as he had public enemies in the field, who sought as much his ruin and destruction privately, and would cast aspersions upon his loyalty and duty, as these did publicly oppose him.

In short, that it may appear the better what loyal and faithful services my Lord has done both for his late Majesty King Charles the First and his now gracious master King Charles the Second, I have thought fit to subjoin both their Majesty's commendations which they were pleased to give him, when for his great and loyal services they conferred upon him the titles and dignities of Marquess, and Duke of Newcastle.[1]

A Copy of the Preamble of my Lord's Patent for Marquess, Englished.

"Rex, &c., Salutem.—Whereas it appears to us, that William, Earl of Newcastle-upon-Tyne, besides his most eminent birth and splendid alliances, hath equalled all those titles with which he is adorned by desert, and hath also won them by virtue, industry, prudence, and a steadfast faith : whilst with dangers and expenses gathering together soldiers, arms, and all other warlike habiliments ; and applying them as well in our affairs, as most plentifully sending them to us (having forethought of our dignity and security), he was ready with us in all actions in Yorkshire, and governed the

---

[1] Given also by Collins, "Historical Collections," p. 31, and there dated Oxford, 27th October 1643.

town of Newcastle, and castle in the mouth of
Tyne, at the time of that fatal revolt of the people
who were got together; and with a band of his
friends did opportunely seize that port, and settled
it a garrison; bringing arms to us (then our only
relief): in which service so strongly going on
(which was of grand moment to our affairs) we do
gratefully remember him still to have stood to:
afterwards, having mustered together a good army
(ourself being gone elsewhere), the rebels now enjoying almost all Yorkshire, and the chiefest fortress
of all the country now appearing to have scarce
refuge or safety for him against the swelling
rebels (the whole country then desiring and praying for his coming, that he might timely relieve
them in their desperate condition): and leading
his said army in the midst of winter gave the
rebels battle in his passage, vanquished them, and
put them to flight, and took from them several
garrisons and places of refuge, and restored health
to the subjects, and, by his many victories, peace
and security to the countries: witness those places,
made noble by the death and flight of the rebels:
in Lincolnshire, Gainsborough and Lincoln; in
Derbyshire, Chesterfield; but in Yorkshire, Peirce-
bridge, Seacroft, Tankerly, Tadcaster, Sheffield,
Rotherham, Yarum, Beverley, Cawood, Selby,
Halifax, Leeds, and above all, Bradford; where,
when the Yorkshire and Lancashire rebels were

M

united, and battle joined with them; when our army, as well by the great numbers of the rebels, as much more the badness of our ground, was so prest upon, that the soldiers now seemed to think of flying; he, their General, with a full career, commanding two troops to follow him, broke into the very rage of the battle, and with so much violence fell upon the right wing of those rebels, that those who were but now certain of victory, turned their backs, and fled from the conqueror, who by his wisdom, virtue, and his own hand, brought death and flight to the rebels, victory and glory to himself, plunder to the soldiery, and twenty-two great guns, and many ensigns to us. Nor was there before this, wanting to so much virtue, equal felicity, for our most beloved Consort, after a dismal tempest coming from Holland, being drove ashore at Burlington, and undergoing a more grievous danger, by the excursions of the rebels, than the tossing and tumbling of the sea; he having heard of it, speedily goes to her with his army, and dutifully receiveth her, in safety brings her, and with all security conducts her to us at Oxford. Whereas therefore the aforesaid Earl hath raised so many monuments of his virtue and fidelity towards us, our Queen, children, and our kingdom; when also he doth at this time establish with safety, and with his power defend, the northern parts of our kingdom against the rebels; when, lastly, nothing more concerns mankind and princes, and nothing can be more just, than that he may receive for his deeds a reward suitable to his name, which requires that he who defends the Borders should be created by us, Governor or Marquess of the Borderers. Know therefore," &c.

A Copy of the Preamble of my Lord's Patent for Duke, Englished.[1]

"REX, &c., SALUTEM.—Whereas our most beloved and faithful cousin and counsellor, William, Earl and Marquess of Newcastle-upon-Tyne, &c., worthy by his famous name, blood, and office, of large honours, has been eminent in so many, and so great services performed to us and our father (of ever-blessed memory) that his merits are still producing new effects, we have decreed likewise to add more honour to his former. And though these his such eminent actions, which he hath faithfully and valiantly performed to us, our father, and our kingdom, speak loud enough in themselves; yet since the valiant services of a good subject are always pleasant to remember, we have thought fit to have them in part related for a good example and encouragement to virtue.

"The great proofs of his wisdom and piety are

---

[1] Collins' " Historical Collections," p. 43, dated 16th March 166⅘.

sufficiently known to us from our younger years,
and we shall always retain a sense of those good
principles he instilled into us; the care of our
youth which he happily undertook for our good,
he as faithfully and well discharged.   Our years
growing up amidst bad times, and the harsh necessities of war, a new charge and care of loyalty, the
kingdom and religion, called him off to make use of
his further diligence and valour.   Rebellion spread
abroad, he levied loyal forces in great numbers,
opposed the enemy, won so many and so great
victories in the field, took in so many towns,
castles, and garrisons, as well in our northern
parts, as elsewhere; and behaved himself with so
great courage and valour in the defending also
what he had got, especially at the siege of York,
which he maintained against three potent armies,
of Scots and English, closely beleaguering, and
with emulation assaulting it for three months (till
relief was brought), to the wonder and envy of the
enemy; that, if loyal and human force could have
prevailed, he had soon restored fidelity, peace, and
his KING to the nation, which was then hurrying
to ruin by an unhappy fate; so that rebellion
getting the upper hand, and no place being left for
him to act further valiantly in, for his King and
country, he still retained the same loyalty and
valour in suffering, being an inseparable follower
of our exile; during which sad catastrophe, his

whole estate was sequestered and sold from him, and his person always one of the first of those few who were excepted, both for life and estate (which was offered to all others). Besides, his virtues are accompanied with a noble blood, being of a family by each stock equally adorned and endowed with great honours and riches. For which reasons we have resolved to grace the said Marquess with a new mark of our favour, he being every way deserving of it, as one who loved virtue equal to his noble birth, and possessed patrimonies suitable to both, as long as loyalty had any place to show itself in our realm ; which possessions he so well employed, and at last for us and our father's service lost, till he was with us restored. Know therefore," &c.

4. *Of his Prudence and Wisdom.*

My Lord's prudence and wisdom hath been sufficiently apparent both in his public and private actions and employments; for he hath such a natural inspection, and judicious observation of things, that he sees beforehand what will come to pass, and orders his affairs accordingly. To which purpose I cannot but mention, that Laud, the then Archbishop of Canterbury (between whom and my Lord interceded a great and entire friendship, which he confirmed by a legacy of a diamond, to the value of £200, left to my Lord when he

died, which was much for him to bequeath; for
though he was a great statesman, and in favour
with his late Majesty, yet he was not covetous to
hoard up wealth, but bestowed it rather upon the
public, repairing the Cathedral of St. Paul's in
London, which, had God granted him life, he
would certainly have beautified, and rendered as
famous and glorious as any in Christendom): this
said Archbishop was pleased to tell his late Majesty,
that my Lord was one of the wisest and prudentest
persons that ever he was acquainted with.

For further proof, I cannot pass by that my
Lord told his late Majesty, King Charles the First,
and her Majesty the now Queen Mother, some
time · before the wars, that he observed, by the
humours of the people, the approaching of a civil
war, and that his Majesty's person would be in
danger of being deposed, if timely care was not
taken to prevent it.

Also when my Lord was at Antwerp, the
Marquess of Montrose, before he went into Scotland, gave my Lord a visit, and acquainted him
with his intended journey, asking my Lord whether
he was not also going for England? My Lord
answered, he was ready to do his Majesty what
service he could, and would shun no opportunity,
where he perceived he could effect something to
his Majesty's advantage; nay, said he, if his
Majesty should be pleased to command my single

person to go against the whole army of the enemy, although I was sure to lose my life, yet out of a loyal duty to his Majesty, and in obedience to his commands, I should never refuse it. But to venture (said he) the life of my friends, and to betray them in a desperate action, without any probability of doing the least good to his Majesty, would be a very unjust and unconscionable act; for my friends might perhaps venture with me upon an implicit faith, that I was so honest as not to engage them without a firm and solid foundation; but I wanting that, as having no ships, arms, ammunition, provision, forts, and places of rendezvous, and what is the chief thing, money; to what purpose would it be to draw them into so hazardous an action, but to seek their ruin and destruction, without the least benefit to his Majesty? Then the Marquess of Montrose asked my Lord's advice, and what he should do in such a case? My Lord answered, that he, knowing best his own country, power, and strength, and what probability he had of forces, and other necessaries for war, when he came into Scotland, could give himself the best advice; but withal told him, that if he had no provision nor ammunition, arms and places of rendezvous for his men to meet and join, he would likely be forced to hide his head, and suffer for his rash undertaking: which unlucky fate did also accordingly befall that worthy person.

These passages I mention to no other end, but to declare my Lord's judgment and prudence in worldly affairs; whereof there are so many, that if I should set them all down, it would swell this history to a big volume. They may in some sort be gathered from his actions mentioned heretofore, especially the ordering of his affairs in the time of war, with such conduct, prudence, and wisdom, that, notwithstanding at the beginning of his undertaking that great trust and honourable employment which his late Majesty was pleased to confer upon him, he saw so little appearance of performing his designs with good success, his Majesty's revenues being then much weakened, and the magazines and public purse in the enemy's power, besides several other obstructions and hindrances; yet as he undertook it cheerfully, and out of pure loyalty and obedience to his Majesty; so he ordered it so wisely, that so long as he acted by his own counsels and was personally present at the execution of his designs, he was always prosperous in his success. And although he had so great an army, as afore-mentioned, yet by his wise and prudent conduct, there appeared no visible sign of devastation in any of the countries where he marched; for first, he settled a constant rule for the regular levy of money for the convenient maintenance of the soldiery. Next, he constituted such officers of his army, that most of them were known to be gentlemen of large and fair estates, which drew a good part of their private revenues, to serve and support them in their public employments ; wherein my Lord did lead them the way by his own good example.

To which may be added his wisdom in ordering the government of the Church, for the advancement of the orthodox religion, and suppression of factions ; as also in coining, printing, knighting, and the like, which he used with great discretion and prudence, only for the interest of his Majesty, and the benefit of the kingdom, as formerly has been mentioned.

The prudent manage of his private and domestic affairs appears sufficiently : (1.) In his marriage ; (2.) in the ordering and increasing his estate before the wars, which, notwithstanding his noble housekeeping and hospitality, and his generous bounty and charity, he increased to the value of £100,000 ; (3.) in the ordering his affairs in the time of banishment, where, although he received not the least of his own estate, during all the time of his exile, until his return ; yet maintained himself handsomely and nobly, according to his quality, as much as his condition at that time would permit ; (4.) in reducing his torn and ruined estate after his return, which, beyond all probability, himself hath settled and ordered so, that his posterity will have reason gratefully to remember it.

In short, although my Lord naturally loves not business, especially those of state (though he understands them as well as anybody), yet what business or affairs he cannot avoid, none will do them better than himself. His private affairs he orders without any noise or trouble, not over-hastily, but wisely. Neither is he passionate in acting of business, but hears patiently, and orders soberly, and pierces into the heart or bottom of a business at the first encounter; but before all things, he considers well before he undertakes a business, whether he be able to go through it or no, for he never ventures upon either public or private business, beyond his strength.

And here I cannot forbear to mention, that my noble Lord, when he was in banishment, presumed out of his duty and love to his gracious master, our now sovereign King, Charles the Second, to write and send him a little book, or rather a letter, wherein he delivered his opinion concerning the government of his dominions, whensoever God should be pleased to restore him to his throne, together with some other notes and observations of foreign states and kingdoms; but it being a private offer to his sacred Majesty, I dare not presume to publish it.[1]

---

[1] Unfortunately this paper does not appear to have survived

5. *Of his Blessings.*

Although my Lord hath been one of the most unfortunate persons of his rank and quality, which this later age did produce; yet Heaven hath been so propitious to him, that it bestowed some blessings upon him even in the midst of his misfortunes, and supported him against Fortune's malice, which otherwise, as it seems, had designed his total ruin and destruction. Of these blessings I may name in the first place,

1. The royal favours of his gracious sovereigns, and the good esteem they had of his fidelity and loyalty; which, as it was the chief of his endeavours, so he esteemed it above all the rest. To repeat them particularly would be too tedious, and they are sufficiently apparent out of the precedent history; only this I may add, that King Charles the First, out of a singular favour to my Lord, was pleased, upon his most humble request, to create several noblemen; the names of them, lest I commit an offence, I shall not mention, by reason most men usually pretend such claims upon the ground of their own merit.

2. That God was pleased to bless him with wealth and power, to enable him the better for the service of his King and country.

3. That He made him happy in his marriage; (for his first wife was a very kind, loving, and

virtuous lady) and blessed him with dutiful and
obedient children, free from vices, noble and
generous both in their natures and actions; who
did all that lay in their power to support and
relieve my Lord their father in his banishment, as
before is mentioned.

4. The kindness and civility which my Lord
received from strangers, and the inhabitants of
those places, where he lived during the time of his
banishment; for had it not been for them, he
would have perished in his extreme wants; but it
pleased God so to provide for him, that although
he wanted an estate, yet he wanted not credit; and
although he was banished and forsaken by his own
friends and countrymen, yet he was civilly received
and relieved by strangers, until God blessed him.

Lastly, with a happy return to his native country,
his dear children, and his own estate; which,
although he found much ruined and broke, yet by
his prudence and wisdom, hath ordered as well as
he could; and I hope, and pray God to add this
blessing to all the rest, that he may live long to
increase it for the benefit of his posterity.

6. *Of his Honours and Dignities.*

The honours, titles, and dignities which were
conferred upon my Lord, by King James, King
Charles the First, and King Charles the Second,

partly as an encouragement for future service, and a reward for past, are following :

1. He was made Knight of the Bath, when he was but fifteen or sixteen years of age, at the creation of Henry, Prince of Wales, King James's eldest son.[1]

2. King James created him Viscount Mansfield, and Baron of Bolsover.

3. King Charles the First constituted him Lord Lieutenant of Nottinghamshire, and

4. Lord Warden of the Forest of Sherwood ; as also,

5. Lord Lieutenant of Derbyshire.

6. He chose him Governor to his son Charles, our now gracious King ; and

7. Made him one of his honourable Privy Council.

8. He constituted him Governor of the town and county of Newcastle, and General of all his Majesty's forces raised, and to be raised, in the northern parts of England ; as also of the several counties of Nottingham, Lincoln, Rutland, Derby, Stafford, Leicester, Warwick, Northampton, Huntingdon, Cambridge, Norfolk, Sussex, Essex, and Hertford, together with all the appurtenances

---

[1] These honours have already been mentioned in their proper places. Newcastle was made one of the Privy Council of Charles I., November 29, 1639. Doyle, "Official Peerage."

belonging to so great a power, as is formerly declared.

9. He conferred upon him the honour and title of Earl of Newcastle, and Baron of Bothal and Hepple.

10. He created him Marquess of Newcastle.

11. His Majesty King Charles the Second was pleased, when my Lord was in banishment, to make him Knight of the most noble Order of the Garter;[1] and

12. After his return into England, Chief-Justice in Eyre Trent-North.[2]

13. He created him Duke of Newcastle and Earl of Ogle.

7. *Of the Entertainments he made for King Charles the First.*

Though my Lord hath always been free and noble in his entertainments and feastings, yet he was pleased to show his great affection and duty to his gracious King, Charles the First, and her Majesty the Queen, in some particular entertainments which he made of purpose for them before the late wars.

When his Majesty was going into Scotland to

---

[1] He was appointed Knight of the Garter 12th January 1650, but not solemnly installed in that dignity till April 15, 1661. Collins' " Historical Collections," pp. 38–42.

[2] July 10, 1661. Doyle, " Official Peerage."

be crowned, he took his way through Nottinghamshire; and lying at Worksop Manor, hardly two
miles distant from Welbeck, where my Lord then
was, my Lord invited his Majesty thither to a
dinner, which he was graciously pleased to accept
of.[1] This entertainment cost my Lord between
four and five thousand pounds; which his Majesty
liked so well, that a year after his return out of
Scotland, he was pleased to send my Lord word,
that her Majesty the Queen was resolved to make
a progress into the northern parts, desiring him to
prepare the like entertainment for her, as he had
formerly done for him. Which my Lord did, and
endeavoured for it with all possible care and industry, sparing nothing that might add splendour to
that feast, which both their Majesties were pleased

---

[1] Clarendon thus describes these entertainments (Rebellion i. 167): "Both King and court were received and
entertained by the Earl of Newcastle, and at his own proper
expense, in such a wonderful manner, and in such an excess
of feasting, as had never before been known in England;
and would still be thought very prodigious, if the same noble
person had not, within a year or two afterwards, made the
King and Queen a more stupendous entertainment; which
(God be thanked), though possibly it might too much whet
the appetite of others to excess, no man ever after imitated."

Jonson's two Masques are entitled, "The King's Entertainment at Welbeck in Nottinghamshire," &c., and "Love's
Welcome—The King's and Queen's entertainment at Bolsover,
the 30th of July 1634."

to honour with their presence : Ben Jonson he employed in fitting such scenes and speeches as he could best devise ; and sent for all the gentry of the country to come and wait on their Majesties ; and, in short, did all that ever he could imagine, to render it great, and worthy their royal acceptance.

This entertainment he made at Bolsover Castle in Derbyshire, some five miles distant from Welbeck, and resigned Welbeck for their Majesties' lodging ; it cost him in all between fourteen and fifteen thousand pounds.

Besides these two, there was another small entertainment which my Lord prepared for his late Majesty, in his own park at Welbeck, when his Majesty came down, with his two nephews, the now Prince Elector Palatine, and his brother Prince Rupert, into the Forest of Sherwood ; which cost him fifteen hundred pounds.

And this I mention not out of a vain glory, but to declare the great love and duty my Lord had for his gracious King and Queen, and to correct the mistakes committed by some historians, who, not being rightly informed of those entertainments, make the world believe falsehood for truth.   But, as I said, they were made before the wars, when my Lord had the possession of a great estate ; and wanted nothing to express his love and duty to his sovereign in that manner ; whereas now he should be much to seek to do the like, his estate being so much ruined by the late Civil Wars, that neither himself nor his posterity will be able so soon to recover it.

8. *His Education.*

His education was according. to his birth; for as he was born a gentleman, so he was bred like a gentleman.[1] To school learning he never showed a

---

[1] In " Nature's Pictures, by Fancy's Pencil," the Duchess describes the education of her day (pp. 273, 333, ed. 1656). In " The Tale' of a Traveller," she thus sketches a boy's bringing up: " His education, in the first place, was to learn the horn-book, from that his primer, and so the Bible, by his mother's chambermaid or the like. But after he came to ten years old or thereabouts, he was sent to a free school, where the noise of each scholar's reading aloud did drown the sense of what they read, burying the knowledge and understanding in the confusion of many words, and several languages; yet was whipt for not learning by their tutors, for their ill teaching them, which broke and weakened their memories with the over heavy burthens, striving to thrust in more learning than could be digested or kept in the brain. . . . After some time he was sent to the University, there continuing from the years of fourteen to the years of eighteen; at last considering with himself that he was buried to the world and the delights therein, conversing more with the dead than the living, in reading old authors, and that little company he had, was only at prayers, and meat; wherein the time of the one was taken up in devotion, the other in eating, or rather fasting; for their prayers were so long, and their commons so short, that it seemed rather an

N

great inclination ; for though he was sent to the University, and was a student of St. John's College in Cambridge, and had his tutors to instruct him ; yet they could not persuade him to read or study much, he taking more delight in sports, than in learning ; so that his father being a wise man, and seeing that his son had a good natural wit, and was of a very good disposition, suffered him to follow his own genius ; whereas his other son Charles, in whom he found a greater love and inclination to learning, he encouraged as much that way as possibly he could.

One time it happened that a young gentleman, one of. my Lord's relations, had bought some land, at the same time when my Lord had bought a singing-boy for £50, a horse for £50, and a dog for £2 ; which humour his father Sir Charles liked so well, that he was pleased to say, that if he should find his son to be so covetous, that he would buy land before he was twenty years of age, he would disinherit him.   But above all the

---

humiliation and fasting, than an eating and thanksgiving. But their conversation was a greater penance than their spare diet ; for their disputations, which are fed by contradictions, did more wrack the brain, than the other did gripe the belly, the one filling the head with vain opinions and false imaginations, for want of the light of truth, as the other with wind and rude humours, for want of a sufficient nourishment.   Where upon these considerations he left the University."

rest, my Lord had a great inclination to the art of horsemanship and weapons, in which later his father Sir Charles, being a most ingenious and unparalleled master of that age, was his only tutor,[1] and kept him also several masters in the art of horsemanship, and sent him to the Mews to Mons. Antoine, who · was then accounted the best master

---

[1] Jonson, in his " Underwoods," has an epigram on the Duke's fencing (No. LXXXIX.) :

"They talk of Fencing and the use of arms,
    The art of urging and avoiding harms,
    The noble science, and the mastering skill
    Of making just approaches how to kill ;
    To hit in angles, and to clash with time :
    As all defence or offence were a chime !
    I hate such measured—give me mettled fire,
    That trembles in the blaze, but then mounts higher
    A quick and dazzling motion ; when a pair
    Of bodies meet like rarefied air !
    Their weapons darted with that flame and force
    As they outdid the lightning in the course ;
    This were a spectacle, a sight to draw
    Wonder to valour !   No, it is the law
    Of daring not to do a wrong ; 'tis true
    Valour to slight it, being done to you,
    To know the heads of danger, where 'tis fit
    To bend, to break, provoke, or suffer it ;
    All this, my Lord, is valour, this is yours,
    And was your father's, all your ancestor's !
    Who durst live great 'mongst all the colds and heats
    Of human life ; as all the frosts and sweats
    Of fortune, when or death appeared, or bands ;
    And valiant were, with or without their hands."

in that art.   But my Lord's delight in those heroic exercises was such, that he soon became master thereof himself, which increased much his father's hopes of his future perfections, who being himself a person of a noble and heroic nature, was extremely well pleased to observe his son take delight in such arts and exercises as were proper and fit for a person of quality.

9. *His Natural Wit and Understanding.*

Although my Lord has not so much of scholarship and learning as his brother Sir Charles Cavendish had, yet he hath an excellent natural wit and judgment, and dives into the bottom of everything ; as it is evidently apparent in the forementioned art of horsemanship and weapons, which by his own ingenuity he has reformed and brought to such perfection, as never any one has done heretofore.   And though he is no mathematician by art, yet he hath a very good mathematical brain, to demonstrate truth by natural reason, and is both a good natural and moral philosopher, not by reading philosophical books, but by his own natural understanding and observation, by which he hath found out many truths.

To pass by several other instances, I'll but mention, that when my Lord was at Paris, in his exile, it happened one time, that he discoursing with some of his friends, amongst whom was also that learned philosopher Hobbes,[1] they began, amongst the rest, to argue upon this subject, namely, Whether it were possible to make man by art fly as birds do; and when some of the company had delivered their opinion, viz., That they thought it probable to be done by the help of artificial wings; my Lord declared, that he deemed it altogether impossible, and demonstrated it by this following reason. Man's arms, said he, are not set on his shoulders in the same manner as bird's wings are; for that part of the arm which joins to the shoulder is in man placed inward, as towards the breast, but in birds outward, as toward the back; which difference and contrary position or shape hinders that man cannot have the same flying action with his arms, as birds have with their wings. Which argument Mr. Hobbes liked so well, that he was pleased to make use of it in one of his books called Leviathan, if I remember well.

---

[1] "I have heard Mr. Edmund Waller say that W. Lord Marquis of Newcastle was a great patron to Dr. Gassendi, and M. Des Cartes, as well as to Mr. Hobbes, and that he hath dined with them all three at the Marquis's table, at Paris."—Aubrey's Letters, iii. 602. I have not succeeded in finding these arguments which the Duchess mentions in the following pages, in the "Leviathan." Hobbes, however, acknowledges Newcastle's patronage by several dedications to him, viz., the dedication of his "Liberty and Necessity," and that of his "Elements of Law."

Some other time they falling into a discourse concerning witches, Mr. Hobbes said, that though he could not rationally believe there were witches, yet he could not be fully satisfied to believe there were none, by reason they would themselves confess it, if strictly examined.

To which my Lord answered, that though for his part he cared not whether there were witches or no; yet his opinion was, that the confession of witches, and their suffering for it, proceeded from an erroneous belief, viz., that they had made a contract with the devil to serve him for such rewards as were in his power to give them; and that it was their religion to worship and adore him; in which religion they had such a firm and constant belief, that if anything came to pass according to their desire, they believed the devil had heard their prayers, and granted their requests, for which they gave him thanks; but if things fell out contrary to their prayers and desires, then they were troubled at it, fearing they had offended him, or not served him as they ought, and asked him forgiveness for their offences. Also (said my Lord) they imagine that their dreams are real exterior actions; for example, if they dream they fly in the air, or out of the chimney top, or that they are turned into several shapes, they believe no otherwise, but that it is really so. And this wicked opinion makes them industrious to perform such ceremonies to the devil, that they adore and worship him as their god, and choose to live and die for him.

Thus my Lord declared himself concerning witches, which Mr. Hobbes was also pleased to insert in his fore-mentioned book. But yet my Lord doth not count this opinion of his so universal, as if there were none but imaginary witches; for he doth not speak but of such a sort of witches as make it their religion to worship the devil in the manner aforesaid. Nor doth he think it a crime to entertain what opinion seems most probable to him, in things indifferent; for in such cases men may discourse and argue as they please, to exercise their wit, and may change and alter their opinions upon more probable grounds and reasons; whereas in fundamental matters, both of Church and State, he is so strict an adherent to them, that he will never maintain or defend such opinions which are in the least prejudicial to either.[1]

---

[1] The Duke, like most of his contemporaries, made occasional scientific experiments and held views of his own about natural science. In a preface written by him to the "Philosophical and Physical Opinions" of his wife he says: "Since it is now *à la mode* to write of natural philosophy, and I know nobody knows what is the cause of anything, and since they are all but guessers, not knowing, it gives every man room to think what he lists, and so I mean to

One proof more I'll add to confirm his natural understanding and judgment, which was upon some discourse I held with him one time, concerning that famous chemist Van Helmont, who in his writings is very invective against the schoolmen, and, amongst the rest, accuses them for taking the

---

set up for myself, and play at this philosophical game as follows, without patching or stealing from anybody." He then proceeds to deliver his opinion concerning the grounds of natural philosophy : "Salt is the life that giveth motion to all things in the world," which he proves, amongst other reasons, by the following experiment :—"The sun, no doubt, is a great fire, and must have something to maintain it ; but before I deliver my opinion to you, I desire leave to make you a little relation, and it is this : Dr. Payn, a divine, and my chaplain, who hath a very witty searching brain of his own, being at my house at Bolsover, locked up with me in a chamber to make Lapis Prunellæ, which is saltpetre and brimstone inflamed, looking at it a while, I said, Mark it, Mr. Payn, the flame is pale, like the Sun, and hath a violent motion in it, like the Sun ; saith he, It hath so, and the more to confirm you, says he, look what abundance of little suns, round like a globe, appear to us everywhere, just the same motion as the Sun makes in every one's eyes. So we concluded the Sun could be nothing else but a very solid body of salt and sulphur, inflamed by his own violent motion upon his own axis. . . .

"This," he concludes, "is my opinion, which I think can as hardly be disproved as proved ; since any opinion may be right or wrong, for anything that anybody knows, for certainly there is none can make a mathematical demonstration of natural philosophy."

radical moisture for the fat of animal bodies. Whereupon my Lord answered, that surely the schoolmen were too wise to commit such an error; for, said he, the radical moisture is not the fat or tallow of an animal, but an oily and balsamous substance; for the fat and tallow, as also the watery parts, are cold; whereas the oily and balsamous parts have at all times a lively heat, which makes that those creatures which have much of that oil or balsam are long lived, and appear young; and not only animals, but also vegetables, which have much of that oil or balsam, as ivy, bays, laurel, holly, and the like, live long, and appear fresh and green, not only in winter, but when they are old. Then I asked my Lord's opinion concerning the radical heat: to which he answered, that the radical heat lived in the radical moisture; and when the one decayed, the other decayed also; and then was produced either an unnatural heat, which caused an unnatural dryness, or an unnatural moisture, which caused dropsies, and these, an unnatural coldness.

Lastly, his natural wit appears by his delight in poetry; for I may justly call him the best lyric and dramatic poet of this age.[1] His Comedies

---

[1] The Duke's poems are represented by songs in his own plays and in those of the Duchess, by dedicatory verses to her different books, and by several pieces in her " Nature's

do sufficiently show his great observation and judgment, for they are composed of these three ingredients, viz., wit, humour, and satire; and his chief design in them is to divulge and laugh at the follies of mankind; to persecute vice, and to encourage virtue.[1]

Pictures" (pp. 65, 79, 94, 97). At the end of her volume of Poems the Duchess says :—

> " A Poet I am neither born nor bred,
>   But to a witty poet married,
>   Whose brain is fresh, and pleasant, as the Spring,
>   Where fancies grow, and where the Muses sing ;
> . There oft I lean my head, and listening hark,
>   T' observe his words, and all his fancies mark ;
>   And from that garden flowers of fancies take,
>   Whereof a posy up in verse I make :
>   Thus I that have no garden of my own
>   There gather flowers, that are newly blown."

[1] The Duke was the author of four Comedies :—
"The Country Captain," 12mo, 1649, said to have been acted with applause at Black Friars and printed at the Hague and at London. On October 26, 1661, Pepys notes seeing this play, "the first time it hath been acted this twenty-five years . . . but so silly a play as in all my life I never saw."
"The Variety," printed with "The Country Captain." 12mo, 1649, London and the Hague. A droll called "The French-Dancing Master," was made out of this play, and is printed in "The Wits, or Sport upon Sport," 1671.
"The Humorous Lovers," acted at the Duke's Theatre. 4to, 1677. Pepys, who attributes it to the Duchess, saw it on

10. *Of his Natural Humour and Disposition.*

My Lord may justly be compared to Titus the deliciæ of mankind, by reason of his sweet, gentle, and obliging nature ; for though his wisdom and experience found it impossible to please all men, because of their different humours and dispositions ; yet his nature is such, that he will be sorry when he seeth that men are displeased with him out of their own ill natures, without any cause ; for he loves all that are his friends, and hates none that are his enemies.[1] He is a loyal subject, a kind

March 30, 1667, and calls it "the most silly thing that ever came upon a stage."

"The Triumphant Widow, or the Medley of Humours," acted at the Duke's Theatre. 4to, 1677. Shadwell thought sufficiently well of this play to incorporate the greater part of it in "Bury Fair."

The Duke also wrote five scenes of "The Lady Contemplation," a play by the Duchess.

He also translated Molière's "L'Etourdi," which Dryden converted into "Sir Martin Mar-All." Though printed in 1668, this play did not appear with Dryden's name till 1697, and was entered in the Stationers' Register under the Duke's name. Pepys saw it on August 16, 1667, and calls it "a play made by my Lord Duke of Newcastle, but, as everybody says, corrected by Dryden. It is the most entire piece of mirth, a complete farce from one end to the other, that was ever writ. I never laughed so in all my life, and at very good wit therein, not fooling."

[1] The Duke's generosity to his political opponents was shown in his treatment of those accused of sharing in the

husband, a loving father, a generous master, and a constant friend.

His natural love to his parents has been so great, that I have heard him say, he would most willingly, and without the least repining, have begged for his daily relief, so God would but have let his parents live.

He is true and just both in his words and actions, and has no mean or petty designs, but they are all just and honest.

He condemns not upon report, but upon proof; nor judges by words, but actions; he forgets not past service, for present advantage; but gives a present reward to a present desert.

He hath a great power over his passions, and hath had the greatest trials thereof; for certainly he must of necessity have a great share of patience, that can forgive so many false, treacherous, malicious, and ungrateful persons as he hath done; but he is so wise, that his passion never outruns his patience, nor his extravagances his prudence; and although his private enemies have been numerous,

---

Yorkshire plot of 1663. He treated Colonel Hutchinson " very honourably," and "dismissed him without a guard to his own house, only engaging him to stay there one week, till he gave account to the Council." Memoirs, ii. 290. Mr. John Cromwell, another sufferer on the same occasion, found a powerful protector in the Duke, who finally secured his release. Kennet's Register, p. 890.

yet I verily believe, there is never a subject more generally beloved than he is.

He hates pride and loves humility; is civil to strangers, kind to his acquaintance, and respectful to all persons, according to their quality; he never regards place, except it be for ceremony: to the meanest person he'll put off his hat, and suffer everybody to speak to him.

He never refuses any petition, but accepts them; and being informed of the business, will give a just, and as much as lies in him, a favourable answer to the petitioning party.

He easily pardons, and bountifully rewards; and always praises particular men's virtues, but covers their faults with silence.

He is full of charity and compassion to persons that are in misery, and full of clemency and mercy; insomuch, that when he was general of a great army, he would never sit in council himself upon causes of life and death, but granted pardon to many delinquents that were condemned by his council of war; so that some were forced to petition him not to do it, by reason it was an ill precedent for others. To which my Lord merrily answered, that if they did hang all, they would leave him none to fight.

His courage he always showed in action, more than in words, for he would fight, but not rant.

He is not vain-glorious to heighten or brag of

his heroic actions; witness that great victory upon Atherton Moor, after which he would not suffer his trumpets to sound, but came quietly and silently into the city of York; for which he would certainly have been blamed by those that make a great noise upon small causes, and love to be applauded, though their actions little deserve it.

His noble bounty and generosity is so manifest to all the world, that I should light a candle to the sun, if I should strive to illustrate it; for he has no self-designs or self-interest, but will rather wrong and injure himself than others. To give you but one proof of this noble virtue, it is known, that where he hath a legal right to felons' goods, as he hath in a great part of his estate, yet he never took or exacted more than some inconsiderable share for acknowledgment of his right; saying, that he was resolved never to grow rich by other men's misfortunes.

In short, I know him not addicted to any manner of vice, except that he has been a great lover and admirer of the female sex; which, whether it be so great a crime as to condemn him for it, I'll leave to the judgment of young gallants and beautiful ladies.

11. *Of his outward Shape and Behaviour.*

His shape is neat, and exactly proportioned; his stature of a middle size, and his complexion sanguine.

His behaviour is such, that it might be a pattern for all gentlemen; for it is courtly, civil, easy and free, without formality or constraint; and yet hath something in it of grandeur, that causes an awful respect towards him.

12. *Of his Discourse.*

His discourse is as free and unconcerned as his behaviour, pleasant, witty, and instructive; he is quick in repartees or sudden answers, and hates dubious disputes, and premeditated speeches. He loves also to intermingle his discourse with some short pleasant stories, and witty sayings, and always names the author from whom he hath them; for he hates to make another man's wit his own.[1]

13. *Of his Habit.*

He accoutres his person according to the fashion, if it be one that is not troublesome and uneasy

---

[1] Shadwell, in his dedication of "The Libertine" to Lord Newcastle, says: "By the great honour I had to be daily admitted unto your Grace's public and private conversation, I observed that admirable experience and judgment surmounting all the old, and that vigorousness of wit, and smartness of expression, exceeding all the young, I ever saw; and not only in sharp and apt replies, but, which is much more difficult, by giving easy and unforced occasions, the most admirable way of beginning one, and all this adapted to men of all circumstances and conditions."

for men of heroic exercises and actions. He is neat and cleanly; which makes him to be some-what long in dressing, though not so long as many effeminate persons are. He shifts ordinarily once a day, and every time when he uses exercise, or his temper is more hot than ordinary.

14. *Of his Diet.*

In his diet he is so sparing and temperate, that he never eats nor drinks beyond his set proportion, so as to satisfy only his natural appetite. He makes but one meal a day, at which he drinks two good glasses of small-beer, one about the beginning, the other at the end thereof, and a little glass of sack in the middle of his dinner; which glass of sack he also uses in the morning for his breakfast, with a morsel of bread. His supper consists of an egg, and a draught of small-beer. And by this temperance he finds himself very healthful, and may yet live many years, he being now of the age of seventy-three, which I pray God from my soul to grant him.

15. *His Recreation and Exercise.*

His prime pastime and recreation hath always been the exercise of manage and weapons; which heroic arts he used to practise every day; but I observing that when he had overheated himself,

RAINING WITH THE LEFT HAND

he would be apt to take cold, prevailed so far, that at last he left the frequent use of the manage, using nevertheless still the exercise of weapons ; and though he doth not ride himself so frequently as he hath done, yet he takes delight in seeing his horses of manage rid by his escuyers,[1] whom he instructs in that art for his own pleasure.[2]   But in the art of weapons (in which he has a method beyond all that ever were famous in it, found out by his own ingenuity and practice) he never taught

---

[1] " Escuyer," groom ; *écuyer,* Fr., the English esquire.

[2] Jonson dedicates the following epigram to Newcastle (Underwoods, LXXII.) :—

> " When first, my Lord, I saw you back your horse,
> Provoke his mettle, and command his force
> To all the uses of the field and race,
> Methought I read the ancient art of Thrace,
> And saw a Centaur past those tales of Greece,
> So seemed your horse and you both of a piece !
> You showed like Perseus upon Pegasus,
> Or Castor mounted on his Cyllarus ;
> Or what we hear our home-born legends tell,
> Of bold Sir Bevis and his Arundel ;
> Nay, so your seat his beauties did endorse,
> As I began to wish myself a horse ;
> And surely, had I but your stable seen
> Before, I think my wish absolved had been,
> For never saw I yet the Muses dwell,
> Nor any of their household, half so well.
> So well ! as when I saw the floor and room,
> I looked for Hercules to be the groom ;
> And cried, Away with the Cæsarian bread !
> At these immortal mangers Virgil fed." .

anybody but the now Duke of Buckingham, whose guardian he hath been, and his own two sons.

The rest of his time he spends in music, poetry, architecture, and the like.

16. *Of his Pedigree.*

Having made promise in the beginning of the first Book that I would join a more large description of the pedigree of my noble Lord and husband to the end of the history of his life, I shall now discharge myself; and though I could derive it from a longer time, and reckon up a great many of his ancestors, even from the time of William the Conqueror, he being descended from the most ancient family of the Gernouns, as Camden relates in his Britannia, in the description of Derbyshire ; [1] yet it being a work fitter for heralds, I shall proceed no further than his grandfather, and show you only . those noble families which my Lord is allied to by his birth.

My Lord's grandfather, by his father (as is formerly mentioned), was Sir William Cavendish, Privy-Counsellor and Treasurer of the Chamber to King Henry the Eighth, Edward the Sixth, and Queen Mary ; who married two wives. [2] By the

---

[1] Camden's Britannia, p. 491, ed. 1695. See also Collins' Peerage, ed. Brydges, i. 303.

[2] Sir William Cavendish married (1.) Margaret, daughter of Edmund Bostock, of Cheshire, who died in 1540 ; (2.)

first he had only two daughters ; but by the second, Elizabeth, who was my Lord's grandmother, he had three sons and four daughters, whereof one daughter died young. She was daughter to John Hardwick of Hardwick, in the county of Derby, Esq. ; and had four husbands : the first was —— Barlow, Esq., who died before they were bedded together, they being both very young ; the second was Sir William Cavendish, my Lord's grandfather, who being somewhat in years, married her chiefly for her beauty. She had so much power in his affection, that she persuaded him to sell his estate which he had in the southern parts of England (for he was very rich) and buy an estate in the northern parts, viz., in Derbyshire, and thereabout, where her own friends and kindred lived, which he did ; and having there settled himself, upon her further persuasion built a manor-house in the same county, called Chatsworth, which, as I have heard, cost first and last above £80,000 sterling. But before this house was finished, he died, and left six

---

Elizabeth, daughter of Thomas Parker, of Poslingford. Suffolk; (3.) Elizabeth Hardwick, August 20, 1547. See Sir William Cavendish's biographical notes in Collins'"Historical Collections," p. 10. Elizabeth Hardwick married Robert Barley, of Barley in Derbyshire; she was then fourteen, and her first husband died in 1532. She herself died on the 13th of February 1607, about the age of eighty-seven. Her will and epitaph are both printed by Collins.

children, viz., three sons and three daughters, which before they came to be marriageable, she married a third husband, Sir William St. Loo, Captain of the Guard to Queen Elizabeth, and Grand Butler of England ; who dying without issue, she married a fourth husband, George, Earl of Shrewsbury, by whom she left no issue.

The children which she had by her second husband, Sir William Cavendish, being grown marriageable ; the eldest son, Henry, married Grace, the youngest daughter of his father-in-law, the said George, Earl of Shrewsbury, which he had by his former wife Gertrude, daughter of Thomas Manners, Earl of Rutland, but died without issue.

The second son William, after Earl of Devonshire, had two wives. The first was an heiress, by whom he had children, but all died save one son, whose name was also William, Earl of Devonshire. His second wife was widow to Sir Edward Wortley, who had several children by her first husband, and but one son by the said William Cavendish, after Earl of Devonshire, who died young.

His son by his first wife (William, Earl of Devonshire) married Christian, daughter of Edward, Lord Bruce, a Scotsman, by whom he had two sons and one daughter. The eldest son William, now Earl of Devonshire, married Elizabeth, the second daughter of William, Earl of Salisbury, by whom he has three children, viz., two sons and one daughter, whereof the eldest son William is married to the second daughter of James, now Duke of Ormond.[1] The second son Charles is yet a youth. The daughter Anne married the Lord Rich, the only son and child to Charles now Earl of Warwick ; but he died without issue.

The second son of William, Earl of Devonshire, and brother to the now Earl of Devonshire, was unfortunately slain in the late Civil Wars, as is before mentioned.

The daughter of the said William, Earl of Devonshire, sister to the now Earl of Devonshire, married Robert, Lord Rich, eldest son to Robert, Earl of

---

[1] Henry Cavendish died October 12, 1616 (Collins, p. 13). William Cavendish, first Earl of Devonshire, died on March 3, 1625 ; he married (1.) Anne, daughter of Henry Kighley, of Kighley, Yorkshire ; (2.) Elizabeth, daughter of Edward Boughton, of Causton, Warwickshire, and widow of Sir Richard (?) Wortley (Collins' Peerage, ed. Brydges, i. 323). William Cavendish, second Earl, died on June 20, 1628. Pomfret's " Life of Christian, Countess of Devonshire," which is largely quoted by Collins and Kennet, well deserves perusal. Some account of the circumstances of her marriage is given in Lodge's " Illustrations of English History," vol. iii. p. 232. "The wench is a pretty red-headed wench, and her portion is £7000," write the Earl and Countess of Arundel to the Earl of Shrewsbury.

William, third Earl of Devonshire, died in 1684 ; his son of the same name, who married the Duke of Ormond's daughter, was the first Duke of Devonshire. Collins, ed. Brydges, vol. i.

Warwick, by whom she had but one son, who married, but died without issue.

The third and youngest son of Sir William Cavendish, Charles Cavendish (my Lord's father), had two wives. The first was daughter and co-heir to Sir Thomas Kidson, who died a year after her marriage without issue. The second was the younger daughter of Cuthbert, Lord Ogle, and after her elder and only sister Jane, wife to Edward, Earl of Shrewsbury, who died without issue, became heir to her father's estate and title; by whom he had three sons, whereof the eldest died in his infancy; the second was William, my dear Lord and husband; the third Charles, who died a bachelor about the age of sixty-three.

My Lord hath had two wives; the first was Elizabeth, daughter and heir to William Basset of Blore, in the county of Stafford, Esq.; and widow to Henry Howard, younger son to Thomas, Earl of Suffolk; by whom he had ten children, viz., six sons and four daughters; whereof five, viz., four sons and one daughter, died young; the rest, viz., two sons and three daughters, came to be married.[1]

His elder son Charles, Viscount of Mansfield, married the eldest daughter and heir of Mr.

---

[1] The statement originally printed in the text was "five sons and five daughters, whereof five, viz., three sons and two daughters, died young." It was corrected by hand before publication.

Richard Rogers, by whom he had but one daughter, who died soon after her birth ; and he died also without any other issue.[1]

His second son Henry, now Earl of Ogle, married Francis the eldest daughter of Mr. William Pierrepont, by whom he hath had three sons and four daughters. Two sons were born before their natural time; the third, Henry, Lord Mansfield, is alive : the four daughters are, the Lady Elizabeth, Lady Frances, Lady Margaret, and Lady Catherine.[2]

My Lord's three daughters were thus married. The eldest, Lady Jane, married Charles Cheiney, Esq., descended of a very noble and ancient family; by whom she hath one son and two

---

[1] Charles, Viscount Mansfield, died in 1659. On June 15, 1659, Nicholas writes to Newcastle condoling with him on his recent loss (Calendar of Domestic State Papers, 1659, p. 374). His widow married Charles Stuart, Duke of Richmond.

[2] This Henry, Earl of Ogle, succeeded to the title of Duke of Newcastle on his father's death in 1676, and died on July 26, 1691. The second Report of the Royal Commission on Historical MSS. gives abstracts of some of his letters now in the possession of Earl Spencer (p. 17). His son Henry, Lord Mansfield, died in 1680. The Duke by his will settled all his real estate on his third daughter Margaret and her heirs, who married John Holles, Earl of Clare, created Duke of Newcastle in 1694. Collins' Historical Collections, pp. 47–179.

daughters. The second, Lady Elizabeth, married John, now Earl of Bridgwater, then Lord Brackley, and eldest son to John, then Earl of Bridgwater; who died in childbed, and left five sons and one daughter, whereof the eldest son John, Lord Brackley, married the Lady Elizabeth, only daughter and child to James, then Earl of Middlesex.

My Lord's third daughter, the Lady Frances, married Oliver, Earl of Bullingbrook, and hath had no child yet.[1]

After the death of my Lord's first wife, who died the 17th of April in the year 1643, he married me, Margaret, daughter to Thomas Lucas of St. John's, near Colchester, in Essex, Esq.; but hath no issue by me.

And this is the posterity of the three sons of Sir William Cavendish, my Lord's grandfather by his father's side. The three daughters were disposed of as followeth:

---

[1] These ladies were left in England when their father retired to the Continent after the battle of Marston Moor; they were in Welbeck when it surrendered to the Earl of Manchester. (Manchester's Quarrel with Cromwell, Camden Society, p. 6.) Lady Jane and Lady Frances wrote to Lord Fairfax on April 17, 1645, thanking him for his favour and protection (Fairfax Correspondence, iii. 194). There is in Davenant's works (p. 291) a short poem on the marriage of Lady Jane. Lady Elizabeth's marriage, which has been before referred to (p. 141), took place in 1639. Lord Brackley performed the elder brother in Milton's "Comus."

The eldest, Frances Cavendish, married Sir Henry Pierrepont of Holm Pierrepont, in the county of Nottingham, by whom she had two sons, whereof the first died young ; the second, Robert, after Earl of Kingston-upon-Hull, married Gertrude, the eldest daughter and co-heir to Henry Talbot, fourth son to George, Earl of Shrewsbury, by whom he had five sons and three daughters, whereof the eldest son, Henry, now Marquess of Dorchester, hath had two wives ; the first Cecilia, eldest daughter to the Lord Viscount Bayning, by whom he had several children, of which there are living only two daughters ; the eldest Anne, who married John Ross, only son to John now Earl of Rutland ; the second, Grace, who is unmarried. His second wife was Catharine, second daughter to James, Earl of Derby, by whom he has no issue living.[1]

The second son of the Earl of Kingston, William, married the sole daughter and heir of Sir Thomas Harries, by whom he had issue five sons and five

---

[1] Robert, Earl of Kingston, died on July 30, 1643, in the manner described on page 53 of this Life. Henry, Marquis of Dorchester, is frequently mentioned in the " Memoirs of Mrs. Hutchinson," see vol. i. 164 ; vol. ii. 168. Lady Roos was divorced by Act of Parliament in 1668. *Vide* Collins' Peerage, ed. Brydges, i. 480, and Clarendon's Life, Continuation, 999–1008.

daughters, whereof two sons and two daughters died unmarried. The other six are :[1]

Robert, the eldest, who married Elizabeth, daughter and co-heir to Sir John Evelyn, by whom he has three sons, and one daughter. The second son George, and the third Gervase, are yet unmarried.

The eldest daughter of William Pierrepont, Frances, is married to my Lord's now only son and heir, Henry, Earl of Ogle, as before is mentioned.

The second, Grace, is married to Gilbert, now Earl of Clare, by whom he hath issue two sons and three daughters.[2]

The third, Gertrude, is unmarried.

---

[1] William Pierrepont, whose character is sketched in the " Memoirs of Colonel Hutchinson," i. 167. The three sons of Robert Pierrepont, mentioned above, grandsons of William Pierrepont, became in succession Earls of Kingston, and the third, Evelyn, was the first Duke of that name and the father of Lady Mary Wortley Montagu. Gervase, third son of William Pierrepont, became in 1703 Lord Pierrepont, but died without issue.

[2] Gilbert, second Earl of Clare, 1633–1689. His son, John Holles, married Margaret, daughter of Henry Cavendish, second Duke of Newcastle ; inherited the estates of his father-in-law, and in 1694 obtained the title of Duke of Newcastle. Grace, fourth and youngest daughter of this Gilbert, Earl of Clare, was the mother of Henry Pelham the statesman, and Thomas Pelham, heir of his uncle, John Holles, created Duke of Newcastle in 1715.

The third son of the Earl of Kingston, Francis
Pierrepont, married Elizabeth the eldest daughter
of Mr. Bray, by whom he had issue one son and
one daughter.[1] The son, Robert, married Anne,
the daughter of Henry Murray. The daughter,
Frances, married William Paget, eldest son to
William, Lord Paget.

The fourth son of the Earl of Kingston, Gervase,
is unmarried.

The fifth son, George Pierrepont, married the
daughter of Mr. Jonas, by whom he had two sons
unmarried, Henry and Samuel.

The three daughters of the said Earl of Kingston
are, Frances the eldest, who was married to Philip
Rolleston ; the second, Mary, died young ; the
third, Elizabeth, is unmarried.

The second daughter of Sir William Cavendish,
Elizabeth, married the Earl of Lennox, uncle to
King James ; by whom she had only one daughter,
the Lady Arabella, who against King James' commands (she being, after him and his children, the
next heir to the Crown) married William, the
second son to the Earl of Hertford ; for which she

---

[1] For some account of Francis Pierrepont see the "Memoirs
of Colonel Hutchinson" in this series, i. 194 ; ii. 177. His widow
Alisamon married Sir John Read in 1662, and was badly
treated by him. See her petition in the Eighth Report of
the Historical Manuscripts Commission, p. 136.

was put into the Tower, where not long after she died.[1]

The youngest daughter, Mary Cavendish, married Gilbert Talbot, second son to George, Earl of Shrewsbury; who after the decease of his father, and his elder brother Francis, who died without issue, became Earl of Shrewsbury; by whom she had issue four sons and three daughters; the sons all died in their infancy, but the daughters were married.[2]

The eldest, Mary Talbot, married William Herbert, Earl of Pembroke, by whom (some eighteen years after her marriage) she had one son, who died young.[3]

The second daughter, Elizabeth, married Sir Henry Gray, after Earl of Kent (the fourth Earl of England) by whom she had no issue.[4]

---

[1] Margaret, sister of Henry VIII., married Matthew, Earl of Lennox, and became the mother of Henry Stuart, Lord, and Charles Stuart, Earl of Lennox. The latter married Elizabeth Cavendish in 1574, against the commands of Queen Elizabeth. Arabella Stuart, born in 1575, married William Seymour in 1610, and died in 1615. Cooper's "Life of Arabella Stuart."

[2] Gilbert, seventh Earl of Shrewsbury, died in 1616.

[3] This marriage took place in 1606. Clarendon in his character of the Earl (Rebellion, i. 120) says, "He paid much too dear for his wife's fortune by taking her person into the bargain."

[4] The Earl of Kent died in 1639, the Countess on December 7, 1651. After the Earl's death, John Selden, according

The third and youngest daughter, Aletheia, married Thomas Howard, Earl of Arundel, the first earl, and Earl Marshal of England; by whom she left two sons, James, who died beyond the seas without issue; and Henry, who married Elizabeth, daughter of Esme Stuart, Duke of Lennox; by whom he had issue several sons and one daughter; whereof the eldest son Thomas (since the restoration of King Charles the Second) was restored to the dignity of his ancestors, viz., Duke of Norfolk, next to the royal family, the first Duke of England.[1]

---

to Aubrey, married the Countess, but "never owned the marriage till after her death upon some law account." Aubrey terms her an "ingeniose lady," and there is in Mercurius Politicus for May 10–17, 1655, a curious advertisement to prove it: "That excellent Cordial, called the Countess of Kent's powder, approved by long experience of the nobility, gentry, and best physicians of this nation, in any malign disease, Plague, Small Pox, Burning Fevers, Wind, Colic, Women in Labour, Children newly born, &c. It is now made by one Mistress Williamson, living in Whitefriars, near the late Countess's house, who was a servant to her, and for many years compounded it by her Lady's direction. The whole stock of powder, and of the ingredients left by the Countess, was, after her death, given to the said Mistress Williamson by Mr. Selden, her Ladyship's executor. This notice is published because of the many counterfeit powders uttered up and down by apothecaries and others, under the same name, to the intent that it may be known where the right powder is to be had."

[1] Thomas, Earl of Arundel, was born in 1592, and died in 1646. He collected the Arundel Marbles, and was com-

And this is briefly the pedigree of my dear Lord and husband, from his grandfather by his father's side. Concerning his kindred and alliances by his mother, who was Katherine, daughter to Cuthbert, Lord Ogle, they are so many, that it is impossible for me to enumerate them all, my Lord being by his mother related to the chief of the most ancient families of Northumberland, and other the northern parts ; only this I may mention, that my Lord is a peer of the realm, from the first year of King Edward the Fourth his reign.[1]

---

mander of the King's army in the campaign of 1639 against the Scots. His character is described by Clarendon (Rebellion, i. 118) and by Sir Edward Walker (Historical Collections, p. 209). His son Henry married Elizabeth Stuart in 1626, became Earl of Arundel on his father's death, and died in 1652. Thomas was restored to the title of Duke of Norfolk in 1664.

[1] Some account of the Ogle family is given by Collins in his " Historical Collections of the Noble Families of Cavendish, Holles, Vere, Harley, and Ogle."

THE LIFE

OF

THE MOST ILLUSTRIOUS PRINCE,

WILLIAM, DUKE OF NEWCASTLE.

—•—

THE FOURTH BOOK:

CONTAINING SEVERAL ESSAYS AND DISCOURSES GATHERED
FROM THE MOUTH OF MY NOBLE LORD AND HUSBAND.

With some few notes of mine own.

———

I have heard my Lord say,

I.

THAT those which command the wealth of a kingdom, command the hearts and hands of the people.

II.

That he is a great monarch, who hath a sovereign
command over Church, laws, and arms; and he a
wise monarch, that employs his subjects for their

own profit (for their profit is his), encourages
tradesmen, and assists and defends merchants.

III.

That it is a part of prudence in a commonwealth or kingdom to encourage drainers; for
drowned lands are only fit to maintain and increase
some wild ducks, whereas being drained, they are
able to afford nourishment and food to cattle,
besides the producing of several sorts of fruit and
corn.

IV.

That, without a well-ordered force, a prince doth
but reign upon the courtesy of others.

V.

That great princes should not suffer their chief
cities to be stronger than themselves.

VI.

That great princes are half-armed, when their
subjects are unarmed, unless it be in time of foreign
wars.

VII.

That the prince is richest, who is master of the
purse; and he strongest that is master of the
arms; and he wisest that can tell how to save the
one, and use the other.

VIII.

That great princes should be the only paymasters of their soldiers, and pay them out of their own treasuries; for all men follow the purse; and so they'll have both the civil and martial power in their hands.

IX.

That great monarchs should rather study men, than books; for all affairs or business are amongst men.

X.

That a prince should advance foreign trade or traffic to the utmost of his power, because no state or kingdom can be rich without it; and where subjects are poor, the sovereign can have but little.

XI.

That trade and traffic brings honey to the hive; that is to say, riches to the commonwealth; whereas other professions are so far from that, that they rather rob the commonwealth, instead of enriching it.

XII.

That it is not so much unseasonable weather that makes the country complain of scarcity, but want of commerce; for whensoever commodities are cheap, it is a sign that commerce is decayed;

P

because the cheapness of them shows a scarcity of money. For example, put the case five men came to market to buy a horse, and each of them had no more but ten pounds, the seller can receive no more than what the buyer has, but must content himself with those ten pounds, if he be necessitated to sell his horse: but if each one of the buyers had an hundred pounds to lay out for a horse, the seller might receive as much. Thus commodities are cheap or dear, according to the plenty or scarcity of money; and though we had mines of gold and silver at home, and no traffic into foreign parts, yet we should want necessaries from other nations, which proves that no nation can live or subsist well, without foreign trade and commerce; for God and nature have ordered it so, that no particular nation is provided with all things.

XIII.

That merchants by carrying out more commodities than they bring in, that is to say, by selling more than they buy, do enrich a state or kingdom with money, that hath none in its own bowels; but what kingdom or state soever hath mines of gold and silver, there merchants buy more than they sell, to furnish and accommodate it with necessary provisions.

XIV.

That debasing, and setting a higher value upon money, is but a present shift of poor and needy princes; and doth more hurt for the future, than good for the present.

XV.

That foreign commerce causes frequent voyages, and frequent voyages make skilful and experienced seamen, and skilful seamen are a brazen wall to an island.

XVI.

That he is the powerfullest monarch that hath the best shipping; and that a prince should hinder his neighbours as much as he can, from being strong at sea.

XVII.

That wise statesmen ought to understand the laws, customs, and trade of the commonwealth, and have good intelligence both of foreign transactions and designs, and of domestic factions; also they ought to have a treasury, and well-furnished magazine.

XVIII.

That it is a great matter in a state or kingdom, to take care of the education of youth, to breed them so, that they may know first how to obey, and then how to command and order affairs wisely.

XIX.

That it is great wisdom in a state, to breed and train up good statesmen : as, first, to let them be some time at the Universities : next, to put them to the Inns of Court, that they may have some knowledge of the laws of the land ; then to send them to travel with some ambassador, in the quality of secretary ; and let them be agents or residents in foreign countries.   Fourthly, to make them Clerks of the Signet, or Council : and lastly, to make them Secretaries of State, or give them some other employment in state affairs.

XX.

That there should be more praying, and less preaching ; for much preaching breeds faction, but much praying causes devotion.[1]

---

[1] A similar opinion about preaching inspired the Royal Declaration against controversial preaching issued in 1628, and the King's instructions in 1629, imposing restrictions on all lecturers and preachers, and substituting catechising of children for afternoon sermons.   See Heylin's remarks on the feeling of the Puritans with respect to these measures (Cyprianus Anglicus, 202).

XXI.

That young people should be frequently cate-chised, and that wise men, rather than learned, should be chosen heads of schools and colleges.

XXII.

That the more divisions there are in Church and State, the more trouble and confusion is apt to ensue : wherefore too many controversies and dis-putes in the one, and too many law cases and pleadings in the other, ought to be avoided and suppressed.

XXIII.

That disputes and factions amongst statesmen are forerunners of future disorders, if not total ruins.

XXIV.

That all books of controversies should be writ in Latin, that none but the learned may read them, and that there should be no disputations but in schools, lest it breed factions amongst the vulgar, for disputations and controversies are a kind of civil war, maintained by the pen, and often draw out the sword soon after. Also that all prayer-books should be writ in the native language ; that excommunications should not be too frequent for every little and petty trespass ; that every clergyman should be kind and loving to his parishioners, not proud and quarrelsome.

XXV.

That ceremony is nothing in itself, and yet doth everything ; for without ceremony there would be no distinction, neither in Church nor State.

XXVI.

That orders and professions ought not to entrench upon each other, lest in time they make a confusion amongst themselves.[1]

XXVII.

That in a well-ordered state or government, care should be taken lest any degree or profession whatsoever swell too big, or grow too numerous, it being not only a hindrance to those of the same profession, but a burden to the commonwealth, which cannot be well if it exceeds in extremes.

XXVIII.

That the taxes should not be above the riches of the commonwealth, for that must upon necessity breed factions and civil wars, by reason a general poverty united, is far more dangerous than a

---

[1] Compare Clarendon's remarks (Book iv. sect. 38) on the encroachments of the common lawyers on the Church.

private purse ; for though their wealth be small, yet their unity and combination makes them strong, so that, being armed with necessity, they become outrageous with despair.

XXIX.

That heavy taxes upon farms ruin the nobility and gentry ; for if the tenant be poor, the landlord cannot be rich, he having nothing but his rents to live on.

XXX.

That it is not so much laws and religion, nor rhetoric, that keeps a state or kingdom in order, but arms ; which if they be not employed to an evil use, keep up the right and privileges both of Crown, Church, and State.

XXXI.

That no equivocation should be used either in Church or Law ; for the one causes several opinions, to the disturbance of men's consciences ; the other long and tedious suits, to the disturbance of men's private affairs : and both do oftentimes ruin and impoverish the state.

XXXII.

That in cases of robberies and murders, it is better to be severe than merciful ; for the hanging of a few will save the lives and purses of many.

XXXIII.

That many laws do rather entrap than help the subject.

XXXIV.

That no martial law should be executed, but in an army.

XXXV.

That the sheriffs in this kingdom of England have been so expensive in liveries and entertainments in the time of their sheriffalty, as it hath ruined many families that had but indifferent estates.[1]

---

[1] In 1647 Sir Anthony Ashley Cooper was Sheriff of Wiltshire. He says, in his Diary, that when the judges came to Salisbury during his term of office, " I had sixty men in livery and kept an ordinary for all gentlemen, four shillings, and two shillings for blue men. I paid for all." Sir Hugh Cholmley also, in his Memoirs, states, that being Sheriff of Yorkshire in 1625 cost Sir Richard Cholmley £1000. Cromwell endeavoured to put a stop to this expenditure. It was ordered by the Council of State on February 13, 1656, "that, as for many years complaints have been made of the excessive charges burdening the office of sheriff, through the example of some, which discourage those employed, the Major-Generals appoint in their respective counties a troop of horse to attend the sheriff at the assizes, to wait on the judge, and perform the services that have been required of the sheriff's men, and to demean themselves with all respect and diligence. That no gratuity be given by any sheriff to the judge's clerks or officers, nor any table or entertainment kept for them or for the justices of the peace at the assizes, at the

XXXVL

That the cutting down of timber in the time of rebellion has been an inestimable loss to this kingdom, by reason of shipping ; for though timber might be had out of foreign countries that would serve for the building of ships, yet there is none of such a temper as, our English oak ; it being not only strong and large, but not apt to splint, which renders the ships of other nations much inferior to ours : and that therefore it would be very beneficial for the kingdom, to set out some lands for the bearing of such oaks, by sowing of acorns, and then transplanting them : which would be like a storehouse for shipping, and bring an incomparable benefit to the kingdom, since in shipping consists our greatest strength, they being the only walls that defend an island.[1]

---

sheriff's charge."—Calendar of Domestic State Papers, 1655–6, p. 175. Heath says that it was pretended indeed that this substitution of troopers for men in livery was to lessen the charge of the place, "but in truth, the Protector, knowing he could not be served faithfully by the gentry, would name such, no matter whom, as he could confide in, and the expense of retinue and treating the judges being taken off, a yeoman or tradesman of the well-affected might serve the turn and make profit of his place, as in all other offices of the Commonwealth."—Heath, Chronicle, p. 730, ed. 1663.

[1] " This," says Mr. Lower, "is the first allusion I have met with to the ' Wooden Walls of Old England.'"

XXXVII.

That the nobility and gentry in this kingdom have done themselves a great injury, by giving away (out of a petty pride) to the commonalty, the power of being juries and justices of peace : for certainly they cannot but understand that that must of necessity be an act of great consequence and power, which concerns men's lives, lands, and estates.

XXXVIII.

That it is no act of prudence to make poor and mean persons governors or commanders, either by land or sea ; by reason their poverty causes them to take bribes, and so betray their trust : at best, they are apt to extort, which is a great grievance to the people. Besides, it breeds envy in the nobility and gentry, who by that means rise into factions, and cause disturbances in a state or commonwealth ; wherefore the best way is to choose rich and honourable persons (or at least, gentlemen) for such employments, who esteem fame and honourable actions above their lives ; and if they want skill, they must get such under-officers as have more than themselves, to instruct them.

XXXIX.

That great princes should consider, before they make war against foreign nations, whether they be able to maintain it : for if they be not able, then it is better to submit to an honourable peace, than to make war to their great disadvantage : but if they be able to maintain war, then they'll force (in time) their enemies to submit and yield to what terms and conditions they please.

XL.

That, when a state or government is ensnarled [1] and troubled, it is more easy to raise the common people to a factious mutiny, than to draw them to a loyal duty.

XLI.

That in a kingdom where subjects are apt to rebel, no offices or commands should be sold ; for those that buy, will not only use extortion, and practise unjust ways to make out their purchase, but be ablest to rebel, by reason they are more for private gain than the public good ; for it is probable their principles are like their purchases.

But, that all magistrates, officers, commanders, heads and rulers, in what profession soever, both in Church and State, should be chosen according to their abilities, wisdom, courage, piety, justice, honesty, and loyalty ; and then they'll mind the public good more than their particular interest.

---

[1] " Ensnarle," *i.e.*, ensnare or entangle.—Halliwell.

XLII.

That those which have politic designs are for the most part dishonest, by reason their designs tend more to interest than justice.

XLIII.

That great princes should only have great, noble, and rich persons to attend them, whose purses and power may always be ready to assist them.

XLIV.

That a poor nobility is apt to be factious; and a numerous nobility is a burden to a commonwealth.[1]

XLV.

That in a monarchical government, to be for the king is to be for the commonwealth; for when head and body are divided, the life of happiness dies, and the soul of peace is departed.

XLVI.

That, as it is a great error in a state to have all affairs put into gazettes (for it over-heats the people's brains, and makes them neglect their private

---

[1] Compare Sir Edward Walker's "Observations upon the inconveniences that have attended the frequent promotions to titles of honour, since King James came to the crown of England" (Historical Discourses, p. 291).

affairs, by over-busying themselves with state business) ; so it is great wisdom for a Council of State to have good intelligences (although they be bought with great cost and charges) as well of domestic, as foreign affairs and transactions, and to keep them in private for the benefit of the commonwealth.[1]

XLVII.

That there is no better policy for a prince to please his people, than to have many holidays for their ease, and order several sports and pastimes for their recreation, and to be himself sometime spectator thereof; by which means he'll not only gain love and respect from the people, but busy their minds in harmless actions, sweeten their natures, and hinder them from factious designs.[2]

---

[1] Burnet praises Cromwell for his excellent intelligence. "He laid it down for a maxim to spare no cost or charge in order to procure intelligence. . . . He had on all occasions very good intelligence : he knew everything that passed in the King's little court, and yet none of his spies were discovered but one only."

[2] The same idea inspired James I. and his son when they published their " Declarations concerning lawful sports" to be used in 1618 and 1633 respectively. The prohibition of lawful sports, says the Declaration, "barreth the common and meaner sort of people from using such exercises, as may make their bodies more able for war when we or our successor shall have occasion to use them ; and in place thereof, sets up filthy tipplings and drunken-

XLVIII.

That it is more difficult and dangerous for a prince or commander to raise an army in such a time when the country is embroiled in a civil war, than to lead out an army to fight a battle; for

---

ness, and breeds a number of idle and discontented speeches in their alehouses." When the Long Parliament abolished the observation of Christmas and other holy-days, it was obliged to ordain days of recreation, "that all scholars, apprentices, and other servants shall, with the leave and approbation of their masters respectively first had and obtained, have such convenient relaxation and recreation from their constant and ordinary labours on every second Tuesday in the month, throughout the year, as formerly they have used to have on such aforesaid festivals, commonly called Holy-days. And that masters of all scholars, apprentices, and servants shall grant unto them respectively such time for their recreations on the aforesaid second Tuesdays in every month, as they may conveniently spare from their extraordinary and necessary services and occasions." This ordinance was passed on June 8, 1647, and on the renewed petition of the apprentices, followed by another on June 28, which made its observance compulsory by ordaining that the windows of all shops and warehouses should be shut from eight in the morning till eight in the evening, and by adding the clause—" That no master shall wilfully detain or withhold his apprentice or other servant within doors, or from his recreation, in his usual duty or service on the said day of recreation, unless market-days, fair days, or other extraordinary occasion ; yet so as such master shall allow unto such apprentice or other servant, one other day instead," &c. Provisions were also added against the abuse of such days by riots or other misconduct.

when an army is raised, he hath strength ; but in raising it, he hath none.

XLIX.

That good commanders, and experienced soldiers, are like skilful fencers, who defend with prudence, and assault with courage, and kill their enemies by art, not trusting their lives to chance or fortune ; for as a little man with skill may easily kill an ignorant giant, so a small army that hath experienced commanders may easily overcome a great army that hath none.

L.

That gallant men having no employment for heroic actions become lazy, as hating any other business ; whereas cowards and base persons are only active and stirring in times of peace, working ill designs to breed factions, and cause disturbances in a commonwealth.

LI.

That there have been many questions and disputes concerning the governments of princes ; as, whether they ought to govern by love, or fear ? But the best way of government is, and has always been, by just rewards and punishments ; for that state which cannot tell how and when to punish and reward, does not know how to govern, by reason all the world is governed that way.

LII.

That if the ancient Britons had had skill according to their courage, they might have conquered all the world, as the Romans did.

LIII.

That it would be very beneficial for great princes to be sometimes present in courts of judicature, to examine the causes of their poor subjects, and find out the extortions and corruptions of magistrates and officers; by which glorious act they would gain much love and fame from the people.

LIV.

That it would be very advantageous for subjects, and not in the least prejudicial to the sovereign, to have a general register in every county, for the entry of all manner of deeds, and conveyance of land between party and party, and offices of record; for by this means, whosoever buys, would see clearly what interest and title there is in any land he intends to purchase, whereby he shall be assured that the sale made to him is good and firm, and prevent many lawsuits touching the title of his purchase.[1]

---

[1] This idea of the desirability of a public register for the transfer of land was very frequently put forward in the seventeenth century. The " Harleian Miscellany " contains

LV.

That there should be a limitation for lawsuits; and that the longest suits should not last above two terms, at length not above a year; which would certainly be a great benefit to the subjects in general, though not to lawyers; and though some politicians object, that the more the people is busy about their private affairs, the less time have they to make disturbance in the public; yet this is but a weak argument, since lawsuits are as apt to breed factions, as anything else; for they bring people into poverty, that they know not how to live, which must of necessity breed discontent, and put them upon ill designs.

LVI.

That power, for the most part, does more than wisdom; for fools, with power, seem wise; whereas wise men, without power, seem fools; and this is

---

"Reasons and Proposals for a Registry of all deeds or encumbrances to be had in every county," &c., by Nicholas Philpot, 1671. There is also a tract in the same collection against such registers by William Pierrepoint. It is one of the proposals made in the pamphlet entitled "The Grand Concern of England Explained," 1673. Yarranton brings forward the same plan in "England's Improvement by Sea and Land," 1677. Sir William Petty, in his "Political Arithmetic," and Sir Robert Moray, also argued in favour of a system of registers.

the reason that the world takes power for wisdom, and the want of power for foolishness.

LVII.

That a valiant man will not refuse an honourable duel; nor a wise man fight upon a fool's quarrel.

LVIII.

That men are apt to find fault with each other's actions; believing they prove themselves wise in finding fault with their neighbours.

LIX.

That a wise man will draw several occasions to the point of his design, as a burning glass doth the several beams of the sun.

LX.

That although actions may be prudently designed, and valiantly performed; yet none can warrant the issue; for Fortune is more powerful than prudence, and had Cæsar not been fortunate, his valour and prudence would never have gained him so much applause.

LXI.

That ill fortune makes wise and honest men seem fools and knaves; but good fortune makes fools and knaves seem wise and honest men.

LXII.

That ill fortune doth oftener succeed good, than good fortune succeeds ill; for those that have ill fortune do not so easily recover it, as those that have good fortune are apt to lose it.

LXIII.

That he had observed, that seldom any person did laugh, but it was at the follies or misfortunes of other men; by which we may judge of their good natures.

LXIV.

I have heard my Lord say, that when he was in banishment, he had nothing left him but a clear conscience, by which he had and did still conquer all the armies of misfortunes that ever seized upon him.

LXV.

Also I have heard him say, that he was never beholding to Lady Fortune; for he had suffered on both sides, although he never was but on one side.

LXVI.

I have heard him say, that his father one time, upon some discourse of expenses, should tell him, it was but just that every man should have his time.

LXVII.

I have heard my Lord say, that bold soliciting
and intruding men shall gain more by their importunate petitions, than modest honest men shall get
by silence (as being loath to offend, or be too
troublesome) both in the manner and matter of
their requests. The reason is, said he, that great
princes will rather grant sometimes an unreasonable
suit, than be tired with frequent petitions, and
hindered from their ordinary pleasures. And
when I asked my Lord, whether the grants of
such importunate suits were fitly and properly
placed? he answered, not so well as those that
are placed upon due consideration, and upon trial
and proof.

LXVIII.

I have heard my Lord say, that it is a great
error and weak policy in a state to advance their
enemies, and endeavour to make them friends, by
bribing them with honours and offices, saying,
" they are shrewd men, and may do the state
much hurt:" and on the other side, to neglect
their friends, and those that have done them great
service, saying, " they are honest men, and mean
the state no harm." For this kind of policy comes
from the heathen, who prayed to the devil, and
not to God, by reason they supposed God was
good, and would hurt no creature; but the devil

they flattered and worshipped out of fear, lest he should hurt them. But by this foolish policy, said he, they most commonly increase their enemies, and lose their friends. For, first, it teaches men to observe, that the only way to preferment, is to be against the state or government. Next, since all that are factious cannot be rewarded or preferred (by reason a state hath more subjects, than rewards or preferments) there must of necessity be numerous enemies; for when their hopes of reward fail them, they grow more factious and inveterate than ever they were at first. Wherefore the best policy in a state or government, said my Lord, is to reward friends, and punish enemies, and prefer the honest before the factious; and then all will be real friends, and proffer their honest service, either out of pure love and loyalty, or in hopes of advancement, seeing there is none but by serving the state.

LXIX.

I have heard him say several times, that his love to his gracious master King Charles the Second was above the love he bore to his wife, children, and all his posterity, nay, to his own life : and when, since his return into England, I answered him that I observed his gracious master did not love him so well as he loved him ; he replied, that

he cared not whether his Majesty loved him again
or not ; for he was resolved to love him.[1]

LXX.

I asking my Lord one time, what kind of fate
it was that restored our gracious King, Charles the
Second, to his throne ? he answered, it was a
blessed kind of fate.   I replied, that I had observed
a perfect contrariety between the fortunes of his
royal father, of blessed memory, and him.   For
as there was a division amongst the generality of
the people, in the reign of King Charles the First,
tending to his destruction ; so there was a general
combination and agreement between them in King
Charles the Second his restoration ; and as there
was a general malice amongst the people against
the father to depose him ; so there was a general
love for the son to enthrone him.   My Lord
answered, I had observed something, but not all ;
for, said he, there was a necessity for the people
to desire and restore King Charles the Second ;
but there was no necessity to murder King Charles
the First.   For the kingdom being through so many

---

[1] In the spirit of Butler's lines—

> "Loyalty is still the same,
> Whether it win or lose the game,
> True as the dial to the sun,
> Although it be not shined upon."

alterations and changes of government, divided into several factions and parties, was at last hurried into such a confusion, that it was impossible in that manner to subsist, or hold out any longer. Which confusion having opened the people's eyes, the generality being tired with the evil effects and consequences of their unsettled governments under unjust usurpers, and frightened with the apprehension of future dangers, began to call to mind the happy times, when in an uninterrupted peace they enjoyed their own, under the happy reign of their lawful sovereigns ; and hereupon with an unanimous consent recalled and restored our now gracious King ; which, although it was opposed by some factious parties, yet the generality of the people outweighed the rest ; neither was the royal party wanting in their endeavours.

LXXI.

Asking my Lord one time, whether it was easy or difficult to govern a state or kingdom? he answered me, that most states were governed by secret policy, and so with difficulty ; for those that govern, are (at least should be) wiser than the state or commonwealth they govern. I replied, that in my opinion, a state was easily governed, if their government was like unto God's ; that is to say, if governors did reward and punish according to the desert. My Lord answered, I said well ;

but he added, the follies of the people are many times too hard for the prudence of the governor; like as the sins of men work more evil effects in them, than the grace of God works good; for if this were not, there would be more good than bad, which, alas, experience proves otherwise.

LXXII.

Some gentlemen making a complaint to my Lord, that some he employed in his Majesty's affairs were too hasty and over-busy, my Lord told them, that he would rather choose such persons for his Majesty's service as were over-active, than such that would be fuller of questions than actions. The same he would do for his own particular affairs.

LXXIII.

Some condemning my Lord for having Roman Catholics and Scots in his army; he answered them, that he did not examine their opinions in religion, but looked more upon their honesty and duty; for certainly there were honest men and loyal subjects amongst Roman Catholics, as well as Protestants; and amongst Scots as well as English. Nevertheless, my Lord, as he was for the King, so he was also for the orthodox Church of England, as sufficiently appears by the care he took in ordering the Church government, mentioned in the history.   To which purpose, when my Lord was walking one time with some of his officers in the church at Durham, and wondered at the greatness and strength of the pillars that supported that structure, my brother, Sir Charles Lucas, who was then with him, told my Lord, that he must confess those pillars were very great, and of a vast strength ; but, said he, your Lordship is a far greater pillar of the Church than all these.   Which certainly was also a real truth, and would have more evidently appeared, had Fortune favoured my Lord more than she did.

LXXIV.

My Lord being in banishment, I told him, that he was happy in his misfortunes, for he was not subject to any state or prince.   To which he jestingly answered, that as he was subject to no prince, so he was a prince of no subjects.

LXXV.

In some discourse which I had with my Lord concerning princes and their subjects, I declared that I had observed great princes were not like the sun, which sends forth out of itself rays of light, and beams of heat, effects that did both glorify the sun, and nourish and comfort sublunary creatures ; but their glory and splendour proceeded rather from the ceremony which they received from their subjects. To which my Lord answered, that subjects were so far from giving splendour to their princes, that all the honours and titles, in which consists the chief splendour of a subject, were principally derived from them; for, said he, were there no princes, there would be none to confer honours and titles upon them.

LXXVI.

My Lord entertaining one time some gentlemen with a merry discourse, told them, that he would not keep them company except they had done and suffered as much for their King and country as he had. They answered, that they had not a power answerable to my Lord's. My Lord replied, they should do their endeavour according to their abilities. No, said they, if we did, we should be like yourself, lose all, and get but little for our pains.

LXXVII.

I being much grieved that my Lord, for his loyalty and honest service, had so many enemies, used sometimes to speak somewhat sharply of them; but he gently reproving me, said, I should do like experienced seamen, and as they either turn their sails with the wind, or take them down, so should I either comply with time, or abate my passion.

LXXVIII.

A soldier's wife, whose husband had been slain in my Lord's army, came one time to beg some relief of my Lord; who told her, that he was not able to relieve all that had been loyal to his Majesty; for, said he, my losses are so many, that if I should give away the remainder of my estate, my wife and children would have nothing to live on. She answered, that his Majesty's enemies were preferred to great honours, and had much wealth. Then it is a sign (replied my Lord) that your husband and I were honest men.

LXXIX.

A friend of my Lord's complaining that he had done the state much service, but received little reward for it; my Lord answered him, that states did not usually reward past services : but if he could do some present service, he might perhaps get something; but, said he, those men are wisest that will be paid beforehand.

LXXX.

I observing that in the late Civil Wars, many were desirous to be employed in state's affairs, and at the noise of war endeavoured to be commanders, though but of small parties, asked my Lord the reason thereof, and what advantage they could make by their employments ?   My Lord smilingly answered, that for the generality, he knew not what they could get, but danger, loss, and labour for their pains.   Then I asked him, whether generals of great armies were ever enriched by their heroic exploits, and great victories ?   My Lord answered, that ordinary commanders gained more, and were better rewarded than great generals. To which I added, that I had observed the same in histories, namely, that men of great merit and power had not only no rewards, but were either found fault withal, or laid aside when they had no more business or employment for them, and that I could not conceive any reason for it, but that states were afraid of their power.   My Lord answered, the reason was, that it was far more easy to reward under-officers than great commanders.

LXXXI.

My Lord having, since the return from his banishment, set up a race of horses, instead of those he lost by the wars, uses often to ride through his park to see his breed.   One time it chanced when he went through it, that he espied some labouring men sawing of woods that were blown down by the wind, for some particular uses ; at which my Lord, turning to his attendants, said, that he had been at that work a great part of his life.   They not knowing what my Lord meant, but thinking he jested; I speak very seriously, added he, and not in jest; for you see that this tree which is blown down by the wind, although it was sound and strong, yet it could not withstand its force; and now it is down, it must be cut in pieces, and made serviceable for several uses; whereof some will serve for building, some for paling, some for firing, &c. In the like manner, said he, have I been cut down by the Lady Fortune; and being not able to resist so powerful a princess, I have been forced to make the best use of my misfortunes, as the chips of my estate.

LXXXII.

My Lord discoursing one time with some of his friends, of judging of other men's natures, dispositions, and actions; and some observing that men could not possibly know or judge of them, the events of men's actions falling out oftentimes contrary to their intentions; so that where they hit once, they failed twenty times in their judgments: my Lord answered, that his judgment in that point seldom did miss, although he thought it weaker than theirs. The reason is, said he, because I judge most men to be like myself, that is to say, fools; when as you do judge them all according to yourself, that is, wise men; and since there are more fools in the world than wise men, I may sooner guess right than you: for though my judgment roves at random, yet it can never miss of errors; which yours will never do, except you can dive into other men's follies by the length of your own line, and sound their bottom by the weight of your own plummet, for the depth of folly is beyond the line of wisdom.

Besides, said he, you believe that other men would do as you would have them, or as you would do to them; wherein you are mistaken, for most men do the contrary. In short, folly is bottomless, and hath no end; but wisdom hath bounds to all her designs, otherwise she would never compass them.

LXXXIII.

My Lord discoursing some time with a learned doctor of divinity concerning faith, said, that in his opinion, the wisest way for a man was to have as little faith as he could for this world, and as much as he could for the next world.

LXXXIV.

In some discourse with my Lord, I told him that I did speak sharpest to those I loved best. To which he jestingly answered, that if so, then he would not have me love him best.

LXXXV.

After my Lord's return from a long banishment, when he had been in the country some time, and endeavoured to pick up some gleanings of his ruined estate ; it chanced that the widow of Charles, Lord Mansfield, my Lord's eldest son, afterwards Duchess of Richmond, to whom the said Lord of Mansfield had made a jointure of £2000 a year, died not long after her second marriage. For whose death, though my Lord was heartily sorry, and would willingly have lost the said money, had it been able to save her life ; yet discoursing one time merrily with his friends, was pleased to say, that though his earthly king and master seemed to have forgot him, yet the King of Heaven had remembered him, for he had given him £2000 a year.

SOME FEW NOTES OF THE
AUTHORESS.

—◆◆—

I.

IT was far more difficult in the late Civil Wars, for
my Lord to raise an army for his Majesty's service,
than it was for the Parliament to raise an army
against his Majesty. Not only because the Parliament were many, and my Lord but one single
person; but by reason a kingly or monarchical
government was then generally disliked, and most
part of the kingdom proved rebellious, and assisted
the Parliament either with their purses or persons,
or both; when as the army which my Lord raised
for the defence and maintenance of the King, and
his rights, was raised most upon his own and his
friends' interest. For it is frequently seen and
known, by woful experience, that rebellious and
factious parties do more suddenly and numerously
flock together to act a mischievous design, than
loyal and honest men to assist or maintain a just

cause ; and certainly 'tis much to be lamented, that evil men should be more industrious .and prosperous than good, and that the wicked should have a more desperate courage, than the virtuous an active valour.

II.

I have observed, that many, by flattering poets, have been compared to Cæsar, without desert ; but this I dare freely and without flattery say of my Lord, that though he had not Cæsar's fortune, yet he wanted not Cæsar's courage, nor his prudence, nor his good nature, nor his wit. Nay, in some particulars he did more than Cæsar ever did ; for though Cæsar had a great army, yet he was first set out by the state or senators of Rome, who were masters almost of all the world ; when as my Lord raised his army (as before is mentioned) most upon his own interest (he having many friends and kindred in the northern parts) at such a time when his gracious King and sovereign was then not master of his own kingdoms, he being overpowered by his rebellious subjects.

III.

I have observed that my noble Lord has always had an aversion to that kind of policy that now is commonly practised in the world, which in plain terms is dissembling, flattery, and cheating, under

R

the cover of honesty, love, and kindness. But I have heard him say that the best policy is to act justly, honestly, and wisely, and to speak truly; and that the old proverb is true, "To be wise is to be honest;" for, said he, that man of what condition, quality, or profession soever, that is once found out to deceive either in words or actions, shall never be trusted again by wise and honest men. But, said he, a wise man is not bound to take notice of all dissemblers and their cheating actions, if they do not concern him; nay, even of those he would not always take notice, but choose his time; for the chief part of a wise man is to time business well, and to do it without partiality and passion. But, said he, the folly of the world is so great that one honest and wise man may be overpowered by many knaves and fools; and if so, then the only benefit of a wise man consists in the satisfaction he finds by his honest and wise actions, and that he has done what in conscience, honour, and duty, he ought to do; and all successors of such worthy persons ought to be more satisfied in the worth and merit of their predecessors, than in their title and riches.

IV.

I have heard that some noble gentleman (who was servant to his Highness, then Prince of Wales, our now gracious sovereign, when my Lord was Governor) should relate, that whensoever my Lord by his prudent inspection and foresight did foretell what would come to pass hereafter, it seemed so improbable to him, that both himself and some others believed my Lord spoke extravagantly; but some few years after, his predictions proved true, and the event did confirm what his prudence had observed.

V.

I have heard that in our late Civil Wars there were many petty skirmishes and fortifications of weak and inconsiderable houses, where some small parties would be shooting and pottering[1] at each other; an action more proper for bandits or thieves than stout and valiant soldiers; for I have heard my Lord say, that such small parties divide the body of an army, and by that means weaken it; whereas the business might be much easier decided in one or two battles, with less ruin both to the country and army. For I have heard my Lord say, that as it is dangerous to divide a limb from the body, so it is also dangerous to divide armies or navies in time of war; and there are often more men lost in such petty skirmishes than in set battles, by reason those happen almost every day, nay, every hour in several places.

---

[1] "Pottering" seems to be used as a synonym for shooting, as we should say "potting," and not in the sense of sauntering, or working inefficiently.

VI.

Many in our late Civil Wars had more title than power; for though they were generals or chief commanders, yet their forces were more like a brigade than a well-formed army; and their actions were accordingly, not set battles, but petty skirmishes between small parties; for there were no great battles fought, but by my Lord's army, his being the greatest and best-formed army which his Majesty had.

VII.

Although I have observed that it is a usual custom of the world to glorify the present power and good fortune, and vilify ill fortune and low conditions, yet I never heard that my noble Lord was ever neglected by the generality, but was, on the contrary, always esteemed and praised by all; for he is truly an honest and honourable man, and one that may be relied upon both for trust and truth.

VIII.

I have observed that many instead of great actions make only a great noise, and like shallow fords, or empty bladders, sound most when there is least in them, which expresses a flattering partiality, rather than honesty and truth; for truth and honesty lie at the bottom, and have more action than show.

IX.

I have observed, that good fortune adds fame to mean actions, when as ill fortune darkens the splendour of the most meritorious ; for mean persons, plied with good fortune, are more famous than noble persons that are shadowed or darkened with ill fortune ; so that Fortune, for the most part, is Fame's champion.

X.

I observe, that as it would be a grief to covetous and miserable persons to be rewarded with honour rather than with wealth, because they love wealth before honour and fame ; so, on the other side, noble, heroic, and meritorious persons prefer honour and fame before wealth ; well knowing, that as infamy is the greatest punishment of unworthiness, so fame and honour is the best reward of worth and merit.

XI.

I observe, that spleen and malice, especially in this age, is grown to that height, that none will endure the praise of anybody besides themselves ; nay, they'll rather praise the wicked than the good ; the coward rather than the valiant ; the miserable than the generous ; the traitor than the loyal ; which makes wise men meddle as little with the affairs of the world as ever they can.

XII.

I have observed, as well as former ages have done, that meritorious persons, for their noble actions, most commonly get envy and reproach, instead of praise and reward ; unless their fortunes be above envy, as Cæsar's and Alexander's were. But had these two worthies been as unfortunate as they were fortunate, they would have been as much vilified as they are glorified.

XIII.

I have observed, that it is more easy to talk than to act ; to forget than to remember ; to punish than to reward ; and more common to prefer flattery before truth, interest before justice, and present service before past.

XIV.

I have observed, that many old proverbs are very true, and amongst the rest, this : " It is better to be at the latter end of a feast than at the beginning of a fray ; " for most commonly, those that are in the beginning of a fray get but little of the feast ; and those that have undergone the greatest dangers have least of the spoils.

XV.

I have observed, that favours of great princes make men often thought meritorious; whereas without them, they would be esteemed but as ordinary persons.

XVI.

I observe, that in other kingdoms or countries, to be the chief governor of a province is not only a place of honour, but much profit ; for they have a great revenue to themselves ; whereas in England, the lieutenancy of a county is barely a title of honour, without profit ; except it be the lieutenancy or government of the kingdom of Ireland ; especially since the late Earl of Strafford enjoyed that dignity, who settled that kingdom very wisely both for militia and trade.

XVII.

I have observed, that those that meddle least in wars, whether civil or foreign, are not only most safe and free from danger, but most secure from losses ; and though heroic persons esteem fame before life, yet many there are, that think the wisest way is to be a spectator, rather than an actor, unless they be necessitated to it ; for it is better, say they, to sit on the stool of quiet, than in the chair of troublesome business.

NATURE'S PICTURES,

DRAWN BY

FANCY'S PENCIL TO THE LIFE.

*Written by the thrice noble, illustrious, and excellent
Princess, the Lady Marchioness of Newcastle.*

IN this volume there are several feigned stories of natural
descriptions, as comical, tragical, and tragi-comical, poetical,
romancical, philosophical, and historical, both in prose and
verse, some all verse, some all prose, some mixt, partly
prose and partly verse.   Also there are some morals, and
some dialogues ; but they are as the advantage loaves of
bread to baker's dozen ; and a true story at the latter end,
wherein there is no feignings.

1656.

(The Life of the Duchess forms the Eleventh and last Book.)

BOOK XI.

AN EPISTLE.

I HAVE heard, that some should say my wit seemed as if it would overpower my brain, especially when it works upon philosophical opinions. I am obliged to them for judging my wit stronger than my brain : but I should be sorry that they should think my wit stronger than my reason : but I must tell them that my brain is stronger than my wit, and my reason as strong as the effeminate sex requires.

Again, I have heard some should say, that my writings are none of my own, because when some have visited me, though seldom I receive visits, they have not heard me speak of them, or repeat some of the chapters or verses; but I believe, if they should desire the best orator to repeat his orations or sermons that he hath spoke *ex tempore*, he shall not do it although but an hour's discourse : for I believe Tully, who I have heard was an eloquent orator, yet could not repeat them over to his auditory. The same is in writers; for I do believe Homer, as great and

excellent poet as it is said he was, could not repeat
his poems by heart, nor Virgil, nor Ovid, or any
other; nor Euclid repeat his demonstrations, nume-
rations, and the like without book, nor Aristotle,
who, I have heard, was a great philosopher, the
explanations of his opinions by heart; for I have
heard that his memory failed in the writing, for
that he hath sometimes contradicted himself; and
my Lord, who hath written hundreds of verses,
songs, and themes, could not repeat three by heart;
and I have heard him say, that after he hath writ
them, he doth so little remember any part in them,
that when they have been a short time by, and
then read them over, they are new to him.   But
he is not so forgetful of other things, for he hath
an extraordinary memory for received courtesies, or
to do any timely good or service, not only to
friends, but to strangers.   Also he hath an excellent memory concerning the general actions of and
in the world.   But certainly they that remember
their own wit least, have the most of it; for there
is an old saying, and surely true, that the best wits
have the worst memory, I mean wit-memory; for
great memories are standing ponds that are made
with rain; so that memory is nothing but the
showers of other men's wits; and those brains are
muddy that have not running springs of their own,
that issue out still fresh and new.   Indeed, it's
against nature for natural wits to remember; for it

is impossible that the brain should retain and create ; and we see in nature, death makes way for life ; for if there were no death there would be no new life or lives.

But say I were so witless I could repeat some of my works, I do think it would seem self-conceitedness to mention them ; but since that report, I have spoken more of them than otherwise I should have done, though truly I condemn myself; for it is an indiscretion, although I was forced to that indiscretion, and I repent it both for the disfiguring of my works, by pulling out a piece here and a piece there, according as my memory could catch hold ; also for troubling, or rather vexing the hearers with such discourses as they delight not in.

Besides, it hath been a long and true observation, that every one had rather speak than listen to what another says; insomuch as for the most part all mankind run from company to company, not to learn, but to talk, and like bells their tongues as the clappers keep a jangling noise all at once, without method or distinction.

But I hope my indiscretion in speaking of my works to my hearers is not beyond a pardon, for I have not spoke of them, nor parts in them, much nor often, nor to many, but to some particularly, as those I thought did understand poetry, or natural philosophy, or moral philosophy, though I fear not always according as their capacities lay. For I have observed, some understand common-wealths, customs, laws, or the like ; others, the distinguishments of passions, and understand nothing of law; others, divinity, that understand nothing of temporal government, and so the like of many several studies ; and some may have a rational capacity to most sciences, yet conceive nothing of natural philosophy, as of the first matter, or innated matter, or motions, or figures, or forms, or infinites, or spirits, or essences, or the like ; nay, for the most part they conceive little further than an almanac to know the time by, of which I am ignorant, for I understand it not. And for poetry, most laugh at it as a ridiculous thing, especially grave statists, severe moralists, zealous priesthood, wrangling lawyers, covetous hoarders, or purloiners, or those that have mechanic natures, and many more, which for the most part account poetry a toy, and condemn it for a vanity, an idle employment ; nor have they so much fancy of their own, as to conceive the poetical fancies of others ; for if they did, they must needs love poetry ; for poetry is so powerful, and hath such an attractive beauty, that those that can but view her perfectly, could not but be enamoured, her charms do so force affection. But surely those that delight not in poetry or music, have no divine souls nor harmonious thoughts. But by those weak observations I have made, I perceive that as most men have particular understandings, capacities, or ingenuities, and not a general; so in their discourses some can speak eloquently, and not learnedly; others learnedly and not eloquently; some wittily, and neither learned nor eloquent; and some will speak neither learnedly, eloquently, wittily, or rationally. Likewise, some can speak well, but 'tis but for a time, some a longer, and some a shorter time, like several sized candles, are longer or shorter ere they come to a snuff; where sometimes some objects or conceits, unexpected objections or questions, or the like, do prove as a small coal got into the tallow of their wit, which makes it bleer [1] out sooner than otherwise it would do. Also some will speak wisely upon some subjects, and foolishly upon others.

Likewise some will speak well as it were by chance; others in one discourse speak mixtly, now rational, then nonsensely, at least weakly or obstructedly. But they are great masters of speech that speak clearly, as I may say, untangled, which can wind their words from off their tongue without a snarl [2] or knot, and can keep even sense, like an even thread, or can work that thread of sense into a flourishing discourse; and they have a quick

[1] Probably "blear," to make dim, used in the sense of to become dim.

[2] Halliwell gives "snarle," a snare, and "snarrel," a hard knot (Cumberland dialect).

wit that can play with, or on any subject, which doubtless some can do of those things they never heard, saw, or thought on, but just when they speak of it. And some have great capacities, as may be perceived in their discourse : but yet their speech is like those that are lame, which limp and halt, although the ground whereon they go is even, smooth, and firm. But some have such large capacities, elevated fancies, illuminated souls, and volubility of speech, that they can conceive, create, enlighten, and deliver with that abundance, curiosity, facility, and pleasure, as their conversible company is a heaven, where all worldly delights reside.

But to return to the ground of this Epistle. I desire all my readers and acquaintance to believe, though my words run stumbling out of my mouth, and my pen draws roughly on my paper, yet my thoughts move regular in my brain ; for the several tracks or paths that contemplation hath made on my brain, which paths or tracks are the several ways my thoughts move in, are much smoother than the tongue in my mouth, from whence words flow, or the paper on which my pen writes ; for I have not spoke so much as I have writ, nor writ so much as I have thought. For I must tell my readers, that nature, which is the best and curiousest worker, hath paved my brain smoother than custom hath oiled my tongue, or variety hath polished my senses, or art hath beaten the paper whereon I write; for my fancy is quicker that the pen with which I write, insomuch as it is many times lost through the slowness of my hand, and yet I write so fast, as I stay not so long as to make perfect letters.

But if they will not believe my books are my own, let them search the author or authoress: but I am very confident that they will do like Drake, who went so far about, until he came to the place he first set out at. But for the sake of after ages, which I hope will be more just to me than the present, I will write the true relation of my birth, breeding, and to this part of my life, not regarding carping tongues, or malicious censurers, for I despise them.

MARGARET NEWCASTLE.

A TRUE RELATION

OF MY

BIRTH, BREEDING, AND LIFE.

By Margaret, Duchess of Newcastle.

—▸+—

My father was a gentleman, which title is grounded
and given by merit, not by princes ; and it is the
act of time, not favour : and though my father was
not a peer of the realm, yet there were few peers
who had much greater estates, or lived more noble
therewith. Yet at that time great titles were to be
sold, and not at so high rates, but that his estate
might have easily purchased, and was pressed for
to take ; but my father did not esteem titles, unless
they were gained by heroic actions, and the kingdom
being in a happy peace with all other nations, and
in itself being governed by a wise king, King James,
there was no employments for heroic spirits ; and
towards the latter end of Queen Elizabeth's reign,
as soon as he came to man's estate, he unfortu-

nately killed one Mr. Brooks in a single duel. For my father by the laws of honour could do no less than call him to the field to question him for an injury he did him, where their swords were to dispute, and one or both of their lives to decide the argument, wherein my father had the better; and though my father by honour challenged him, with valour fought him, and in justice killed him, yet he suffered more than any person of quality usually doth in cases of honour; for though the laws be rigorous, yet the present princes most commonly are gracious in those misfortunes, especially to the injured: but my father found it not, for his exile was from the time of his misfortunes to Queen Elizabeth's death.   For the Lord Cobham being then a great man with Queen Elizabeth, and this gentleman, Mr. Brooks, a kind of a favourite, and as I take it brother to the then Lord Cobham, which made Queen Elizabeth so severe, not to pardon him.[1]   But King James of blessed memory graciously gave him his pardon, and leave to return home to his native country, wherein he lived happily, and died peaceably, leaving a wife and eight children, three sons, and five daughters, I being the youngest child he had, and an infant when he died.

---

[1] This was probably George Brooke, the brother of Lord Cobham, executed for his share in the plot called "The Bye," in 1603.   I have not been able to find any mention of this duel.

As for my breeding, it was according to my birth, and the nature of my sex ; for my birth was not lost in my breeding. For as my sisters was or had been bred, so was I in plenty, or rather with superfluity. Likewise we were bred virtuously, modestly, civilly, honourably, and on honest principles. As for plenty, we had not only for necessity, conveniency, and decency, but for delight and pleasure to a superfluity ; it is true we did not riot, but we lived orderly ; for riot, even in kings' courts and princes' palaces, brings ruin without content or pleasure, when order in less fortunes shall live more plentifully and deliciously than princes that lives in a hurlyburly, as I may term it, in which they are seldom well served. For disorder obstructs ; besides, it doth disgust life, distract the appetites, and yield no true relish to the senses ; for pleasure, delight, peace, and felicity live in method and temperance.

As for our garments, my mother did not only delight to see us neat and cleanly, fine and gay, but rich and costly ; maintaining us to the height of her estate, but not beyond it. For we were so far from being in debt, before these wars, as we were rather beforehand with the world ; buying all with ready money, not on the score. For although after my father's death the estate was divided between my mother and her sons, paying such a sum of money for portions to her daughters, either at the day of their marriage, or when they should come to age; yet by reason she and her children agreed with a mutual consent, all their affairs were managed so well, as she lived not in a much lower condition than when my father lived. 'Tis true, my mother might have increased her daughters' portions by a thrifty sparing, yet she chose to bestow it on our breeding, honest pleasures, and harmless delights, out of an opinion, that if she bred us with needy necessity, it might chance to create in us sharking[1] qualities, mean thoughts, and base actions, which she knew my father, as well as herself, did abhor. Likewise we were bred tenderly, for my mother naturally did strive, to please and delight her children, not to cross or torment them, terrifying them with threats, or lashing them with slavish whips; but instead of threats, reason was used to persuade us, and instead of lashes, the deformities of vice was discovered, and the graces and virtues were presented unto us. Also we were bred with respectful attendance, every one being severally waited upon, and all her servants in general used the same respect to her children (even those that were very young) as they did to herself; for she suffered not her servants, either to be rude before us, or to domineer over us, which all vulgar servants are apt, and ofttimes which some

---

[1] Shark, to swindle, to trick dishonestly, to sponge on a person.

have leave to do. Likewise she never suffered the vulgar serving-men to be in the nursery among the nursemaids, lest their rude love-making might do unseemly actions, or speak unhandsome words in the presence of her children, knowing that youth is apt to take infection by ill examples, having not the reason of distinguishing good from bad. Neither were we suffered to have any familiarity with the vulgar servants, or conversation: yet caused us to demean ourselves with an humble civility towards them, as they with a dutiful respect to us. Not because they were servants were we so reserved; for many noble persons are forced to serve through necessity; but by reason the vulgar sort of servants are as ill bred as meanly born; giving children ill examples and worse counsel.[1]

As for tutors, although we had for all sorts of

---

[1] The Duchess elsewhere describes the evils of familiarity with servants:—" Others through carelessness make their children fall into the same errors, not instructing them with noble and honourable principles, but suffering them to run about into every dirty office, where the young master must learn to drink and play at cards with the kitchen-boy, and learn to kiss his mother's dirty maid for a mess of cream. The daughters are danced upon the knee of every clown and serving-man, and hear them talk scurrilous to their maids, which is their compliment of wooing; and then dancing Sellinger's Round with them in Christmas time, and many other such things, which makes them become like unto like; and their parents think no harm in it because they are young."—The World's Olio, p. 79.

virtues,[1] as singing, dancing, playing on music, reading, writing, working, and the like, yet we were not kept strictly thereto, they were rather for formality than benefit; for my mother cared not so much for our dancing and fiddling, singing and prating of several languages, as that we should be bred virtuously, modestly, civilly, honourably, and on honest principles.

As for my brothers, of which I had three, I know not how they were bred. First, they were bred when I was not capable to observe, or before I was born; likewise the breeding of men were after different manner of ways from those of women. But this I know, that they loved virtue, endeavoured merit, practised justice, and spoke truth; they were constantly loyal, and truly valiant. Two of my three brothers were excellent soldiers, and martial discipliners, being practised therein; for though they might have lived upon their own estates very honourably, yet they rather chose to serve in the wars under the States of Holland, than to live idly at home in peace: my brother, Sir Thomas Lucas, there having a troop of horse;

---

[1] Virtues, accomplishments. According to Mr. Jenkins, in his reprint of this relation in " The Cavalier and His Lady," in the copy of this book in the King's Library at the British Museum, the Duchess has with her own hand altered virtues into virtuosos. Accordingly he reads " As for tutors, although we had all sorts of virtuosos."

my brother (the youngest) Sir Charles Lucas, serving therein. But he served the States not long, for after he had been at the siege and taking of some towns, he returned home again ; and though he had the less experience, yet he was like to have proved the better soldier, if better could have been, for naturally he had a practical genius to the warlike arts, or arts in war, as natural poets have to poetry.[1] But his life was cut off before he could arrive to the true perfection thereof ;[2] yet he writ

---

[1] Sir Charles Lucas, according to Clarendon (Rebellion, xi. 108), was held as good a commander of horse as the nation had. " He had been bred in the Low Countries, and always amongst the horse,' so that he had little conversation in that court, where great civility was practised and learned. He was very brave in his person, and in a day of battle a gallant man to look upon, and follow ; but at all other times and places of a nature not to be lived with, of an ill understanding, of a rough and proud nature, which made him during the time of their being in Colchester more intolerable than the siege, or any fortune that threatened them ; yet they all desired to accompany him in his death." See also the note on his life in the Appendix.

[2] The Duchess wrote the following poem on her brother's death.

An Elegy upon the Death of my Brother.

" Dear Brother,—
        Thy idea in my mind doth lie,
And is entombed in my sad memory,
Where every day I to thy shrine do go,
And offer tears, which from my eyes do flow ;

"A Treatise of the Arts in War," but by reason it was in characters, and the key thereof lost, we cannot as yet understand any thing therein, at least not so as to divulge it. My other brother, the Lord Lucas,[1] who was heir to my father's estate, and as it were the father to take care of us all, is not less valiant than they were, although his skill in the discipline of war was not so much, being not bred therein. Yet he had more skill in the use of the sword, and is more learned in other arts and sciences than they were, he being a great scholar, by reason he is given much to studious contemplation.[2]

> My heart the fire, whose flames are ever pure,
> Shall on Love's altar last while life endure ;
> My sorrow incense strews of sighs fetched deep,
> My thoughts keep watch o'er thy sweet spirit's sleep.
> Dear blessed soul, though thou art gone, yet lives
> Thy fame on earth, and man thee praises gives :
> But all's too small : for thy heroic mind
> Was above all the praises of mankind."
>
> —*Poems*, p. 271, ed. 1664.

[1] Sir John Lucas was created Baron Lucas of Shenfield by patent dated 3d May 20 Charles I. (Collins, vii. 114). Clarendon gives an account of the manner in which he bought his peerage. John Ashburnham acted as broker. Clarendon, Life, iii. 62, 63.

[2] John, Lord Lucas, is included in Walpole's " Royal and Noble Authors," his title to inclusion being a speech in the House of Lords in 1671 against the burdens of taxation and the extravagance of the Government. It was

Their practice was, when they met together, to exercise themselves with fencing, wrestling, shooting, and such like exercises, for I observed they did seldom hawk or hunt, and very seldom or never dance, or play on music, saying it was too effeminate for masculine spirits. Neither had they skill, or did use to play, for aught I could hear, at cards or dice, or the like games, nor given to any vice, as I did know, unless to love a mistress were a crime, not that I knew any they had, but what report did say, and usually reports are false, at least exceed the truth.

As for the pastime of my sisters when they were in the country, it was to read, work, walk, and discourse with each other. For though two of my three brothers[1] were married (my brother the Lord

---

printed, and burnt by the hands of the hangman. The speech is contained in State Tracts, vol. i. p. 454, and is also reprinted in Park's edition of Walpole, vol. iii. p. 119.

[1] Sir Egerton Brydges gives the following pedigree :—
Sir Thomas Lucas of St. John's, near Colchester, married Mary, daughter of Sir John Fermor of Eston-Neston, in Northamptonshire, by whom he had Thomas Lucas of St. John's, near Colchester, Esq., who by Elizabeth, daughter and co-heir of John Leighton of London, Gent., had three sons and five daughters, viz.—

1. John Lucas of St. John's, near Colchester, afterwards Lord Lucas, who married Anne, daughter of Sir Christopher Neville, Kt., younger brother of the Lord Abergavenny, by whom he had John, his son and heir, born about 1624.

2. Sir Thomas Lucas, a captain in London, who married

Lucas to a virtuous and beautiful lady, daughter
to Sir Christopher Nevil, son to the Lord Abergavenny ; and my brother Sir Thomas Lucas
to a virtuous lady of an ancient family, one Sir
John Byron's daughter), likewise three of my four
sisters (one married Sir Peter Killegrew, the other
Sir William Walter, the third Sir Edmund Pye,
the fourth as yet unmarried), yet most of them lived
with my mother, especially when she was at her
country-house, living most commonly at London
half the year, which is the metropolitan city of
England.   But when they were at London, they
were dispersed into several houses of their own,
yet for the most part they met every day, feasting
each other like Job's children.   But this unnatural
war came like a whirlwind, which felled down their
houses, where some in the wars were crushed to
death, as my youngest brother Sir Charles Lucas,
and my brother Sir Thomas Lucas.   And though

---

a daughter of Sir John Byron, Kt., by whom he had a son,
Thomas.

3. Sir Charles Lucas.
4. Mary, wife of Sir Peter Killegrew, Kt.
5. Anne.
6. Elizabeth, wife of William Walter, Esq.
7. Catherine, wife of Sir Edmund Pye of London, Kt.
8. Margaret, afterwards Duchess of Newcastle.*
Arms.—Argent, a fess between six annulets, gules.

---

* Harl. MSS. 1541, f. 59.

my brother Sir Thomas Lucas died not immediately of his wounds, yet a wound he received on his head in Ireland shortened his life.

But to rehearse their recreations. Their customs were in winter time to go sometimes to plays, or to ride in their coaches about the streets to see the concourse and recourse of people ; and in the spring time to visit the Spring Garden, Hyde Park, and the like places ;[1] and sometimes they would have music, and sup in barges upon the water. These harmless recreations they would pass their time away with ; for I observed they did seldom make visits, nor never went abroad with strangers in their company, but only themselves in a flock together, agreeing so well that there seemed but one mind amongst them. And not only my own brothers and sisters agreed so, but my brothers and sisters in law, and their children, although but young, had the like agreeable natures and affectionable dispositions. For to my best remembrance I do not know that ever they did fall out, or had

---

[1] A description of Hyde Park a few years later is quoted on page 302. The same author thus describes Spring Garden :—" The manner is as the company returns (*i.e.*, from Hyde Park), to alight at the Spring Garden, so called in order to the Park, as our Thuilleries is to the course : the inclosure not disagreeable for the solemness of the grove, the warbling of the birds, and as it opens into the spacious walks at St. James's."—Evelyn's " Character of England."

any angry or unkind disputes. Likewise, I did observe that my sisters were so far from mingling themselves with any other company, that they had no familiar conversation or intimate acquaintance with the families to which each other were linked to by marriage, the family of the one being as great strangers to the rest of my brothers and sisters as the family of the other.

But sometime after this war began, I knew not how they lived. For though most of them were in Oxford, wherein the King was, yet after the Queen went from Oxford, and so out of England, I was parted from them. For when the Queen was in Oxford I had a great desire to be one of her maids of honour, hearing the Queen had not the same number she was used to have. Whereupon I wooed and won my mother to let me go ; for my mother, being fond of all her children, was desirous to please them, which made her consent to my request. But my brothers and sisters seemed not very well pleased, by reason I had never been from home, nor seldom out of their sight ; for though they knew I would not behave myself to their or my own dishonour, yet they thought I might to my disadvantage, being inexperienced in the world. Which indeed I did, for I was so bashful when I was out of my mother's, brothers', and sisters' sight, whose presence used to give me confidence—thinking I could not do

amiss whilst any one of them were by, for I knew
they would gently reform me if I did; besides, I
was ambitious they should approve of my actions
and behaviour—that when I was gone from them,
I was like one that had no foundation to stand, or
guide to direct me, which made me afraid, lest I
should wander with ignorance out of the ways of
honour, so that I knew not how to behave myself.
Besides, I had heard that the world was apt to lay
aspersions even on the innocent, for which I durst
neither look up with my eyes, nor speak, nor be
any way sociable, insomuch as I was thought a
natural fool. Indeed I had not much wit, yet I
was not an idiot, my wit was according to my
years; and though I might have learnt more wit,
and advanced my understanding by living in a
Court, yet being dull, fearful, and bashful, I neither
heeded what was said or practised, but just what
belonged to my loyal duty, and my own honest
reputation. And, indeed, I was so afraid to dishonour my friends and family by my indiscreet
actions, that I rather chose to be accounted a fool
than to be thought rude or wanton. In truth, my
bashfulness and fears made me repent my going
from home to see the world abroad, and much I
did desire to return to my mother again, or to my
sister Pye, with whom I often lived when she was
in London, and loved with a supernatural affection.
But my mother advised me there to stay, although

I put her to more charges than if she had kept me at home, and the more, by reason she and my brothers were sequestered from their estates, and plundered of all their goods, yet she maintained me so, that I was in a condition rather to lend than to borrow, which courtiers usually are not, being always necessitated by reason of great expenses Courts put them to. But my mother said it would be a disgrace for me to return out of the Court so soon after I was placed; so I continued almost two years, until such time as I was married from thence. For my Lord the Marquis of Newcastle did approve of those bashful fears which many condemned, and would choose such a wife as he might bring to his own humours, and not such a one as was wedded to self-conceit, or one that had been tempered to the humours of another; for which he wooed me for his wife; and though I did dread marriage, and shunned men's company as much as I could, yet I could not, nor had not the power to refuse him, by reason my affections were fixed on him, and he was the only person I ever was in love with. Neither was I ashamed to own it, but gloried therein. For it was not amorous love (I never was infected therewith, it is a disease, or a passion, or both, I only know by relation, not by experience), neither could title, wealth, power, or person entice me to love. But my love was honest and honourable, being placed upon merit, which affection joyed at the fame of his worth, pleased with delight in his wit, proud of the respects he used to me, and triumphing in the affections he professed for me, which affections he hath confirmed to me by a deed of time, sealed by constancy, and assigned by an unalterable decree of his promise, which makes me happy in despite of Fortune's frowns. For though misfortunes may and do oft dissolve base, wild, loose, and ungrounded affections, yet she hath no power of those that are united either by merit, justice, gratitude, duty, fidelity, or the like. And though my Lord hath lost his estate, and banished out of his country for his loyalty to his King and country, yet neither despised poverty, nor pinching necessity could make him break the bonds of friendship, or weaken his loyal duty to his King or country.

But not only the family I am linked to is ruined, but the family from which I sprung, by these unhappy wars. Which ruin my mother lived to see, and then died, having lived a widow many years; for she never forgot my father so as to marry again. Indeed, he remained so lively in her memory, and her grief was so lasting, as she never mentioned his name, though she spoke often of him, but love and grief caused tears to flow, and tender sighs to rise, mourning in sad complaints. She made her house her cloister, inclosing

T

herself, as it were, therein, for she seldom went abroad, unless to church. But these unhappy wars forced her out, by reason she and her children were loyal to the King ; for which they plundered her and my brothers of all their goods, plate, jewels, money, corn, cattle, and the like, cut down their woods, pulled down their houses, and sequestered them from their lands and livings ; but in such misfortunes my mother was of an heroic spirit, in suffering patiently where there is no remedy, or to be industrious where she thought she could help. She was of a grave behaviour, and had such a majestic grandeur, as it were continually hung about her, that it would strike a kind of an awe to the beholders, and command respect from the rudest (I mean the rudest of civilised people, I mean not such barbarous people as plundered her, and used her cruelly, for they would have pulled God out of heaven, had they had power, as they did royalty out of his throne).[1] Also her beauty

---

[1] An account of the plunder of the house of Sir John Lucas at Colchester is given in " Mercurius Rusticus," No. 1 :—" On August 22, 1642, Sir John Lucas intended with some horse and arms to begin his journey towards the north to wait upon the King." This was discovered to the leaders of the local parliamentarians by a treacherous servant, and the roads were beset, and a guard set on his house. On his attempt to start the town was raised, the volunteers and train-band assembled, and a crowd of 2000

was beyond the ruin of time, for she had a well-favoured loveliness in her face, a pleasing sweetness in her countenance, and a well-tempered complexion, as neither too red nor too pale, even to her dying hour, although in years. And by her dying, one might think death was enamoured with her, for he embraced her in a sleep, and so gently, as if he were afraid to hurt her. Also she was an affectionate mother, breeding her children with a most industrious care, and tender love ; and having

---

people broke into the house to search for arms and the suppressed garrison of cavaliers. "The people lay hands on Sir John Lucas, his lady, and sister, and carry them, attended with swords, guns, and halberts to the common gaol. Last of all they bring forth his mother, with the like or greater insolency, who, being faint and breathless, hardly obtained leave to rest herself in a shop by the way ; yet this leave was no sooner obtained, but the rest of that rude rabble threatened to pull down the house, unless they thrust her out ; being by this means forced to depart from thence, a countryman (whom the alarm had summoned to this work) espies her, and pressing with his horse through the crowd, struck at her head with his sword so heartily, that if an halbert had not crossed the blow, both her sorrows and her journey had there found an end." After this the house was thoroughly plundered, deeds and papers destroyed, garden defaced, deer killed, and cattle driven away. This was largely caused by a rumour that 200 armed men were discovered in a vault at Sir John Lucas's, had killed nine men already, and were issuing forth to destroy the town. "And to show that their rage will know no bounds, and that nothing is so sacred and venerable

eight children, three sons and five daughters, there was not any one crooked, or any ways deformed, neither were they dwarfish, or of a giant-like stature, but every ways proportionable; likewise well featured, clear complexions, brown hairs (but some lighter than others), sound teeth, sweet breaths, plain speeches, tunable voices (I mean not so much to sing as in speaking, as not stuttering, nor wharling [1] in the throat, or speaking through the

---

which they dare not to violate, they break into St. Giles's Church, open the vault where his (Sir John's) ancestors were buried, and with pistols, swords, and halberts transfix the coffins of the dead." Sir John was sent a prisoner to London, committed to the Gatehouse, and after a short time released on giving bail to appear on summons. His eight horses and his arms were employed for the service of the Parliament. Parliament also published two Declarations, the one a general prohibition to soldiers and others to break into and search the houses of persons suspected of disaffection and popery (August 27), the other entitled " A Declaration concerning abuses lately done by several persons in the county of Essex."—Husband's " Exact Collection," pp. 590, 592, 605. In this latter Declaration it is stated that the people, on the order of the parliamentary commissioners, withdrew themselves peaceably, " and as they were required, did make restitution of plate, money, and many other goods." However, the Parliament's Commissioners did not come down till Thursday, and the riot took place on Monday, and the worst feature of these outrages was the amount of wanton destruction.

[1] Wharling—I can find no other use of the word. Halli-well explains " wharling " to mean " an inability in any-

nose, or hoarsely, unless they had a cold, or squeakingly, which impediments many have) : neither were their voices of too low a strain, or too high, but their notes and words were tunable and timely. I hope this truth will not offend my readers, and lest they should think I am a partial register, I dare not commend my sisters, as to say they were handsome ; although many would say they were very handsome. But this I dare say, their beauty, if any they had, was not so lasting as my mother's, Time making suddener ruin in their faces than in hers. Likewise my mother was a good mistress to her servants, taking care of her servants in their sickness, not sparing any cost she was able to bestow for their recovery : neither did she exact more from them in their health than what they with ease or rather like pastime could do. She would freely pardon a fault, and forget an injury, yet sometimes she would be angry ; but never with her children, the sight of them would pacify her ; neither would she be angry with others but when she had cause, as negligent or knavish servants, that would lavishly or unnecessarily waste, or subtly

---

one to pronounce the letter R " (Dictionary of Archaic and Provincial Words). Shakespeare uses a somewhat similar word in " King Lear," iv. 6 :—

> " We came crying hither ;
> Thou know'st, the first time that we smell the air,
> We wawl and cry."

and thievishly steal. And though she would often complain that her family was too great for her weak management, and often pressed my brother to take it upon him, yet I observe she took a pleasure, and some little pride, in the governing thereof. She was very skilful in leases, and setting of lands, and court keeping, ordering of stewards, and the like affairs.[1] Also I observed that my mother nor brothers, before these wars, had never any lawsuits, but what an attorney despatched in a term with small cost, but if they had it was more than I knew of. But, as I said, my mother lived to see the ruin of her children, in which was her ruin, and then died : my brother Sir Thomas Lucas soon after, my brother Sir Charles Lucas after him, being shot to death for his loyal service, for he was most constantly loyal and courageously active, indeed he had a superfluity of courage. My eldest sister died some time before my mother, her death being, as I believe, hastened through grief of her only daughter, on which she doted, being very pretty, sweet natured, and had an extraordinary wit for her age. She dying of a consumption, my sister, her mother, died some half a year after of the same disease ; and though time is apt to waste remembrance as a consumptive body, or to wear it

[1] This refers to the management of manors and manorial courts. See Roger North's "Life of Lord Guilford," pp. 34–6, ed. 1826.

out like a garment into rags, or to moulder it into dust, yet I find the natural affections I have for my friends are beyond the length, strength, and power of time : for I shall lament the loss so long as I live, also the loss of my Lord's noble brother, which died not long after I returned from England, he being then sick of an ague, whose favours and my thankfulness ingratitude shall never disjoin. For I will build his monument of truth, though I cannot of marble, and hang my tears and scutcheons on his tomb. He was nobly generous, wisely valiant, naturally civil, honestly kind, truly loving, virtuously temperate ; his promise was like a fixed decree, his words were destiny, his life was holy, his disposition mild, his behaviour courteous, his discourse pleasing ; he had a ready wit and a spacious knowledge, a settled judgment, a clear understanding, a rational insight ; he was learned in all arts and sciences, but especially in the mathematics, in which study he spent most part of his time ; and though his tongue preached not moral philosophy, yet his life taught it, indeed he was such a person, that he might have been a pattern for all mankind to take. He loved my Lord his brother with a doting affection, as my Lord did him, for whose sake I suppose he was so nobly generous, carefully kind, and respectful to me ; for I dare not challenge his favours as to myself, having not merits to deserve them. He was for a time the preserver of my life, for after I was married some two or three years, my Lord travelled out of France, from the city of Paris, in which city he resided the time he was there, so went into Holland, to a town called Rotterdam, in which place he stayed some six months. From thence he returned to Brabant, unto the city of Antwerp, which city we passed through when we went into Holland, and in that city my Lord settled himself and family, choosing it for the most pleasantest and quietest place to retire himself and ruined fortunes in. But after we had remained some time therein, we grew extremely necessitated, tradesmen being there not so rich as to trust my Lord for so much, or so long, as those of France; yet they were so civil, kind, and charitable as to trust him for as much as they were able. But at last necessity enforced me to return into England to seek for relief. For I, hearing my Lord's estate, amongst the rest of many more estates, was to be sold, and that the wives of the owners should have an allowance therefrom, it gave me hopes I should receive a benefit thereby. So, being accompanied with my Lord's only brother, Sir Charles Cavendish (who was commanded to return, to live therein, or to lose his estate, which estate he was forced to buy with a great composition before he could enjoy any part thereof), so over I went. But when I came there I found their hearts as hard as my fortunes, and their natures as cruel as my miseries, for they sold all my Lord's estate, which was a very great one, and gave me not any part thereof, or any allowance thereout, which few or no other was so hardly dealt withal. Indeed, I did not stand as a beggar at the Parliament door, for I never was at the Parliament House, nor stood I ever at the door, as I do know, or can remember, I am sure, not as a petitioner. Neither did I haunt the committees, for I never was at any, as a petitioner, but one in my life, which was called Goldsmiths' Hall,[1] but I received neither gold nor silver from them, only an absolute refusal, I should have no share of my Lord's estate. For my brother, the Lord Lucas,

---

[1] The committee sitting at Goldsmiths' Hall was that for compounding with delinquents. "Its object was to receive from delinquents themselves, either such against whom no information had been made, or such as were already under sequestration—

(1.) A confession of their delinquency.
(2.) A pledge of adherence to the present Government.
(3.) A full account on oath of their possessions, real and personal.

Whereupon a legal report was made, and they were admitted to compound in proportions, according to their guilt ; half the estate was exacted from any delinquent Member of Parliament ; one-sixth from those who had taken part either in the former or latter war ; two-sixths or one-third from those who had been active in both wars, &c. Those who were in cities that surrendered on articles of war compounded according to the tenor of those articles " (Mrs. Greene's Preface to the Calendar of Domestic State Papers,

did claim in my behalf such a part of my Lord's estate as wives had allowed them, but they told him that by reason I was married since my Lord was made a delinquent, I could have nothing, nor should have anything, he being the greatest traitor to the State, which was to be the most loyal subject to his King and country.   But I whisperingly spoke to my brother to conduct me out of that ungentlemanly place, so without speaking to them one word good or bad, I returned to my lodgings, and as that committee was the first, so was it the last, I ever was at as a petitioner.   'Tis true I went sometimes to Drury House to inquire how the land was sold, but no other ways, although some reported I was at the Parliament House, and at this committee and at that committee, and what I should say, and how I was answered.   But the customs of England being changed as well as the laws, where women become pleaders, attornies,

---

1649, p. ix.).   The songs of the Cavaliers are naturally full of allusions to this committee :—

> " Under the rose be it spoken, there's a damned committee,
>   Sits in Hell (Goldsmiths' Hall) in the middle of the city,
>   Only to sequester the poor Cavaliers,
>   The devil take their souls and the hangman their ears."

Another song says in allusion to the oaths :—

> " They force us to take
>   Three oaths, but we'll make
>   A third, that we ne'er meant to keep 'em."

petitioners, and the like, running about with their several causes, complaining of their several grievances, exclaiming against their several enemies, bragging of their several favours they receive from the powerful, thus trafficking with idle words bring in false reports and vain discourse. For the truth is, our sex doth nothing but jostle for the pre-eminence of words (I mean not for speaking well, but speaking much) as they do for the pre-eminence of place, words rushing against words, thwarting and crossing each other, and pulling with reproaches, striving to throw each other down with disgrace, thinking to advance themselves thereby. But if our sex would but well consider, and rationally ponder, they will perceive and find, that it is neither words nor place that can advance them, but worth and merit. Nor can words or place disgrace them, but inconstancy and boldness : for an honest heart, a noble soul, a chaste life, and a true speaking tongue, is the throne, sceptre, crown, and footstool that advances them to an honourable renown. I mean not noble, virtuous, discreet, and worthy persons whom necessity did enforce to submit, comply, and follow their own suits, but such as had nothing to lose, but made it their trade to solicit. But I despairing, being positively denied at Goldsmiths' Hall (besides, I had a firm faith, or strong opinion, that the pains was more than the gains), and being unpractised in public employments, unlearned in their uncouth ways, ignorant of the humours and dispositions of those persons to whom I was to address my suit, and not knowing where the power lay, and being not a good flatterer, I did not trouble myself or petition my enemies. Besides I am naturally bashful, not that I am ashamed of my mind or body, my birth or breeding, my actions or fortunes, for my bashfulness is my nature, not for any crime, and though I have strived and reasoned with myself, yet that which is inbred I find is difficult to root out. But I do not find that my bashfulness is concerned with the qualities of the persons, but the number ; for were I to enter amongst a company of Lazaruses, I should be as much out of countenance as if they were all Cæsars or Alexanders, Cleopatras or Queen Didos. Neither do I find my bashfulness riseth so often in blushes, as contracts my spirits to a chill paleness. But the best of it is, most commonly it soon vanisheth away, and many times before it can be perceived ; and the more foolish or unworthy I conceive the company to be, the worse I am, and the best remedy I ever found was, is to persuade myself that all those persons I meet are wise and virtuous. The reason I take to be is, that the wise and virtuous censure least, excuse most, praise best, esteem rightly, judge justly, behave themselves civilly, demean themselves respectfully, and speak modestly when fools or unworthy persons are apt to commit absurdities, as to be bold, rude, uncivil both in words and actions, forgetting or not well understanding themselves or the company they are with.   And though I never met such sorts of ill-bred creatures, yet naturally I have such an aversion to such kind of people, as I am afraid to meet them, as children are afraid of spirits, or those that are afraid to see or meet devils ; which makes me think this natural defect in me, if it be a defect, is rather a fear than a bashfulness, but whatso-ever it is, I find it troublesome, for it hath many times obstructed the passage of my speech, and perturbed my natural actions, forcing a constrained-ness or unusual motions.   However, since it is rather a fear of others than a bashful distrust of myself, I despair of a perfect cure, unless nature as well as human governments could be civilised and brought into a methodical order, ruling the words and actions with a supreme power of reason, and the authority of discretion : but a rude nature is worse than a brute nature by so much more as man is better than beast, but those that are of civil natures and gentle dispositions are as much nearer to celestial creatures, as those that are of rude or cruel are to devils.   But in fine, after I had been in England a year and a half,[1] in which time

---

[1] Supply, to complete the sense, " I resolved to return," from p. 304.

I gave some half a score visits, and went with my
Lord's brother to hear music in one Mr. Lawes his
house,[1] three or four times, as also some three or
four times to Hyde Park with my sisters, to take
the air,[2] else I never stirred out of my lodgings,

---

[1] This was Henry Lawes, for his elder brother William
was killed at the siege of Chester in October 1645. He
composed the music for " Comus," and acted in it the parts
of Thyrsis and the Attendant Spirit. Milton addressed to
him on 9th February 1646 the well-known sonnet :—

To my Friend, Mr. Henry Lawes.

" Harry, whose tuneful and well-measured song
   First taught our English music how to span
   Words with just note and accent."
                          —Masson, "Life of Milton," iii. 464.

[2] In Evelyn's " Character of England," 1651, Hyde
Park is thus described :—

" I did frequently in the spring accompany my Lord N.
into a field near the town, which they call Hyde-Park ;
the place not unpleasant, and which they use, as our
Course ; but with nothing that order, equipage, and
splendor, being such an assembly of wretched jades and
hackney-coaches, as next a regiment of car-men there is
nothing approaches the resemblance. This Park was (it
seems) used by the late King and Nobility for the freshness of the air, and the goodly prospect : but it is that
which now (besides all other excises) they pay for here
in England, though it be free in all the world beside ;
every coach and horse which enters buying his mouth-
ful, and permission of the publican who has purchased it,
for which the entrance is guarded with porters and long
staves."

unless to see my brothers and sisters, nor seldom did I dress myself, as taking no delight to adorn myself, since he I only desired to please was absent, although report did dress me in a hundred several fashions. 'Tis true when I did dress myself I did endeavour to do it in my best becoming, both in respect to myself and those I went to visit, or chanced to meet. But after I had been in England a year and a half, part of which time I writ a book of poems,[1] and a little book called my " Philosophical Fancies," [2] to which I have writ a

---

[1] The book called " Poems and Fancies " was published in 1653, dedicated to Sir Charles Cavendish, the " World's Olio " in 1655.

[2] "Philosophical Fancies," published in 1653, was afterwards expanded into "Philosophical Opinions,"which passed through two editions, 1655 and 1663. In one of the Epistles to the Reader in the edition of 1663, the Duchess writes :—
" The ground of these my philosophical and physical opinions was printed in the year 1653, to which in the year 1655 I made an addition, but after I returned with my noble Lord into England, I have since recovered my former work, and finding it not so perfect, as I wish it had been, I have employed part of my idle time to make it more intelligible for my readers."
At the end of the same book she informs her readers, that it is her favourite work (p. 457) :—

> " Of all my works this work which I have writ,
> My best beloved and greatest favourite,
> I look upon it with a pleasing eye.
> I pleasure take in its sweet company ;

large addition, since I returned out of England, besides this book and one other. As for my book entitled "The World's Olio," I writ most part of it before I went into England, but being not of a merry, although not of a froward or peevish disposition, became very melancholy, by reason I was from my Lord, which made my mind so restless, as it did break my sleep, and distemper my health, with which growing impatient of a longer delay, I resolved to return, although I was grieved to leave Sir Charles, my Lord's brother, he being sick of an ague, of which sickness he died. For though his ague was cured, his life was decayed, he being not of a strong constitution could not, as it did prove, recover his health, for the dregs of his ague did put out the lamp of his life. Yet Heaven knows I did not think his life was so near to an end, for his doctor had great hopes of his perfect recovery, and by reason he was to go into the country for change of air, where I should have been a trouble, rather than any way serviceable, besides, more charge

---

I entertain it with a grave respect,
And with my pen am ready to protect
The life and safety of it 'gainst all those
That will oppose it, or profess it foes:
But I am sure there's none condemn it can,
Unless some foolish and unlearned man,
That hath no understanding, judgment, wit,
For to perceive the reason that's in it."

the longer I stayed, for which I made the more haste to return to my Lord, with whom I had rather be as a poor beggar, than to be mistress of the world absented from him, yet, Heaven hitherto hath kept us, and though Fortune hath been cross, yet we do submit, and are both content with what is, and cannot be mended, and are so prepared that the worst of fortunes shall not afflict our minds, so as to make us unhappy, howsoever it doth pinch our lives with poverty. For, if tranquillity lives in an honest mind, the mind lives in peace, although the body suffer. But patience hath armed us, and misery hath tried us, and finds us fortune-proof. For the truth is, my Lord is a person whose humour is neither extravagantly merry nor unnecessarily sad, his mind is above his fortune as his generosity is above his purse, his courage above danger, his justice above bribes, his friendship above self-interest, his truth too firm for falsehood, his temperance beyond temptation. His conversation is pleasing and affable, his wit is quick, and his judgment is strong, distinguishing clearly without clouds of mistakes, dissecting truth, so as it justly admits not of disputes : his discourse is always new upon the occasion, without troubling the hearers with old historical relations, nor stuffed with useless sentences. His behaviour is manly without formality, and free without constraint, and his mind hath the same freedom. His nature is

U

noble, and his disposition sweet ; his loyalty is proved by his public service for his King and country, by his often hazarding of his life, by the loss of his estate, and the banishment of his person, by his necessitated condition, and his constant and patient suffering. But, howsoever our fortunes are, we are both content, spending our time harmlessly, for my Lord pleaseth himself with the management of some few horses, and exercises himself with the use of the sword ; which two arts he hath brought by his studious thoughts, rational experience, and industrous practice, to an absolute perfection. And though he hath taken as much pains in those arts, both by study and practice, as chymists for the philosopher's-stone, yet he hath this advantage of them, that he hath found the right and the truth thereof and therein, which chymists never found in their art, and I believe never will. Also he recreates himself with his pen, writing what his wit dictates to him, but I pass my time rather with scribbling than writing, with words than wit. Not that I speak much, because I am addicted to contemplation, unless I am with my Lord, yet then I rather attentively listen to what he says, than impertinently speak. Yet when I am writing any sad feigned stories, or serious humours, or melancholy passions, I am forced many times to express them with the tongue before I can write them with the pen, by reason those thoughts that are sad, serious, and melancholy are apt to contract and to draw too much back, which oppression doth as it were overpower or smother the conception in the brain. But when some of those thoughts are sent out in words, they give the rest more liberty to place themselves in a more methodical order, marching more regularly with my pen on the ground of white paper; but my letters seem rather as a ragged rout than a well armed body, for the brain being quicker in creating than the hand in writing or the memory in retaining, many fancies are lost, by reason they ofttimes outrun the pen, where I, to keep speed in the race, write so fast as I stay not so long as to write my letters plain, insomuch as some have taken my handwriting for some strange character, and being accustomed so to do, I cannot now write very plain, when I strive to write my best; indeed, my ordinary handwriting is so bad as few can read it, so as to write it fair for the press; but however, that little wit I have, it delights me to scribble it out, and disperse it about. For I being addicted from my childhood to contemplation rather than conversation, to solitariness rather than society, to melancholy rather than mirth, to write with the pen than to work with a needle, passing my time with harmless fancies, their company being pleasing, their conversation innocent (in which I take such pleasure as I neglect my health, for it is as great a grief to leave their society as a joy to be in their company), my only trouble is, lest my brain should grow barren, or that the root of my fancies should become insipid, withering into a dull stupidity for want of maturing subjects to write on. For I being of a lazy nature, and not of an active disposition, as some are that love to journey from town to town, from place to place, from house to house, delighting in variety of company, making still one where the greatest number is ;—likewise in playing at cards, or any other games, in which I neither have practised, nor have I any skill therein :—as for dancing, although it be a graceful art, and becometh unmarried persons well, yet for those that are married, it is too light an action, disagreeing with the gravity thereof ;—and for revelling, I am of too dull a nature to make one in a merry society ;—as for feasting, it would neither agree with my humour or constitution, for my diet is for the most part sparing, as a little boiled chicken, or the like, my drink most commonly water; for though I have an indifferent good appetite, yet I do often fast, out of an opinion that [1] if I should eat much, and exercise little, which I do, only walking a slow pace in

---

[1] Supply " I should injure myself," or some phrase to that effect.

my chamber, whilst my thoughts run apace in my
brain, so that the motions of my mind hinders
the active exercises of my body; for should I
dance or run, or walk apace, I should dance my
thoughts out of measure, run my fancies out of
breath, and tread out the feet of my numbers.
But because I would not bury myself quite from
the sight of the world, I go sometimes abroad,
seldom to visit, but only in my coach about the
town, or about some of the streets, which we call
here a tour, where all the chief of the town go to
see and to be seen, likewise all strangers of what
quality soever, as all great princes or queens that
make any short stay. For this town being a passage or thoroughfare to most parts, causeth many
times persons of great quality to be here, though
not as inhabitants, yet to lodge for some short
time; and all such, as I said, take a delight, or
at least go to see the customs thereof, which
most cities of note in Europe, for all I can hear,
hath such like recreations for the effeminate sex,
although for my part I had rather sit at home
and write, or walk, as I said, in my chamber and
contemplate; but I hold necessary sometimes to
appear abroad, besides I do find, that several
objects do bring new materials for my thoughts
and fancies to build upon. Yet I must say this
in the behalf of my thoughts, that I never found
them idle; for if the senses bring no work in,

they will work of themselves, like silk-worms that spins out of their own bowels. Neither can I say I think the time tedious, when I am alone, so I be near my Lord, and know he is well.

But now I have declared to my readers my birth, breeding, and actions, to this part of my life (I mean the material parts, for should I write every particular, as my childish sports and the like, it would be ridiculous and tedious); but I have been honourably born and nobly matched; I have been bred to elevated thoughts, not to a dejected spirit, my life hath been ruled with honesty, attended by modesty, and directed by truth. But since I have writ in general thus far of my life, I think it fit I should speak something of my humour, particular practice and disposition. As for my humour, I was from my childhood given to contemplation, being more taken or delighted with thoughts than in conversation with a society, insomuch as I would walk two or three hours, and never rest, in a musing, considering, contemplating manner, reasoning with myself of everything my senses did present. But when I was in the company of my natural friends, I was very attentive of what they said or did; but for strangers I regarded not much what they said, but many times I did observe their actions, whereupon my reason as judge, and my thoughts as accusers, or excusers, or approvers and commenders, did plead, or appeal to accuse, or complain thereto. Also I never took delight in closets, or cabinets of toys, but in the variety of fine clothes, and such toys as only were to adorn my person. Likewise I had a natural stupidity towards the learning of any other language than my native tongue, for I could sooner and with more facility understand the sense, than remember the words, and for want of such memory makes me so unlearned in foreign languages as I am.[1] As for my practice, I was never very active, by reason I was given so much to contemplation; besides my brothers and sisters were for the most part serious and staid in their actions, not given to sport or play, nor dance about, whose company I keeping, made me so too. But I observed, that although their actions were staid, yet they would be very merry amongst themselves, delighting in each other's company: also they would in their discourse express the

---

[1] In the preface to her Philosophical Letters the Duchess says :—" The authors whose opinions I mention I have read, as I found them printed, in my native language, except Des Cartes, who being in Latin, I had some few places translated to me out of his works." And again, in the same place : " My error was I began to write so early, that I had not lived so long as to be able to read many authors."

general actions of the world, judging, condemning, approving, commending, as they thought good, and with those that were innocently harmless, they would make themselves merry therewith. As for my study of books it was little, yet I chose rather to read, than to employ my time in any other work, or practice, and when I read what I understood not, I would ask my brother, the Lord Lucas, he being learned, the sense or meaning thereof. But my serious study could not be much, by reason I took great delight in attiring, fine dressing, and fashions, especially such fashions as I did invent myself, not taking that pleasure in such fashions as was invented by others. Also I did dislike any should follow my fashions, for I always took delight in a singularity, even in accoutrements of habits.[1] But whatsoever I was

---

[1] This is quite borne out by the remarks of Pepys and other contemporaries, and by her portraits. For instance, Pepys on April 11, 1667, speaks of her coming to court, "her footmen in velvet coats and herself in antique dress. . . . There is as much expectation of her coming to court, so that people may see her, as if it were the Queen of Sheba." On April 26 he notes : " Met my Lady Newcastle going with her coaches and footmen all in velvet ; herself (whom I never saw before), as I have heard her often described, for all the town talk is now-a-days of her extravagances, with her velvet cap, her hair about her ears, many black patches because of pimples about her mouth, naked-necked, without anything about it, and a black just-

addicted to, either in fashion of clothes, contemplation of thoughts, actions of life, they were lawful, honest, honourable, and modest, of which I can avouch to the world with a great confidence, because it is a pure truth. As for my disposition, it is more inclining to be melancholy than merry, but not crabbed or peevishly melancholy, but soft, melting, solitary, and contemplating melancholy. And I am apt to weep rather than laugh, not that I do often either of them. Also I am tender natured, for it troubles my conscience to kill a fly, and the groans of a dying beast strike my soul. Also where I place a particular affection, I love extraordinarily and constantly, yet not fondly, but

---

au-corps. She seemed to me a very comely woman ; but I hope to see more of her on May-day." On May-day, accordingly, Pepys went with Sir William Penn to the Park. " That which we and almost all went for, was to see my Lady Newcastle ; which we could not, she being followed and crowded upon by coaches all the way she went, that nobody could come near her ; only I could see she was in a large black coach, adorned in silver instead of gold, and so white curtains, and everything else black and white, herself in her cap." See also May 8, 1667.

Evelyn on April 18, 1667, "went to make court to the Duke and Duchess of Newcastle at their house in Clerkenwell, being newly come out of the north. They received me with great kindness, and I was much pleased with the extraordinary fanciful habit, garb, and discourse of the Duchess." On April 27 he saw her again, and remarks that her dress was " very singular."

soberly and observingly, not to hang about them as a trouble, but to wait upon them as a servant ; but this affection will take no root, but where I think or find merit, and have leave both from divine and moral laws. Yet I find this passion so troublesome, as it is the only torment to my life, for fear any evil misfortune or accident, or sickness, or death, should come unto them, insomuch as I am never freely at rest. Likewise I am grateful, for I never received a courtesy,—but I am impatient and troubled until I can return it. Also I am chaste, both by nature and education, insomuch as I do abhor an unchaste thought. Likewise I am seldom angry, as my servants may witness for me, for I rather choose to suffer some inconveniences than disturb my thoughts, which makes me wink many times at their faults ; but when I am angry, I am very angry, but yet it is soon over, and I am easily pacified, if it be not such an injury as may create a hate. Neither am I apt to be exceptious or jealous, but if I have the least symptom of this passion, I declare it to those it concerns, for I never let it lie smothering in my breast to breed a malignant disease in the mind, which might break out into extravagant passions, or railing speeches, or indiscreet actions ; but I examine moderately, reason soberly, and plead gently in my own behalf, through a desire to keep those affections I had, or at least thought to have. And truly I am so vain, as to be so self-conceited, or so naturally partial, to think my friends have as much reason to love me as another, since none can love more sincerely than I, and it were an injustice to prefer a fainter affection, or to esteem the body more than the mind. Likewise I am neither spiteful, envious, nor malicious. I repine not at the gifts that Nature or Fortune bestows upon others, yet I am a great emulator; for, though I wish none worse than they are, yet it is lawful for me to wish myself the best, and to do my honest endeavour thereunto. For I think it no crime to wish myself the exactest of Nature's works, my thread of life the longest, my chain of destiny the strongest, my mind the peaceablest, my life the pleasantest, my death the easiest, and the greatest saint in heaven; also to do my endeavour, so far as honour and honesty doth allow of, to be the highest on Fortune's wheel, and to hold the wheel from turning, if I can. And if it be commendable to wish another's good, it were a sin not to wish my own; for as envy is a vice, so emulation is a virtue, but emulation is in the way to ambition, or indeed it is a noble ambition. But I fear my ambition inclines to vainglory, for I am very ambitious; yet 'tis neither for beauty, wit, titles, wealth, or power, but as they are steps to raise me to Fame's tower, which is to live by remembrance in after-ages. Likewise I am that the vulgar calls proud, not out of self-conceit, or to slight or condemn any, but scorning to do a base or mean act, and disdaining rude or unworthy persons; insomuch, that if I should find any that were rude, or too bold, I should be apt to be so passionate, as to affront them, if I can, unless discretion should get betwixt my passion and their boldness, which sometimes perchance it might, if discretion should crowd hard for place. For though I am naturally bashful, yet in such a cause my spirits would be all on fire. Otherwise I am so well bred, as to be civil to all persons, of all degrees, or qualities. Likewise I am so proud, or rather just to my Lord, as to abate nothing of the quality of his wife, for if honour be the mark of merit, and his master's royal favour, who will favour none but those that have merit to deserve, it were a baseness for me to neglect the ceremony thereof. Also in some cases I am naturally a coward, and in other cases very valiant. As for example, if any of my nearest friends were in danger I should never consider my life in striving to help them, though I were sure to do them no good, and would willingly, nay cheerfully, resign my life for their sakes : likewise I should not spare my life, if honour bids me die. But in a danger where my friends, or my honour is not concerned, or engaged, but only my life to be unprofitably lost, I am the veriest coward in nature, as upon the sea, or any dangerous places, or of thieves, or fire, or the like. Nay the shooting of a gun, although but a potgun,[1] will make me start, and stop my hearing, much less have I courage to discharge one ; or if a sword should be held against me, although but in jest, I am afraid. Also as I am not covetous, so I am not prodigal, but of the two I am inclining to be prodigal, yet I cannot say to a vain prodigality, because I imagine it is to a profitable end ; for perceiving the world is given, or apt to honour the outside more than the inside, worshipping show more than substance ; and I am so vain (if it be a vanity) as to endeavour to be worshipped, rather than not to be regarded. Yet I shall never be so prodigal as to impoverish my friends, or go beyond the limits or facility of our estate. And though I desire to appear to the best advantage, whilst I live in the view of the public world, yet I could most willingly exclude myself, so as never to see the face of any creature but my Lord as long as I live, inclosing myself like an anchorite, wearing a frieze gown, tied with a cord about my waist. But I hope my readers will not think me vain for writing my life, since there have been many that have done the like, as Cæsar, Ovid, and many more, both men and women, and I know no reason I may not do it as well as they : but I verily believe some censuring readers will scornfully say, why hath this Lady writ her own life ? since none

---

[1] Pop-gun.

cares to know whose daughter she was, or whose wife she is, or how she was bred, or what fortunes she had, or how she lived, or what humour or disposition she was of. I answer that it is true, that 'tis to no purpose to the readers, but it is to the authoress, because I write it for my own sake, not theirs. Neither did I intend this piece for to delight, but to divulge ; not to please the fancy, but to tell the truth, lest after-ages should mistake, in not knowing I was daughter to one Master Lucas of St. Johns, near Colchester, in Essex, second wife to the Lord Marquis of Newcastle ; for my Lord having had two wives, I might easily have been mistaken, especially if I should die and my Lord marry again.

APPENDIX.

APPENDIX.

---+---

I.

CORRESPONDENCE OF THE EARL OF NEWCASTLE WITH STRAFFORD.

A FEW letters between the Earl of Newcastle and Strafford have been printed by Dr. Knowler in the Strafford Papers. Dr. Knowler's notes on the Strafford Papers, now in my possession, show that the letters he has printed are merely a small portion of those which passed between the two noblemen, and were when he wrote still in existence. It is to be hoped that Earl Fitzwilliam will some time or other reconsider his objections to their publication, but as they are at present inaccessible, I am reduced to the necessity of merely reprinting two of Newcastle's letters to Strafford, from the Strafford Papers, and referring the reader to Strafford's letters to Newcastle printed in the same collection.

The letters from Strafford to Newcastle are five in number : —

July 19, 1634, vol. i. p. 274; April 9, 1635, vol. i. p. 410 ; June 1, 1638, vol. ii. 210 ; December 10, 1638, vol. ii. 246 ; February 10, 163$\frac{8}{9}$, vol. ii., 281.

Those from Newcastle to Strafford are only the two following ; the first written under his earlier title of Mansfield.

The Lord Viscount Mansfield to Sir Thomas Wentworth, Bart.

NOBLE SIR,—I think myself much bound to you for your favours to me in my absence, and your kind letter with your good counsel, which I have taken, and writ my mind at full to my Lord Duke, and, I protest to God, no more sparing the old Cavalier or his nature than I would speak of him to you, nor mincing my desires or my nature, which is not to do courtesies for injuries. Mr. Endymion Porter, Mr. Richard Oliver, with Dr. More are my agents, and all with my own letters to my Lord Duke, but to let things stand as they were, which I hope is so reasonable a suit, since I am not repaired in the Keepership, that I shall not be denied. When that is done, I beseech you, sir, give this bearer Thomas Bamford leave to wait of you, with one Robin Butler to advise but how to make a ground to bring him into the Duchy, and have a suit of it, and then I make no doubt but to have the better of him. There is no man gladder than myself of your absolute liberty, and I hope now we shall not be long without a Parliament, which God grant. And so I rest affectionately, your most faithful kinsman and humble servant,

W. MANSFIELD.

WELBECK, *Jan.* 24, 1627.

The Earl of Newcastle to the Lord Deputy.

MY MOST HONOURED LORD,—I heartily congratulate your Lordship's safe arrival in Ireland, next I am to beg your pardon for not presenting my service to you by letter all this while ; but in good faith, my Lord, the reason was, I daily heard you were going. I give your Lordship humble thanks for your noble and kind counsel; the truth is, my Lord, I have waited of the King the Scottish journey both diligently, and, as Sir Robert Swift said of my Lord of Carlisle, it was of no small charge unto me. I cannot find by the King but he seemed to be pleased with me very well, and never used me better or more graciously ; the truth is, I have hurt my estate much with the hopes of it, and I have been put in hope long, and so long as I will labour no more in it, but let nature work and expect the issue at Welbeck ; for I would be loth to be sick in mind, body, and purse, and when it is too late to repent, and my reward laughed at for my labour. It is better to give over in time with some loss than lose all, and mend what is to come, seeing what is past is not in my power to help. Besides, my Lord, if I obtained what I desire, it would be a more painful life, and since I am so much plunged in debt, it would help very well to undo me ; for I know not how to get, neither know I any reason why the King should give me anything. Children come on apace, my Lord, and with this weight of debt that lies upon me, I know no diet better than a strict diet in the country, which, in time, may recover me of the prodigal disease. By your favour, my Lord, I cannot say I have recovered myself at Welbeck this summer, but run much more in debt than ever I did, but I hope hereafter I may. The truth is, my Lord, for my court business, your Lordship with your noble friends and mine have spoken so often to the King, and myself refreshed his memory in that particular, so that I mean not to move my friends any more to their so great trouble ; but what-soever pleases his Majesty, be fully contented, and look after some other little contentments within myself, which shall well serve me during my life, and if the King command me, I am at all times ready to serve him ; if no commands, pray for him heartily. For, by my troth, my Lord, I know no man in the whole world more bound unto his Majesty than myself. For that point to try your Lordship's friends in my behalf, I humbly thank you for the motion, and I desire your Lordship to follow it. For the King's particular liking of my proper person, I think my Lord of Carlisle would do best, or what doth your Lordship think to his Lady, for further I would not willingly have it go ; but I assure your Lord-ship I am most confident of the King's good opinion of me : and about my Lord Savile's business and mine, his Majesty pleased me extremely, being never moved by me or any friend in my behalf that I desired. My Lord Treasurer used me extreme well and ex-traordinary kindly ; my Lord of Carlisle for your Lordship's sake, but the greatest news is my Lord of Holland courted me extremely ;

and so to conclude with this business, I intend to be quiet, and not press the King at all, but to leave his Majesty to his own time, and rest quietly here in the country; and this I assure your Lordship is my resolution and my full intention, and except it be to the purpose, their greatest friendship is to let me rest here. I humbly thank your Lordship for your noble favours to my old servant; for my groom, my Lord, I beseech you keep him, and I am sorry your Lordship will use such ceremony with me. For La Roche, I always told your Lordship my opinion of him, and, in good faith, he is no such horseman, neither for anything I ever saw, but got a great reputation with doing little: I would your Lordship had taken Porter, but I know not how he is disposed of. I assure your Lordship that horse you pleased to accept, I thought him the fittest horse in the world for that purpose, but your Lordship doth not write how you approve of him. My Lord, in a word, I desire no man's favour and love more than yours, or would be beholding to any man sooner; for, I protest to God I honour and love you heartily, and I vow without any end or particular in the whole world; your Lordship's favours to me are merely your own goodness, for I shall never be useful to you in any kind, which makes my obligation such that I must ever be faithfully,—Your Lordship's most humble servant,

W. NEWCASTLE.

WELBECK, *the 5th of August* 1633.

II.

NEWCASTLE AS GOVERNOR OF PRINCE CHARLES.

Mr. Secretary Windebank to the Earl of Newcastle.

MY LORD,—His Majesty having a purpose, according to the precedents of former times, to settle the government both of the person and family of the Prince in a way answerable to his state and years, and having deliberately advised upon some person of honour and trust to be near his Highness, and to be a chief director in so weighty a business, hath been pleased, in his gracious opinion of your Lordship, to make choice of you to be the only gentleman of his Bedchamber at this time, and hath commanded me to give you knowledge of this his princely resolution. And withal his Majesty's pleasure is, that you prepare yourself to come to the Court in diligence, and to attend his Majesty before the Sunday fortnight after Easter, which will be the eighth day of April. And lastly his Majesty hath expressly commanded me to let your Lordship know, that you have no particular obligation to any whatsoever in this business, but merely and entirely to the King's and Queen's Majesties alone ; who of their own mere and special grace and goodness have made this choice, and vouchsafed you this honour ; the countenance and increase whereof, and of much happiness with it, I wish to your Lordship, and so rest,— Your Lordship's humble and faithful servant,

FRAN. WINDEBANK.

At the COURT at WHITEHALL,
   19th of March, 1637.

The Earl of Newcastle to Mr. Secretary Windebank.

NOBLE SIR,—I beseech you to present me in the most humble manner in the world to his sacred Majesty, and to let his Majesty know I shall as cheerfully as diligently obey his Majesty's commands. Truly, the infinite favour, honour and trust his Majesty is pleased to heap on me in this princely employment, is beyond anything I can express. It was beyond a hope of the most partial thoughts I had about me : neither is there anything in me left, but a thankful heart filled with diligence, and obedience to his sacred Majesty's will.

It is not the least favour of the King and Queen's Majesties to let me know my obligation : and I pray, sir, humbly inform their Majesties it is my greatest blessing that I owe myself to none but their sacred Majesties. God ever preserve them and theirs, and make me worthy of their Majesties' favours !

I have had but seldom the honour to receive letters from you; but such as these you cannot write often. But truly I am very proud I received such happy news by your hand, which shall ever oblige me to be inviolably,—Sir, your most faithful and obliged servant, W. NEWCASTLE.

WELBECK, *the 21st of March*, 1637.

(Clarendon State Papers, vol. ii. p. 7.)

With these letters should be read that of Strafford to the Earl of Newcastle, dated June 1, 1638, in which he gives him advice concerning the line of conduct to be followed in the Court (Strafford Letters, ii. 174).

The Earl of Newcastle's letter of instructions to Prince Charles for his studies, conduct, and behaviour.

[From a copy preserved with the Royal Letters in the Harleian MS., 6988, Art. 62. Printed by Ellis, Original Letters, ser. i. vol. iii. p. 288.]

MAY IT PLEASE YOUR HIGHNESS,—Since it pleased your most gracious father, his sacred Majesty, to think me worthy to be your Governor, I will justify his Majesty's choice; for, what I may want in abilities I will make up with fidelity and duty to his Majesty, in diligence and service to you. Then for your education, sir, it is fit you should have some languages, though I confess I would rather have you study things than words, matter than language; for seldom a critic in many languages hath time to study sense, for words; and at best, he is, or can be, but a living dictionary. Besides, I would not have you too studious, for too much contemplation spoils action, and virtue consists in that. What you read, I would have it history, and the best chosen histories, that so you might compare the dead with the living; for the same humours is now as was then; there is no alteration but in names, and though you meet not with a Cæsar for Emperor of the whole world, yet he may have the same passions in him; and you are not to compare fortunes so much as humours, wit, and judgment ; and thus you shall see the excellency and errors both of Kings and subjects; and though you are young in years, yet living by your wading in all those times, be older in wisdom and judgment than Nature can afford any man to be without this help.

For the arts, I would have you know them so far as they are of use, and especially those that are most proper for war and use ; but whensoever you are too studious your contemplation will spoil your government, for you cannot be a good contemplative man and a good commonwealth's man; therefore, take heed of too much book.

Beware of too much devotion for a King, for one may be a good man, but a bad King ; and how many will history represent to you that in seeming to gain the kingdom of heaven have lost their own ; and the old saying is, that short prayers pierce the heaven's gates; but if you be not religious (and not only seem so, but be so), God will not prosper you ; and if you have no reverence to Him, why should your subjects have any to you. At the best, you are accounted, for your greatest honour, His servant, His deputy, His anointed, and you owe as much reverence and duty to Him as we owe to you ; and why, nay justly, may not He punish you for want of reverence and service to Him, if you fail in it, as well as you to punish us : but this subject I leave to the right reverend Father in God, Lord Bishop of Chichester, your worthy tutor : your tutor, sir, wherein you are most happy, since he hath no pedantry in him ; his learning he makes right use of, neither to trouble himself with it or his friends ; reads men as well as books ; and goes the next way to everything that he should, and that is what he would, for his will is governed by that law : the purity of his wit doth not spoil the serenity of his judgment ; travelled, which you shall perceive by his wisdom and fashion more than by his relations ; and in a word strives as much discreetly to hide the scholar in him, as other men's follies to show it ; and is a right gentleman, such a one as man should be.

But, sir, to fall back again to your reverence at prayers, so far as concerns reason and your advantage is my duty to tell you ; then I say, sir, were there no heaven or hell, you shall see the disadvantage for your government ; if you have no reverence at prayers, what will the people have, think you ? They go according to the example of the Prince ; if they have none, then they have no obedience to God ; there they will easily have none to your Highness ; no obedience, no subjects ; no subjects—then your power is off that side, and whether it be in one or more then that's King, and thus they will turn tables with you. Of the other side, if any be Bible mad, over much burned with fiery zeal, they may think it a service to God to destroy you and say the Spirit moved them and bring some example of a king with a hard name in the Old Testament. Thus one way you may have a civil war, the other a private treason ; and he that cares not for his own life is master of another man's.

For books thus much more : the greatest clerks are not the wisest men ; and the great troublers of the world, the greatest captains, were not the greatest scholars ; neither have I known bookworms great statesmen ; some have heretofore and some are now, but they study men more now than books, or else they would prove but silly statesmen. For a mere scholar, there is nothing so simple for this world. The reason is plain, for divinity teaches what we should be, not what we are ; so doth moral philosophy ; and many philosophical worlds' and Utopia's scholars have made and fancied to themselves such worlds as never was, is, or shall be ; and then I dare say if they govern themselves by those rules what men should be, or not what they are, they will miss the cushion very much.

But, sir, you are in your own disposition religious and not very apt to your book, so you need no great labour to persuade you from the one, or long discourses to dissuade from the other.

The things that I have discoursed to you most is to be courteous and civil to everybody ; set to, make difference of cabinges,[1] and, believe it, the putting off of your hat, and making a leg pleases more than reward or preservation, so much doth it take all kind of people. Then to speak well of everybody, and when you hear people speak ill of others reprehend them and seem to dislike it so much, as do not look of them so favourably for a few days after, and say something in favour of those that have been spoke against ;

---

[1] So in the MS.—Ellis.

for you may say something of everybody to the best; the other which is railing, scorn, and jeering, is fitter for porters, watermen, and carmen, than for gentlemen; how much more then for a Prince, whose dislike is death, and kills any subject. Besides, you may be sure the parties will hear of it, and though they dare do nothing because they want power, nor say nothing for fear of being troubled, yet believe it, sir, they are traitors in their hearts to you, and of your own making, and so are all their friends. Of the other side, to speak well of them will be told too, and that wins them as much; the other loses them; and this way you will get their hearts, and then you have all they have, and more you cannot have. And how easy a way is this to have the people. To lose your dignity and set by your state, I do not advise you to that, but the contrary: for what preserves you Kings more than ceremony. The cloth of estates, the distance people are with you, great officers, heralds, drums, trumpeters, rich coaches, rich furniture for horses, guards, marshal's men making room, disorders to be laboured by their staff of office, and cry "now the King comes;" I know these maskers[1] the people sufficiently; aye, even the wisest though he knew it and not accustomed to it, shall shake off his wisdom and shake for fear of it, for this is the mist is cast before us, and maskers the Commonwealth. Besides authority doth what it list, I mean power that's the stronger, though sometimes it shifts sides, therefore the King must know at what time to play the King, and when to qualify it, but never put it off; for in all triumphs whatsoever or public showing yourself, you cannot put upon you too much king; yet even there sometimes a hat or 'smile in the right place will advantage you, but at other times you may do more, and civil speeches to people and short doth much win of them: and certainly, sir, civility cannot unprince, you, but much] advantage you. To women you cannot be too civil, especially to great ones: what hurt were it to send them a dish from your table when they dine with some of your great lords, and to drink their health? Certainly, sir, you cannot lose by courtesy. I mean not you should be so familiar as to bring you to contempt, for I mean you should

---

[1] Here and four lines lower down I should suggest "masters" instead of "maskers."

keep yourself up Prince still, and in all your actions, but I would not have you so seared with majesty as to think you are not of mankind, nor suffer others or yourself to flatter you so much. The incommodities to life and the sustaining of it, and the same things the meanest do, you must do the like or not live ; these things when you are pleased to think of them will persuade you that are of the lump of man, and mortal, and the more you repeat these thoughts the better Prince you will be, both to serve God and for distributive justice to your people ; for being a Prince you ought rather to give Almighty God thanks for the advantage-ground you have of other people, than to be proud. I mean not by repeating your mortality to have a death's head set always before you, or to cry every morning that you are mortal, for I would not have you fall into a divine melancholy, to be an anchorite or a capuchin, or with a philosophical discourse to be a Diogenes in your tub; but to temper yourself so by this means, as to be a brave, noble, and just King, and make your name immortal by your brave acts abroad and your unspotted justice at home, qualified by your well temper and mercy."

In the Patent creating Newcastle a Duke, quoted in the Life, p. 180, King Charles II. says : " The great proofs of his wisdom and piety are sufficiently known to us from our younger years, and we shall always retain a sense of those good principles he instilled into us."

III.

NEWCASTLE'S MISSION TO HULL IN JANUARY 1642.

The following are the two letters mentioned in the note on p. 17 :—

MAY IT PLEASE YOUR MOST SACRED MAJESTY,—I am here at Hull according to your Majesty's commands, but the town will not admit of me by no means, so I am very flat and out of countenance here, but will stay until I know your Majesty's further pleasure,

which I hope I shall soon do. God preserve your Majesty,—Your
Majesty's most faithful creature, W. NEWCASTLE.

HULL, *the 15th of January* 1642.

SIR,—My first address, in these parts, was to Sir Thomas
Metham with his Majesty's directions, but I found him altogether
incapable of any power to secure the Magazine or town of Hull, as
being neither Deputy-Lieutenant or Colonel of the Trained-bands.
When that hope was taken from me I conceived the best means
I had was to prevail with the burgesses of the town, by themselves,
to secure the place for his Majesty's service, and that work is very
well brought to pass, for last night here arrived an express from Sir
John Hotham, with an order from the Parliament for him to be
Governor, and a power to draw in such forces as he thought fit,
likewise a letter from him to the Magistrates for preparing lodging
and billet for his regiments : his admission was quite denied, and
a letter to the Parliament despatched with the hands of the chief
burgesses to excuse themselves from receiving any garrison, they of
the town being able to secure the place for his Majesty's service.
This afternoon arrived here the Earl of Newcastle with his
Majesty's commission for the Government, to which I shall (for my
own part) be ever obedient, but I perceive not the townsmen be
willing to receive him unto their command, but insist upon their
own affections and readiness to serve his Majesty with all faithfulness. Now the means of present strength from Sir Thomas
Metham or any near hand, being taken away, there is no mean
for us but to assure the people of this town to his Majesty by hold-
ing off any other from the power of the place, and if ever his
Majesty appear in person all will be absolutely at his disposing.
When I received his Majesty's command, he told me his directions
should be derived by (me from) you, and therefore I humbly
beseech you to give him this account of me ; and I shall to my
utmost power labour nothing but his Majesty's service ; and shall
ever be ready (as obliged) to express myself,—Your Honour's most
humble and obedient servant, WILL. LEGGE.

HULL, 14th Jan. 1642.

(Endorsed as received on Jan. 18.)

On January 21, 1642, Nicholas writes to Roe that the Earl of Newcastle is Governor of Kingston upon Hull, where the townsmen have manifested great affections to the King, and excused their not receiving Sir John Hotham, commanded to that charge by the Parliament. S. P. Dom. vol. 488, No. 80. The following are the entries in the Journals of the House of Lords referred to in the note on p. 18 :—

The Earl was ordered, on January 20, to attend the House of Lords at once. The Earl was absent at a call of the House on February 9.

On February 14 it was moved, "That the Earl of Newcastle, being sent for to come and give his attendance on this House, hath daily attended this House, and now desires that he might have leave to go into the country for his health sake." Hereupon the House ordered, " That the Earl of Newcastle shall deliver in his commission, granted to him under the King's manual, by which he was to have raised forces to go into the town of Hull, and to be Governor ; and that his Lordship be ready to attend this House when he shall have notice upon any occasion " (L. J., February 14, 1642).

The commission was delivered by the Earl on the afternoon of the same day. It is given in full in the Journals (p. 585).

The Earl was then excused attendance, and granted leave to go into the country.

IV.

A NEW DISCOVERY OF HIDDEN SECRETS

In several letters, propositions, articles, and other writings concerning the Earl of Newcastle, Captain John Hotham, and many other malignant gentry of the northern counties. All lately found in Pomfret Castle ; the original whereof remain now in York, where they may be seen of any who desire it. With a declaration of the committee of Yorkshire and some observations there-upon to undeceive their deluded and oppressed country-men.

LONDON, 1645.

(Dated November 3d, by Thomason, E. 267 (2). British Museum, King's Pamphlets.)

The Declaration is omitted.

It states that "the letters are being examined by some of the committee appointed for that purpose, and the originals remain in safe hands to be seen by any man that shall desire it."

MY LORD,—It is the desire of us, and the most of the gentry of this country to crave assistance from your Lordship in this time of Mr. Hotham's infesting the country ; which favour we shall always acknowledge from your Lordship, and we are the bolder in this business, because we know it to be a great service to his Majesty, by the preservation of this country, and will be much to your honour, to preserve in peace and safety, my Lord,—Your Lordship's most humble servants,

SAVILE.	WILLIAM SAVILE.
HENRY SLINGSBY.	JOHN KEY.
FERDINAND LEIGH.	FRANCIS NEVILE.
JOHN GOODRICKE.	WILLIAM INGRAM.
GEORGE WENTWORTH.	THO. GOWER, Vi. Co.
PETER MIDDLETON.	JOHN RAMSDEN.
JOHN MALLORY.	THO. INGRAM.
RICHARD HUTTON.	ROBERT ROCKELEY.

YORK, *September* 26, 1642.

NOBLE GENTLEMEN,—I have received from you a letter of invitation by the hands of Sir Mar. Langdale, and Mr. Aldburgh, and shall (for the esteem and affection I bear in general to the country, being my native country, and in particular to many of you whom I have the honour to be known) be ready to contribute my best aid and assistance in that work, since it is likely to conduce to his Majesty's service, and peace and quiet of all his good subjects, and to conclude this agreement, I have sent you inclosed certain propositions which by way of articles should be drawn and signed and sealed by you, and as many more as you shall engage in that work, which I shall expect from you before I march. And so pre-senting my service to you all,—I remain your most faithful servant,

W. N.

NEWCASTLE, *September* 30, 1642.

To the Right Honourable, and my noble friends the nobility and gentry now assembled at York for his Majesty's present service. Propositions in answer to your letter of invitation :—

First, that I have all your consents and promises that the army be paid whilst they are in that county.

That an assessment be laid upon the country to enable you for that undertaking, and that if money be not gotten in time, that I may have free billet for the soldiers, for which billet you are to engage yourself to the quarters, and that the officers be paid according to his Majesty's present establishment, out of that assessment.

That there be some of the gentry of that county appointed as a committee, enabled by the rest of the gentry to agree and conclude of such further propositions as may happen to be necessary for this service, and not here mentioned, and to march along with the army, whose counsel and assistance from time to time I am resolved to use.

That I have assurance that all manner of provisions fit for an army be prepared and brought to the army the first day it enters.

That since this army was levied a purpose to guard her Majesty's person, that it shall not be held a breach of any engagement betwixt us if I retire with such numbers as I shall think fit for that service.

W. N.

MY LORD,—We have received from your Lordship an answer to
our letter of invitation, noble as yourself, which we hope shall
make you the master of such a work of honour, as besides your
great service it will be to his Majesty, shall both enable yourself
farther and oblige us. We have signed and sent unto your Lordship, articles proportionable to your Lordship's desire, as we conceive, besides a particular power to those gentlemen now with you
more fully to declare ourselves. My Lord, believe this, that we
suffer here no distresses, but for our loyalty to the King, and your
Lordship's favour to us will equally oblige both : therefore, good
my Lord, make all possible speed to march hither, or to send some
force before, lest a little delay make all our endeavours fruitless ;
and in the general believe there is nothing in the power of us, or of
this country, which shall not faithfully serve you ; and more you
cannot expect from, my Lord, your most faithful and humble
servants,

H. CUMBERLAND.	GEORGE WENTWORTH.
SAVILE.	CONYERS DARCY.
THOMAS GOWER, Vi. Co.	ROBERT STRICKLAND.
WILLIAM SAVILE.	WILLIAM WENTWORTH.
HENRY GRIFFITH.	INGRAM HOPTON.
HENRY SLINGSBY.	JOHN GOODRICKE.
EDWARD STANHOPE.	WILLIAM WENTWORTH.
JOHN KEY.	JOHN BATTY.
JOHN MALLORY.	RICHARD HUTTON.
FERDINANDO LEIGH.	FRANCIS MONCKTON.
WILLIAM INGLEBY.	ROBERT ROCKLEY.
JOHN RAMSDEN.	W. THORNTON.

The answer of the nobility and gentry of Yorkshire assembled at York for his Majesty's service, to the propositions sent unto them by the Right Honourable the Earl
of Newcastle.

1. That your Lordship shall have our consents and promises, the
army which your Lordship shall bring with you into this country
for the defence thereof shall be paid by this country.

2. There is an assessment of £8000 already laid upon this country, which shall be levied as soon as by your Lordship's assistance we are enabled to do it, and that till money be gotten in, your soldiers shall have free billet, for which we will engage ourselves to the quarters ; and for the payment of your officers for the army, it is referred to the committee for this county who have instructions and power to treat and conclude with your Lordship in that particular.

3. There shall be a committee of some of the gentry of the county appointed and enabled by the rest to agree, and conclude of such further propositions as may happen to be necessary for this service, not here mentioned, and to march along with your Lordship's army, whose counsel and assistance we desire your Lordship may use, the names of which committee we send your Lordship herewithal, who are appointed to attend you at Newcastle, and to march along with your army when you enter into the county.

4. That as soon as we have notice of your Lordship's march, we will use all possible means to bring to your army all such provisions as this country can afford.

5. We are tender of the safety of her Majesty's person, that we shall not only consent to your Lordship's performance of that service but will also contribute our utmost endeavours to assist your Lordship therein.

6. Lastly, we have appointed our committee to be, Sir Edward Osborne, Baronet, Sir Marmaduke Langdale, Knight, Francis Tindall and Richard Aldburgh, Esquires, and given them instructions and power to treat with your Lordship, and to conclude in such particulars as may further conduce to this service, or in these propositions admit a doubtful interpretation.

H. CUMBERLAND,

(and the rest signing before with the addition of Walter Hawkesworth).

MY LORDS AND GENTLEMEN,—I am to give you many thanks for your favourable letter by Mr. Aldburgh, and the signing so far my desired articles, which had no other end than the better to enable me to serve you. And I beseech you to give me leave as I intend faithfully to serve you, so to deal clearly and freely with you, which I hold a duty; the truth is, I am very sorry you pleased to leave out the article for the officers' pay, or coldly referred it to your committee, being the principal thing in all the articles, for you know the soldier is encouraged with nothing but money, or hopes of it, and truly last night when I was going to bed, there came colonels and lieutenant-colonels, and said they heard you had left it out, and for their parts that they must think that if you were so cautious not to grant it in paper before we came in, they doubted very much of it in money when they were there, and that the workman was worthy of his hire, and such like discontented words; so the truth is, rather than not come cheerfully to serve you, I will not come at all, for I see beforehand I shall either disband with a mutiny, or fall of plundering without distinction, either of which would be destructive to me: and besides, I hold myself free, since my articles are not signed, for I never understood any of those articles to be referred to the committee, but such things as we could not remember, and the present occasion offered. Could I pay them or his Majesty, you should not have had such an article, but since that cannot be, you will pardon me in telling you how I am capable to serve you, and how not, and so I rest in a huge disposition to be really your most faithful servant,   W. N.

NEWCASTLE, *October* 30, 1642.

V.

MISCELLANEOUS LETTERS RELATING TO THE CIVIL WAR IN YORKSHIRE.

THE first of these letters was captured when Guilford Slingsby, to whom it was addressed, was defeated by Sir Hugh Cholmley at Guisborough on January 16, 1643. (Rushworth, III. ii. 125.) Slingsby was severely wounded, and died a few days afterwards. (Rushworth, Strafford's Trial, 773.) The letter was sent up to Parliament, and is now amongst the papers of the House of Lords, together with the instructions given to Slingsby which accompany it.

SIR,—I have received your letters this day, and return you thanks for the very good service you have done, and should be very glad to give you all the assistance you desire, and more, to prosecute your present levies, but I was informed that you had of your own levies 400 foot besides your troop of horse. And as the case stands I cannot furnish you with any more forces for the present. For these reasons, first, the forces of the Bishoprick were levied upon condition to remain in the country for the security thereof; and besides, they are appointed to guard the ammunition through their country, and if need be further; which I hope they will obey, for I hear Colonel Huddleston nor Colonel Clavering can either of them march for that convoy as was intended, and therefore I have appointed Sir Robert Strickland and his forces to wait upon that service, and I desire you will do so too, for I hear they have a design to surprise it if they can, and it deserves our best cares to secure it. When that service is done, I shall be ready to give you all the assistance I can. For the lady you mention use your own discretion towards her, for I have not been ever used to take ladies prisoners. For any goods or arms you shall take of disaffected persons or in their possession, keep them to your own use, the goods upon account for paying your soldiers (for we can get no money here to supply you) and the arms for arming your men, and though they be part of the Trained-band arms, yet being taken by you as a prize, they shall be accounted so. For your fortifying those castles you mention, I do not understand of what consequence it can be to you, except it be some one for your retreat and place of residence whilst you are levying your regiment. For the 500 arms you desire a warrant for, it will be very inconvenient to serve it upon their way, and therefore for it you must have a little patience. For the paying of your troop you propose one of three ways, but to resolve of which of them is to no end unless there was money to pay, but in that you shall have all the right that may best be, in time. Till then, as I told you before, you may make use of such moneys and goods you take of delinquents, or so much thereof as will serve you, for I perceive you meet with good store. And thus much for answer to your letters from,—Your very affectionate friend, W. NEWCASTLE.

POMFRET, *8th Jan.* 1642.

(Papers of the House of Lords.)

Instructions taken with Colonel Slingsby.

The county (York) to be universally disarmed of all private arms, both of horse and foot, and those not borne in service to be brought into a magazine at York. The trained bands that rose with Hotham to be compelled to rise again, and serve in their persons, or every man to send an able-bodied man to serve for him. Considering her Majesty intends to commit her person into the protection of this county, a magazine is to be made at York to enable an army to subsist there in case of extremity or necessary retreat. All the gentry of Yorkshire to be unanimously moved to resort thither with their families and movables, as the contrary faction do daily to Hull, by which means the persons and estates of such as are not well affected will be secured, as such as refuse or decline it shall discover themselves, and every man's fortune and family being there engaged they will more actually move with a joint concurrence for the preservation of the place, which must be the retreat for the safety of the Queen's person, no other place being defensible and considerable to balance Hull. Those that decline this proposition are to understand that they must at their own peril undergo the plunder of the soldiers, if any fall out. The garrison in York shall be daily employed in making regular works upon the avenue and outworks, and encroachments upon the hills and other places commanding the town. No markets or fairs to be held in any place in the county except York. Some of the iron ordnance, sent over by the Queen, to be sent for at the charge of the county to place upon the avenues and fortifications.

(From Report V. of the Historical MSS. Commission, p. 69. For " encroachments " in l. 21 we should most likely substitute "intrenchments.")

Summons to Hull.

When the news of the arrest of Sir John Hotham reached the Earl of Newcastle he wrote from Bowling Hall, near Bradford, where he was staying, after the capture of that town, the following letter to the Mayor of Hull :—

Sir,—I hear there is some alteration in the government of the garrison of Hull, and because I have some prisoners there which I may have occasion to treat for, I desire to know in what condition it now stands, and whether I am to treat with his Majesty's loyal and faithful subjects or such as are in opposition to him, or neutrals, to that end that I may accordingly apply myself. So expecting your answer, I remain, your very affectionate friend to serve you,

W. Newcastle.

Bowling Hall, 4th July 1643.

To my very worthy friend, the Mayor
    of the town of Hull.

The Mayor answered :—

Right Honourable,—It is true there is some alteration here of governor, not government ; though the power of exchanging persons is not such as we assume for the present, nor know we any neutral or opposite here to his Majesty, all being, for aught we understand, as dutiful as ever, and as constant, and resolute to keep what we have hitherto defended for King and Parliament (God assisting), in confidence whereof we rest your Lordship's humbly devoted servants.

Kingston-upon-Hull,
    the 5th July 1643.

(Tanner MSS., lxii. 144, 151.)

There is in the same collection a commission to Colonel Thomas Haggerston to be colonel of a regiment of 500 harquebusiers, April 14, 1643 (lxii. 51); and a warrant to arrest certain delinquents in Durham, dated 25th April 1643 (lxii. 80).

A Declaration and Summons sent by the Earl of New-castle to the town of Manchester to lay down their arms, &c.

I presume you are not ignorant of the success it hath pleased Almighty God to give unto his Majesty's army under my command, and the great desire I have to avoid the effusion of Christian blood, which moves me before I proceed any further towards you, to make you an offer of his Majesty's grace and mercy. If you will submit yourselves, lay down your arms, so unjustly taken up in contempt of the laws of this kingdom, and immediately return to your due allegiance, his Majesty is graciously pleased to authorise me to receive you into his favour and protection, which I am as willing to do as to enforce your obedience. If you will refuse, I cannot but wonder, while you fight against the King and his authority, you should so boldly offer to profess yourselves for King and Parliament, and most ignominiously scandalise this army with the title of Papists, when we venture our lives and fortunes for the true Protestant religion established in this kingdom. Be no longer deceived, for the blood that shall be shed in this quarrel will assuredly fall on your own heads. I have no other ends in this but to let you see your error, if you please; for my condition is such that I need not court you; if not, let me receive your answers by this messenger, and you may expect to find little favour (if you force my nature), but such as is due to high contemners of his Majesty's grace and favour now offered to you by   W. NEWCASTLE.

BRADFORD, *5th July* 1643.

Appended to this letter is the answer of Manchester, dated Rochdale, 7th July 1643. It ends :—

SIR,—We are nothing dismayed at your force, but hope that God, who hath been our Protector hitherto, will so direct our just army that we shall be able to return the violence intended into their bosoms that shall assay the prosecution of it, which shall be the endeavour of his Majesty's most humble and obedient subjects.

In " Certain Informations for Thursday, July 13," we are told that the Lancashire men " have placed a garrison of 1200 men in Rochdale, and 500 more upon Blackstone Edge, to guard the passage into their country out of Yorkshire, and that they have sent away Colonel Goring and their other prisoners, but whither it was not known, yet is supposed to be Liverpool, to be conveyed thence by sea to London ; but it is now said they are brought to Nottingham."

Letter to Lord Loftus, July 6, 1643.

To Edward, Viscount Loftus of Ely, or the Commander-in-Chief at Middleham Castle.

You cannot be ignorant of the good success it hath pleased Almighty God to give unto the army under my command. And that you may see the desire I have to avoid the effusion of more blood before I proceed any further, I have thought it my duty to God and the King to signify unto you that if you shall upon sight hereof submit yourselves, lay down your arms most unjustly taken up against your dread Sovereign, and immediately return to your due allegiance, his Majesty is graciously pleased to authorise me to receive you into his mercy and favour, which I shall as willingly do as to bring you to obedience by force if you shall refuse. And I cannot but wonder, whilst you fight against the King and his authority, you should so boldly presume to profess yourself for the King and Parliament. Be no longer deceived, for that blood that shall be shed in this quarrel will fall upon your own head. I have no other ends in this treaty but to let you see your error, if you please ; if not, let me receive your answer, and that without delay. And if you resolve to persist in your obstinacy, then I do hereby advise you to remove out of the castle all women and children, unto whom and all others well affected I do promise safe and free passage without any interruption. And then you may expect no other than what is due to so high a contemner of his Majesty's grace and favour offered. Given under my hand the sixth day of July 1643.   ·   W. NEWCASTLE.

(Ninth Report of the Historical MSS. Commission, Part II.,
p. 317. From the Marquis of Drogheda's Papers.)

VI.

A TRUE RELATION OF THE PASSAGES OF THE ARMY UNDER THE COMMAND OF HIS EXCELLENCY THE MARQUESS OF NEWCASTLE, SINCE HIS COMING INTO DERBYSHIRE.

(Printed at York by Stephen Bulkley, 1643.)

Sir Thomas Fairfax and his forces being at Chesterfield, a part of our horse marched near unto them and beat in their scouts, and a troop of their horse, and showed themselves upon a hill within the view of the town a little before sunset, where they remained till it grew dark; then the soldiers set the whins and gorse on fire upon that hill, which gave them such an alarm in the town, that Sir Thomas Fairfax presently called to horse, and about twelve o'clock in the night they quit both that town and a garrison they had in Sir Henry Humlock's house, and in great disorder away they fled to Nottingham without any stay, having lost many of their men, most of which are now our prisoners. About Broxtowe their men so straggled, that two parties met with one another in a lane, and conceiving they had met a party of ours, gave fire upon one another, and killed a lieutenant of their own. They passed to Nottingham extremely tired and wearied, and there remained three or four days; from thence they went to Melton-Mowbray in Leicestershire, and stayed but a while there, not liking to remain long in one place. But we had no sooner possessed Chesterfield, before the rebels possessed themselves of a strong house at Alfreton and the church there, against which we sent two hundred musquetiers, who fell upon the church and took it by assault (without any loss on our part), and about twenty men in it, together with their arms; whereupon the house and arms were surrendered with this condition, that they might march away to their own houses, making first protestation never again to bear arms against his Majesty.

About that time Colonel Dudley, Major-General of the Dragoons, was sent with a commanding party of horse and foot, into the Peak Country, where at the first, about Ashford, he encountered with at least five hundred foot and three troops of horse, which he charged home, and presently routed them; some of them he killed, and took about twenty prisoners, but being late and growing dark the rest escaped, and in great disorder ran away to save themselves.

About the same time Commissary Windham going out with a party of horse and dragoons into Craven, was there encountered by some rebels, which he presently forced into a house (belonging to Sir William Savile) called Aireton Hall, where though he had some few men hurt, and himself shot through the shoulder (not without good hopes of recovery), yet continuing their assault, they took the house and sixty men in it (together with all their arms), whom now they have prisoners at the Earl of Cumberland's castle in Skipton.

Not long after this, about the twenty-seventh day of November, the Governor of Newark having intelligence from Belvoir that the committee of Leicester was at Melton raising money, with a guard of two or three troops of horse, and some dragoons (which town is sixteen miles distant from Newark), he drew forth about four troops of horse from thence, and having one from Belvoir to join with them, they marched away all night, and coming to Melton about break of day, they presently fell into the town, and without the loss of one man they took the committee (one Haslerig, Stanley, and Hatcher), three troops of horse (every troop consisting of seventy), two troops of dragoons, and one company of foot, with all their commanders both horse and foot (except one Cornet), which are now prisoners at Belvoir Castle.

There comes news again from Colonel Dudley, who in the morning about three of the clock on the seven and twentieth day of this instant November marched out with all the horse and foot he had (excepting four companies of foot and two troops of horse, which he left to secure and attend the Commissioners of Array then sitting at Bakewell), and went towards the enemy's quarters about Hartington towards Staffordshire, with an intention to beat up those quarters ; but not coming so soon as to perform that intention, the rebels drew out a body of two thousand horse and foot (such as they were), and with a hideous noise, proclaimed the expectation they had of a sudden victory. But it pleased God otherwise to dispose of them; for Colonel Dudley (leaving only a good reserve of foot and one troop of horse) charged the rebels with all the rest of his horse and foot in a full body at once, which was so home, that with his horse he beat quite through their rear of foot into the midst of their horse, and forced them to a disorderly retreat ; and not willing to give them time to recollect, he pursued and slew above one hundred of them upon the place, following the chase into Staffordshire near five miles together (almost to Leek), and doing sharp execution all the way. Then he drew up his horse in order, and made a stand, and sent back a messenger to know the success of the foot, who had by that time routed all the rebels' foot, only three hundred or thereabouts retreated into the church which they had prepared with strong baragadoes, but before this messenger came thither, the foot had forced one of the church doors, and taken and slain every man of them. They took ten officers, three colours of foot, and one of horse, and among others the brother of Colonel Ashenhurst.

About this time, upon the left hand, a body of three hundred horse appeared from Derby to join with the rebels, but they found that they came too late, and our horse, marching towards them, they fled away into Staffordshire.

And Colonel Dudley having then secured the prisoners, and given the soldiers the pillage of the field, marched again that night to Bakewell to his quarters there. In this whole action he knows not any one man slain on our part, and but five hurt, whereof not one officer but Lieutenant-Colonel Preston, and he not dangerously.

Upon the nine-and-twentieth day of November, so soon as the rebels who possessed Chatsworth House (the principal seat of the Earl of Devonshire), then under the command of Captain Stafford, heard of this news, though the place was very strong, and three hundred well provided to defend it, yet not adventuring either an assault or a summons, they quit their hold and are fled away.

VII.

THE CAMPAIGN OF THE MARQUIS OF NEW-CASTLE AGAINST THE SCOTS IN FEBRUARY, MARCH, AND APRIL 1644.

The best account of this campaign is that given by Rushworth, III. ii. 612–16; it is a summary of the different news-

letters published at the time, and seems to be derived
entirely from writers favourable to the Parliamentary cause,
and based mainly on letters from the Scottish camp. The
object of this note is to collect some materials for the history
of the campaign from Royalist sources. Some of the letters
of the Marquis during the campaign are printed in Warburton's " Prince Rupert." A long despatch which I have printed
here in full is from a copy amongst the Conway papers, now in
the Record-office, and an extract from " Mercurius Aulicus "
represents another despatch which has now disappeared.

Newcastle writes to Prince Rupert from York on January
28, 1644, telling him that his marching army amounted to
only 5000 foot, and that his horse was not well armed, whilst the
Scots numbered 14,000 and had advanced as far as Morpeth
(Warburton, ii. 368.) He concludes by regretting that he is
to be left to fight the Scots unaided. A day or two later he
set out for Newcastle; the Scots appeared before that town
and summoned it on February 3d, and the same day the
Marquis arrived within its walls. Of the attack which
followed, and the condition of their forces, Newcastle and
King sent the following account to Charles.

*A true and perfect representation of the state of your
Majesty's army under our command and the condition
we are in at this present.*

Your Majesty may be pleased to understand that the greatest
part of this winter was necessarily spent in suppressing the rebellion
in Derbyshire, which otherwise had grown to an irresistible head.
And by the time we had reduced that county, and put it in a
defensible posture, the disorders in Yorkshire, together with the
rumour of the Scots' invasion, called us back into Yorkshire very
much wearied and toiled, both horse and foot, where we had hopes
to have refreshed and clothed our men, which were discouraged
both for want of clothes and money. We remained there not above

a fortnight, but the Scots had invaded the kingdom with a very great army, although the season of the year and a great snow at the very instant did persuade us that it was impossible for them to march. Yet not trusting to that, my Lord-Lieutenant-General hasted away with all expedition with such horse and foot as were quartered nearest to those parts, and, receiving intelligence of the Scots continuing their march, he hasted to Newcastle in his own person some days before his forces could possibly get thither; where truly he found the town in a very good posture, and that the mayor, who had charge of it, had performed his part in your Majesty's service very faithfully; and all the aldermen and best of the town well disposed for your service. And though our charge was very tedious, by reason of floods occasioned by the sudden thaw of the snow, yet I came thither the night before the Scots assaulted the town, which was done with such a fury as if the gates had been promised to be set open to them; but they found it otherwise; for the truth is, the town soldiers gave them such an entertainment (few of our forces being then come into the town, and those extremely wearied in their march), as persuaded them to retire a mile from the town, where they have remained ever since quartered in strong bodies, and raising the whole country of Northumberland, which is totally lost, all turned to them, so that they daily increase their army, and are now striving to pass part of it over the river, so to environ us on every side, and cut off all provision from us. But we have hitherto made good the town and river, and shall do our best endeavour still to do so. But your Majesty may be pleased to know that the enemy's army consists of at least fourteen thousand foot and two thousand horse, and daily increase their numbers; and we cannot possibly draw into the field full five thousand foot and about three thousand horse: and besides, Sir Thomas Fairfax's success in Cheshire hath made him capable of drawing from Lancashire a very great force into the West Riding of Yorkshire, which he is ready to do. My Lord Fairfax hath sent forth of Hull into the East Riding two thousand foot and five hundred horse, all threatening to march towards us, which will make them a great body. And by this your Majesty may perceive where the seat of the war is likely to be.

ı The letter from which this is extracted is dated February 13, and signed by the two generals. They concluded by desiring the King's express commands—"whether we shall still continue in a defensive posture, and expect some assistance as well of force, as ammunition, from your Majesty, or whether upon this great inequality, we shall adventure to hazard the loss of the army, and so of all the north, by giving them battle" (Warburton's "Prince Rupert," ii. 481). This was followed by another letter of Newcastle's dated February 16, pointing out the advances of Sir Thomas Fairfax and his father in Yorkshire, and begging earnestly for aid. "If your Majesty beat the Scots, your game is absolutely won; which can be no other way but by sending more forces, especially foot, and either diverting Manchester, and those forces about Newark" (Warburton, iii. 381). The letter of March 9 gives an account of the progress of the campaign from February 19 to March 8, including the three days' manœuvring and skirmishing near Sunderland on the 6th, 7th, and 8th of March. The skirmish near Corbridge which in the letter is said to have taken place on Feb. 19, is said by Rushworth to have taken place on Feb. 5.

March 9, 164¾.

Despatch communicating the doings of the army under the Marquis of Newcastle to the King. It is headed, "A true relation of all the observable accidents and passages that have happened in these northern parts since my last to your Majesty and before the 9th of this month; with the reason of the impossibility of making good the river of Tyne against the Scots":—

SIR,—Thomas Riddell sent about 50 musketeers from Tynmouth Castle to destroy some corn in the enemy's quarters, from whence they were drawn out as he was informed. But it seems his intelligence betrayed them to the enemy, and about 45 of them were taken prisoners, who being carried to Leslie he sent them to me as a token, and I returned him thanks for his civility with this answer, that I hoped very shortly to repay that debt with interest : which I did within a few days. The 19th of February 1643 Sir Marmaduke Langdale fell upon their quarters at Corbridge in Northumberland, but the enemy having timely notice of his coming were drawn into the field. He thereupon sent some troops to second those that first entered the towns, who charged the enemy, but the enemy with their lancers forced them to retreat. He sent more, but the enemy charged them gallantly, but durst not pursue them because of our reserve. At last he rallied his forces and took about 200 foot with him and forced the enemy to retreat. He routed them totally and followed the chase three miles, killed above 200, took above 150 prisoners, besides divers officers slain whereof one named Captain Haddon. The prisoners Major Agnew, major to the Lord Kirkcudbright, dangerously hurt, Archibald Magee his Quartermaster, Haddon's Cornet Carr, grandchild to the Lord Roxburgh. There was 15 of their troops of horse, whereof Leslie's life-guard was one, and 3 troops of dragooners, and that Leslie's son was their general, who is shot through the shoulder. There is 2 horse colours and a dragoon colour taken. The same morning Colonel Dudley from his quarters about Prudhoe marched over the river with some horse and dragoons and fell into a quarter of the enemy's in Northumberland and slew and took all that was in it, which was 55 prisoners, and gave such an alarm to four of their quarters that they quit the same with disorder and some loss; in which neither had we suffered any loss at all had not Colonel Brandling been taken prisoner by the unfortunate fall of his horse ; and Colonel Dudley, perceiving a greater force preparing to assault him, retreated, and in his retreat took eight of the Scots prisoners, both horse and men, but they took four of his dragoons, whose horse were so weak they could not pass the river. First, after I had made true inquisition of the passes over the river Tyne, I found that there was so many fordable places betwixt Newburn and Hexham, about twelve miles distant one from the other, that it was impossible with my small number of foot to divide them so as to guard and make good every place, but to hazard the loss of them at any one place, and yet not do the work; so I resolved of two evils to choose the less, and left them to their own wills : so they passed the river, and after some days' quartering upon the high moors which was beyond the river Derwent, so that I could by no means march to them, for the situation of these quarters gave them great advantage against our approaches, they marched thence over the new bridge near Chester (le Street) to Sunderland, which pass our horses in respect of the inclosures could not hinder them nor charge them. Upon Wednesday the 6th of this instant March, at one o'clock afternoon, our first troops passed Newbridge, and within a while after the enemy appeared with some horse; when they advanced towards us with more than they first discovered, after some bullets had been exchanged and they appeared again with a greater body, we backed our party with my Lord Henry's regiment, Lieutenant-Colonel Scrimsher commanding them—being part of Colonel Dudley's brigade, with which he drew up after them—with whom also we sent some musketeers; which caused the enemy that day to look upon us at a further distance, we judged they were about 500 horse when they appeared most, yet they continued most of that day in our sight, which satisfied us extremely in hopes the rest were not far off, yet far from troubling us except it were sometimes to make use of our perspectives.

The next morning, from the hill from whence the day before they viewed us, we discovered them, from whence setting ourselves in order we marched towards them, but they still upon our advance fell something obliquely from us on our right hand, bending towards Sunderland, placing their army upon a hill called ——, which was on the left hand of the town from the sea, there ranked themselves for their best advantage to display their own strength, and for their own security, upon which finding them thus backward to join, which truly we little expected, considering what great brags they had made, we resolved to march towards the town, either to possess ourselves of it or a piece of ground near unto it, which would have hindered them from coming back again to the town without fighting with us, upon which piece of ground they had left a good part of their horse and a strong party of their musketeers; which they per-

ceiving made them to draw down again to the same place with all
the haste they could make, where again they possessed themselves
before they could put over any troops. The convenient passage
we could find to it being through some fields of furze and whin
bushes, where we were to make our way with pioneers through three
thick hedges with banks, two of which they had lined with musketeers, there also being a valley betwixt us and them, besides they
had possessed themselves of a house, wherein as we guess they had
put 200 musketeers and a drake, which flankered those hedges
which were betwixt us, and from thence there ran a brook, with a
great bank, down to the river Wear ; behind these places was this
plain above-mentioned, where they stood in their best postures to
receive us, having the sea behind them and on the left hand the town,
the hill and inaccessible places, by which we must have fetched so
great a compass about, that they would have been upon the same
hill again to have received us that way. By this time the evening
caused us to withdraw towards the higher ground, where being
saluted with cold blasts and snow, our horses sufferance with hunger,
that we seemed so far to become friends as in providing against
those common enemies. The next morning both the armies drew
up again into batalia, when with the continual snow that fell all that
day, and by reason of the great fatigation of the horse, it being the
third day they had received little or no sustenance, it was thought
by the consent of all the general officers not expedient that the army
should suffer such extremity or for that time seek any further occasion to engage an enemy whom we found so hard to be provoked,
who found from us I believe, contrary to their expectations, so much
forwardness as they might plainly perceive we endeavoured what
we could to fight with them, and were confident enough of our own
strength could we have come unto them upon any indifferent terms
of equality. And truly the forwardness of the soldiers was such
as we would have been contented to have 'given them some advantages to boot rather than to have deferred it. But upon such disadvantages we had no manner of reason, being the ground would
not permit us to draw up the fourth part of the army, by which we
had been defeated of the advantage we had over them with our
horse, and besides we should have been forced to have fought for

that ground which afterwards we should have stood upon. We being now resolved to march off, and they having been so niggardly to afford us occasion to try what mettle each other was made of, in some measure to satisfy the great forwardness we found in our people, and also to give the enemy warning that they should not be too bold upon our retreat. For these reasons we sent off 120 horse to entertain them near their own leaguer, Sir Charles Lucas his major commanding them, where, meeting with 200 of the enemy's, the first that charged them not passing 60 of this one regiment, notwithstanding the enemy was so placed before a hedge, where they had some dragooners as it seems, they were confident ours would not have come up unto them ; but when they saw that their muskets could not prevent the courage of our men, they turned their backs and leaped over their dragooners, affording our men the execution of them to a great body of theirs, in which chase our men killed some 40 of them, and had taken near 100 men, but they advanced so suddenly that we could bring off but 20 of them, of whom there were three English—one of them were handed (was hanged ?) immediately, having formerly served in our army : their lancers did seem to follow eagerly upon our men in their retreat in great numbers, but we had not passing six men hurt, whereof one died, and not any of the rest miscarried or are missing. In the meantime we were drawing back our army, and the enemy, when they saw the greatest of our number to be marching, made a show as if they would have followed us : they therefore sent down about 600 horse and as many musketeers to try, as I suppose, our behaviour in our retreat, as also to requite us if they could, sending three bodies of horse into the field next the moor, by the side of which we passed, but still under the favour of their musketeers, which lined the hedges ; but we, being content to play with them at their own game, whilst we amused them by presenting some horse before them, our musketeers, which in the meantime stole down upon their flank towards their passage, gave them such a peal, that it made the passage which they retired over seem I believe a great deal straiter, and the time much longer than at their coming over, after which they were a great deal better satisfied with our retreat, and this was all we could do with the enemy. I must confess we

z

brought our horse home very weary, which did us more harm than the enemy could have done, until they be again refreshed, which we make no doubt will be in a very short time. We could entreat the world to be content with further expectation.

A summary of this letter is given in "Mercurius Aulicus" for March 14, 1644. After the events narrated in the letter, Newcastle retired to Durham, and devoted himself to endeavouring to straiten the quarters of the Scots and cut off their provisions, in which he was very successful (Rushworth, III. ii. 615). The Scots succeeded, however, in taking a fort at South Shields on March 20, and in surprising on the same day a detachment of Newcastle's horse at Chester le Street. On March 23 Newcastle marched from Durham to Hilton near Sunderland, and unsuccessfully endeavoured to bring on a general engagement. The skirmishes which took place on March 24 and 25 are narrated from a despatch of Newcastle's in "Mercurius Aulicus" for March 30.

"It being expressly certified from the noble Marquis of Newcastle that on Sunday last (March 24) he got the Scots out to West Bedwick near Hilton Castle in the Bishopric of Durham, where they sat fast upon Bedwick Hill: my Lord Marquis had often invited them to fight, with overtures of many advantageous opportunities; but could not possibly draw them out: on this hill four regiments of his Excellency's foot fell to work with six regiments of the rebels. The fight began about three in the afternoon (March 24) and continued from that time till night, and continued more or less till next morning, the rebels all this while being upon their own *Mickle Midding*, and there they lay all night; next morning (being Monday) the Lord Marquis followed them till afternoon, and then they vanished instantly into their trenches and retirements in Sunderland. Then his Excellency (seeing no hope of getting them out) drew off towards his quarters, and they being sensible of so many provocations, came on his rear (which was 500 horse) with all the horse they had (for as yet they never looked the Lord Marquis in the face), but the rear (with the loss of some thirty (men killed and taken) presently faced about, being seconded by that valiant knight, Sir Charles Lucas, with his brigade of horse, who fell on so gallantly that he forced all their horse (which is about 3000) to hasten up the hill to their cannon, all the way doing sharp execution upon them so as their Lancers lay plentifully upon the ground (many others being taken and brought away prisoners) their cannon all that while playing upon the Lord Marquis his horse with so little success as is not easily imagined. In both these fights (on Sunday and Monday) they that speak least reckon a full 1000 Scots killed and taken which cost the Lord Marquis 240 of his common soldiers, scarce an officer being either killed or taken, though many of their leaders are certainly cut off. Their foot ran twice, and would not stand longer than their officers forced them on with the sword ; the Lord Marquis hath taken many of their arms, especially of their Scottish pistols. Next morning (Tuesday) his Excellency drew towards them again, faced them a long while, but they had too much of the two days before, and would by no means be entreated to show themselves."—(Mercurius Aulicus, March 30, 1644.)

On the 25th of March, after this unsuccessful attempt to bring on a battle, Newcastle wrote to congratulate Rupert on his successful relief of Newark and to urge again his own need of assistance. " I must assure your Highness," he says, "that the Scots are as big again in foot as I am, and their horse, I doubt, much better than ours are, so that if your Highness do not please to come hither, and that very soon too, the great game of your uncle's will be endangered, if not lost" (Warburton, ii. 397 ; see also 399). In his old quarters at Durham, Newcastle awaited the arrival of aid and continued his former tactics. The Scots established their headquarters at Easington, midway between Hartlepool and Durham, where they continued till the 8th of April, and then marched to Quarendon Hill, within two miles of Durham. On the 11th of April took place the defeat of Bellasis at Selby, and on the 13th Newcastle commenced his retreat to York. His next letter is dated from York, 18th April (Warburton, ii. 433); he says that Fairfax and the Scots are too strong for him, and "have put themselves in such a posture as will ruin soon us, unless there be some speedy course taken to give us relief." I have not been able to find any letter of Newcastle giving an account of the latter part of the campaign, or the retreat to York.

VIII.

SEVEN LETTERS WRITTEN BY THE MARQUIS OF NEWCASTLE DURING HIS EXILE TO SECRETARY NICHOLAS.

NOBLE SIR,—I desire you will be pleased to put his Majesty in mind that he will be graciously pleased to renew those offices and places unto me, that the King his father of blessed memory gave me, that others may not possess them, his Majesty not knowing of it; and those I have had and desire to have are the following :—

1. Lord Lieutenant of the County of Nottingham.
2. Lord Lieutenant of the Forest of Sherwood, which that worthy person the Earl of Clare hath had from the Parliament ever since my misfortune.
3. Then Custos Rotulorum of the County of Nottingham.
4. And Custos Rotulorum of the County of Northumberland.

Then if please God his Majesty come to his throne, which I make no doubt of, certainly all my land that the rebels have possessed themselves of I may lawfully take possession of without troubling his Majesty; but whereas my traitorous servant hath sold any land to any of those rebels, that I may have my land again, since it was but in trust, which the law will give me. But I speak of it only in this case, that any of the rebels that the King might give to any courtier or others, if they have any of my land I shall have great trouble with them, though justly they cannot possess it; and therefore I humbly desire his Majesty there may be an exception made in my particular, and in acquainting his Majesty with these particulars you will oblige me very much,—Your most faithful servant, W. NEWCASTLE.

ANTWERP, *the 15th of August* 1654.

To Sir ED. NICHOLAS.

(Domestic State Papers. Record Office.)

NOBLE SIR,—I received yours of the 22d, and give you many hearty thanks for the favour, for I assure you there could nothing rejoice me more in the whole world than the King and the Duke of York to be so kind, and my daily prayers shall be that it may ever continue. Now I will give you my intelligence. I hear my friend and neighbour, Sir Gervase Clifton, who at least is seventy years old, hath lately married, as I take it her name is the Lady Alice Hastings, sister I believe to the Lord Loughborough, with £4000 portion, Sir Gervase his second wife, so that off the next wife he comes eight, and then I believe the mark will be out of his mouth. I speak like an experienced horseman. This lady, I believe, is in years for a maid, a pretty tough hen for this Lent without eggs. I am so tormented about my book of horsemanship as you cannot believe, with a hundred several trades I think, and the printing will cost above £1300, which I could never have done but for my good friends Sir H. Cartwright and Mr. Loving; and I hope they shall lose nothing by it, and I am sure they hope the like. I hope this next summer I may be so happy as to see you, and believe me,—I am affectionately your most faithful servant, W. NEWCASTLE.

ANTWERP, *the 15th of Feb.* 1656.

(Domestic State Papers. Record Office).

NOBLE SIR,—I received the favour of yours of the 22d, and you have obliged me very much, not only by your own letter, but by sending that of Sir Henry Bennet. I beseech you put his Majesty in mind of his gracious promise to me, in giving Sir Henry Bennet thanks for his favours to me. I hope by your news that the Swede will go down. We have it here very confidently reported, that the peace between the two crowns is very far advanced (and truly I am not so wise as not to believe it, for all things considered, methinks it is very probable), and then I hope the King cannot fail of their aid. There are many noblemen, or at least lords, that are comed over to Paris it is true, but those lords that can take such sudden apprehensions of fears so far off, I doubt will hardly have the courage to help our gracious Master to his throne —woful people—and the next generation of lords they tell me are fools. It will be a brave Upper House! Pray present my humble service to my Lord Chancellor. I have been indisposed this week, but I thank God I am much better now. And in all conditions I shall be entirely your most faithful servant, W. NEWCASTLE.

ANTWERP, 23d *Jan.* 1659.

I write with so much freedom to you that I pray burn this.

(Egerton MSS. British Museum.)

Newcastle to Nicholas.

NOBLE SIR,—I thank you for your last and your favour to me in presenting my humble thanks to the King. I thank God I am for the time very much mended; for age, I am in less than a year of you, and hope we may both live to see better times, for I will always hope the best. The Duke of Gloucester went away this morning, and the Earl of Norwich galloping along with him, as also my Lord Berkeley; the young lady, Mrs. Hyde, her brother, and Doctor Morley went away this morning too. The noble Lord of Ormond and his company will be with you to-morrow. The Earl of Nòrwich within a few days will be with you too. I spoke with a young gentleman, one Mr. Smith, newly comed (coumde) out of England: he thinks that Cromwell and the Parliament will agree but I think he knows little. But I spoke with another, an elderly man and a stout, that served in my army, and he says they will fall to pieces, and that there will be great factions and divisions in England. The merchants have it here that certainly there will be no peace between the two crowns and that the treaty is absolutely broke ; others say that it is piecing again : they report confidently that some English ships have met with some Spanish ships and sunk them, but I do not believe it. Now if you can make anything out of all this you do very well, for I protest I cannot. Pray remember my service to Lord Chancellor and thank him for his favours, and so I rest constantly your most faithful servant,

W. NEWCASTLE.

ANTWERP, *the 2d of April* 1659.

(Egerton MSS. 536, f. 336.)

Newcastle to Nicholas.

NOBLE SIR,—I now have two petitions to you—one to present this enclosed humbly to his Majesty, the next that you would favour me so much as to give me the most timely notice of the assurance of the peace between Spain and France. The reason is, the Burgo-masters and Governors of this town desired me to let them know if I could the certainty of it. I told them that my King's principal secretary was my very noble friend, and I would write unto him ; thus, by your favour, I shall ingratiate myself very much to this town. Pardon me thus trespassing upon you and believe me, I am very constantly your most faithful servant, W. NEWCASTLE.

ANTWERP, *the 18th of April* 1659.

My service to my Lord Chancellor.

(Egerton MSS. British Museum.)

Newcastle to Nicholas.

NOBLE SIR,—I received yours of the 30th last, and give you many thanks for the favour of your most excellent news. I am sure we cannot be worse than we are, and I hope in God that this peace may prove considerable for the advantage of our gracious King. But your son writ to Mr. Topp that the Lower House was divided and that the two Houses could not agree, and that it was thought they would be dissolved—this may be considerable indeed. We have it here by some letters that the army stands upon terms of their own, that is considerable and to the purpose if it be so ; but we have so many lies here at Antwerp that we know not what to believe, for this morning the Lord Wentworth and Sir Cecil Howard came to me and told me that Major Wood told them that one of the Prince of Condé's followers told him that Sir Robert Welsh his son, and three or four more had a plot to kill my gracious Master, and they had no sooner said it but I received your letter dated yesterday, so then they saw there was no such thing : God ever preserve my gracious Master from all knaves, fools, and bloody rascals. My service to your younger son, with many thanks for his favours to me about Monsieur Juliane (?) ; though he hath not answered it I do not care, so that now he knows my mind, which is sufficient. It was about a truck for horses, and I would be loth to give a good horse for a jade ; and though there is none that is a piece of a horseman amongst them, riders or others, yet I assure you the greatest of them are horse coursers beyond any in Smith-field, and so they are in France, for it is two professions, a good horseman and a horse courser. I pretend to the first, but know nothing of the second, for I'll cozen nobody ; I only take care not to be cozened, which they find I can do reasonable well at that. Believe me it is not an easy thing to have a good horse nor a rare man in any quality.

ANTWERP, *May Day* 1659.

(Egerton MSS. British Museum.)

Newcastle to Nicholas.

NOBLE SIR,—I received yours of the 12th, and give you many thanks for your excellent good news. We have it here that the Parliament is dissolved by Cromwell, but he was forced to it by the army, who told him if he would not dissolve they would, and then they say they came to Cromwell and took away all the dishes of meat he had but one. Cromwell went presently to Hampton Court, and letters from the Venetian ambassador say that he believes by this time there is a guard set upon him. Fleetwood is made General of the Army, and Lambert Lieutenant-general, and this is the red-coats which I always said would do what they list. Some talks the Presbyterians begin to appear in divers parts of the kingdom, but I doubt that yet. Great confusions and alterations is daily looked for, and I hope in God it will produce excellent things for the King, for certainly Fleetwood and Lambert can never make their advantage and settlement so well as to serve the King. My service to my Lord Chancellor, and tell him that now I hope to wait on him to Westminster to see him take possession of the Chancery, and upon one of my horses of manage which will be the quietest, safest, and surest he or any man can have. You see how my hopes transports me with the passion I have for my gracious Master. God send us a good meeting at Whitehall, and so I rest constantly your most faithful servant   W. NEWCASTLE.

ANTWERP, *the* 13*th May* 1659.

(Egerton MSS.   British Museum.)

IX.

TO THE TWO MOST FAMOUS UNIVERSITIES OF ENGLAND.

MOST FAMOUSLY LEARNED,—I here present to you this philosophical work, not that I can hope wise school-men and industrious, laborious students should value it for any worth, but to receive it without scorn, for the good encouragement of our sex, lest in time we should grow irrational as idiots, by the dejectedness of our spirits, through the careless neglects and despisements of the masculine sex to the female, thinking it impossible we should have either learning or understanding, wit or judgment, as if we had not rational souls as well as men, and we out of a custom of dejectedness think so too, which makes us quit all industry towards profitable knowledge, being employed only in low and petty employments which take away not only our abilities towards arts, but higher capacities in speculations, so as we are become like worms that only live in the dull earth of ignorance, winding ourselves sometimes out by the help of some refreshing rain of good education, which seldom is given us, for we are kept like birds in cages, to hop up and down in our houses, not suffered to fly abroad to see the several changes of Fortune, and the various humours ordained and created by nature, and wanting the experience of nature, we must needs want the understanding and knowledge, and so consequently prudence and invention of men. Thus by an opinion, which I hope is but an erroneous one in men, we are shut out of all power and authority, by reason we are never employed either in civil or martial affairs, our counsels are despised and laughed at, the best of our actions are trodden down with scorn by the overweening conceit men have of themselves, and through a despisement of us.

But I, considering with myself that if a right judgment and a true understanding and a respectful civility live anywhere, it must be in learned universities, where nature is best known, where truth is oftenest found, where civility is most practised, and if I find not a resentment here, I am very confident I shall find it nowhere, neither shall I think I deserve it, if you approve not of me; but if I deserve not praise, I am sure to receive so much courtship from your sage society as to bury me in silence, that thus I may have a quiet grave, since not worthy a famous memory, for to lie entombed under the dust of an university will be honour enough for me, and more than if I were worshipped by the vulgar as a deity. Wherefore, if your wisdoms cannot give me the bays, let your charity strew me with cypress ; and who knows but, after my honourable burial, I may have a glorious resurrection in following ages, since time brings strange and unusual things to pass —I mean unusual to men, though not in nature. And I hope this action of mine is not unnatural, though unusual for a woman to present a book to the university, nor impudent, for it is honest, although it seem vainglorious. But if it be, I am to be pardoned, since there is little difference between man and beast, but what ambition and glory makes.

(Dedication by the Duchess of "Philosophical and Physical Opinions," 1663.)

X.

SIR CHARLES LUCAS.

Sir Charles was the youngest son of Sir Thomas Lucas, of St. John's, Colchester. The Duchess gives an account of his youth in her own autobiography. He served, like most young soldiers of his time, in the wars of the Low Countries. In the second Scotch war he commanded a troop of horse (Calendar of Domestic State Papers, 1640-1, 318). From the beginning of the Civil War he served in the King's army. He was wounded at the battle of Powick Bridge, September 22, 1642 (Warburton's "Prince Rupert," i. 409). He served under Prince Rupert also at the capture of Cirencester, February 2d, 1643, and a contemporary account notices his mercy in taking prisoners ("Bibliotheca Gloucestrensis," 170). On July 1, 1643, with three troops of his own regiment, he defeated Colonel Middleton with 400 horse and dragoons at Padbury, taking 40 prisoners and killing above 100 of the enemy ("Mercurius Aulicus"). In the autumn of the same year he served for some months in Lincolnshire and Nottinghamshire, and commanded in an attack on Nottingham on January 16, 1644. The committee, describing the attack in a letter to Gilbert Millington, say that he "reports himself General of this county and Lincolnshire" (Memoirs of Colonel Hutchinson, vol. i. pp. 298, 388). Immediately after this Lucas was ordered into Yorkshire. A remonstrance of the committee of Newark complains that the recent capture of Gainsborough and the Isle of Axholm "have moved his Excellency the Lord Marquis of Newcastle to engarrison Doncaster now in fortifying, and to command Sir Charles Lucas with his own regiment, and the Lincolnshire horse, in all about 1400, to quarter thereabouts for securing that fortification, which is like to be a work of time, and so to procrastinate Sir Charles Lucas his coming into these parts (whom we hoped to have been sent by your Majesty for our immediate assistance) to the apparent hazard of this garrison and these two counties" (Rushworth, III. ii. 305). From Doncaster, on February 2, 1644, Lucas wrote to Rupert a very interesting letter, thanking him for his recommendation to Lord Newcastle (Warburton, ii. 370). He joined Newcastle in the north some time before March 6th, and distinguished himself in the skirmish at Hilton on March 25th (Rushworth, III. ii. 615-16). When the Marquis was obliged to shut himself up in York, Lucas in command of the horse was sent to quarter in Nottinghamshire and the Midland counties, and to take part in any attempts at the relief of the besieged. He accordingly joined Rupert in his march to York, and was one of the commanders of the left wing of the Prince's horse at Marston, in which defeat he was taken prisoner, although his division successfully routed that of Sir Thomas Fairfax, which was its immediate opponent. Rupert as soon as possible negotiated the exchange of Sir Charles, which probably took place in the winter of 1644-5 (see letter in Warburton's "Prince Rupert," iii. 38). He was certainly released before March 1645, for in a letter of March 5 Digby discusses the question of his appointment to the government of Berkeley Castle (Warburton, iii. 66).

In July 1645 Lucas writes to Rupert from Berkeley complain-

ing of the inadequacy of the garrison, and the disaffection
of his soldiers, and of the people of the neighbouring country
(Hist. MSS. Rep. ix. pt. ii. p. 437). Berkeley Castle was
stormed by Colonel Rainsborough on September 25, 1645
(Sprigge, Anglia Rediviva, p. 136, ed. 1854). According to
Sprigge it had endured nine days' siege, but the capture of
the church and outworks, and the planting of cannon thereupon, forced the Governor to sound a parley and treat. " The
castle was surrendered upon these articles : the soldiers to
march out without arms ; the Governor, Sir Charles Lucas,
with three horses and arms and not above £50 in money ;
every field officer with two horses, and but £5 in money ;
foot captains with swords but no horse ; the soldiers with
not above 5s. apiece." In the castle were taken provisions
for six months. Lucas had answered to the first summons
"that he would eat horse flesh before he would yield, and
man's flesh when that was done," and returned an equally
peremptory answer to the second summons. The garrison
marched out about 500 strong, but probably the disaffection before mentioned by Lucas still existed and contri-
buted to the surrender, and it is not likely that it had been
increased in numbers since he complained of its inadequacy
to Rupert in July. The table at the end of Sprigge's work
seems to imply that forty of the garrison were killed and
ninety taken prisoners during the siege. Mr. Markham
speaks of the "weak and unintelligent defence" of Berkeley,
but the facts of the defence are almost entirely unknown and
hardly justify this condemnation. Sprigge in his account of
the surrender speaks of Lucas as "a soldier of reputation
and valour," hence it has been argued that he could not
have been thus spoken of by a Parliamentary historian if
he had broken his parole to Fairfax in taking up arms in
1648. But as Sprigge's book was published in 1647 this
inference is obviously absurd. Before many weeks passed
Lucas was again actively employed. In the diary of Richard
Symonds for December 23, 1645, it is stated " Lord Astley

came to Worcester, being General of these four counties, Sir Charles Lucas with him, Lieutenant-general of the horse." His career came to an end three months later with the defeat of Astley's army at Stow in the Wold in the following March. The name of Lucas is not mentioned in the list of prisoners given in many reports of the battle ; for instance, in the letter of Colonel Morgan to the speaker. This is explained by a circumstance mentioned by Vicars. "Sir Charles Lucas, as was credibly reported, was also taken in the fight, but immediately after rescued by a party of fire-locks of the enemy, and on his rescue fled into the wood hard by for hoped safety ; but after the fight our forces searching the wood for stragglers found there the said Sir Charles Lucas" (Burning Bush, 399). Thus Lucas became a prisoner, and it is presumed that he obtained his liberty by engaging himself to Fairfax not to serve again against the Parliament. The sole evidence for this fact, probable enough in itself, is in the letters exchanged between Fairfax and Lucas on June 19, 1648. Soon after the siege of Colchester began, Fairfax sent a letter to the besieged "to acquaint them that Sir Charles Lucas had forfeited his parole, his honour and faith, being his prisoner upon parole, and therefore not capable of command or trust in martial affairs" (Rushworth, IV. ii. 1160). To which Lucas replied : "Sir, I wonder you should question me of any such engagement, since I purchased my freedom and estate at a high rate by a great sum of money, which I paid into Gold-smith's Hall, for which according to the ordinances of the two Houses I was to enjoy my freedom and estate. When I conceived myself in this condition, I sent a letter to your secretary, desiring him to advertise your Lordship that I had punctually performed my engagements as they stood in relation to your Lordship. Upon which I had notice from him that you accepted of my respects to you, which truly have never been wanting to your person. But, my Lord, besides my inclinations and duty to the service I am in at present, be

pleased to examine whether the law of nature hath not insti-
gated me to take my sword again into my hand, for when I
was in peaceable manner in London, there was a price set
upon me by the committee of Derby House, upon which I
was constrained to retire myself into my own country, and to
my native town, for refuge" (Fairfax Correspondence, iii. 57).

In this letter Lucas admits that such an engagement as
the one supposed to have been contracted after his capture
at Stow had actually existed. At the same time he puts
forward two pleas : the first, that his engagement to Fairfax
had been ended by his payment of a composition for his
estates ; the second, that the action of the Parliament against
him had justified him in taking up arms in self-defence. With
regard to the first it may fairly be held that the personal
obligation to Fairfax had been superseded and ended by
the arrangement with the civil government ; from being a
prisoner Lucas had become a citizen, and substituted for
his former obligation to the commander-in-chief a new obligation to the civil power. In Dring's list of compounders
Sir Charles Lucas, knight, of Horsley, Essex, appears as
having paid a composition of £508,10s. But the committee
at Goldsmith's Hall, to which this composition was paid,
exacted from delinquents the taking of the Covenant and
an oath not to assist the King against the Parliament, "nor
any forces raised without the consent of the two Houses of
Parliament in this cause or war " (*Vide* Husbands' " Collection of Ordinances," fol. 1646, pp. 636, and 739). The action
of Sir Charles in taking up arms again in 1648 was a distinct breach of this engagement.

With reference to the second plea it may be stated that
Lucas more than any other man was responsible, if Matthew
Carter is to be trusted, for the refusal by the loyalists of
Essex of the indemnity offered them by Parliament if they
laid down their arms. (Passed in the House of Commons,
June 5, 1648). Rushworth gives the following news from
Essex under June 7 : " That the Parliament's commissioners

having published the indemnity at Bow to those that should lay down arms, Sir William Hicks and divers others of the gentlemen submitted, and the Lord Goring retreated back from thence. But Sir Charles Lucas, that eminent cavalier, is come into them, and keeps up the soldiers, making great promises to them ; and by his insinuations hath prevailed with the discontented party not to lay down arms."   It must be admitted that this circumstance, confirmed by the evidence of Rushworth and Carter, does not seem to bear out the statement of Sir Charles Lucas that he took up arms in self-defence. At the same time he expressly states that the committee of Derby House put a price upon his head, and till the truth or falsehood of that statement is ascertained a final judgment on this second plea is hardly possible.

For a detailed account of the siege the reader must be referred to Mr. G. F. Townshend's Siege of Colchester, to Mr. Markham's Life of Fairfax, and to the anonymous author of " The History and Antiquities of Colchester Castle " (Colchester, 1882). Carter's " True Relation of the Honourable though Unfortunate Expedition of Kent, Essex and Colchester," together with the contemporary diurnals and the extracts in Rushworth, supply a full account of the incidents of the struggle. The pamphlet entitled " Colchester's Tears " charges Sir Charles Lucas with cruelty to the inhabitants of the town during the siege, but it deserves very little credit. However, Clarendon in the extract quoted on p. 281 accuses Lucas of considerable harshness. But Rushworth quotes a letter saying, " the Lords Goring and Capel carry things very high and peremptorily, but Sir Charles Lucas more moderate " (1181).

Colchester capitulated on August 27, 1648, and Lisle and Lucas were shot on August 28 by sentence of a court-martial. By the terms of the capitulation (quoted in the note to p. 95), the superior officers had rendered themselves to mercy, so this execution was not a breach of the terms of the capitulation. Fairfax gives two reasons for the execution : the first, "satisfaction of military justice ;" the second, "avenge for the innocent blood they have caused to be spilt, and the trouble, damage, and mischief they have brought upon the town, this country, and the kingdom " (Rushworth, p. 1243). The first of these reasons evidently refers to the breach of parole with which Fairfax charged Lucas. If the argument stated above holds good, this had been superseded by an engagement to the Parliament, and it would have been juster to leave the punishment of the breach of that engagement to the Parliament. The second reason given for the sentence, the punishment for raising a civil war (satisfaction of political justice, as it might be termed), is obviously a subject which should have been reserved for the judgment of a political authority like the Parliament rather than decided by a General, or a council of war. Parliament might have condemned Lucas, as it afterwards condemned Hamilton and Capel, and the justice of the sentence could hardly have been impeached except by those who are prepared to hold that it is in no case just to impose the penalty of death on the leaders of a civil war. With reference to the personal share of Fairfax in this sentence, it may be pointed out that Clarendon says that "the manner of taking the lives of these worthy men was generally imputed to Ireton, who swayed the General, and was upon all occasions of an unmerciful and bloody nature " (Rebellion, xi. 109). In " Mercurius Pragmaticus " for October 3–10, 1648, the following statement is made : " In (that) unworthy act it's said his Excellency had no hand, but only the council of war, by the special instigation of Ireton, Rainsborough, and Whalley." An account of the death of Lucas is given in " Mercurius Pragmaticus " for August 29 to September 5, 1648. It will be seen that the conclusion here adopted differs from that arrived at in the note to p. 95, in granting that the composition might be fairly considered to put an end to the engagement of Sir Charles to Lord Fairfax.

2 A

XI.

GENERAL JAMES KING, LORD EYTHIN.

General King was the son of Sir James King, knight, of Barracht, in Scotland. Like so many Scots he early entered foreign service. His name appears in Monro's " List of the Scottish officers in chief (called the officers of the field) that served his Majesty of Sweden, anno 1632," as General-Major James King. (Monro's Expedition, part i.) In 1638 King, who was then commanding in Munster under Baner, had orders to join Rupert and the Prince Palatine, who had raised a small army. But Hatzfeldt, the Austrian General, routed them at the battle of Lemgo or Flota. Warburton, on the authority of Bennet's narrative, charges King with misconduct and treachery (" Prince Rupert," i. 452), but it appears from other sources that Rupert was attacked before his army was collected, and defeated before King could bring up the foot to support the cavalry, and that finally King rallied and skilfully conducted the retreat of the remainder of the troops. In December 1640 he was recalled to England by Charles I., and the Calendar of Domestic State Papers contains two letters from King to Vane on the subject of his recall (pp. 320, 579). Henrietta Maria, writing to Charles on December 18, 1641. mentions King's alacrity for his service (Letters, p. 149). Charles himself wrote to Newcastle on December 29 of the same year, saying that he heard King had landed, and desired Newcastle to use him in his army (Ellis' Original Letters, vol. iii. p. 297). King's influence with Newcastle seems to have been exerted throughout in order to carry out the regular method of warfare with which his continental experience had made him familiar, and opposed to the dashing attacks and bold movements popular amongst amateur soldiers. At the siege of Leeds in April 1643

"General King, and all the old officers from Holland, were of an opinion that an assault was too dangerous," and in favour of raising the siege (Letters of Henrietta Maria, 189). Again, he is said to have been the chief advocate of the policy of reducing Hull, rather than marching south to join the King (Warwick's Memoirs, p. 264). He is said by the same authority to have been the inspirer of Newcastle's defensive strategy during the campaign against the Scots, and is accused of a treacherous leaning towards his fellow-countrymen (Warwick, p. 277). So much did these complaints and accusations weigh with King that in April 1644 he seriously thought of retiring from the royal service and returning to the Continent. Both Charles and Henrietta pressed him to stay. "I hope that he will not leave us in the present state of our affairs," wrote the Queen, "and that if anybody has said any foolish thing he is too gallant to mind it" (Letters of Queen Henrietta, p. 238). "If either you or Lord Ethyn leave my service," wrote Charles to Newcastle, "I am sure all the North is lost (Ellis, Original Letters, iii. 298).

During the siege of York even the hostile Warwick admits that "Lieutenant-General King so demeaned himself, that as he showed eminency in soldiery and personal stoutness, so there appeared now no want of loyalty; for now he fought not singly against his own nation" (p. 278). His share in the battle of Marston Moor, his opposition to Rupert's desire to engage, his criticism of the plan of battle, have been mentioned in this life (p. 77). After the battle King accompanied Newcastle to Hamburg. Upon King, says Clarendon, "they who were content to spare the Marquis poured out all the reproaches of infidelity, treason, and conjunction with his countrymen; which, without doubt, was the effect of the universal discontent, and the miserable condition to which the people of those northern parts were on the sudden reduced, without the least foundation or ground for any such reproach; and as he had, throughout the whole course of his life, been generally reputed a man of honour, and had exercised the highest commands under the King of Sweden with extraordinary ability and success, so he had been prosecuted by some of his countrymen with the highest malice, from his very coming into the King's service ; and the same malice pursued him after he had left the kingdom, even to his death " (Rebellion, viii. 87). Amongst those who gave countenance to these charges, seems to have been Prince Rupert, to whom King wrote a letter defending himself. (Pythouse Papers, p. 21.) King's last services in the royalist cause seem to have been performed in connection with the expedition of Montrose. The Calendar of Domestic State Papers contains a warrant dated March 19, 1650, appointing Lord Eythin Lieutenant-General under Montrose. A letter of March 13, 1650, shows that he had also been engaged in some negotiations for the coming of Charles II. in person to Sweden. (Calendar, 1650, pp. 52, 611.) General King was created a peer of Scotland on March 28, 1643, by the title of Lord Eythin, or Ethyn, the title being probably derived from the river Ythan in Aberdeenshire.

On July 26, 1644, the Scottish Parliament passed a decreet of forfaulture against him which was rescinded on January 14, 1647, and on the 19th February following, another act in his favour was passed. (Douglas' Peerage of Scotland.) A letter from King to the Earl of Forth may be found in Mr. Macray's edition of Patrick Ruthven's Correspondence, p. 81. (Ruthven Correspondence, Roxburgh Society.) King died in Sweden some time between October 1651 and April 1652. (Ibid., p. xxxviii., note).

XII.

LORD NEWCASTLE'S ACCOUNT OF THE BATTLE OF ATHERTON MOOR.

The original of the despatch in which Lord Newcastle announced his victory has not survived, but it appears to me to be contained in the following pamphlet. The pamphlet does not bear on its title the name of any place, but the device of an Oxford printer shows it to have been printed at Oxford. No author's name is attached to it, nor is there any signature; but it is evidently an official relation, and the use of the first person ("I sent troops, &c.") shows it to have been written by the royalist commander-in-chief. Its style also rather resembles that of Newcastle's despatch on his campaign against the Scots, printed earlier in the Appendix. For these reasons I insert it here, but as being doubtful, have given it the last place in the Appendix.

"An Express Relation of the Passages and Proceedings of his Majesty's Army, under the Command of his Excellence the Earl of Newcastle, against the Rebels under the Command of the Lord Fairfax and his Adherents.

[Printed in the year 1643.]

"We marched from Pomfret towards Bradford, and in our way thither we summoned Sir John Savile, commander of Howley, to deliver up that house, and lay down his arms so unjustly taken up, who returned an uncivil answer, and that he would keep it maugre our forces, whereupon we planted our cannon against that house, and environed it upon Wednesday the 21st of June in the afternoon, and next

morning took it by assault, and in it the said commander-
in-chief and all his officers and soldiers, about 245, some
few whereof were slain, the rest taken prisoners; where, by
the unseasonableness of the weather, we were enforced to
remain till Friday the 30th of June, from whence we
marched early towards Bradford, and when we had marched
two miles or thereabouts we found a great body of men, a
greater number of foot than we, and almost all musketeers,
and some twenty troops of horse, and had possessed a place
called Adderton Moor, and taken the most advantageous
places thereof, and lined several hedges with musketeers, and
played so fiercely upon us, and that before the whole body
of our foot could be drawn up, and their horse likewise
possessing a plain field and a great ditch betwixt us lined
with musketeers, and keeping our horse in a ground full of
pits, that for the space of two hours or thereabouts, we
were forced to give ground, though very little; but when
our cannon was well placed, and our foot once drawn up,
within half-an-hour we put their foot on the right wing of
the battle to retire, and pursued them so hotly, that they
presently were put into a disorderly retreat; whereupon,
part of our horse fell upon that wing, and the cannon playing
upon the body of their horse killed many and routed them,
together with our horse charging at that time, so we pursued them, killing and taking them to Bradford town end,
which was more than two miles, in which chase was slain
(as is supposed) about 500 of the enemies, and about 1400
taken prisoners, amongst which many officers, together with
three filed pieces, and all their ammunition there, which
was not much. We had many soldiers hurt, two colonels
of horse slain, Heron and Howard, and some officers hurt,
as Colonel Throckmorton, Colonel Carnaby, and Captain
Maison, all recoverable, and not above twenty common
soldiers slain.

"That night we came before Bradford, a strong town, and
ill approaching to it, yet we made our approaches that

night. The next day we had placed our cannon and made
places of batteries very near the town and church, where
they had two drakes upon the top of the steeple, and lined
the steeple with woolpacks; yet our cannon dismounted
their drakes upon the top of the steeple, and battered the
steeple so as none could stay on it, where they had many
musketeers, and so we got both the ends of the town before
Sunday night; and in the night-time Sir Thomas Fairfax,
governor of the town, his lady, Major Gifford, and Sir
Henry Fowlis, escaped out of the town, and upon a moor
was forced to charge with their party a party of our horse,
where his lady and his cornet were taken prisoners, but he
and the other two being well horsed escaped, though pursued very near Leeds, which was above five miles; and
that morning our men entered the town, took prisoners—

1. Colonel Malliver (Mauleverer ?).
2. Sergeant-Major Willshire.
3. Captain Mudd.
4. Captain Rogers.
5. Captain Bland.
6. Captain O'Neal.
7. Captain White.
8. Captain Smith.
9. Captain Dent.
10. Captain Stanley.
11. Captain Feure.
12. Lieutenant Popler.
13. Lieutenant Loveday.
14. Lieutenant Moore.
15. Lieutenant Sad.
    Sergeant Floyd.
    Sergeant Brabant.
    William Lowden and Nathaniel Goffe, gunners,

with all or most of the common soldiers, which are in
number 300 or thereabouts, besides the enlarging of 200

prisoners of ours there, and taking of arms which are yet uncertain in number.

"That very day, within three hours after, came a captain of ours, who among divers other prisoners at Leeds, finding that my Lord Fairfax and his son were inclined to leave the town (as they did) attended with three or four troops of horse, 200 dragooners, and 300 foot, broke out of prison, possessed themselves of the magazine, took all the arms, which were 1500 at least, eight barrels of powder, and 12 pieces of ordnance, with a very great proportion of match and ball, and so kept the town till I sent forces into it, besides the enlarging of 700 prisoners there. The Lord Fairfax and his son marched towards Selby, in which march his 300 foot run away from him ; and his forces left, being discovered by our forces at the garrison of Cawood were charged by them, and they fled into the town of Selby. Our forces being too weak for them were forced to retire ; so my Lord, his son Sir Thomas, Major Gifford, Sir Henry Fowlis, and Sir Thomas Mauleverer, took a boat and passed themselves therein ; and swimming their horses over the river, and as their men were passing over some of them were drowned with crowding the boats, and so they fled, we conceive, to Hull or to Nottingham, but to which is not certain.

"The same day news was brought us from Halifax, that all the forces were run from thence, and have taken with them all our prisoners that remained there, and so we are possessed of that town, as also of Denton House, my Lord Fairfax, his house, wherein there was a small garrison, two drakes, 200 men and arms."

INDEX.

INDEX OF OBSOLETE WORDS AND PHRASES.

PRINTED BY BALLANTYNE, HANSON AND CO.
EDINBURGH AND LONDON.

14 KING WILLIAM STREET, STRAND, W.C.,
LONDON, MARCH 1886.

JOHN C. NIMMO'S

LIST OF NEW BOOKS

FOR

THE SPRING OF 1886.

A New Edition, in Three Volumes, medium 8vo, cloth,
fine paper, price 31s. 6d. net.

BURTON'S
ANATOMY OF MELANCHOLY.

THE ANATOMY OF MELANCHOLY:

WHAT IT IS,

WITH ALL THE KINDS, CAUSES, SYMPTOMS, PROGNOSTICS,
AND SEVERAL CURES OF IT.

In Three Partitions.

WITH THEIR SEVERAL SECTIONS, MEMBERS, AND SUBSECTIONS,
PHILOSOPHICALLY, MEDICINALLY, HISTORICALLY
OPENED AND CUT UP.

By DEMOCRITUS JUNIOR
[ROBERT BURTON].

Burton's Anatomy at the time of its original publication obtained a great
celebrity, which continued more than half a century.   During that period few
books were more read or more deservedly applauded.   It was the delight of
the learned, the solace of the indolent, and the refuge of the uninformed.   It
passed through at least eight editions, by which the bookseller, as Wood
records, got an estate ; and, notwithstanding the objection sometimes opposed
against it, of a quaint style and too great an accumulation of authorities, the
fascination of its wit, fancy, and sterling sense have borne down all censures,
and extorted praise from the first writers in the English language.   The grave
Johnson has praised it in the warmest terms, and the ludicrous Sterne has
interwoven many parts of it into his own popular performance.   Milton did
not disdain to build two of his finest poems on it ; and a host of inferior
writers have embellished their works with beauties not their own, culled from
a performance which they had not the justice even to mention.   Change of
times and the frivolity of fashion suspended, in some degree, that fame
which had lasted nearly a century ; and the succeeding generation affected
indifference towards an author who at length was only looked into by the
plunderers of literature, the poachers in obscure volumes.   The plagiarisms
of "Tristram Shandy," so successfully brought to light by Dr. Ferriar, at
length drew the attention of the public towards a writer who, though then
little known, might, without impeachment of modesty, lay claim to every
mark of respect ; and inquiry proved, beyond a doubt, that the calls of justice
had been little attended to by others as well as the facetious Yorick.   Wood
observed, more than a century ago, that several authors had unmercifully
stolen matter from Burton without any acknowledgment.

THE SONG OF SONGS.

SUPER ROYAL QUARTO.

Illustrated with Twenty=six Full=page Original
Etchings from Designs

By BIDA.

*ETCHED BY EDMOND HÉDOUIN AND
ÉMILE BOILVIN.*

Also Twelve Culs=de=Lampes from Designs

By GUSTAVE GREUX.

Bound in half morocco extra, price Three Guineas *net.*

———

Two Hundred and Fifty copies printed, each numbered.

———

NOTE.—" The Song of Songs " is printed from the REVISED
VERSION, the copyright of which belongs to the authorities
of the Oxford and Cambridge University Presses, who have
courteously granted the publisher permission to use it for this
purpose.

The twenty-six full-page etchings are beautifully printed on
fine Japanese paper, and carefully mounted on white vellum
paper, same as the text is printed on.

No finer specimens than these of BIDA's wonderful designs
have hitherto appeared.

OCTAVE UZANNE'S NEW WORK.

The Frenchwoman of the Century.

FASHIONS—MANNERS—USAGES.

By **OCTAVE UZANNE,**

Author of "The Fan," "The Sunshade, Muff, and Glove."

Illustrations in Water Colours by ALBERT LYNCH.

Engraved in Colours by EUGÈNE GAUJEAN.

Super royal 8vo, cloth, price Two Guineas *net.*

Only 500 copies are printed, 300 for England and 200 for America.
Type distributed.

NOTE.—"The Frenchwoman of the Century," written by Octave Uzanne, gives a description of the principal fashions in France, its customs, manners, and usages from the earliest years of the Revolution to the present time. With the history of the dress is pleasantly intermingled a history of the most notable people of this eventful period. The book sparkles with vivid allusions to the principal men and women of the epoch. Napoleon is photographed in his habit as he lived, and the inner life of the Empress Josephine appears as in a delicate miniature. The work, comprehensive in extent, is at the same time minute in detail. The fashions of the Directory and the First Empire are, as it were, underlined. To the assistance of the letterpress has been called, not without sufficient reason in description of the intricate complexity of Parisian fashions, the able pencil of M. Albert Lynch, who has been careful to supply his water colour illustrations exactly in those places where they were most wanted. These pictures have been subsequently engraved in colours by the skilful hand of Eugène Gaujean.

The work, careless and superficial it may seem, is in reality a marvel of profound research and exact investigations. Though copious it is not prodigal, though anecdotal it is seldom trifling, though learned it is never dull. Its expression is polished and lively, its plan precise and duly defined. The best writers of the time for the subject in hand, such as George Duval, Madame d'Abranté, Emile de Girardin, and others of equal reputation have been diligently consulted. The volume is a suitable, almost indeed a necessary, appendage to the other works of Uzanne, viz., "The Fan" and "The Sunshade, Muff, and Glove," recently published.

14 King William Street, Strand, London, W.C.

An elegant and choicely Illustrated Edition of

The Vicar of Wakefield.
By OLIVER GOLDSMITH.

With Prefatory Memoir by GEORGE SAINTSBURY, and One Hundred and Fourteen Coloured Illustrations by V. A. POIRSON (Illustrator of "Gulliver's Travels").

Royal 8vo, cloth extra, printed in colours and gilt top, price 12s. 6d.

NOTE.—This edition of Oliver Goldsmith's famous English classic is illustrated and produced in so sumptuous a form and at so moderate a price, the publisher feels confident the entire edition will be speedily disposed of. It is uniform in size and style of illustration to "Gulliver's Travels" recently published, and of which three thousand copies were sold in two months.

Edinburgh and its Neighbourhood
IN THE DAYS OF OUR GRANDFATHERS.

A series of Illustrations of the more remarkable Old and New Buildings and Picturesque Scenery of Edinburgh, as they appeared about 1830. With Historical Introduction and Descriptive Sketches by JAMES GOWANS.

Royal 8vo, Eighty Illustrations, fine paper, cloth elegant, price 12s. 6d.

NOTE.—The leading feature of this book will be a series of views of Edinburgh and its neighbourhood from the original steel plates after drawings by Mr. Thomas H. Shepherd, and published in 1833. Some of these views are of special interest, as they give vivid representations of historical and other edifices now swept away in the course of improvements which have so much altered the features of "the grey metropolis of the north." A few of the original descriptions of the views will be preserved, but most of the others will be superseded by fresh sketches, whilst the original introduction will be recast, and in great part rewritten. Numerous incidents will be supplied illustrative of the social life of the period, when Scott was still the typical representative of the literary life of Scotland and Christopher North and his associates were exercising a mighty influence in the domain of literature and politics by their diatribes and searching yet sympathetic criticisms in the brilliant pages of *Maga*.

A new and beautiful edition of the "IMITATION OF CHRIST," in demy 8vo, with the text and quaint borders printed in brown ink, and illustrated with Fifteen Etchings, ten by J. P. LAURENS and five by CH. WALTNER, price 21s. *net*, bound in full parchment, gilt top.

THE IMITATION OF CHRIST.
FOUR BOOKS.

Translated from the Latin by Rev. W. BENHAM, B.D.,
Rector of St Edmund, King and Martyr, Lombard Street, London.

NOTE.—The etchings to this new edition of the "IMITATION," fifteen in number, and printed on fine Japanese paper, make it one of the most beautiful at present to be had.

14 King William Street, Strand, London, W.C.

𝔑𝔢𝔴 𝔖𝔢𝔯𝔦𝔢𝔰 𝔬𝔣 𝔥𝔦𝔰𝔱𝔬𝔯𝔦𝔠𝔞𝔩 𝔐𝔢𝔪𝔬𝔦𝔯𝔰.

The Autobiography of Edward,

LORD HERBERT OF CHERBURY.

With Introduction, Notes, Appendices, and a Continuation of the Life. By SYDNEY L. LEE, B.A., Balliol College, Oxford. With Four Etched Portraits, fine paper, medium 8vo, cloth, 21s. *net.*

One Thousand copies printed, 600 for England and 400 for America.

NOTE.—"Lord Herbert of Cherbury's Autobiography" is one of the most fascinating and entertaining books of its class. The author is devoid of self-consciousness, and keeps no secrets from his readers. He dwells as complacently on his failings as on his virtues; his childlike vanity keeps his self-esteem intact in the least promising circumstances. But the book does more than throw a steady light on an attractive personality, it illustrates the habits and customs of English and French society at the beginning of the seventeenth century. No other work so fully describes the contemporary practice of duelling. Abundant reference is made to politics, and it thus forms an important commentary on the history of James the First's reign. Incidentally Lord Herbert enunciates his religious, educational, and metaphysical theories, and substantiates his claim to be regarded as the father of English deism. The autobiography only carries the writer's life as far as the year 1624, and Lord Herbert died in 1648. The book has been reprinted two or three times since its first publication by Horace Walpole in 1764, but it has never been fully edited. In the present edition the editor endeavours to explain the allusions to the historical events, and gives brief accounts of the numerous terms and books mentioned in the text, and interprets the obscure words and phrases. He will also continue Lord Herbert's life until the date of his death, print some of his correspondence, and will attempt to define his place in English literature, philosophy, history, and religion.

MEMOIRS OF

The Life of William Cavendish,

DUKE OF NEWCASTLE,

To which is added the True Relation of My Birth, Breeding, and Life. By MARGARET, DUCHESS OF NEWCASTLE. Edited by C. H. FIRTH, M.A. (Editor of "Memoirs of the Life of Colonel Hutchinson.") With Four Etched Portraits, fine paper, medium 8vo, cloth, price 21s. *net.*

Five Hundred copies printed, 300 for England and 200 for America.

NOTE.—The Memoirs of the Duke of Newcastle by the Duchess has been judged by Charles Lamb a book "both good and rare," "a jewel which no casket is rich enough to honour or keep safe." The first edition of these Memoirs is, however, difficult to obtain, and the later reprint in form hardly worthy of the original. The aim of the present edition is to supply a book which shall be in type, print, and paper attractive. At the same time, preface, notes, letters, and an index are added to increase its use to the student of seventeenth century history, and to all who are interested in the records of our great civil war. As in the corresponding edition of Mrs. Hutchinson's Memoirs, the spelling is modernised and explanations of obsolete words given.

A Chronicle History of the Life and Work of William Shakespeare,

PLAYER, POET, AND PLAYMAKER.

By F. G. FLEAY, M.A. With Two Etchings of interest. Fine paper,
Roxburghe binding, medium 8vo, gilt top, price 15s.

NOTE.—The theatrical side of the career of Shakespeare has never yet
received any adequate consideration, his connection with the theatres and
acting companies in his earlier years not having been traced or even investi-
gated. His relations with other dramatists, especially with Jonson, have
also been grossly misrepresented. While every idle story of mythical gossip
has been carefully collected, and the pettiest details of his commercial
dealings have been garnered, little attention has hitherto been given to his
dealings with the plays by other men with whom he was fellow-worker, and
a large group of evidences bearing on the chronology of his work, derived
from the early production of English plays in Germany, has been cast aside
as valueless. In this work an attempt is made to collect this neglected
material, to throw new light on the Sonnets, and to determine the dates of
the production of all his works. A complete list of all plays published with
due authority anterior of 1640 by any dramatic writer is given from the
Stationers' Registers. Many unfounded hypotheses of Collier, Halliwell, and
others are for the first time exploded, and the work of ten years investigation
is condensed in a single volume. In many instances one paragraph represents
months of labour, and it is hoped that a permanent addition of value is thus
made to Shakespearian literature. The arrangement of the book is made so as
to appeal not merely to the specialist, but to every one who feels an interest in
the greatest writer of any literature, and the crowning glory of our own.

VOLUMES RECENTLY ISSUED.

MEMOIRS OF THE LIFE OF COLONEL HUTCHINSON. By his
Widow, LUCY. Revised and Edited by CHARLES H. FIRTH, M.A.
With Ten Etched Portraits. Two Volumes, fine paper, medium 8vo,
and handsome binding, 42s. *net.*
NOTE.—Only 500 copies are printed, 300 for England and 200 for America.
Type distributed.

OLD TIMES: A Picture of Social Life at the End of the Eighteenth
Century. Collected and Illustrated from the Satirical and other
Sketches of the Day. By JOHN ASHTON, Author of "Social Life in
the Reign of Queen Anne." One Volume, fine paper, medium 8vo,
handsome binding, Eighty-eight Illustrations, 21s. *net.*

THE LIFE OF GEORGE BRUMMELL, Esq., commonly called BEAU
BRUMMELL. By Captain JESSE, unattached. Revised and Annotated
Edition from the Author's own Interleaved Copy. With Forty Portraits
in Colour of Brummell and his Contemporaries. Two Volumes, fine
paper, medium 8vo, and handsome cloth binding, 42s. *net.*
NOTE.—Only 500 copies are printed, 300 for England and 200 for America.
Type distributed.

MEMOIRS OF COUNT GRAMMONT. By ANTHONY HAMILTON. A
New Edition, Edited, with Notes, by Sir WALTER SCOTT. With
Sixty-Four Portraits engraved by EDWARD SCRIVEN. Two Volumes,
8vo, Roxburghe binding, gilt top, 30s. *net.*

14 King William Street, Strand, London, W.C.

NEW SERIES OF HISTORICAL MEMOIRS—continued.

SOME NOTICES OF THE PRESS.

HUTCHINSON.
Athenæum.

" Is an excellent edition of a famous book. Mr. Firth presents the ' Memoirs ' with a modernised orthography and a revised scheme of punctuation. He retains the notes of Julius Hutchinson, and supplements them by annotations—corrective and explanatory—of his own. Since their publication in 1805, the ' Memoirs' have been a kind of classic. To say that this is the best and fullest edition of them in existence is to say everything."

Times.

" Beautifully printed upon fine paper, with rough edges, and with margins which will delight the heart of the book-lover, we announce with pleasure a new edition of Colonel Hutchinson's ' Memoirs,' revised, with additional notes, by Mr. C. H. Firth. This edition, which is in two handsome volumes, contains ten etched portraits of eminent personages. As the editor remarks in his introduction, none of the ' Memoirs' which relate to the troubled history of the English Civil Wars have obtained a greater popularity than those of Colonel Hutchinson compiled by his wife."

OLD TIMES.
Daily Telegraph.

" That is the best and truest history of the past which comes nearest to the life of the bulk of the people. It is in this spirit that Mr. John Ashton has composed ' Old Times,' intended to be a picture of social life at the end of the eighteenth century. The illustrations form a very valuable, and at the same time quaint and amusing, feature of the volume."

Saturday Review.

" ' Old Times,' however, is not only valuable as a book to be taken up for a few minutes at a time ; a rather careful reading will repay those who wish to brush up their recollections of the period. To some extent it may serve as a book of reference, and even historians may find in it some useful matter concerning the times of which it treats. The book is in every respect suited for a hall or library table in a country house."

BEAU BRUMMELL.
Morning Post.

" The editor of the present edition has been enabled to add much new matter which had been excluded from the original by reason of many of the persons therein referred to being alive at the time. . . . And readers who plod through these two handsome volumes will be rewarded with an admirable picture of English and French society in the days of the Regency."

Notes and Queries.

" The book, which is on beautiful paper, is worthy of a place in most collections, and the privilege of possessing it in a form so artistic and handsome is a subject for gratitude."

GRAMMONT.
Hallam.

" The ' Memoirs of Grammont,' by Anthony Hamilton, scarcely challenge a place as historical ; but we are now looking more at the style than the intrinsic importance of books. Every one is aware of the peculiar felicity and fascinating gaiety which they display."

T. B. Macaulay.

"The artist to whom we owe the most highly finished and vividly coloured picture of the English Court in the days when the English Court was gayest."

Travels

INTO SEVERAL REMOTE NATIONS OF THE WORLD BY LEMUEL GULLIVER, First a Surgeon and then a Captain of Several Ships. By JONATHAN SWIFT, Dean of St. Patrick. With Prefatory Memoir by GEORGE SAINTSBURY, and One Hundred and Eighty Coloured and Sixty Plain Illustrations. Royal 8vo, cloth extra, price 12s. 6d., 450 pages.

SOME NOTICES OF THE PRESS.

The Saturday Review.

"Mr. Saintsbury, in editing the fascinating volume before us, wisely refrains from hinting at any matter that may become matter of controversy. The remarks with which he introduces this beautiful edition of one of the masterpieces of the world's literature breathe the very spirit of true criticism. . . . But we have barely alluded to the distinctive features of this edition which make it a book to be coveted and purchased by all true bibliophiles. M. Poiron's pictures, in their delicacy and subtle humour, are in every way worthy of the story. Those which illustrate the Voyage to Lilliput are perhaps the most dainty and delightful in their quaint poetical design and colouring. But there are some uncoloured head and tailpieces which, to all true lovers of art, will appear simply delicious."

Daily News.

"No handsomer edition of Swift's renowned work than that which Mr. Nimmo has just published of 'The Travels into Several Remote Nations of the World, by Lemuel Gulliver,' is recorded in the annals of bibliography. Mr. George Saintsbury furnishes a brief biographical and critical introduction."

Scotsman.

"The charm of the book, besides the excellence of the printing and generally attractive appearance, lies in the illustrations. They are charmingly drawn bits, some interwoven, so to speak, into the page, others of them occupying the whole page, and all of them marked by a delicacy and refinement which are delightful. Take the edition altogether and it is one of the most remarkable books of its kind that has been published."

Times.

"For this handsome edition of 'Gulliver's Travels' we have nothing but praise. Paper and type are unexceptionable, while there is a profusion of quaintly grotesque illustrations."

The Guardian.

"This is in every respect one of those sumptuous volumes which are now being devoted to our standard authors. Every luxury of paper and type have been freely spent upon it, and the numerous illustrations, both plain and coloured, especially perhaps the latter, display a spirit and humour and wealth of delicate and graceful fancy which it would be difficult to surpass. Possibly some of our readers may have a very vague remembrance of what Swift really allowed himself to write. If so, they will be tolerably certain to be attracted by the grace and beauty of this edition of his most popular work."

Spectator.

"Of all Swift's works, 'Gulliver's Travels' is the most satisfactory and complete, as it is the most famous; and it follows, therefore, that all lovers of English literature will be pleased at the production of so handsome a reprint as that published by Mr. J. C. Nimmo. A special feature of this edition is the pictures. There is no doubt that 'the process by which they are produced is extremely delicate and beautiful, the colours being as transparent as water colours, and laid with perfect clearness of outline and precision of detail. And we reinvite those who have not read 'Gulliver's Travels' since childhood to study once more one of the profoundest and most brilliant satires, one of the greatest of imaginative creations, and one of the noblest models of style in the English language."

The Elizabethan Dramatists.

NOTE.—This is the first instalment towards a collective edition of the Dramatists who lived about the time of Shakespeare. The type will be distributed after each work is printed, the impression of which will be four hundred copies, post 8vo, and one hundred and twenty large fine-paper copies, medium 8vo, which will be numbered.

One of the chief features of this New Edition of the Elizabethan Dramatists, besides the handsome and handy size of the volumes, will be the fact that *each Work will be carefully edited and new notes given throughout.*

ALGERNON CHARLES SWINBURNE

(IN THE *NINETEENTH CENTURY*, JANUARY 1886)

ON THE

Elizabethan Dramatists.

"If it be true, as we are told on high authority, that the greatest glory of England is her literature, and the greatest glory of English literature is its poetry, it is not less true that the greatest glory of English poetry lies rather in its dramatic than its epic or its lyric triumphs. The name of Shakespeare is above the names even of Milton and Coleridge and Shelley ; and the names of his comrades in art and their immediate successors are above all but the highest names in any other province of our song. There is such an overflowing life, such a superb exuberance of abounding and exulting strength, in the dramatic poetry of the half century extending from 1590 to 1640, that all other epochs of English literature seem as it were but half awake and half alive by comparison with this generation of giants and of gods. There is more sap in this than in any other branch of the national bay-tree ; it has an energy in fertility which reminds us rather of the forest than the garden or the park. It is true that the weeds and briars of the underwood are but too likely to embarrass and offend the feet of the rangers and the gardeners who trim the level flower-plots or preserve the domestic game of enclosed and ordered lowlands in the tamer demesnes of literature. The sun is strong and the wind sharp in the climate which reared the fellows and the followers of Shakespeare. The extreme inequality and roughness of the ground must also be taken into account when we are disposed, as I for one have often been disposed, to wonder beyond measure at the apathetic ignorance of average students in regard of the abundant treasure to be gathered from this widest and most fruitful province in the poetic empire of England. And yet, since Charles Lamb threw open its gates to all comers in the ninth year of the present century, it cannot but seem strange that comparatively so few should have availed themselves of the entry to so rich and royal an estate. Mr. Bullen has taken up a task than which none more arduous and important, none worthier of thanks and praise, can be undertaken by any English scholar."

The Elizabethan Dramatists.

The Works of Christopher Marlowe.
Edited by A. H. BULLEN, B.A.
IN THREE VOLUMES.

Post 8vo, cloth.   Published price, 7s. 6d. per volume *net*; also large fine-paper edition, medium 8vo, cloth.

The Works of Thomas Middleton.
Edited by A. H. BULLEN, B.A.

In Eight Volumes, post 8vo, 7s. 6d. per volume *net*; also large fine-paper edition, medium 8vo, cloth.

NOTE.—The next issue of this series will be *The Works of John Marston*, in Three Volumes, and *The Works of Thomas Dekker*, in Four Volumes. The remaining dramatists of this *Period* will follow in due order.

Some Press Notices of the Elizabethan Dramatists.

Saturday Review.
"Mr. Bullen has discharged his task as editor in all important points satisfactorily. Marlowe needs no irrelevant partisanship, no 'zeal of the devil's house,' to support his greatness. . . . Mr. Bullen's introduction is well informed and well written, and his notes are well chosen and sufficient. . . . We hope it may be his good fortune to give and ours to receive every dramatist, from Peele to Shirley, in this handsome, convenient, and well-edited form."

Scotsman.
"Never in the history of the world has a period been marked by so much of literary power and excellence as the Elizabethan period ; and never have the difficulties in the way of literature seemed to be greater. The three volumes which Mr. Nimmo has issued now may be regarded as earnests of more to come, and as proofs of the excellence which will mark this edition of the Elizabethan Dramatists as essentially the best that has been published. Mr. Bullen is a competent editor in every respect."

The Academy.
"Mr. Bullen is known to all those interested in such things as an authority on most matters connected with old plays. We are not surprised, therefore, to find these volumes well edited throughout. They are not overburdened with notes."

The Spectator.
"That Marlowe should take precedence in Mr. Bullen's arduous undertaking is matter of course. He is the father of the English drama, and the first poet who showed the capabilities of the language when employed in blank verse. His line is not only mighty ; it is sometimes most musical, giving us a foretaste of what English verse was to become in the masterful hands of Shakespeare. We cannot part with Mr. Bullen without congratulating him on his success."

Contemporary Review.
"Mr. Bullen relates the little that is known of Marlowe's life with much care, leaving all that he tells us of him beyond the region of doubt ; for with great pains he has succeeded in verifying his statements."

The Elizabethan Dramatists.

SOME PRESS NOTICES—continued.

Athenæum.

'' Mr. Bullen's edition deserves warm recognition. It is intelligent, scholarly, adequate. His preface is judicious. The elegant edition of the dramatists of which these volumes are the first is likely to stand high in public estimation. . . . The completion of the series will be a boon to bibliographers and scholars alike."

Pall Mall Gazette.

''. . . Marlowe has indeed passed the age of simple eulogy, and has reached that of comment. The task set before him by Mr. Bullen is that of supplying a text which shall be as clear and intelligible as the conditions under which plays were printed in the sixteenth and early seventeenth centuries render possible. In this he has been successful. . . . If the series is continued as it is begun, by one of the most careful editors, this set of the English Dramatists will be a coveted literary possession."

Notes and Queries.

''Passages of Marlowe are as nervous, as pliant, as perfect as anything in Shakespeare or any succeeding writer. The same may be said of Marlowe's dramatic inspiration. Much mirth has been made over the grandiloquence of his early plays. None the less Marlowe is, in a sense, the most representative drama-tist of his epoch. . . . Appropriately, then, the series Mr. Bullen edits and Mr. Nimmo issues in most attractive guise is headed by Marlowe, the leader, and in some respects all but the mightiest spirit, of the great army of English Dramatists."

Illustrated London News.

'' It is perhaps, a bold venture on the part of the publisher, or would be if he had chosen an editor less competent than Mr. A. H. Bullen. Marlowe's power was felt by Shakespeare, and felt also by Goethe; and Mr. Bullen is not, perhaps, a rash prophet in saying that, 'so long as high tragedy continues to have interest for men, Time shall lay no hands on the works of Christopher Marlowe!'"

The Standard.

'' Throughout Mr. Bullen has done his difficult work remarkably well, and the publisher has produced it in a form which will make the edition of early dramatists of which it is a part an almost indispensable addition to a well-stocked library."

The Quarterly Review.—*October* 1885.

'' We gladly take this opportunity of directing attention to an edition of Marlowe's complete works recently edited by Mr. A. H. Bullen. If the volumes which follow are as carefully edited as this the first instalment of the series is, Mr. Bullen will be conferring a great boon on all who are interested in the Early English Drama."

The Spectator.—*October* 17, 1885.

'' Probably one of the boldest literary undertakings of our time, on the part of publisher as well as editor, is the fine edition of the Dramatists which has been placed in Mr. Bullen's careful hands; considering the comprehensiveness of the subject, and the variety of knowledge it demands, the courage of the editor is remarkable."

The Antiquary.

'' Mr. Swinburne calls Marlowe 'the greatest discoverer, the most daring and inspired pioneer, in all our poetic literature.'"

Manchester Examiner.

'' Not Shakespeare, not Milton, not Landor, not our own Tennyson, has written lines more splendid in movement or more wealthy in sonorous music than these, from ' The Tragical History of Dr. Faustus '—

> ' Have I not made blind Homer sing to me
> Of Alexander's love and Œnon's death?
> And hath not he who built the walls of Thebes,
> With ravishing sound of his melodious harp,
> Made music with my Mephistophilis?'"

Uniform with " Characters of La Bruyère" and a " Handbook of Gastronomy."

Robin Hood:

A COLLECTION OF ALL THE ANCIENT POEMS, SONGS, AND BALLADS now extant relative to that celebrated English Outlaw ;

To which are prefixed Historical Anecdotes of his Life.

By JOSEPH RITSON.

Illustrated with Eighty Wood Engravings by BEWICK, *printed on China Paper.*

Also Ten Etchings from Original Paintings by A. H. TOURRIER and E. BUCKMAN.

8vo, half parchment, gilt top, 42s. *net.*

NOTE.—300 copies printed, and each numbered. Also 100 copies on fine imperial paper, with etchings in two states, and richly bound in Lincoln Green Satin. Each copy numbered. Type distributed.

This edition of "ROBIN HOOD" is printed from that published in 1832, which was carefully edited and printed from Mr. RITSON's own annotated edition of 1795.

The Guardian.

"This reprint of the Robin Hood ballads will be welcome to many who have loved from childhood the rude romance of the famous outlaw ; it will not be the less welcome to them by reason of its excellent paper and print and the reproduction in China paper of Bewick's original woodcuts. A novel and interesting feature of the book is the old musical settings which are appended to some of the songs."

Pall Mall Gazette.

" Robin Hood has lived in the old ballads of England for many centuries ; his own exploits and those of his merry men have been sung in every town ; the Elizabethan dramatists made him the hero of many of their plays. Southey proposed to write an epic poem on him, Walter Scott brought a faint echo of his life into 'As You Like It,' his bower is still carried through the streets on the first of May, while Maid Marian dances on the pavement for pennies, and still in the pleasant summer afternoons worthy tradesmen flock to the Crystal Palace in doublets of Lincoln green, and with horns that won't blow and bows that won't bend wander through the refreshment-room and the Pompeian Court of that amazing structure in a laudable attempt to combine respectability and picturesqueness."

Notes and Queries.

"The shape in which this work is presented is uniform with La Bruyère and Brillat-Savarin, the appearance of which has already been noticed. Pickering's edition of 1832, which contains the additions of Ritson and of his editor and nephew, including the tale of Robin Hood and the Monk, the existence of which was ignored by Ritson, has been followed, and the woodcuts of Bewick have been retained. These are now printed upon India paper, with a view of communicating greater softness. To these indispensable illustrations have been added nine etchings which now first see the light, from original paintings by A. H. Tourrier and E. Buckman. Some of these, which are also on India paper, are very spirited in design and rich in execution. A handsomer edition of Ritson's Robin Hood, or a more coveted possession to the bibliophile, is not to be expected."

The Literary World.

"Any who cherish a love for mediæval lore will find much to delight them in Ritson's Robin Hood, and an edition more desirable than the one Mr. Nimmo has given us could hardly be demanded by the most fastidious of book collectors. The print and paper superb, and the illustrations have all the freshness of originals."

A. B. FROST'S NEW ILLUSTRATED WORK.

100 *Illustrations.*   *Crown 8vo, cloth, gilt top,* 5s.

Rudder Grange.

By FRANK R. STOCKTON.

The new "Rudder Grange" has not been illustrated in a conventional way. Mr. Frost has given us a series of interpretations of Mr. Stockton's fancies which will delight every appreciative reader,—sketches scattered through the text; larger pictures of the many great and memorable events, and everywhere quaint ornaments and headpieces. It is, on the whole, one of the best existing specimens of the complete supplementing of one another by author and artist.

SOME PRESS NOTICES.

The Times.—"Many of the smaller drawings are wonderfully spirited; there are sketchy suggestions of scenery, which recall the pregnant touches of Bewick; and the figures of animals and of human types are capital, from the row of roosting fowls at the beginning of the chapter to the dilapidated tramp standing hat in hand."

Scotsman.—"Externally it is an uncommonly pretty volume, and the pencil of Mr. A. B. Frost has been employed to brighten its pages with a hundred capital illustrations."

Daily Telegraph.—"Allured by the graphic illustrations, no fewer than a hundred, which the pencil of Mr. A. B. Frost has furnished, the reader who takes in hand Mr. Frank R. Stockton's 'Rudder Grange' will have no reason to regret the fascination, or to wish he had resisted it; altogether the book is full of quiet and humorous amusement."

Morning Post.—"It will be welcomed in its new dress by many who have already made the acquaintance of Euphemia and Pomona, as well as by many who will now meet those excellent types of feminine character for the first time."

Saturday Review.—"The new edition of 'Rudder Grange' has a hundred illustrations by Mr. A. B. Frost; they are extremely good, and worthy of Mr. Stockton's amusing book."

Court and Society Review.—"After looking at the pictures we found ourselves reading the book again, and enjoying Pomona and her reading, and her adventure with the lightning rodder, and her dog-fight as much as ever. And to read it twice over is the greatest compliment you can pay to a book of American humour."

Figaro.—"The volume contains no less than a hundred illustrations large and small, all charming, and what is even better, all appropriate. There is no doubt that it will be very popular."

Society.—"Mr. Stockton's story is quaintly conceived and thoroughly American in style, the characters being most amusing types, and Mr. Frost has provided a host of quaintly grotesque illustrations, large and small, adding much to the intrinsic merit of the work."

Guardian.—"The illustrations by Mr. A. B. Frost to the new edition are extremely humorous and the edition itself is handsome both in type and paper. No one who cares to know what American humour is at its best should be without a copy of 'Rudder Grange.'"

A VERY FUNNY ILLUSTRATED HUMOROUS BOOK.

Stuff and Nonsense.

By A. B. FROST,

The Illustrator of Stockton's " Rudder Grange."

Small 4to, illustrated boards, price 6s.

Mr. Frost has made a wonderfully amusing and clever book. There are in all more than one hundred pictures, many with droll verses and ludicrous jingles. Others are unaccompanied by any text, for no one knows better than Mr. Frost how to tell a funny story, in the funniest way, with his artist's pencil.

Standard.—"This is a book which will please equally people of all ages. The illustrations are not only extremely funny, but they are drawn with wonderful artistic ability, and are full of life and action.

"It is far and away the best book of 'Stuff and Nonsense' which has appeared for a long time."

Times.—"It is a most grotesque medley of mad ideas, carried out nevertheless with a certain regard to consistency, if not to probability."

Figaro.—"The verses and jingles which accompany some of the illustrations are excellent fooling, but Mr. Frost is also able to tell a ludicrous story with his pencil only."

Press.—"The most facetious bit of wit that has been penned for many a day, both in design and text, is Mr. A. B. Frost's 'Stuff and Nonsense.' 'A Tale of a Cat' is funny, 'The Balloonists' is perhaps rather extravagant, but nothing can outdo the wit of 'The Powers of the Human Eye,' whilst 'Ye Æsthete, ye Boy, and ye Bullfrog' may be described as a 'roarer.' Mr. Frost's pen and pencil know how to chronicle fun, and their outcomes should not be overlooked."

Graphic.—"Grotesque in the extreme. His jokes will rouse many a laugh."

Daily News.—"There is really a marvellous abundance of fun in this volume of a harmless kind."

Athenæum.—"Clever sketches of grotesque incidents."

Literary World.—"A hundred and twenty excruciatingly funny sketches."

CONTENTS.

LIMITED EDITIONS

OF

The Two Guinea Half-Bound Parchment Series of Choice Works.

A Handbook of Gastronomy.

(BRILLAT-SAVARIN'S "Physiologie du Goût.") New and Complete Translation, with 52 original Etchings by A. LALAUZE. Printed on China Paper. 8vo, half parchment, gilt top, 42s. *net.*
NOTE.—300 *copies printed, and each numbered. Type distributed.*
[*Out of print.*

The Characters of Jean de La Bruyère.

NEWLY RENDERED INTO ENGLISH. With an Introduction, Biographical Memoir, and Copious Notes, by HENRI VAN LAUN. With Seven Etched Portraits by B. DAMMAN, and Seventeen Vignettes etched by V. FOULQUIER, and printed on China paper. 8vo, half parchment, gilt top, 42s. *net.*
NOTE.—300 *copies printed, and each numbered. Type distributed.*
[*Out of print.*

The Complete Angler;

OR, THE CONTEMPLATIVE MAN'S RECREATION, of IZAAK WALTON and CHARLES COTTON. Edited by JOHN MAJOR. A New Edition, with 8 original Etchings (2 Portraits and 6 Vignettes), two impressions of each, one on Japanese and one on Whatman paper; also, 74 Engravings on Wood, printed on China Paper throughout the text. 8vo, cloth or half parchment elegant, gilt top, 31s. 6d. *net.*
NOTE.—*500 copies printed.*
[*Out of print.*

Robin Hood:

A COLLECTION OF ALL THE ANCIENT POEMS, SONGS, AND BALLADS now extant relative to that celebrated English Outlaw ; to which are prefixed Historical Anecdotes of his Life. By JOSEPH RITSON. Illustrated with Eighty Wood Engravings by BEWICK, printed on China paper. Also Ten Etchings from Original Paintings by A. H. TOURRIER and E. BUCKMAN. 8vo, half parchment, gilt top, 42s. *net.*

NOTE.—300 copies printed, and each numbered. Also 100 copies on fine imperial paper, with etchings in two states, and richly bound in Lincoln Green Satin. Each copy numbered. Type distributed.
This edition of "ROBIN HOOD" is printed from that published in 1832, which was carefully edited and printed from Mr. RITSON'S own annotated edition of 1795.

Carols and Poems

FROM THE FIFTEENTH CENTURY TO THE PRESENT TIME.

Edited by **A. H. BULLEN, B.A.**

Post 8vo, cloth, elegant gilt top, price 5s.

NOTE.—120 copies printed on fine medium 8vo paper, with Seven Illustrations on Japanese paper. Each copy numbered.

Saturday Review.

"Since the publication of Mr. Sandys' collection there have been many books issued on carols, but the most complete by far that we have met with is Mr. Bullen's new volume, 'Carols and Poems from the Fifteenth Century to the Present Time.' The preface contains an interesting account of Christmas festivities and the use of carols. Mr. Bullen has exercised great care in verifying and correcting the collections of his predecessors, and he has joined to them two modern poems by Hawker, two by Mr. William Morris, and others by Mr. Swinburne, Mr. Symonds, and Miss Rossetti. No one has been more successful than Mr. Morris in imitating the ancient carol : —

> 'Outlanders, whence come ye last ?
> The snow in the street and the wind on the door.
> Through what green sea and great have ye past ?
> Minstrels and maids stand forth on the floor.'

Altogether this is one of the most welcome books of the season."

Morning Post.

"Good Christian people all, and more especially those of artistic or poetic inclinations, will feel indebted to the editor and publisher of this fascinating volume, which, bound as it is in elegant cloth, ornamented with sprigs of holly, may fairly claim to be considered *par excellence* the gift-book of the season. 'Carols and Poems' are supplemented by voluminous and interesting notes by the editor, who also contributes some very graceful dedicatory verses."

Spectator.

"Mr. Bullen divides his 'Carols and Poems from the Fifteenth Century to the Present Time' into three parts—' Christmas Chants and Carols,' 'Carmina Sacra,' and 'Christmas Customs and Christmas Cheer.' These make up together between seventy and eighty poems of one kind and another. The selection has been carefully made from a wide range of authors. Indeed, it is curious to see the very mixed company which the subject of Christmas has brought together—as, indeed, it is quite right that it should. Altogether the result is a very interesting book."

Notes and Queries.

"Mr. Bullen does not indeed pretend to cater for those who regard carols from a purely antiquarian point of view. His book is intended to be popular rather than scholarly. Scholarly none the less it is, and representative also, including as it does every form of Christmas strain, from early mysteries down to poems so modern as not previously to have seen the light."

The Times.

"Is very exceptionally a Christmas book, and a book at which we may cut and come again through this sentimentally festive season. It forms a 'Christmas Garland' of the sweetest or the quaintest carols, ancient and modern."

Athenæum.

"Is an excellent collection of ancient and modern verse, mostly religious and sentimental, formed with much learning, research, and taste by Mr. A. H. Bullen."

Illustrated London News.

"The atmosphere of these plain-speaking songs is of the rarest purity. They come from the heart, and appeal to it, when the way is not choked up by the thorns and briers of conventional propriety. The reader accustomed to more artificial strains may not see the beauty of these songs at first, but it will grow upon him by degrees ; and possibly he will look with something like regret to the old-world days when verses so pure and quaint were household words in England."

14 King William Street, Strand, London, W.C.

Old Spanish Romances.

Old English Romances.

Romances of Fantasy and Humour.

Illustrated with Etchings, crown 8vo, parchment boards or cloth,
7s. 6d. per vol.

The Times.

"Among the numerous handsome reprints which the publishers of the day vie
with each other in producing, we have seen nothing of greater merit than this
series of volumes. Those who have read these masterpieces of the last century in
the homely garb of the old editions may be gratified with the opportunity of perusing
them with the advantages of large clear print and illustrations of a quality which is
rarely bestowed on such reissues. The series deserve every commendation."

THE HISTORY OF DON QUIXOTE DE LA MANCHA.
Translated from the Spanish of MIGUEL DE CERVANTES SAAVEDRA by
MOTTEUX. With copious Notes (including the Spanish Ballads), and
an Essay on the Life and Writings of CERVANTES by JOHN G. LOCK-
HART. Preceded by a Short Notice of the Life and Works of PETER
ANTHONY MOTTEUX by HENRI VAN LAUN. Illustrated with Sixteen
Original Etchings by R. DE LOS RIOS. Four Volumes.

LAZARILLO DE TORMES. By Don DIEGO MENDOZA. Trans-
lated by THOMAS ROSCOE. And **GUZMAN D'ALFARACHE.**
By MATEO ALEMAN. Translated by BRADY. Illustrated with Eight
Original Etchings by R. DE LOS RIOS. Two Volumes.

ASMODEUS. By LE SAGE. Translated from the French. Illustrated
with Four Original Etchings by R. DE LOS RIOS.

THE BACHELOR OF SALAMANCA. By LE SAGE. Translated
from the French by JAMES TOWNSEND. Illustrated with Four Original
Etchings by R. DE LOS RIOS.

VANILLO GONZALES; or, The Merry Bachelor. By LE SAGE.
Translated from the French. Illustrated with Four Original Etchings
by R. DE LOS RIOS.

THE ADVENTURES OF GIL BLAS OF SANTILLANE.
Translated from the French of LE SAGE by TOBIAS SMOLLETT. With
Biographical and Critical Notice of LE SAGE by GEORGE SAINTSBURY.
New Edition, carefully revised. Illustrated with Twelve Original Etch-
ings by R. DE LOS RIOS. Three Volumes.

THE LIFE AND OPINIONS OF TRISTRAM SHANDY,
GENTLEMAN. By LAURENCE STERNE. In Two Vols. With Eight
Etchings by DAMMAN from Original Drawings by HARRY FURNISS.

THE OLD ENGLISH BARON: A GOTHIC STORY. By CLARA
REEVE. **THE CASTLE OF OTRANTO:** A GOTHIC STORY.
By HORACE WALPOLE. In One Vol. With Two Portraits and Four
Original Drawings by A. H. TOURRIER, Etched by DAMMAN.

THE ARABIAN NIGHTS ENTERTAINMENTS. In Four
Vols. Carefully Revised and Corrected from the Arabic by JONATHAN
SCOTT, LL.D., Oxford. With Nineteen Original Etchings by AD.
LALAUZE.

14 King William Street, Strand, London, W.C.

ILLUSTRATED ROMANCE SERIES—continued.

THE HISTORY OF THE CALIPH VATHEK. By WM. BECKFORD. With Notes, Critical and Explanatory. **RASSELAS, PRINCE OF ABYSSINIA.** By SAMUEL JOHNSON. In One Vol. With Portrait of BECKFORD, and Four Original Etchings, designed by A. H. TOURRIER, and Etched by DAMMAN.

ROBINSON CRUSOE. By DANIEL DEFOE. In Two Vols. With Biographical Memoir, Illustrative Notes, and Eight Etchings by M. MOUILLERON, and Portrait by L. FLAMENG.

GULLIVER'S TRAVELS. By JONATHAN SWIFT. With Five Etchings and Portrait by AD. LALAUZE.

A SENTIMENTAL JOURNEY. By LAURENCE STERNE. **A TALE OF A TUB.** By JONATHAN SWIFT. In One Vol. With Five Etchings and Portrait by ED. HÉDOUIN.

THE TALES AND POEMS OF EDGAR ALLAN POE. With Biographical Essay by JOHN H. INGRAM, and Fourteen Original Etchings, Three Photogravures, and a Portrait newly etched from a life-like Daguerreotype of the Author. In Four Volumes.

WEIRD TALES. By E. T. W. HOFFMAN. A New Translation from the German. With Biographical Memoir by J. T. BEALBY, formerly Scholar of Corpus Christi College, Cambridge. With Portrait and Ten Original Etchings by AD. LALAUZE. In Two Volumes.

Imperial 8vo, Extra Illustrated Edition of

The Complete Angler;

OR, THE CONTEMPLATIVE MAN'S RECREATION OF
IZAAK WALTON AND CHARLES COTTON.

Edited by JOHN MAJOR.

Full bound morocco elegant (Zaehnsdorf's binding), price Five Guineas *net.*

This Extra-illustrated Edition of THE COMPLETE ANGLER is specially designed for Collectors of this famous work; and in order to enable them either to take from or add to the Illustrations, it is also supplied unbound, folded and collated.

The Illustrations consist of **Fifty Steel Plates,** designed by T. STOTHARD, R.A., JAMES INSKIP, EDWARD HASSELL, DELAMOTTE, BINKENBOOM, W. HIXON, SIR FRANCIS SYKES, Bart., PINE, &c. &c., and engraved by well-known Engravers. Also **Six Original Etchings and Two Portraits,** as well as **Seventy-four Engravings on Wood** by various Eminent Artists.

To this is added a PRACTICAL TREATISE on FLIES and FLY HOOKS, by the late JOHN JACKSON, of Tanfield Mill, with **Ten Steel Plates,** coloured, representing 120 Flies, natural and artificial.

One Hundred and Twenty copies only are printed, each of which is numbered.

The Fan. By OCTAVE UZANNE.

ILLUSTRATED WITH DESIGNS BY PAUL AVRIL.

Royal 8vo, cloth, gilt top, 31s. 6d. *net.*

The Sunshade—The Glove—The Muff.

By OCTAVE UZANNE.

ILLUSTRATED WITH DESIGNS BY PAUL AVRIL.

Royal 8vo, cloth, gilt top, 31s. 6d. *net.*

NOTE.—*The above are English Editions of the unique and artistic works. " L'Eventail" and " L'Ombrelle," recently published in Paris, and now difficult to be procured, as no new Edition is to be produced. 500 copies only are printed.*

Saturday Review.

"An English counterpart of the well-known French books by Octave Uzanne, with Paul Avril's charming illustrations."

Standard.

"It gives a complete history of fans of all ages and places ; the illustrations are dainty in the extreme. Those who wish to make a pretty and appropriate present to a young lady cannot do better than purchase 'The Fan.'"

Athenæum.

"The letterpress comprises much amusing 'chit-chat,' and is more solid than it pretends to be. This *brochure* is worth reading ; nay, it is worth keeping."

Art Journal.

"At first sight it would seem that material could never be found to fill even a volume ; but the author, in dealing with his first subject alone, 'The Sunshade,' says he could easily have filled a dozen volumes of this emblem of sovereignty. The work is delightfully illustrated in a novel manner by Paul Avril, the pictures which meander about the work being printed in varied colours."

Daily News.

"The pretty adornments of the margin of these artistic volumes, the numerous ornamental designs, and the pleasant vein of the author's running commentary, render these the most attractive monographs ever published on a theme which interests so many enthusiastic collectors."

Glasgow Herald.

"'I have but collected a heap of foreign flowers, and brought of my own only the string which binds them together,' is the fitting quotation with which M. Uzanne closes the preface to his volume on woman's ornaments. The monograph on the sunshade, called by the author 'a little tumbled fantasy,' occupies fully one-half of the volume. It begins with a pleasant invented mythology of the parasol ; glances at the sunshade in all countries and times ; mentions many famous umbrellas : quotes a number of clever sayings. . . . To these remarks on the spirit of the book it is necessary to add that the body of it is a dainty marvel of paper, type, and binding, and that what meaning it has looks out on the reader through a hundred argus-eyes of many-tinted photogravures, exquisitely designed by M. Paul Avril."

Westminster Review.

"The most striking merit of the book is the entire appropriateness both of the letterpress and illustrations to the subject treated. M. Uzanne's style has all the airy grace and sparkling brilliancy of the *petit instrument* whose praise he celebrates, and M. Arvil's drawings seem to conduct us into an enchanted world where everything but fans are forgotten."

Copyright Edition, with Ten Etched Portraits. In Ten Vols., demy 8vo, cloth, £5, 5s.

Lingard's History of England.

FROM THE FIRST INVASION BY THE ROMANS TO THE ACCESSION OF WILLIAM AND MARY IN 1688.

By JOHN LINGARD, D.D.

This New Copyright Library Edition of "Lingard's History of England," besides containing all the latest notes and emendations of the Author, with Memoir, is enriched with Ten Portraits, newly etched by Damman, of the following personages, viz. :—Dr. Lingard, Edward I., Edward III., Cardinal Wolsey, Cardinal Pole, Elizabeth, James I., Cromwell, Charles II., James II.

The Times.

"No greater service can be rendered to literature than the republication, in a handsome and attractive form, of works which time and the continued approbation of the world have made classical. . . . The accuracy of Lingard's statements on many points of controversy, as well as the genial sobriety of his view, is now recognised."

The Tablet.

"It is with the greatest satisfaction that we welcome this new edition of Dr. Lingard's 'History of England.' It has long been a desideratum. . . . No general history of England has appeared which can at all supply the place of Lingard, whose painstaking industry and careful research have dispelled many a popular delusion, whose candour always carries his reader with him, and whose clear and even style is never fatiguing."

The Spectator.

"We are glad to see that the demand for Dr. Lingard's *England* still continues. Few histories give the reader the same impression of exhaustive study. This new edition is excellently printed, and illustrated with ten portraits of the greatest personages in our history."

Dublin Review.

"It is pleasant to notice that the demand for Lingard continues to be such that publishers venture on a well-got-up library edition like the one before us. More than sixty years have gone since the first volume of the first edition was published ; many equally pretentious histories have appeared during that space, and have more or less disappeared since, yet Lingard lives—is still a recognised and respected authority."

The Scotsman.

"There is no need, at this time of day, to say anything in vindication of the importance, as a standard work, of Dr. Lingard's 'History of England.' . . . Its intrinsic merits are very great. The style is lucid, pointed, and puts no strain upon the reader ; and the printer and publisher have neglected nothing that could make this—what it is likely long to remain—the standard edition of a work of great historical and literary value."

Daily Telegraph.

"True learning, untiring research, a philosophic temper, and the possession of a graphic, pleasing style were the qualities which the author brought to his task, and they are displayed in every chapter of his history."

Weekly Register.

"In the full force of the word a scholarly book. Lingard's history is destined to bear a part of growing importance in English education."

Manchester Examiner.

"He stands alone in his own school ; he is the only representative of his own phase of thought. The critical reader will do well to compare him with those who went before and those who came after him."

Imaginary Conversations.

By WALTER SAVAGE LANDOR.

In Five Vols. crown 8vo, cloth, 30s.

FIRST SERIES—CLASSICAL DIALOGUES, GREEK AND ROMAN.

SECOND SERIES—DIALOGUES OF SOVEREIGNS AND STATESMEN.

THIRD SERIES—DIALOGUES OF LITERARY MEN.

FOURTH SERIES—DIALOGUES OF FAMOUS WOMEN.

FIFTH SERIES—MISCELLANEOUS DIALOGUES.

NOTE.—*This New Edition is printed from the last Edition of his Works, revised and edited by John Forster, and is published by arrangement with the Proprietors of the Copyright of Walter Savage Landor's Works.*

The Times.

"The abiding character of the interest excited by the writings of Walter Savage Landor, and the existence of a numerous band of votaries at the shrine of his refined genius, have been lately evidenced by the appearance of the most remarkable of Landor's productions, his 'Imaginary Conversations,' taken from the last edition of his works. To have them in a separate publication will be convenient to a great number of readers."

The Athenæum.

"The appearance of this tasteful reprint would seem to indicate that the present generation is at last waking up to the fact that it has neglected a great writer, and if so, it is well to begin with Landor's most adequate work. It is difficult to overpraise the 'Imaginary Conversations.' The eulogiums bestowed on the 'Conversations' by Emerson will, it is to be hoped, lead many to buy this book."

Scotsman.

"An excellent service has been done to the reading public by presenting to it, in five compact volumes, these 'Conversations.' Admirably printed on good paper, the volumes are handy in shape, and indeed the edition is all that could be desired. When this has been said, it will be understood what a boon has been conferred on the reading public; and it should enable many comparatively poor men to enrich their libraries with a work that will have an enduring interest."

Literary World.

"That the 'Imaginary Conversations' of Walter Savage Landor are not better known is no doubt largely due to their inaccessibility to most readers, by reason of their cost. This new issue, while handsome enough to find a place in the best of libraries, is not beyond the reach of the ordinary bookbuyer."

Edinburgh Review.

"How rich in scholarship! how correct, concise, and pure in style! how full of imagination, wit, and humour! how well informed, how bold in speculation, how various in interest, how universal in sympathy! In these dialogues—making allowance for every shortcoming or excess—the most familiar and the most august shapes of the past are reanimated with vigour, grace, and beauty. We are in the high and goodly company of wits and men of letters; of churchmen, lawyers, and statesmen; of party men, soldiers, and kings; of the most tender, delicate, and noble women; and of figures that seem this instant to have left for us the Agora or the Schools of Athens, the Forum or the Senate of Rome."

In One Volume, 8vo, cloth, price 7s. 6d.

The Teaching of the Twelve Apostles

(ΔΙΔΑΧΗ ΤΩΝ ΔΩΔΕΚΑ ΑΠΟΣΤΟΛΩΝ).

Recently Discovered and Published by PHILOTHEOS BRYENNIOS, *Metropolitan of Nicomedia.*

Edited, with a Translation, Introduction, and Notes, by ROSWELL D. HITCHCOCK and FRANCIS BROWN,

Professors in Union Theological Seminary, New York.

Revised and Enlarged.

Extract from the Preface.

" Among the special features of this edition may be noticed the discussions as to the integrity of the text ; as to the relations between the ' Teaching ' and other early Christian documents, with translations of these *in extenso*, so far as seemed desirable for purposes of comparison ; the presentation, entire, with annotations, of Kramutzcky's now famous reproduction of ' The Two Ways ;' the sections on the peculiarities of the Codex, the printed texts, and the recent literature ; and the care expended on the history of the characteristic Greek words ' of the Teaching.'

" The editors feel sure that continued study will only add to the interest felt by scholars in this unique product of early Christianity, and enhance their estimate of its importance. "

Westminster Review.

" This enlargement of the hastily prepared edition brought out last year by the same editors seems to us one of the most complete and valuable of the numerous commentaries on the ' Teaching.' The matter of the discourse need not again be dealt with ; it may suffice to say that these introductions and notes show thoroughly sound and scholarly work, and the reproduction of the conjectural restoration of ' The Two Ways ' by Kramutzcky, with which our editors incline to identify the document, may be read with interest, even by non-theologians, as a justification of ' reconstructive criticism.' The commentary, too, though mainly for experts, may be read with profit by any who are interested in scholarship. We cordially welcome this new evidence of the activity of America in theological learning."

Spectator.

" Of the several editions of the ' Teaching' none is more worthy of the student's attention than this. A very full introduction gives an account of this very remarkable work of Christian antiquity (certainly the first in intrinsic value of the sub-Apostolic writings), of the circumstances of its discovery, &c. Then follows, first, the text, with a translation on the opposite pages, then notes, and then an appendix."

The Scotsman.

" There are few literary discoveries of recent years which have been so interesting to ecclesiastical scholars, or which have aroused more discussion, than that by Bryennios, Metropolitan of Nicomedia, of a manuscript in the library of the Monastery of the Holy Sepulchre in Constantinople. Found in 1873, it was published in 1883, and for the first time scholars became acquainted with a work which they had seen tantalisingly referred to, quoted, and used by early Christian writers."

The Bookseller.

" If genuine, and apparently there is no reason to doubt its being so, this is one of the most important documents connected with historical theology that has been discovered for many years. It professes to be a summary of the Christian religion as taught by the Apostles themselves. . . . If the editors be correct in their conjectures, the ' Teaching' must have been written about the end of the first century or very early in the second."

www.ingramcontent.com/pod-product-compliance
Lightning Source LLC
Chambersburg PA
CBHW052331110726
47901CB00005B/1199